VALLEDERA
SILVIS
TERROWIN
TENBRIS FOREST
N
ABOLEND
I0714800

"I realized about 50 pages into this book that it was quickly becoming my favorite fantasy book of the year.

I was immersed in the suspenseful ending, and cannot wait to read the next book in this series. I will be anticipating it, and championing this series for a long time to come. The magic system, prophetic lore, and a kingdom poised to enter a revolutionary war, are all elements of a truly exciting world that hinges on one special girl with purple eyes. A girl who grew up beaten into submission until even she believed she was no one."

- Sasha Klimchock
REEDSY DISCOVERY, 5 STARS

♦

"The plot and keeping the story moving with no stagnant parts. The characters were very relatable and fun to learn. Great read!"

-Kayla W.
Teen Librarian

♦

"A captivating exploration of the power of acceptance and understanding."

-Madison L.
Blogger, 5 STARS

♦

"Excellent story."

-Kat N.
Librarian, 5 STARS

♦

"Great writing style."

-Kathryn M.
Blogger, 5 STARS

TOLERANT

TOLERANT

A NOVEL BY

C.J. SPARROW

First published in 2023.
Knoxville, Tennessee.

Library of Congress Control Number:
2022919632

International Standard Book Numbers:
Paperback: 978-1-951987-11-4
Hardcover: 978-1-951987-73-2
eBook: 978-1-951987-67-1

For Robert, who never stopped believing in me.

Also, to my little girl whose beans sat on my

hands while I typed every letter.

I love you.

Prologue

An infant's cry shattered the stillness of the night. In the empty tavern, Breena dropped the earthenware tankard she'd been polishing. Though she'd been expecting the child's arrival, the sound of the babe's voice in the night breathed life into her mission. It had begun. She mopped her brow with her apron, shuffling around vacant wooden tables to investigate the wailing on the other side of the entrance.

The iron hinges squealed as the wooden plank door swung open, revealing a pink-faced babe lying abandoned on the steps. A gust of wind carried snow flurries, dusting the child, whose cries became stifled by hiccups, lulled by the heat from the hearth steaming out into the dark. Scooping the child with one arm, Breena grazed the golden blindfold shielding the infant's eyes. The Shadow Fray had succeeded. They'd delivered the girl.

Breena shot a glance down the empty streets. The lights were extinguished. Not even the guards were still out at this hour. Whoever had delivered the babe was nothing more than another shadow in the night. Good. Their plan was working.

The barmaid had been prepared for this moment. However, she wished it hadn't come so soon. Breena's tightly kept brown-peppered bun fell into disarray as she blotted her face on her sleeve. Breena didn't dare cast a glance at the child's eyes. She knew they shined the color of amethyst beneath the shroud, and that was all she needed to know.

"Nadia," Breena called out to her daughter.

A child no older than seven skipped from behind the bar, where she had been playing with makeshift dolls, used to her mother's late hours. The young girl had chestnut hair and olive eyes that matched her skin. The child gasped with awe the moment her eyes fell on the flaxen-haired babe. Nadia's almost-perfect teeth glimmered as she smiled at the child.

"The Diablerie has risen." Breena gestured to the infant. "We've been waiting a long time to meet her."

Nadia's head bobbed.

"Do you remember the story?" Breena asked.

"Yes, Mommy. It is my job to be a brave girl and take care of my new little sister!" Nadia squealed.

"Nadia, she isn't your sister. She is a Diablerie." Breena's gaze penetrated the girl.

Nadia frowned, eyes darting from her mother to the babe. Breena worried her daughter was too young, too innocent to handle a task so paramount that even a trained warrior of the Shadow Fray may not have been able to succeed.

"Listen, Nadia, let me tell you the story one more time."

Breena sat on the floor, settling close to the crackling hearth. The heat from the flames licked their backs, soothing like a mother cat to her kitten. Breena rested the babe on her lap, her crossed legs cradling the infant. Nadia scooted close, putting a plump hand on the babe.

"A long time ago, Mommy and Daddy were warriors, much like the guards, but we didn't work for the king. We worked for the . . ." Breena paused. This was too much information. Nadia needed to know enough to ensure her survival, nothing more. Nothing about the Shadow Fray. Breena coughed as she breathed in the sooty air, hoping Nadia wouldn't notice her diversion. "We wanted to protect the people and bring fairness and peace, like great warriors from a very long time ago—before King Mallum, before collectives, back in the beginning of the rise of Abolend.

"But as time passes, people forget history. Bad things that happened grow less and less important. Atrocities occurred too long ago for people to remember and too long ago to care. But that kind of thinking is dangerous because then those bad things happen again and again. We are doomed to repeat the same mistakes. Commit horrible acts. And now, Nadia, we must fight against those bad things.

"But before your mommy and daddy could make real change, Daddy got sick. He became a part of the stars that watch over you every night. When Daddy died, King Mallum was very mad. You see, women aren't allowed to own property. King Mallum wanted to take the tavern away from us, but Mommy makes the best drinks, and the people were in an uproar and wanted me to stay.

"King Mallum, at that time, was having a rough year. The winter was long and cold, farmers didn't grow enough food, and pressure was on King Mallum to take care of the people. He was worried. With fear and doubt growing in the people's hearts, he didn't want to lose the favor of the people by taking away something that made that tough year a little easier. Many in the highest ranks did not want to see me go, so he allowed me to keep the bar, for a cost, of course . . . You.

"He declared that by your tenth birthday, you must go and join a collective to give your life in service to Abolend for payment. He wanted the people to know that Mommy didn't have a choice. Keeping the bar became a sentence of pain, not a badge of honor. He knew losing you would be the worst thing any mother could imagine." Breena wiped a tear from her eye.

"It's all right, Mommy. Don't be sad. We have a secret." Nadia glanced at the babe. "That's you."

"Yes, Nadia, we do have a secret. You had a mission to go to a collective anyway. Mommy and Daddy always knew you would be brave enough and strong enough to go on a great quest. There were rumors that a child with purple eyes and hair of gold was coming."

Nadia stroked the hair of the child carefully.

"And she would be the key."

"A key for what, Momma?"

"You will learn what she will unlock in time. For now, that is a secret even from you."

"But why?" Nadia protested.

"Because too many secrets can be hard to remember. Don't forget the babe isn't allowed to know any of them."

Nadia's brow furrowed.

"That's right. It is for her protection," Breena continued. "But your mission is to bring the babe to the collective, the one on the hill surrounded by trees. We've walked the path that leads to the collective nearly every morning for the past year. It is important you two stay at that one. It is the farthest away from Abolend's walls. Do you remember what the collectives are for?" Breena wanted to ensure Nadia knew the true history before the trainers tried to manipulate her understanding of how they worked.

"The collective is where children go. Abandoned children, the unwanted, and the volunteers. And if there aren't enough children to go, servants will have new babies, right?" Nadia eyeballed Breena for approval.

"You're right." Breena seethed. It was deplorable. Mallum would breed a guard and a servant, then rip their child away to be trained as a collective pupil. Human fodder. "And why would anyone volunteer?" Breena asked, knowing the answer.

"Because volunteers receive money for their families or are forgiven for crimes. Or because King Mallum said so, like he did with me. I know more, Mommy." She straightened her shoulders. "The collectives are important to Abolend. Some collectives teach soldiers to protect us, and others teach servants to keep Abolend happy and clean. And when you are sixteen, you can start being tested to graduate. Then you are assigned to a permanent position in Abolend. The better you behave, the better placement you are given."

Breena swallowed bile while listening to the innocent view of her daughter. The collectives kept the lower class oppressed, the middle class complacent, and the upper class entertained—a sick game of control. King Mallum tortured young minds into the embodiment of loyal citizens.

Mallum told the people it was a privilege to be a part of the collective. The kingdom had become convinced this was the best way to keep the masses safe, the best way to maintain order for the past 132 years. Anyone who disagreed had been silenced by death long ago. Or so Mallum thought.

Trainers at the collectives would whip the girls into the molded image they needed servants to be. They were starved into obedience, deprived of sleep to weaken their judgment. King Mallum declared the trainers could be as brutal as necessary to mold the minds of the young.

The trainers were desperate to be loved by the king. They were high enough in status to escape the collective but low enough not to be considered noble. Still, even the trainers weren't trusted enough to hold a blade, only a whip. He told them to imagine the children as clay. If the children did not press into shape, they were to force it—force them to forget logic, forget freedom, forget their loved ones.

It was time for the establishment to end.

"And remember, Nadia, you mustn't graduate. You must stay as long as possible to be with the babe until we meet again. Tell them you don't know how old you are, and let them think you are much younger. It will buy you more time." The barmaid lowered her voice so it was barely audible in the still night. "And if it becomes too dangerous to stay any longer, or if you are forced to graduate and leave the girl, or if you are afraid there is no other option, you must defect and bring the child with you." She peered into her daughter's wide eyes.

"Yes, Mommy." Nadia's face was serious, too serious for a child.

Breena grabbed Nadia's little hands, which trembled in her grasp. "Mommy won't be able to visit you for a little while, but sooner than you know, we will be together again. All three of us." Nadia inched closer, hanging on to every word. "And you remember when that is, right?"

"Yes, Nadia and Mommy will meet at the path that makes a Y seventeen whole winters past today." Nadia held ten wiggling fingers in the air before realizing she didn't have enough to show seventeen. A frown washed away her excitement.

"No frowns. Before you know it, you will have enough fingers to count down the years." Breena forced enthusiasm into her voice. She ran her fingers through her daughter's silky mane, comforting her. "As long as you find me, all will be well. Be good and listen to the trainers. But never forget that you are smart, kind, beautiful, and most of all, important."

Breena paused, contemplating her next words. "Nadia, the trainers might ask you to do something bad. Even if it seems wrong, you must do it. But remind yourself that you only are doing the wrong because it is a mission, not because you think it is the right thing to do."

Fear and confusion washed over Nadia's face. "How will I know if I am bad or good?" Nadia asked, her face the color of chalk.

"You will know in your heart." Guilt washed through Breena's body, wrenching at her organs like she had been poisoned. Her throat swelled, preventing her from speaking. She stilled, letting several moments pass before she forcefully spoke. "Always know I am right here waiting for you, Nadia. You are strong, you are brave, and you will be the best role model she could ever wish for. I know it!"

Nadia smiled, her chest filled with pride, the fear gone like a dandelion seed in the wind.

VII

"Come eat." Breena stood and placed a steaming vegetable soup in front of her girl. Shame ached at the back of Breena's skull. Her child was too proud to understand the fear and too little to know this was the last meal she would enjoy eating, the last time she would be loved by an elder, the last time she could be herself inside and out without fear, without condemnation. The barmaid turned her back, sucking in tears that burned at her eyes like coals in the fire. Breena swaddled the babe in a warm blanket.

"It is time for you to serve our kingdom. And don't forget you can never, ever let anyone remove her impairment."

"Why?" Nadia's forehead turned to mountains of wrinkles as she slurped on steaming soup.

Breena pointed to her eyes. "You know the story. She has purple eyes. It's unusual."

Nadia groaned. "Not even when no one is looking?"

"Not even when no one is looking."

"Yes, Mommy." Nadia's eyebrows wove together. "I will keep it a secret."

Breena scooped Nadia into her arms, kissing her head a dozen times, yet it never seemed to be enough. She forced herself away, tongue-tied with sadness, choking any other words she wished to utter into silence. Opening the door to the darkest night, she prayed she would see Nadia once more.

Nadia held the babe tight to her body as her feet scuttled through the snowfall on the moonless solstice night. Evergreens were dusted with fresh snow, and barren woody branches leered in the dark forest. The walk was scarier at night than in the mornings she and Momma had practiced on. Her muscles ached. Over and over, she shifted the babe from arm to arm. The bundle was much heavier than Nadia had imagined. Nearly every day for the past year, Nadia had practiced carrying bread, mead, and all sorts of bulky items along this path, but tonight the babe was still pushing her strength to the limit.

Leaving the towering gap-toothed walls encasing Abolend, Nadia navigated to the dirt path that led to the collective. A shiver of ice canvassed her body. She'd never gotten this close. With a puff in her chest, she stepped forward onto the avenue she had never traversed before. Breena had never taken her all the way to the collective, and Nadia wasn't sure what to expect. She moved like a ghost through the woods until a haunting torchlit cobbled home appeared in the distance.

It had a thatched roof weathered away in the corners from battering storms and glass windows that sat into the stone every five feet or so. It stood two stories tall. The house seemed empty and was deathly still in the swaying forest. An undersized well sat fifty feet from the house. The wind swung a squealing bucket, slapping the stone hollowly in the night. Nadia ground her teeth, stopping her jaw from trembling.

Trampled mud paths wiped away any glimmer of hope that grass could grow in the somber meadow. Her pace hastened as she made her way to the entrance, practicing what her mother had always told her to say. She was a volunteer. The babe was an orphan. Easy.

The doorway flashed open, the light too bright in the night. Scowling deeply with thin lips, a stern woman with straight black hair stood in the entrance, watching the girls approach. Nadia's heart raced fearfully. She stepped closer to the stranger.

"I am here to escort this babe to the collective. I volunteer to serve Abolend," Nadia said strongly, sure to steady her wavering voice.

"Enter," the greasy woman hissed.

Nadia stepped into the filth-ridden chamber. Scorch marks from torches left sooty marks on the cobbled walls, and the smell of something putrid burning curled the hair in Nadia's nose. The home was silent, so much so that Nadia was sure she could hear the papery twitch of a cockroach scuttling on the ground in the corner.

Nadia wondered if the home was empty. No. She knew the other girls here must have been asleep somewhere. Mother had said there were almost one hundred girls in a collective, though the house didn't seem large enough to fit that many. Nadia wanted to explore, but she didn't dare move her eyes from the trainer or the roach for long.

"Who gave this one her impairment?" the woman barked at Nadia.

"Highborns of Abolend," Nadia answered, having been trained by Breena to answer in specific responses. It wasn't unusual for those destined to serve to arrive impaired. Momma had always said highborns enjoyed being cruel to servants. She'd said they thought it was fun.

"Replace it with this one." Dry hands shoved rough fabric into Nadia's chest, the woman's knuckles twisting into Nadia's sternum. "And you . . ." She knelt, leveling herself eye to eye with Nadia, rot emitting from her mouth.

Nadia held her breath.

"Well, there is nothing notable about you, is there?" she sneered. "Lucky day."

A chill rushed through Nadia's body. She had always imagined she was unique in many ways, inside and out. She was kind, had her mother's thick hair, and was the best at keeping secrets. Best of all, she had a piece of her dad. She had his olive eyes, full of passion and as rich as the leaves in summer. Mother had always told her so.

Momma had warned her of impairments and pointed them out on servants they passed in the streets. Some had scars, and some had missing fingers. There was no limit on how many someone could receive, and they kept them for life. King Mallum had emboldened the trainers to pick at the qualities that gave servants confidence, designed to rip away any shred of uniqueness, tear away the light in their souls, keep them fearful of stepping out of the image the trainers whipped them to be. Momma had said impairments kept the girls tolerant.

Confidence was a dangerous thing in collectives. But Nadia hadn't realized impairments were so easy to get. This trainer already wanted to find something to destroy. She should slouch, or she'd have to carry rocks. She should frown, or her smile could be carved away with a kitchen knife. She shouldn't run lest her feet be lashed or pebbles put in her shoes. She shouldn't do anything. It had seemed easy when Mother had told her about it, but now it seemed like it was going to be hard—too hard.

Nothing was out-of-bounds for the wickedness of the trainers. Nadia's gaze froze on the woman, and she tried hard to suck in her tears. The trainer was right. If they didn't think she needed impaired, she was lucky. She didn't want to be hurt. But somehow, she didn't feel that way, didn't feel lucky. Momma was wrong. Maybe she wasn't special. Maybe she wasn't brave enough for this.

A wicked smile flicked around the woman's face like a flame. Nadia gripped the babe tighter in her arms as the babe cried. The trainer lurched forward, a sharpened fingernail cutting Nadia's arm. Nadia gripped the babe tighter, still and silent. Nadia's face felt hot with rage.

"Ah. There it is." The trainer gripped Nadia's face hard in her hand. "You may be silent now, but those eyes aren't. Here." She ripped a piece of hemp from a cloth spread across the table behind her. "You, like this miserable lump, will be permanently blindfolded. Your eyes disgust me, and I never want to see that look on your face again."

Nadia's lip quivered. She was mad at herself. Momma had always said she could think whatever she wanted, but this trainer seemed to know that she had awful musings about her. She knew Nadia was mad that she wasn't special. Fuming, Nadia bowed her head and laid the babe in the corner of the room, grateful to relieve her aching arms of the weight.

"And if you ever remove it, Servant, I'll cut your eyes out." She laughed as she left the girls abandoned in the hall.

Nadia waited a few more moments to be sure she was alone before touching the babe's blindfold. She prodded the golden fabric carefully, removing the child's impairment. The babe locked her gaze on Nadia. She had bright lilac eyes emitting the faintest glow, like a firefly in the night. Nadia's smile grew as the baby cooed.

"Pretty," Nadia sang softly to the child. "Those will be our secret, little lilac." Nadia's fingers flashed, fastening the new blindfold around the babe's head before anyone could see the glow. Nadia pulled on the scrap, and the blindfold didn't waver.

Tears rushed to Nadia's eyes as she surveyed the blindfold. "Permanent?" she muttered. She held the fabric to her eyes. She could still see through it, though it wasn't easy. Her gaze bolted toward the door. She could run. She knew the way home.

Nadia shook her head. Mother had told her to stay, no matter how hard or how scary. The babe needed to be here. She needed to be hidden. Seventeen winters past today, she would meet Momma. It was the plan, though she wasn't sure why the plan even existed. Nadia marveled at the little lilac already blindfolded and cooing. If her sister could be happy, she could be happy too. She had to be brave.

Fumbling, Nadia placed a blindfold around her head, knowing her eyes were beautiful too. Even behind the fabric, they would be lively and truthful. Breena had told her the trainers would be mean, but this was worse than Nadia had imagined. She craned her neck and wrinkled her nose, squirming against the vile shroud, scolding herself for being bad. She pressed her hand to the cut with fury.

"No, little lilac, I was not bad. I was good. I didn't drop you. That lady wanted me to drop you, but I protected you, sister. I will always protect you." Nadia kissed the babe's forehead in the same fashion Breena had constantly pecked her own. "I will be strong, Momma." Nadia lifted her chin to the moonless night, praying her mother could hear her.

The trainer returned, her arms cradling two gray gowns. "Bring her up the stairs and find space to sleep. Your training starts tomorrow. Be dressed in these when the sun rises, and bring your old clothes. Tomorrow you will burn them."

Nadia shuddered. She loved the dress she wore. Breena had made it herself. She had stitched a sun inside the sleeve so she would remember her mother's warmth no matter where she went. Momma always liked hiding little secrets for Nadia.

Crying, Nadia scooped her little lilac into her arms and forced herself to climb the stairs. Tripping over herself, unable to see the next step, Nadia hobbled, sure to protect the babe. That was all that mattered now.

A torch-lined hall was before her with eight wooden doors embedded in the cobblestone walls. She pushed the first door on her left open to see a room filled with girls from newborn to eighteen or so, all asleep in piles of hay strewn across the stone floor. Several sat asleep propped against the wall with others lying over their legs. A space the size of two baking sheets was open in the hay.

Nadia tiptoed over the girls, who all wore the same gray gowns. Nadia peeked beneath her blindfold to see the room more clearly. There were eleven girls. They were bruised and beaten and whimpered in their sleep. Nadia scrunched her nose at the rotted fruit stench, unsure if it was the hay or the poor souls who lay on it. She curled next to her sister, wiggling her finger into the babe's fist.

She studied the soft bends of the baby's face. Worry bubbled in her belly. Mother had not told her the babe's name. Nadia searched her mind as excitement buzzed in her chest. She was able to name her baby sister! Nadia thought of a constellation Mother had pointed out to her once. It was an ancient warrior, a lady Mother said had brought fairness to the land, and Nadia needed a warrior like that now.

"I will call you Tovey."

1

The forest was still as death. Even the trees held their breath, leaves frozen in the early fall. The only noise was the erratic drumming of Tovey's heartbeat. She ran blindfolded, letting her soft boots glide through the woods. Aside from gathering duties, which allowed them an extra four-hundred-foot radius into the trees, servants were never to leave the five acres surrounding the collective. But even gathering was done in doubles, sometimes tied together with a rope. Being alone was strictly forbidden. And Tovey had already shattered both rules.

Paranoia encased Tovey's thoughts. She swore she heard someone speak, but it was nothing. She thought she could sense someone running beside her, but no. She was truly, unquestionably alone. Itching at the blindfold, Tovey cursed the wretched thing. She had worn the blindfold for nearly eighteen years, but it still felt foreign to her, like a strange attachment on her face that didn't belong. Even so, she couldn't imagine a day without it.

Nadia told her to wear it as a badge of honor, not as a burden. Impairments highlighted their strengths, but Nadia saw beauty in the mundane in a way Tovey couldn't. To Tovey, it was shameful, a sign to all who glanced her way that she was offensive, a failure, a stain on society.

The blindfold wasn't as bad when it was freshly knotted, dipped in water, and formed to her face. But after a few days of sweat and nightmare-filled sleep loosening the scrap, it would nag at her worse than the trainers.

Every few moments, she would pause, ears perked. Craning her neck, she detected nothing more than a few woodland creatures skittering across dried leaves. Butterflies tickled at her ribs, giving her new hope. She wasn't alone after all. There were squirrels, tree squeaks, rabbits, and wisps. She cantered, careful not to let a heavy breath escape her cracking lips. Being silent was something she had grown accustomed to, something that was more useful now than ever.

Tovey had been planning on defecting since she'd failed graduation the second time. It was something she'd hoped she'd never have to do. *Defecting* was a word that she had prayed would never become a reality. Tovey aspired to graduate and be assigned to somewhere wonderful in Abolend. She dreamt of a fine house perched in the middle of a city full of life, sound, and sweet smells. But outside of her dreams, she was nothing but a failure who couldn't be as perfect as the trainers wanted, needed.

Nadia would laugh at the trainers behind their backs, but Tovey took them seriously. The trainers were her family. They knew what was best. They knew how to ensure the girls had a safe and fulfilling life. They were cruel at times, yes, but family all the same.

Tovey yearned to be someone they were proud of, someone the other young girls aspired to be like, someone the trainers would tell stories about to inspire the young ones to work harder, be better. But she was incapable: slow, lazy, dim-witted.

Nadia had told Tovey to never fail, to defect. Though Nadia had only told her once, her sister's words burned like fire in Tovey's ears, an irritating buzzing she couldn't stifle.

Nadia had said when servants failed their third test, they were shipped away for use in some other way than a servant. It was said to be something from a nightmare, though no one ever talked of it, not even the trainers. Tovey had three options: graduate, fail, or defect. Since failure was not an option and graduation would not happen no matter how hard she tried, she ran.

Tonight the trainers were spread thin. Three had fallen ill from a seasonal cold that had swept through the house. The other two, Vivian and Lisha, were scrambling to keep up with monitoring the servants. After three months of preparing and minutes of debating, Tovey had to decide: now or never.

Tovey had an hour before Vivian rang the midnight bell. They'd ring bells every hour, even through the night. The new girls would cry at the disturbance, but Tovey had learned to ignore it. The older girls knew there was no use being upset over circumstances they couldn't change. Accept it and sleep.

Vivian would check on the sleeping servants during her rounds, where Tovey should've been at this precise moment. Vivian would count the heads in eight rooms only to realize she was one short.

She'd think it was a miscount. Lisha would count again before they realized one was missing, that Tovey was a defector of Abolend.

Tovey hesitated. She hoped the trainers wouldn't hate her. She hoped they would forgive her, though she knew they would never. They would shun her.

What if she ran back and begged for forgiveness? Would they take her? No. They couldn't. It was against the rules. Defectors were dead, burned out of the hearts of anyone who'd ever loved them. She had to keep running.

Powering forward, Tovey pushed herself, muscles aching for a break. At this point, the radius the trainers would have to search would be far too vast for the collective to find her. She couldn't stop now.

If Tovey were caught within the gathering radius, she would be flogged before the other girls, made an example of. She would be punished, likely deprived of food. The trainers fed them enough to stay healthy but not enough to be strong. She would survive, and her only option would be to succeed in graduating. It was worth the risk. Nadia would have wanted her to at least try.

But now that Tovey had breached the gathering area, she would be killed. Her body would be hung to rot for the other servants-in-training to see daily as a reminder of why defecting wasn't an option. Punishment was common for the most mundane actions. Only a few managed to escape the wrath of Vivian, but even then, no one left the collective without scars.

Untamed foliage darkened the night. Tovey relied on her other senses to fill in the gaps she couldn't see, something she had done her entire life. Through fuzzy vision, the world formed in her mind's eye. Each tree, stone, and leaf painted itself in a hazy vibration as sound echoed from them, telling her their exact placement.

Tovey moved with grace, bouncing from stone to stone, landing in a grassy patch if there were no leaves to crunch beneath her weight. She had practiced moving through the forest surrounding the collective on gathering days for the past few months, hoping she wouldn't make a mistake when this day came. She'd pushed herself to balance on unstable rocks, climb trees, and sprint in her dress, letting herself trust her next steps as she barreled through the thicket. She cursed herself for not trying harder to move even faster. Her attempts at preparedness were laughable.

Her gathering partner, Jack, had scolded her. She knew what Tovey was practicing for, though she'd never report Tovey to the trainers. Jack was three or four years older than Tovey, one of the oldest girls at the collective. She stood three inches above Nadia and had fiery red hair that was kept trimmed by the trainers. Jack acted sad when they cut it in punishment for missing the morning bell, but Jack seemed to like it that way. Though impairments were meant to prevent servants from being seen or loved, they did the opposite for Jack.

Tovey would watch Jack and Nadia hold hands at night, speaking silently as they read each other's lips. Jack would push her finger beneath Nadia's blindfold, tracing her eyes. Tovey thought she'd seen them kiss once. Relationships were forbidden. Touching was forbidden. Now burns covered Jack's shoulder and half of her face, but Tovey refused to remember how she'd gotten them. Ever since the burning, Jack had a soft spot for Tovey's antics.

The air was still, and Tovey was unable to follow the taste of the nearby musky river. Tovey caressed the wet moss on the side of a craggy stone, but without clear vision, she had no idea if following the moss northward would lead her to danger. The patter of stumbling footsteps sounded to her right. Tovey's brow wrinkled, and she wondered if it was another defector. No one from her collective had defected in seven years. Listening closer, Tovey blinked hard through the hemp, struggling to see through the coarse weave in the night. Though the blindfold wasn't intended to blind, assigned to Tovey by a highborn to wear because of her unsightly eyes, it inhibited her sight enough to be a burden. The footsteps sounded in an arching pattern, circling back to her left. They were light, stepping quickly and without question—human.

Shutting her eyes, Tovey contemplated the options: ignore the footsteps or follow them. No one should've been out in these woods. It was forbidden. Plus, Tovey had listened to each of the trainers step through the cobbled halls every night. She knew the sound of their footsteps better than the sound of her heartbeat. These didn't belong to any of them.

She had to track the noise. There was a chance she wouldn't be alone after all. There could've been another defector out there. Someone could have followed her. She prayed it wasn't Jack. Maybe it was someone from another collective. She couldn't be sure unless she tracked the stranger. But she wouldn't find the person while impaired by the irksome blindfold. With a deep breath, Tovey wedged slender fingers into the hardened knot of hemp tied over her eyes, prodding it until it unraveled.

Tovey felt thin lines that'd scarred her cheeks where the material pushed against them. The collective restricted any tampering with their required impairments. If Tovey had ever removed it, she'd have lost an eye or two. Nadia had told Tovey that a girl named

Hallie once removed her blindfold in front of a trainer in order to refasten it. Lisha snapped, drawing her whip faster than the flick of a horse's tail. Lisha wrestled the girl, digging at her face. It ended with Hallie's eye tumbling across the floor like a marble. Hallie survived at the collective another three years before she stole bread from the trainers and lost a hand. She died from an infection at fourteen years old. While it was a privilege to be a servant, they were also replaceable.

Vivian would know Tovey was missing by now. Tovey knew breaking one more rule didn't matter anymore. If she was caught, death was her only option. She'd be strung in front of the collective as they had done with the last group of defectors. Three girls had run during a gathering assignment and hadn't made it ten steps outside the radius before one of their collective sisters reported them. They were nine, twelve, and thirteen. Their bodies were hung in the trees before the sun set that evening. Bile filled Tovey's throat at the thought. Shaking her head, she knew she had to commit to defecting. She would do it for Nadia.

Tovey unveiled herself, adjusting to the faint luminescent glow of waxy leaves. Heart stuttering, she blinked rapidly, in awe of the forest teeming with life. Fireflies twinkled like the stars scattered in the sky above her as they filled their bodies with splotches of warm color in the dying leaves. For a moment, the birth and death of the fireflies' little suns was the singular thought in her mind. A gentle breeze tickled her skin, and she reveled in the sweet kiss of humidity. Stomach lurching with regret, Tovey wondered how much of the world she'd missed from behind the fabric.

Her chest swelled with sadness and happiness, tears teeming in her eyes at the beauty of the world. Never had something been more beautiful or felt more like home. With newfound determination, she began undressing. No longer could she risk wearing her required gray gown, the uniform of a servant. It would hinder her pace or snag on a thorn and leave a thread of evidence behind. She should have stripped it long ago, but she hadn't been ready to accept what she had already committed to.

Tovey slipped out of her bulky dress before twirling it into a ball and tucking it beneath her arm, her blindfold tucked in the dress pocket. Wearing only her undergarments, she crouched in the brush behind a tree. She was thankful the late summer heat melded into fall this year, keeping her warm. Tovey shifted her weight across all limbs before squatting. She tied her long hair into a knot. Her legs reflected moonlight as she launched forward, weaving through the thicket. She tracked the footsteps that had disappeared like fog in the night.

Tilting her head, she took in the sounds of the forest. Insects chirped as finger-size rodents scampered. Farther was a whispering creek, south down the mountainside, with the faintest clink of pebbles shifting beneath the glassy surface. Tovey attempted to moisten her lips without success. Abandoning tracking her potential comrade, she descended the mountain in a swift motion as if she were dancing, limbs stretching as she leaped, ducked, and spun in crisp calculated movements.

Her hands met the icy liquid. She swallowed thankfully, sucking in the cool puddle cupped in her palms. Once more, she lapped at the water, catching her amethyst eyes staring back at her. Nadia had always said they were like lilacs, having seen them once when she was a babe. The leaves rustled behind her. Fine hair rose on her neck, the sensation stopping her from sipping the water. She bent her toes, gripping the smooth rock where she perched.

Snap.

Tovey trapped air in her lungs, and her body turned to stone.

Snap.

Heavy leather boots trudged on the hardened ground, crushing twigs and leaves beneath them as a man's bellowing groan ricocheted off the trees. Not a defector. A muffled click whispered as a symphony of strained wood met her ears. A bowman! Flattening herself on the edge of the creek bed, Tovey wriggled into the nearby brush surrounding the river's edge.

Plong.

The string of a bow rattled nearby. Tovey covered her head as an arrow whirred through the air. The death stick stuttered to the ground, falling in the opposite direction of where she lay. Tension escaped her muscles as she rested her hollow cheek against the moist soil, grateful the bowman wasn't on her trail. He was, however, on a hunt heading somewhere. She hadn't heard a defector earlier, but a hunter. Great.

Tovey hadn't accounted for anything aside from running. She'd considered finding a river and following it until she found a safe place she could rest. But after that, she wasn't sure what defectors did. There were rumors that they turned into wild women and lived off the land. Perhaps she could do that.

She had put her faith into trusting her instincts after defecting, considering she didn't know what else was out there. She would need food and shelter. Tracking the bowman would lead her to town. Anxiety filled Tovey's chest as her breathing quickened. She no longer wanted to accept her new lifestyle. This was a bad idea.

She shouldn't have run. She could have done it, graduated, if she had tried hard enough.

She winced at the thought of killing an animal. She'd be filled with the same cruelty as the trainers if she showed any malice toward the innocent. Often, she would trade hunting and foraging assignments for cleaning duties to avoid taking a life. When the trainers had commanded her to kill a fawn, she'd faltered—reason number one Tovey had failed graduation the first time. The second time, she was too slow to respond to commands. Vivian's tea was to be brought in under ninety seconds. It took Tovey ninety-three. A sign of defiance. For her incompetence, she was punished for a week without food. Not that eating stewed rat was anything to be missed. Still, it was better than the pain that tore at her stomach and the lethargy that overcame her body.

Tightening her grip on the drab dress, she crouched in the shadows, soundlessly slithering forward, hunting the hunter. Narrowing the space between them, she tracked him west before getting close enough to glimpse the man behind the arrow.

The internal drumming within her chest started again, and her fingertips shuddered. Her gaze was glued upon the golden dragon insignia sewn to his leather tunic, the symbol of Abolend. Jaw falling agape, she processed that he wasn't a rogue arrow-flinging archer but an official Abolend bowman commissioned by the king-dom. He was much more dangerous than others and was indeed on a westward trail, heading toward the city. Her gut swirled with panic.

The faint click of the arrow mounting the string shattered her thoughts as she scurried up the gnarled bark of an evergreen to peer upon the hunter. She squinted, observing him with an unobstructed view. His arrow pointed toward a soft fern that shivered with a gentle whisper in the still night. Tovey wouldn't have noticed it had it not been for his keen sense of awareness.

Gurgling and gasping sounded from the creature, and the fern rustled as an injured body fell to the ground.

Tovey's stomach twisted. The arrow had hit something fleshy. The broad-shouldered man scoffed with pleasure, balling his fingers with a thrust into the air. Tovey's arms tightened, and she shifted higher in the branches to see the creature he had hit. Her stomach rumbled with endless hunger. He was indeed an expert, and if she tracked him long enough, she might be able to steal a bit of his meal.

Perched on a bough, she watched the bowman wrap his fingers around the thin leg of his kill. He pulled a limb from the bushes, tossing a mass over his shoulder. It was pale and gangly. It was human. She squinted and leaned forward in the tree. Tovey's heart stuttered, her eyes falling to a bare foot dangling from beneath rough wool. The gray fabric draped on the victim had darkened red from the fragile body lying carelessly over his shoulder—a defector.

Her heart dropped to her feet, rushing waves of flushed fear through her body. She tilted sideways, limbs hugging the tree, spinning herself beneath the branch before dropping. Her instincts told her to run to the girl, but she couldn't. Not now. It was too late.

The bowman paused, broad shoulders shifting toward the gentle sound resonating from Tovey's fall. His heavy brow ridge lurched forward with his torso, his eyes scanning the tree line. Tovey pulled herself into the ground, stilling her chest once more. She squeezed her eyes shut, body covered with uncontrollable chills, praying she wasn't next.

"Back off, you vile bear!" A gravelly growl escaped the bowman's lips. "This one is mine!" He grunted, befalling to laughter. Returning to the death march of his victory whistle, he paraded on, following a game trail to the main path.

Tovey froze as his footsteps faded, shock stiffening her muscles. Though he was no longer visible, she could still hear his death song. Tovey leaped toward the soft fern. She caressed the bloody leaves, evidence of a once-sister from the collective. Tovey scoured her memories of any recent defectors. There had been none. Everyone at her collective had graduated for the past four years—well, until now.

With sticky blood-covered hands, she feverishly searched the fern for evidence. A torn square of gray wool was pinned to the ground with a twig. Tovey balled the soiled fabric in the pocket of her uniform. It was common to try to save something from the dead, a secret ritual for the sisters. They would bury a piece of them, not letting every bit of their memory be wiped into oblivion.

Hunger poked at her stomach despite the gruesome scene. Her glare darted away from where the bowman had traveled, and she contemplated running once more into the unknown. No. She would never survive. Kill or be killed. She wanted neither. Tovey moved with haste to stay on the bowman's trail.

She snuck over branches like a ghost, following the game trail until it opened onto the widened path the bowman was on. Though his whistle had faded, his giant boot steps had left clear prints. Tovey stepped inside the pressed dirt to avoid leaving breadcrumbs.

Over some distance, she gained on his pace, squatting behind cover, straining to see the girl whose life he'd taken. The memory of her true sister plagued her mind. She'd never be able to wash Nadia's lifeless face from the backs of her eyelids.

Nadia had died seven years ago after her last attempt at graduating. After Nadia's failure, Tovey had watched the trainers pull Nadia by her wrists to the well, where they'd whipped her repeatedly. She stood still alongside the rest of the servants at the collective. During punishments, the girls were forced to stop their duties and watch silently. If a tear or whimper escaped, they would meet the same fate: lashings.

Thirty lashings cut at Nadia's back before Vivian barked at the whipping trainer to stop. Tovey's heart wrenched. She hoped that was enough to please the trainers, but it wasn't. Instead, Vivian directed Nadia's punishers to dunk her face in the well bucket.

Over and over again, the trainers pushed her face into the water. And over and over again, they would let her gulp air before shoving her back under the unforgiving surface. Nadia's thrashing became more violent. Steam built pressure like a boiling kettle in Tovey's heart, and she was unable to stay silent any longer. Screams ripped through Tovey's throat, yet despite her pleas, the trainers gagged her and made her listen. Shock stilled Tovey's bones as Nadia lifted her head for the last time.

"Never fail, Tovey," Nadia commanded, her neck straining as she fought the trainers. Her lips paled as she gave up. "Defect!" Her face went under the water for the last time. The trainers weren't going to let her survive, not after saying *that* word. *Defect*.

The trainers threw Nadia's body into the woods like trash. They forced all the servants inside while they wrapped her discarded body in linens, preparing it for burning. Each servant carried a piece of firewood to the clearing, and one by one, they tossed the wood into a roaring flame. Four servants carried the sack and tossed it into the flames. Jack panicked. She lunged into the fire after Nadia's body. Jack's dress melted around her as her infernal scream shattered the night.

Tovey watched, still as stone. Her sister burned. Jack howled into the night.

Never fail. Defect. Defect.

The words echoed in Tovey's mind with every punishment she had to endure after Nadia's death. Screaming got her gagged for the week. Sympathizing with servants being punished was five lashings. With each lashing, Tovey promised her sweet sister she wouldn't fail. By the fifth lashing, Tovey had vowed she'd honor Nadia's wish and defect before failure.

Tovey followed a hundred feet behind the bowman, breaking from her memory, avoiding the drips of blood coming from the defector's body. The bowman tired after some time. He tossed his kill to the dirt, his knees meeting earth. His shoulders hunched as he rubbed a stick against another, starting a fire. After peeling the socks from his feet, he sat, casually roasting his toes in front of the coals. Some time later, he slumped into a pile of leaves, his heavy eyes sliding shut. Mutely, Tovey waited for stertorous breathing to start before approaching the dead girl.

Crawling with careful movements around the outskirts of the clearing, Tovey inched toward the girl. Filthy tattered fabric wrapped the body. Tovey's eyes met the dead servant's lifeless milky gaze. A knot twisted in Tovey's stomach, bringing bitter bile to her tongue. Tovey's bony hands clasped over her mouth as she whimpered, unable to control herself, recognizing the corpse. Sylvia.

She had left the collective weeks ago. The girls were told Sylvia had graduated early and was sent to her assignment in the night because her placement required a qualified servant immediately. Sylvia had been one of the most loyal trainees at the collective. Her impairment attacked her silvery hair, draped like waves of silken fabric atop her head. The trainers had made her burn it off because she would fiddle with it. It had brought her comfort, and it was not allowed to stay.

Since they were young, Sylvia had been promised a place serving the highest highborns, King Mallum and his court. Rarely ever beaten, Sylvia was a shining example of what was expected of them: to obey. Tovey brushed strands of hair from the girl's face, wondering how she'd ended up a defector. Her eyebrows scrunched, and she contemplated if the collective had lied about her graduation and if they'd bring Sylvia's body back to be strung up in the trees around the collective. No, they couldn't.

If shining-star Sylvia hadn't graduated, bringing her back to the collective would mean they'd lied, and lying was against the rules, punishable by having your tongue removed. The trainers weren't even allowed to lie. If guards heard, they would have stormed the collective and removed the concern promptly. Tovey's mind raced, wondering how many times she had been lied to by the collective before. Her fingers combed Sylvia's hair, pressing it flat once more.

Swallowing dry air, Tovey knew she could have been the defector on the bowman's back instead of dear Sylvia. She was lost, unprepared, and unskilled. She could wander the woods for weeks until a bowman struck an arrow through her heart. Bowing her head, Tovey thanked Sylvia for what she knew she had to do.

Begrudgingly, Tovey swallowed her bile. She smacked the ground, testing how asleep the bowman was. He didn't stir.

Tipping her head back, she let out a hushed yell. His foot flinched. Her cheeks puffed with air in a stress-relieving hope that she could muster a sense of bravery from her rattled bones.

Tovey pressed her lips to Sylvia's forehead, as Nadia had always done to her. Tovey whispered through whimpering cries, "I'm so sorry, but you have saved my life, and you will never know."

Tovey took a scrap of fabric from Sylvia's dress. She wrapped it around the dead girl's head, shielding her eyes. She pressed her palm into the wound in Sylvia's chest, covering her fingers in thick blood before matting Sylvia's singed silvery hair with the sticky liquid. Shoveling with her nails, she pulled dirt from the ground and mixed it with mud to cover the rugged ends. Through scattered breaths and broken tears, Tovey clasped both hands together. "You will not be forgotten."

Wolves howled in the distance. They must have smelled death. Tovey filled her lungs, tilted her head toward the sky, and mimicked the howl of the wolves, calling them to a fresh kill. Her eyes darted to the bowman, tossing side to side as his sleep thinned.

She pecked Sylvia's head one last time, dirt and blood covering her lips. Tovey lunged into the trees, following the road a bit farther. Paws plummeted on the soft soil behind her, running toward the fresh corpse. The bowman's barbaric yell echoed through the valley, sending a ripple of yelps from the wolves. Tovey ignored the plunder, forcing her limbs to keep pushing toward Abolend.

Crumbling, Tovey stumbled toward a gulley with the faintest stream of water passing between its walls. Her chin rested at the water's edge, body spent. Between tearless cries, she washed the dirt, blood, and sweat from her body, the dawn lighting the forest with pink tones of wildflowers.

She gripped a jagged rock, flashing a long wave of hair across a flat stone. Forcefully, she hammered the rock, yanking at her hair. Her steady fist chopped her waist-length locks into a ragged bob brushing a smidge above her shoulders, identical to Sylvia's.

She dressed in her collective uniform, grateful it had avoided staining. She dipped the blindfold into the lilting stream, wetting it before tying it around her skull. It dried, sculpting painfully to her face, but it was the requirement for ensuring it would never slip. She was now Sylvia.

Assignments weren't based on the girls' impairments, though it was the best method the collective had for identification. Any extreme body modifications were logged—at least they were supposed to be. It was plausible Sylvia's short hair and Tovey's blindfold had not been recorded. Identification of bodies didn't matter much when they desecrated the remains anyway. If word reached her trainers that a mauled body had been found with a blindfold, they'd assume it was Tovey. They were similar enough, and no further investigation would be necessary. It was a shot worth taking.

But Tovey couldn't leave her blindfold behind. Impairments were for life. Plus, Nadia hadn't liked the rules, aside from one. Never remove your blindfold, no matter what. It was so serious that if Tovey ever needed to fasten the knot again, Nadia would make her hide in a closet and close her eyes while she did it. Tovey hadn't seen anyone question impairments. They just were. Even with a new life, the thought of abandoning her impairment made her stomach knot. If she were to commit to a life of servitude, she needed to start following the rules. At least a little.

"May the light guide you," Tovey whispered into the wind. She followed the path, her dress fluttering carelessly, devoid of any sign that she had witnessed a horrific death and held in her pocket a bloodied piece of fabric. Wiping the sweat from her cheeks, she softened her lips into a slight smile, hands folded in front of her with a straight spine.

"Abolend, here I come."

2

Ash filled the thick air, choking out the warmth of the sun. A monolithic sandstone wall with decorative battlements as tall as a mature pine bordered the village growing from the mist as Tovey neared the arched opening. Fires from cobbled homes heated the fall breeze with scents of roasting meats. A growl emanated from Tovey's stomach, saliva leaking from under her tongue, filling her mouth.

Ironclad guards lined the archway, ten or more leaning over the top with others littered around the base. The men observed the forest coming to life with morning gatherers leaving dressed in pocketed aprons and carrying woven baskets. Tovey suppressed a smile at the people. It was familiar, like home. Dirt pathways turned to shell the farther she emerged from the forest. She yearned to lean over and touch the strange-shaped pebbles she had never seen before, but that wouldn't be wise. Not here. Not with Abolend guards so near.

She wasn't supposed to be alone, and with so many guards, she wouldn't go unnoticed. Escorts were assigned to girls who'd graduated. Sometimes guards came, sometimes townspeople, and sometimes the girls left with the man and donkey who delivered weekly supplies. Tovey's eyes flicked from person to person, searching for one who was returning from the woods.

Static buzzed like lightning in her chest as her eyes fell upon a young man with a basket full of firewood. He was fit, with a linen tunic tucked messily into the trousers that bunched around his waist. The basket he carried strained with the weight of the wood. He popped the basket higher on his arm, and the handle snapped, sending wood dancing across the ground. He was frazzled, and his hands rushed across his braided hair. Swiftly, he filled his arms with the wood, struggling to see in front of him.

Tovey neared the gatherer, standing a few feet behind him on the right—the rightful place of a servant. She followed the man, who was too busy adjusting the wood stack in his arms to notice he had a servant tailing him. Tovey hoped it would appear to the guards as if the gatherer were her escort.

Tovey trembled as she walked through Abolend's arch. Her training kicked in, and she clasped her fingers in front of her, head bowed to show her obedience and commendation to the guardsmen. Vivian would've been proud.

Shutting her eyes briefly, she took in the kingdom's air, tasting a slight saltiness in the ashen skies. Nibbling her lip, she grew ashamed that she wasn't skilled enough to survive in the wilderness, yet a life of servitude would provide for her, and she would be satisfied. She had to be. Sylvia had given her the chance to defect and honor Nadia's dying wish. Tovey had survived failure, so she'd met Nadia's expectations. The rest was up to her. Wandering the forest for weeks only to be skewered by a bowman was not how she wanted her life to end.

The guardsmen watched her. They wouldn't know she was an impostor. They couldn't. Sylvia was supposed to arrive at the kingdom, and here Tovey was, a little late, but here all the same. Tovey, the defector, was dead in the woods. If they discovered the truth, she would die. No one had ever taken the face of another—at least no one she had heard of.

Stomach churning, Tovey knew she would break a rule and lie. Survival was all that mattered now. She formulated a story in her head. Sylvia had been needed at the collective for a few more weeks. After all, she was so advantageous it was hard for the trainers to let her go.

Sylvia was the perfect servant, and that is what Tovey would be. Girls had chatted at night, telling stories of how Sylvia was assigned to the highest position, serving the highest of the highborns—King Mallum and his court. They dreamt about how glamorous it would be to be in the service of the highest, how proud the trainers would be that they had achieved the ultimate status of servitude. A handful of girls had even gotten to see highborns before and told tall tales of their unmatched beauty and the impractical sparkling objects they adorned themselves with. The girls always giggled at the idea, though Tovey found it fascinating.

The town rustled with people, who were like leaves in the wind, all moving toward different places. It was a stone jungle. The ground was flat, much different than the hills around the collective, and not a single tree stood inside, allowing the sun to graze every surface. The dew-covered walls gleamed like gemstones.

Fresh bread filled the kingdom with a decadent scent that Tovey swore she could taste. It was magnificent.

Shells grumbled beneath her feet as she strode past guards with a false sense of confidence. They turned their thick necks with tilted heads, watching the pair pass. Deep muffled whispers traveled through the guards. Tovey bit her tongue. Something was off.

A metallic clang of boots trailed behind her. She was not to stop unless addressed, though she yearned to turn around and see who was stalking her heels.

"Aye! Servant!" One of the men spat, a wad of slime falling beside her skirt.

Tovey's muscles clenched. She was frozen in her boots, knowing she was not permitted to move if someone spoke to her. Moving or starting a conversation without being commanded to do so could be seen as threatening, not to mention disrespectful, which was why servants were forbidden.

"You're fresh from the collective? I didn't see you leave this mornin', and I also didn't know we were expecting anyone today," he mumbled.

Tovey watched the clumsy firewood man stumble away, unaware that he was her protection. Though her insides were screaming, she did not quiver an inch. Questions were not to be responded to unless commanded to do so. The guard's eyes paused on her as he frowned.

"I command you to report to me your name, post, and why the hell your escort left you," the man growled into Tovey's face, his sour breath stroking her cheeks.

"Boy! You better get back here!" another guard yelled at the man carrying firewood.

The man continued to stumble into a wave of people, lost in the crowd.

"Servant, answer your commands."

She prayed he couldn't hear the erratic beating from her chest. Forcing herself steady, she said, "I am Servant. I have come from the collective. I have been assigned to King Mallum and his court. And I assume my escort could not see that I was still following." Tovey bit her tongue, forcing herself steady. Lies and truths. Truths and lies. She prayed the guards wouldn't notice.

"I lost her escort, boss. He's got dung for brains, that one."

The guard's brows turned upward, his shoulders spinning to a nearby guard for answers.

"Let him go," the lead guard said. "This one's going to the king. She could have walked here without an escort. They've got them trained so well. Like dogs."

Tovey's lips wavered, and she fought the instinct to purse them. It was always a battle to keep her face still, calm, and serene.

"All hail King Mallum!" the guard shouted in her face.

"Hail! Hail King Mallum, leader of the brave, father of the land," echoed the surrounding guardsmen.

Tovey listened to the chorus of men, captivated by their unsettling unity. If she were a dog, then these men were wolves, howling the king's name like ravenous animals.

"It ain't every day they assign one of them to King Mallum. Let her go before we delay his swine for too long," a guard hissed. "You are commanded to continue directly to your post."

Tovey bowed her head, taking meticulous steps forward, unsure where the castle was. Still, she would travel to the center, hoping it made sense to have the castle fortified in the middle, the same as the collective.

"Aye! Servant!" the guard shouted once more.

A sharp breath jolted her. The gig was up; she must have done something wrong. Cursing the man silently, Tovey fell into a frozen stillness.

"I command you to tell me your real name." A deep growl licked between his teeth. With an unwavering grimace plastered on his face, he turned toward his fellow guards.

"Servant. We don't have names." Her monotone voice was calm. It was true. The trainers never used their names, though they knew them secretly. The girls whispered them to one another in the shroud of night like the sound of a bat's wings. Sylvia. Jack. Nadia. Tovey.

"Continue on," he grumbled, satisfied with the answer.

Tovey faltered. He *hadn't* commanded. Disobeying a guard could lead to whippings.

"Wow! She is highborn servant material!" He spat another goopy puddle before lowering his voice so the rest of the guards couldn't hear. "Tell me, do you have to obey *all* commands?" A grimy sneer crossed his face. He drew a slimy tongue over crusted lips. Fire filled her veins. This guard knew she had to obey every command—even the vile. "I'm joking. Go on, go on. I command you to leave!"

Tovey scurried away with a bit more haste. She couldn't blame them, the guards. Their collective was rumored to make them behave not only obediently but boisterously enough to have a false sense of power. They were playing a game precisely as she was. Everyone was a cog in the machine of Abolend.

As she wove through the knotted streets, people emerged from shelled homes. It was hard not to smile. Forcing a frown, she tried with all her might to stifle the upward turn of her mouth, settling for a tightened line.

Aside from the people at the collective, she had never seen anyone else. People were noisy, shouting as if the people in front of them couldn't hear them with talk of trades and strange topics Tovey couldn't comprehend. Vivian would have beaten Tovey if she'd spoken like that.

The people were rich rainbows of color. Dressed in tunics of varying fabrics and patterns, they looked like migratory birds visiting for spring. Some appeared soft as jackalopes, while others shined like spiderwebs in the rising light. Men, women, and children all clamored on the streets in an unchained melody of immeasurable beauty.

Tovey had always assumed there were exclusively highborns and servants, though she imagined there were servants with higher standing, like where she assumed Nadia had come from. But there appeared to be another class of middle people who roamed the streets in a strange position between servant and highborn. Tovey tilted her head, captivated by the idea of being a middle person.

The scent of lavender spiraled in steamy wafts as she passed a washing house, pushing the familiar smell of the collective's washrooms into her hair. Even the piles of soiled clothing towering in the washing house were beautiful. Her eyebrows stitched. If she dressed as a middle person, she could blend in and survive, relinquishing her duties as a servant—no hiding beneath the mask of Sylvia, and no becoming a defector. She wouldn't have to live in the woods or have any guidelines to stick to. It seemed perfect.

Ducking through the narrow alley, Tovey turned to walk behind the washing house. She peered above the stone wall into the open-air washroom. Eight wooden tables sat in rows, preventing the sorted piles of clothing from touching the cobbled floor. The washing woman turned her back to Tovey, carrying a heavy bundle to an oversize stone basin sunken in the ground.

The woman heaved the pile, turning to toss in fresh lavender sprigs from a nearby shelf. She stirred the mixture with a wooden pole, humming a haunting tune. Like clockwork, she worked, tossing a log on the fire as steam blurred the space between them.

The sun crossed mid-sky as afternoon came. Tovey bolted inside the building toward one of the tables, examining the wares closer. Her fingers snagged a petite emerald dress. The fabric was soft and smooth in her hands, unlike the crunchy collective uniform she wore. The washwoman turned back toward Tovey. Ducking, Tovey's knees clashed against the stone floor. The washwoman's song danced in the steam. She turned her back to Tovey, spinning more clothes in the basin.

The silk was smooth, like water on her skin. Fabrics, scents, and colors she didn't even know existed were right here in Abolend. Tovey ran her fingers through the cracks in the stone floor, admiring the broken shells lying in the crevices.

One was a broken conch shell in the shape of a rose. It was beautiful, and she didn't understand what it was made from. Perhaps a stone of sorts. She pushed it into her pocket. Her heartbeat accelerated. It was invigorating to take, to have an object that was hers. She'd not been allowed to keep items like this before, and now she had an object with no use, like a highborn.

Tovey cradled the dress, contemplating wearing it. If she did, she would be a middle person. They still did servants' duties, but they weren't in doubles, weren't in uniform, and weren't under the eye of trainers. They didn't seem impaired, though Tovey knew some impairments were invisible to the eye. Holding the fabric to her nose, she breathed deeply, sucking in the floral notes. This dress was an opportunity, a way to avoid being found out to be a fraud, a way to avoid future trouble.

Nadia had been somewhere before the collective. Girls who came to the collective were prohibited from talking of anything before they arrived. No talk of places, people, or names. Even Nadia hadn't liked talking about her life before Tovey, like it hadn't even existed. Had she been a middle person before she'd brought Tovey to the collective? Tovey cursed Nadia for keeping a secret.

Her options were thin. Be a middle person and try to survive here in Abolend, or be a servant and try to survive until they discovered that Tovey was not Sylvia. Either way, her days were numbered, but one way seemed intriguing.

Tovey waited for the washwoman's footsteps to still by the washbasin.

Silence.

Tovey scampered, slipping out into the alleyway. She darted to a crevice between two buildings that was just bigger than a garbage bin. Catching her breath, she pressed the dress against her bosom. Her chest was going to explode with excitement. She had done it. She had stolen the dress. It was wrong. She should've felt guilty. Instead, her heart danced.

"There you are!"

Before Tovey even processed the voice, an Abolend guard stood before her. His potato nose poked out from beneath a metal helmet. The guard's sausage fingers wrapped around her neck, pushing her against the shelled sandpaper-like wall. Rocks tore at her back, unraveling exhausted threads.

"Master Daleen has been awaiting your arrival, and you are late."

Tovey bowed her head in defeat, though her chin barely moved in his grip.

"You are assigned to King Mallum and the court, correct? We heard of your arrival this morning and have been awaiting you."

Tovey attempted to bow her head again, but her chin was unable to lower. The man tightened his hand around her neck as she gasped for air.

"You were to arrive weeks ago, and now today you are loitering. I don't care if a lousy escort kept you behind or whatever bollocks you want to use as an excuse." He growled deep and low. "Don't be late again."

He released his hand. Air rushed like rapids back into her chest.

"And what is *this?*" He snatched the dress out of Tovey's hand, pressing his branded forearm into her chest, forcing her hollow body against the wall again, the beating not yet over. This time the wall cut at her skin.

Instead of focusing on the pain, Tovey turned her eyes to his brand. It was a circular dragon insignia, the symbol of Abolend. Servants were never branded—they were mutilated in other ways instead—and Tovey wondered if the brand from the men's collective was somehow worse, marking the men as property, as weapons. She wasn't either of those.

A meager crowd formed around the guard, anxious to see the repercussions. Servants disobeying was a rarity, so everyone wanted a front-row seat to the festivities. Tovey's nostrils flared as a woman in a sweat-covered apron approached, the woman's eyes bulging from her skull. She pushed her way to the front of the crowd. For a moment, Tovey thought the woman was Nadia, running to berate her for being so reckless. But she was too old. And Nadia was dead.

"Thank you for grabbing this for me, dearie." She ripped the dress from the guard's hand. "Is there a problem?"

"You *asked* her to do this?"

"Yes, she is a servant, is she not?"

"To the king!"

The woman fell silent, cocking her peppered bun toward Tovey. "I did not know that. She was out here, and I put her to use. What is she going to do, refuse?"

"Don't challenge me, Breena."

Tovey raised an eyebrow. The name was familiar somehow, like one from a story told to her long ago. The guard's hand tightened around her neck, and her thoughts began fading like smoke.

"Oh, calm down, Gorv. I'm not threatening your almighty power." She lowered her voice to a whisper. "Just don't expect me to sneak you or your men drinks anymore."

With a huff, Gorv released Tovey. She filled her lungs once more, grateful for the kind stranger. Breena spun, disappearing into the alley, her apron fluttering as she turned around to glance at Tovey with a penetrating gaze.

"But for your defiance . . ." Gorv turned his hand backward with sweaty glory. It swung toward Tovey's face, blowing her cheek sideways into the wall. Her sunken face split against the warm stone, draining her body, and she collapsed onto the ground.

The crowd dispersed around them, satisfied with the outcome. The guard pulled Tovey to her feet, guiding her forward by the small of her neck. Her feet fumbled in circular patterns beneath her stained dress, and the hope of becoming a middle person leaked from her wounds. Blackness spun in a cloud of doom, impairing her vision as her unsteady legs wobbled.

Gorv shepherded Tovey to the center of town. The streets became more expansive, reflected in the buildings that towered above those around them. If the structures had noses, they would've been upturned at their neighbors.

Tovey and Gorv made their way toward the castle. She could barely make out the features. It stood taller than most of the trees in the forest, an impressive feat for builders. He led her to a scrubby wooden door embellished with wrought iron fixtures in the back of the massive structure. The rusty hinges screamed at his hand as the wooden door opened. The guard shoved her still-swaying body into the filth before slamming the door and locking it behind her.

Face full of dirt, Tovey crawled to the stone wall and rested against it for a moment. She sat on the floor in a tenebrous hall. Biting her tongue, she stumbled to the servants' quarters.

"Eat dung, Gorv," she mumbled beneath her breath.

The collective taught the girls that the servants' dwellings were in the deepest level of the residence, always the last door at the end of the hindmost hallway. The farther away the servants were, the more suitable it was for the highborns. If they remained out of sight, it prevented the servants from being seen for who they were in their hearts. Highborns were too important to worry about the woes of a servant.

The servants' quarters were dim, and a few bales of hay were strewn across the dirty cobble floor. Night had come and most of the servants were asleep, hair disheveled across exhausted faces, the pungent scent of sweat filling the room. It was just like home.

Tovey didn't recognize any of the women, and a twinge of relief warmed her bones. Her disguise might last her one more day. Tovey pressed the inside of her sleeve to her bloody cheek. She took an open spot near the cobwebbed corner, letting her body collapse.

Blinking in the dim room, she wept silently. Her thoughts were dizzy with fright. She cried until there were no more tears. Eyes burning, they forced themselves shut. Sleep and nightmares formed into one while one thought crossed her mind: What in the name of Abolend had she done?

3

Whistling from a distant kettle woke Tovey from a heavy slumber. She pulled the sleeve of her dress away from the crusted split on her cheek, which was tender and swollen. Digging dried tears from her eyes, she shook away the nightmares of Sylvia's bloodied corpse.

She wobbled to her feet, brushing stray hay from her dress. The chamber was empty. Brittle cropped hair laced around her fingers as she mourned the loss of the extra length she had grown accustomed to. But her hair was a fair price to pay for a safe home. At least now she knew this was her only shot.

"Sylvia, I assume?" A slender woman with a braid pressed against her head stepped in front of Tovey, wearing a crimson gown that shimmered with a warm glow in the torchlit halls.

Tovey bowed her head, wondering how she knew Sylvia's name.

"Rumors, darling. The castle's servants know everything, and I like to use names. Our real names. Come here." The woman spun from the sleeping chamber, leading Tovey two doors down to the laundry room. The woman was the same height as a broomstick. Her face was angular, the vision of strength, but her smile was kind. She grabbed a crimson dress in Tovey's size. "Change into this. Servants of the castle wear a separate color from the masses—no more gray. Congratulations on graduating from the collective. It is not every day someone is well-mannered enough for court."

Tovey's mouth turned upward, and she imagined for a blissful moment that she had passed. She'd never know if she had what it took to be a servant or what assignment her scores would've allowed her to take, if any. Her final test was next week, but Tovey would never risk failing the promises she'd made to Nadia: to never let anyone see her eyes and defect before failure.

Nadia had been complicated. She'd hated rules but loved one. She'd never mentioned defecting but then told Tovey she must. It didn't make much sense, but the blood of the collective was thicker than the water of the womb. Finally, Tovey had fulfilled both promises.

Tovey undressed, scooping the shell fragment and torn wool from Sylvia's dress into the pocket of her new gown, careful not to let Master see it.

Masters were the highest position of servants. With additional power, they received improved food and housing. But if a servant misbehaved beneath their watch, it was their head—a risky but honored position to hold. Master swirled the washing linens, sending the scent of fresh spring gardens into the air, a luxury held for trainers at the collective.

The crimson dress was soft on Tovey's skin and flattered her in areas where the gray sack hadn't before. For the first time in forever, Tovey was light on her feet, glowing with pride. She spun, and the dress billowed around her in a silken wave of red.

"Ahem." Master scowled at Tovey before cracking a smile. "I remember when I first came here. It is a nice reward. I'm Daleen." She leaned in close, whispering, "And while you are down here, you don't need to wait for commands. Relax a bit, but no mistakes when serving, got it?"

Tovey's head bobbed as a slight smile crept across her face. She was grateful for a kind master.

"Is this from trainers?" Master Daleen's eyebrows rose. Her long fingers wrapped Tovey's chin, turning it this way and that, examining the cut in the torches' glow.

Tovey hesitated, unsure if she was truly permitted to speak without a command. "No, Master Daleen. It was an Abolend guard."

"A guard?"

"Yes, Master. One called Gorv." Guards were still allowed names. They were regarded as heroes. "I was lost and did not arrive promptly. My escort did not realize guards were questioning me and disappeared into the crowd." Tovey spoke carefully, sure to strengthen her cover story.

Daleen huffed, face turning the color of a tomato. She stomped across the hall to a cabinet. The hinges spat rust as the squealing cabinet opened. Daleen's finger dipped into a pocket-size jar, pulling out a dollop of salve. She pressed the ointment to Tovey's cheek. Wincing, Tovey bit her tongue, locking her spine.

"This will help keep infection away. And don't mess up again. Servants of the castle are under strict watch for the protection of the king. What took you so long to get an escort, anyway? I've been waiting for your arrival."

"They needed me to stay longer."

Confusion crossed Master's face.

"There was a defector, and a few trainers were ill. They needed my assistance." Tovey wove truth and lies again, hoping it would work.

"A defector? Hmm."

Tovey remained silent.

"Let's go over your assignment." Daleen's eyes flickered, head swaying as she gathered her thoughts. Tovey let her shoulders relax.

"Every morning, you will wake at four and begin laundry. Never enter a highborn's room, but take the pile of clothes their servants leave outside the door after they retire. It is their personal servant's responsibility to leave it out for you. They are the only help allowed to interact with that direct highborn. Understand?"

Tovey bobbed her head.

"Bring the laundry here to the basement and begin washing. At five, you will start scrubbing floors, corridors, statues, everything in sight. They must shine in the morning light. And at seven, you will wait outside the kitchen. The cooks will prepare and leave trays of food, which you will carry to the dining hall. Set the table and leave. Serving servants are the only attendants allowed within the chamber during dining. The honor must be earned, and since you are new, you will remain on standby until they finish.

"That's when you will enter and clean the room. Then return the plates to the kitchen, where kitchen servants will polish them."

Tovey smiled.

"Yes, no dishes for you!" Daleen chuckled. "At nine, you will return to the laundry and finish it no later than eleven. That is when you will fold the clothing to deliver through a hidden corridor. Give the wares to the highborns' servants for them to return to their rooms. Do that by twelve. Scrub the north hall. Then return to the kitchen by hour sixteen and carry trays to the dining hall for dinner. You are to wait until they have finished and then clean the dining hall. At hour eighteen, sweep the floors of the main hallway and retire at hour twenty.

"Oh, if you need food, you may find scraps brought to us by kitchen servants around hour thirteen in the door across the hall. The latrine is at the end of the corridor." Daleen smiled. "We don't have chamber pots here. The chutes drain right out into the pond outside. Fascinating, castles." Daleen's eyes were bright.

Tovey bowed her head, amused by Daleen's utter joy over the latrines, though they were admittedly impressive compared to the buckets at the collective. Tovey followed Master to a map, where Daleen relayed her duties again, solidifying the schedule in stone. Daleen's long fingers pointed to various halls and paths to use. Tovey memorized it quickly, as she knew Sylvia would have done.

"All right now, to work! You woke late. It is hour six already. I always give new girls a break. A gift for your first day. Never again though." Daleen flashed a smile before turning away. Tovey was grateful for Master Daleen being the exact opposite of greasy-haired Vivian, who would poke the girls awake with sewing needles in the night because rest was for the wicked.

4

Each day passed with simple stillness. The food was edible, tastier than at the collective, and the sun was unable to burn her nose since she was no longer allowed outside. But Tovey was grateful to leave the trampled dirt surrounding the collective behind. In still moments, she would admire the shell she had taken, which was smooth and beautiful in her hand. Though it was broken, it was brilliant.

The week passed seamlessly. Tovey finessed her chores into a streamlined relay, sometimes even finishing by hour twenty. Efficiency was not explicitly rewarded, but accumulating extra sleeping hours was something Tovey couldn't resist striving for. Tovey would wake at hour three to wash and dress. She would follow her morning routine by rushing through laundry duties to linger during serving times, where she often admired the main hall. The sandstone walls were carved with ornate floral groupings, gold-plated dragons, and arches that folded in crisscrossed patterns atop towering halls.

Sweetness tickled Tovey's tongue as she followed the decadent scent of the morning's meal. She adored watching the kitchen servants as they loaded reflective trays with exotic foods before carrying them into the dining hall. There, she and a fellow servant would fill the table with delicacies laid out in a pleasurable and presentable manner.

The girl refused to speak to Tovey, but she hadn't been offended. It took time to build trust with other servants. Some girls at the collective Tovey never spoke to even though she grew up with them. The serving girl was a few years older than Tovey. A jagged scar ran diagonally from her brown hair across her nose before curving from the corner of her mouth. Tovey winced, imagining the pain.

"You're the new servant, right?"

"Yes."

"Well, Servant, you better make sure these pastries are perfectly aligned with alternating toppings." The girl pointed to Tovey's display with each type grouped together.

"I didn't know."

"Now you do." The girl pursed her full lips. "I find it hard to believe your trainers didn't go over pastry patterns with you."

Tovey remained silent. She had never gotten that far. The trainers knew she wouldn't ever be assigned a position where she'd be in the presence of such fine food.

"Where are you from?" the girl asked.

"A collective . . . well, I'm not sure where. Surrounded by trees."

"Mountains?"

"Some hills."

"I'm from one near the coast. You could smell the salt in the air."

"I've never seen the coast," Tovey admitted.

"You're on it now. If you ever get the chance to serve on a higher floor, look south out a window."

Smiling, Tovey imagined a vast bath of water before shivering from the idea of drowning like Nadia. "You serve during breakfast, right?" Tovey asked. "I haven't seen you waiting in the corridors while they eat."

"Yes, and it's almost time for you to go." The girl gripped Tovey's arm, pulling Tovey's ear close to her mouth. "I'm Marka."

Tovey's heart raced when she heard the girl's name. A sign of trust.

"Sylvia," Tovey whispered.

Tovey made her way to the kitchen to watch the servants. Tovey wasn't allowed to assist, but the kitchen servants were always falling behind. Their fingers bled and peeled from the lasting moisture of the water. Tovey pitied one of the older servants, a walking skeleton who constantly struggled with her duties. Tovey hated seeing the kitchen servants in pain. It seemed useless to stand around and wait. But those were her commands, and she needed to obey for once.

Marka and three other servants waited on the nobles, moving like a clock. When they stopped filling glasses or answering commands, they stood like statues in the corner of the room. Afterward, Tovey returned to the dining hall to help clear the crumb-ridden table and scrub the boot-scuffed floors alongside Marka.

※

Days passed as she moved like a puppet through the halls. Each moment was more draining than the last. Her soul died a little every time she discarded the highborns' pastries. And every moment she watched the kitchen servants suffer, her blood simmered until she couldn't stop it from boiling over.

She piled the scraps from the highborns on her tray. They didn't go to the servants; they went to the trough for the pigs. Servants got burnt bread, eggs that tasted a little too sour, cabbage soup—which consisted of wilted heads—and leftover broth from whatever meal they'd made. It was infuriating that pigs were served more lavish meals and that middle people would, on rare occasions, indulge in higher-quality meals, but never the servants.

"Don't you wonder what they taste like?" Tovey whispered close to Marka, soaking in the newfound friendship.

"No."

"Yes, you do."

Marka shook her head. Tovey pinched a minuscule crumb into the pocket of her dress.

"What are you doing?" Marka's eyes widened.

Tovey bounced her shoulders, returning the dishes to the kitchen with Marka. The two twirled into a nearby hidden passageway for servants.

"Here, take a bite." Tovey pinched a crumb into each of their palms.

"We shouldn't."

"No one will know; it was scrap, garbage. The highborns don't hurt us for hunting rats. They are also garbage to the highborns. There is no difference."

"But I will know that there *is* a difference."

Tovey rolled her eyes, but Marka couldn't see that behind Tovey's blindfold.

"Sylvia, I will report you to Master Daleen. Put it back."

"I will put it back," Tovey lied. She wished Marka would take a risk. Nadia would have. "But smell it first, up close." Tovey lifted the teeniest morsel to her nose, breathing in the crumb. "Whoops." Tongue melting, drool spread the fragrant jellied notes across her taste buds, which relished the sweetness. "Oh my Abolend. That is amazing. Eat yours."

Marka shook her head. "I cannot believe you. There are rules for a reason. Why are you doing this?"

Tovey remained silent. Guilt made her skin crawl. She shouldn't have eaten the crumb. Sylvia wouldn't have. It was exhausting to be so perfect all the time. The floggings weren't anything to be missed, but the trainers had missed half the offenses she and Nadia could get away with. What was the worst that could happen anyway? She'd die. Great.

What was wrong with dying? Then she could be with Nadia and hug her sister again. This Sylvia disguise was temporary. It'd be over the day someone from her collective got assigned here. The day a trainer received word that Sylvia had reached Abolend and was serving. The day the man and the donkey who delivered supplies recognized her. Any second she could die, so why not live?

"You won't report me, will you?"

"Not today, Sylvia."

"Then tomorrow I will take another," Tovey joked.

A stern line formed on Marka's scowling face.

"Or not."

5

News of a dead defector infiltrated the castle on Tovey's twelfth day. The news swarmed into the highborns' conversations like a mosquito, forcing them to itch. They couldn't handle the idea that someone had been unwilling to honor the kingdom with service. It was the juiciest gossip they'd had since one of the ladies had found a snake in her bedchamber. Rumor said it was the young prince who had placed it there after she offended him somehow.

King Mallum was said to wreak havoc on the castle when someone defected. That was part of the reason the highborns couldn't keep the news out of their mouths. It was a strange combination of wanting to tear the defector down to stroke King Mallum's ego while also hoping he would snap and someone's head would fly. Entertainment.

The king took the act of defecting as a personal attack against him. Tovey hadn't had a single thought about the king when she defected. She had, however, worried about how Vivian and the other trainers would feel toward her. In fact, she'd not thought about the king at all, only the guilt of the trainers' disappointment that seventeen years of effort hadn't paid off. Tovey hadn't left because she wanted to. If it weren't for Nadia's final wish, she would have tried graduation one last time. Tovey had left because she *had* to do one last thing for Nadia, no matter how irrevocable the choice was.

The highborns chattered ceaselessly, rumors of the defector spreading throughout the kingdom like wildfire. A handful of the highborns lived in the castle as King Mallum's court, while others lived in nearby dwellings. But today they were all present, dressed as if a caravan of fabric had vomited on them. Sweat beaded on Tovey's lip as she mulled over the thought of another defector dead, or worse, news of Sylvia. She ambled toward the kitchen, craning her neck to catch conversations that echoed in the barren halls.

"Yes, a defector!" A woman in a gown giggled to a man in shiny armor.

"The dumb thing got mauled by wolves." Another lady hysterically laughed as she grabbed the first woman to pull her toward the breakfast hall. High-pitched squeals reverberated like nails on a chalkboard. Their dresses billowed behind them like clouds in the breeze, beautiful despite the vile people that wore them.

Sylvia, Tovey thought. *They have to be talking about Sylvia.*

Tovey spun on her heel, heading back toward the breakfast hall. She needed to hear what they knew, to hear if her plan had worked. If they thought it was Tovey, she was free. But if they knew it was Sylvia, Tovey's safety would be gone before nightfall. If she was in danger, she needed to know, no matter the risk.

Her fingers rubbed the fabric from Sylvia's dress, which was tucked in her pocket. Tovey's cheeks flamed as her boots shuffled through the threshold of the dining hall. She wouldn't watch the kitchen servants today. No. Today she would serve the king. She stiffened her spine, taking Marka's position in the leftmost corner of the hall and stilling her body like one of the lifeless suits of armor that stood at attention with her.

Marka entered the dining hall. Her eyes widened, and veins reddened in her eyes at the sight of Tovey standing in her place. Tovey tilted the crown of her head toward the door, signaling Marka to leave. Marka didn't listen. Instead, she moved toward Tovey like a wrathful spirit.

"Leave now," Marka commanded.

"I cannot."

"Now, Sylvia. Whatever it is, it is not worth risking whippings. Or worse, losing our positions here. Go."

Tovey faltered, wishing Marka would let her stay.

"Go," Marka hissed.

Tovey clenched her jaw and turned toward the door into the bosom of Master Daleen. Tovey shivered as fear washed over her like ice.

"Servant, today's breakfast will have more nobles than expected. Stay and serve. Take a position at the end of the table here." Daleen smiled. "You can do this. You've earned it."

Tovey couldn't help but smirk at Marka as she took her place serving the highborns.

It felt like hours passed as Tovey stood, her feet aching from the stillness. The highborns dawdled into the hall, wearing extravagant dressings in a vibrant palette of colors, leaving a trail of sparkling glitter behind them. More garbage to sweep. Lovely. Even the men wore embroidered tunics that shimmered with the morning sun's light dripping from them like golden sap. The cathedral windows were oriented on all walls to capture the sun no matter the time of day. Even obstructed by the hemp blindfold, the scene was alluring. Tovey thought of her shell, imagined wearing it as a necklace or in her hair. She swooned at the thought.

As if instructed, the highborns stood with squared shoulders, smiling toward the door. Their teeth were polished with smooth lips immune to chapping. The men's hair lacked the frizzy strands that Tovey could never stop from sprouting like weeds. Tovey envied them. She followed the lead of the other servants posted in the cardinal corners and knelt to the floor, her head bowed. She fluffed her crimson dress to cover her legs adequately, sure not to let a worn shoe show.

Tovey narrowed her vision as heavy polished boots prodded the floor. A man with piercing eyes and hair dark as night stepped into the chamber. His face was hardened, jaw strong. Though he wasn't young, he was fierce, dignified in his carriage. Though not in battle, the man wore a shining cuirass and a longsword attached to his hip. He marched to the head of the table, positioned opposite from where Tovey was stationed. King Mallum. Tovey swallowed air. She'd never seen how terrifying he was before.

King Mallum towered at the table. Two men, highborns, moved to his sides, removing his cuirass to reveal a doublet embroidered with the dragon insignia, a symbol of power. Tight woven pants wrapped around his waist, where layers of shirts wove in and out in endless shades of red. The gold embroidered cape laced around his neck lay behind him like a fox's tail.

The room remained still as another pair of polished black boots strode in. This man's steps were lighter than the ones before them. A few highborn women drew in sharp breaths that shifted into sighs of admiration. Tight tan trousers hugged the prince's sturdy legs as a bloodred doublet clung to his torso, tapering into his narrow waist with a leather belt. Golden chains hung with ease around his neck. Dark golden-brown hair lay like clouds on a still day upon his head, his face supple and smooth, no more than twenty.

He didn't have the hardened sneer of the king, but it was apparent this was one of his sons by the way the women swooned over him, desperate to gain his favor. He was average, nothing to gush over, though there wasn't a point in thinking like that anyway. Servants didn't marry. They didn't love. It wasn't permitted. The dragon insignia of Abolend beaded into his tunic shined in the morning light, brighter than the sun itself. He paused at the head of the table opposite King Mallum, closest to Tovey.

"Let us be seated and feast!" the king roared.

At once, the room filled with the clamoring of wooden legs against the polished floor, which left streak marks behind. Tovey winced at how quickly highborns destroyed the floors she had spent an hour polishing. She stood frozen along with the rest of the servants—a mindless observer.

The highborns tore into the pastries, crumbs dancing on the table. They ate fruits with juices so fragrant Tovey prayed her stomach wouldn't growl in protest. Servants poured aromatic wine. Kitchen servants carried fresh fish, inciting gasps of joy. Tovey understood why it was so hard to serve the highborns during meals. The scent alone was enough to drive someone mad with hunger, and she had to fight the urge to rip the roasted meat from their mouths.

"Prince Cullus, did you hear of the body they found?" The rumor-filled woman batted her thick lashes at the prince. Tovey's chest rose as her eyes widened.

Finally, say it.

"No, do tell."

"Apparently, one of the swine ran from the collective." Tension rose in the servants, but the highborns didn't notice. They didn't care. "A bowman caught her, skewering her heart. And afterward, a pack of wolves mauled her to pieces! All that was left was her poor little impairment—a blindfold."

The prince's mouth was in a hard line as he grabbed a pastry. He grazed Tovey with an apologetic gaze, noting her blindfold. The chatter stole his attention back to the table. Her heart sped, uncomfortable with the weight of his gaze. She shouldn't have been seen. She must have done something wrong or had made a noise. Guilt seeped through her pores as sweat beaded at her hairline.

"I don't understand why they don't just behave and save themselves the trouble of receiving impairments," one of the men muttered.

Tovey bit her tongue. Behaving was not enough to spare them lashings.

"I for one couldn't imagine living with my eyes covered. It would be such a shame to deprive the world of these." The annoying woman gestured to her dull eyes, blinking rapidly.

"We all know you have the most beautiful eyes, Lady Rena," a highborn man swooned from across the table.

"You are too gracious." She pouted at the lord while still eyeing the prince like he was her next meal.

Tovey grew irritated. How did the highborns not understand

how servants were treated or why they were punished? Impairments were to humiliate, to silence, to oppress them into obedience. Tovey's brain swelled with confusion, pushing at her skull. No, the impairments were for a reason, to remind them to be idealistic servants, to be able to have the honor of serving. Was standing in a room, hungry, while highborns chastised the people surrounding them an honor? This seemed like punishment.

"How bad do you think she must have smelled to pull in an entire pack of wolves?" the woman next to Rena interjected, and the highborns burst into uncontrollable laughter. All of them except the prince. He smiled half-heartedly. Tovey couldn't tell if he was sympathetic or bored.

"Your Majesty, will her body hang at her collective to teach them a lesson?" a man asked.

"No. There was nothing but bits left of the brute. Don't pay the bowman. The body is what teaches the lesson. They will serve the kingdom either as a servant or a scarecrow," the king said in a monotone voice.

Bitter liquid filled Tovey's mouth as the room spun. Her cheeks burned like she had sat next to a fire for too long. Tovey suppressed the heat rising in her chest as her jaw clenched, promising herself that hearing they'd found a blindfold was a good thing. Her disguise had worked. Sylvia was her hero, and Tovey had been pronounced dead.

A ballet of movement commenced. The servants in the cardinal corners moved in unison, each filling the chalice of the nearest highborn in front of them. Tovey mirrored their movements like a silent dance as she filled two men's cups along with the prince's. A crooked smile flicked across his face like lightning. Her fingers shook as she filled the cup. He smiled at someone, surely not her. It wasn't appropriate. She traced his jaw with her eyes, her gaze falling to the dimple centered on his chin before she backed away, taking her position once more.

Chatter of local politics filled the room. Nothing noteworthy. It was dull, and Tovey had heard what she needed to know. She was safe, for now.

"This is the second defector in the month, correct?" the man on the king's left asked meekly.

Tovey's mind raced. The *second* defector? Others were leaving from nearby collectives too.

"Yes. It is as if the servants don't love me, don't love that I provide for them," King Mallum said, a glimpse of disappointment in his eyes. It was the first time Tovey thought he appeared weak, human.

"Why is it that the rats run?" Lady Rena asked, raising the eyebrows of many highborns around the table. "They get what they need. It isn't like you make them pay to be in the collective. They are cared for, fed, housed. They are greedy."

"How could one know the reason they run? You can't put yourself in that low of a mindset," a man interjected.

Tovey's chest tightened. She had always assumed the highborns and the kingdom adored the servants. While they couldn't show it, she thought they did. It was an honor. Vivian said this was the most respectable position in the entire kingdom, yet these high-borns spoke of the servants like they were nothing but a pebble in their shoe. A nuisance. It was absurd.

"It is strange that even seeing the death of their friends means nothing anymore. If they do not fear death, then what is left? It is as if they are growing even more inhuman by the second," another man suggested.

It is because the brutality makes you numb, Tovey thought.

"Does anyone know what's causing the increase of defectors?" One of the men squinted, twisting his ornate mustache between soft fingers.

The room fell silent. The highborns glanced at one another as if there was a mutual knowing. An uncomfortable shift ran through the room as their eyes avoided the king, and they prodded the food left on their plates. The highborn man's eyes locked on the prince, begging him to break the silence.

Tovey knew that look. It was the same expression the girls had when the trainers knew they had a secret, a knowing they pretended to forget. Tovey's neck ached, and the air became heavy. Another highborn man forced a cough, winking not so subtly toward the prince, urging him to speak.

The king sat still, watching every highborn like this was a game of chess. Who would move first? The pawn? The knight? Who would risk their neck? If they were the girls at the collective, it would have been Nadia. She always took the fall when the trainers hunted for someone to slay.

The prince cocked his neck side to side, tongue gliding over his teeth. "Servants, leave," he commanded. "No need to return. Leave it to the servants who clean to come after we exit."

Without a noise, the four other crimson-gowned girls tiptoed out of the hall through a servants' entrance across from Tovey. The castle was riddled with narrow hallways to keep the servants as invisible as possible. Tovey was the last to fold in. The other servants spiraled from the corridor to the basement, catching up on other duties. Pausing, Tovey stilled behind the tapestry that covered the hall to listen.

Marka turned back, wrapping her fingers around Tovey's arm and pulling her toward the basement.

"We don't eavesdrop."

"I need to hear this. Just go, Marka, please."

"It's your head. I'm not covering for you. If Master Daleen ever asks, I will be honest. You aren't fit for this."

Tovey's nose tingled, embarrassed. "Marka, listen, this is about someone I knew. A sister at my collective. Just this once."

Marka hesitated before nodding and turning into the passageway.

After a few moments of silence, the prince gestured toward the nearest highborn on his right. "Please share the intel you brought to me this morning."

The man sat upright and began speaking. "There is word the prophecy is nearing fruition."

Gasps echoed in the room, pastries falling to the plates before them. Tovey's mouth watered.

"But these are merely rumors amongst the commoners, right?" the woman next to Lady Rena questioned.

"No. Sadly, they are not, but we mustn't let them know." The man to the prince's left stood and cleared his throat. "We all remember the song." He began to recite it.

> *The demon comes, heart of cold.*
> *She'll rise as the seers have foretold.*
> *With purple eyes, hair of gold,*
> *She'll bring the final war.*

Tovey gasped, reaching for her face.

"Though it is centuries old, it isn't just a lullaby to keep children out of the woods. Nearly eighteen years ago, the seers all had visions of the babe being born of this earth. The prophecy is true, and the time has come for us to prepare."

"Oh, codswallop. There is no such thing as purple eyes. Have you ever seen anything even close?" Lady Rena pouted, fishing for a compliment yet again.

A wooden clamor echoed across the table as the king's fist bellowed into the deadwood, the plates rattling from the quake. "If we are approaching the final war, we will stop her, hunt her, and kill her before she can wreak chaos amongst us! The demon will not shake our kingdom!" he roared like the dragon embellished on his tunic. "I tried to kill the rumors of her birth years ago, executing every single seer who claimed the legend had risen. But still the roaches talk, still they run. If they want a hero, then they will get one. We will mount the demon's body in the square, saving them all from its treachery."

Tovey crashed into the passageway's stone wall and slid to the floor as her face fell between her knees. Her body grew tense to the point of shaking. She leaned to her side, peering through the tapestry.

Prince Cullus tilted his head toward the corridor, his eyebrows stitched together. "Silence this talk for now. Keep it amongst yourselves." He looked at Lady Rena. "We don't want to cause a panic. We will stop the final war. We will find her, and we will kill her." He echoed his father, searching for approval. King Mallum's scowl didn't falter.

The highborns shuffled out of the room as Tovey's mind spun

with thousands of questions. They beat against her skull like tiny hammers, reminding her of Nadia's demand that she run before anyone could ever see her eyes. She wondered if Nadia had known the prophecy. She would have told her, wouldn't she? Nadia couldn't have kept something like that a secret.

Tovey tried to reassure herself as she recalled the eyes of everyone she had ever seen. No one had ever had purple eyes, but that was what the blindfolds were for, right? Impairments for servants with offensive eyes? But the highborns had shades of blue, brown, black, gray, and green. Nothing even remotely close to purple. This prophecy wasn't referring to her. It couldn't be.

Purple eyes? Yes. Hair of gold? Sort of. But it wasn't her. She wasn't a demon. It was a coincidence, surely. But if it wasn't . . . if she was evil, there was one plausible thing to do: turn herself in. It was what the trainers would want. It was what Master Daleen would command. It was what Marka would persuade her to do. It was the right choice, the honorable choice, the reasonable choice.

The dining hall emptied except for Prince Cullus and King Mallum. Tovey pressed her nose to a wee crack between the passage and the tapestry. She watched them, taking in every word, praying they would defuse her fear.

"Will you tell me, Father, what we are up against?"

"Don't whine, boy. Elias is better mannered than you, and he is twelve!"

Prince Cullus turned his cheek as if the words had slapped him. "I apologize, *Your* Majesty. I want to prove myself to you."

"Then do it, but I doubt you can."

"Father . . . King Mallum, I will. I don't understand what we are facing. I have heard the prophecy time and time again but have no idea what it means. A demon with purple eyes and hair of gold? It is rubbish."

"Stop searching for the blasted meaning in everything! You are just like your mother, always wanting to know more. You know what I've told you, and if I wanted to tell you more, I would have done so. Are you questioning my rule, boy?" King Mallum stood, fists beating the table. Prince Cullus shook his head, sitting in the opposing chair. "What do we do with threats, Cullus?"

"Eliminate them."

"That's right," King Mallum sneered. "No doubt our enemies are growing their armies as we speak. War means war with everyone, not just a demon. Abolend will destroy any threats, no matter how many lives it costs." The king crossed the dining hall. "And that's all you need to know." He exited the hall.

Prince Cullus sat at the table, resting his face in his palms. After a few moments, his head cocked toward the tapestry Tovey crouched behind. His brow furrowed, the chair squeaking beneath him. Like a mouse, Tovey darted through the passageway, turning a corner before she paused, eyes wide.

She perked her ears, hearing the prince's steps inching toward the tapestry. The heavy shuffle of woven fabric brushed against the ground. Light burst from the dining hall into the corridor, casting a perfect silhouette of the prince on the stone wall before her. Holding her chest steady, she locked in place until he released the tapestry and left the hall. A sigh of relief blew past her lips, and she waited several extra minutes before moving. Abandoning her duties, Tovey pummeled forward, throwing her body around every twisted curve of the passageway. Her boots burned the stone beneath her in a heated race toward the basement, toward Marka.

6

Fire from the torchlit hallway cast dark shadows across Marka's scowling face, illuminating her scar. She towered like a pile of bricks in the basement galley, arms crossed. Her foot erratically tapped against the earthen ground. The tidy crimson dress matched the heat trapped in her face, deepening while Tovey approached. Marka's hand lashed out, squeezing Tovey's wrist, pulling her into a nearby supply closet and slamming the door behind them.

"You do realize you could have had us both killed for that little game you played back there? What in the name of Abolend were you thinking?" She berated Tovey in hushed tones, eyes darting from side to side, searching for any spectators.

"I wanted to hear more. But, like I said, it was about someone from my collective. I had to; it's important."

Marka rolled her eyes, head shaking.

"I'm sorry."

"You're sorry? Sylvia, that doesn't cut it. I left you because dragging you down that hall would have alerted the highborns that we were stalking them. Suppose any of those other servants noticed? What if one of the highborns heard us talking and questioned it? We will be severely punished. And that girl from your collective didn't die."

Tovey winced, giving Marka a dangerous look.

"No, she didn't." Marka's lips pursed as a frustrated grunt exited. "No one *died*. A betrayer was killed. Good people die. Evil people are killed."

Tovey tightened her jaw, grinding her teeth together, the bone-on-bone grating sending a shiver through her core. Sylvia *wasn't* evil. Nadia wasn't wicked either.

"You weren't friends with the defector, were you?"

Tovey stood silent, fighting tears. Marka knew the answer. It was pointless to ask.

"Sylvia, how could you even associate yourself with someone who wouldn't trust the process? Servitude is an honor. Living here is a blessing. We aren't dead, are we?"

Tovey swallowed hard.

"Defecting is something cowards do."

Tovey shook her head as a lump of emptiness formed in her throat. Unable to find words, she snatched a bucket from the wooden shelf and stomped toward the dining hall. Speaking when angry was like throwing accelerant on a rambling fire: useless and explosive. Marka had every right to be upset, but Tovey couldn't help but think one thing: defecting wasn't for cowards; it was for the brave.

Tovey's heart stuttered. Was it true? Was defecting the brave and honorable choice to make? Tovey shook the questions out of her mind. She took her frustrations out on the scuff marks from the chairs the highborns had so carelessly raked across the marble. She cursed the wretched floors she polished multiple times a day. Dirt and grime from the men's boots littered the floor alongside crumbs and little glittery bits from the dresses.

Her blood boiled. She bit her tongue, pushing her teeth into her flesh hard. It was the best way to remind herself that speaking would cause her more pain than her teeth would. Tovey tossed the situation around in her mind. If the demon could only be identified by their eyes, it would be a matter of time before they ripped off every blindfold in the kingdom. The prince had already questioned her with his maddening hazel eyes.

Maybe they would assume Sylvia had been the purple-eyed demon. The disguise had worked, so the wolves could have ended the problem, and all was saved. Shaking the thought from her mind, Tovey scrubbed harder. Surely the prophecy could see behind fake masks, and Tovey knew within the essence of her soul that the Sylvia charade wouldn't last forever. Someone was bound to find out, especially now.

If she surrendered, the highborns would know how to stop the final war, and all would be well. The prophecy would mean nothing if she stopped it. A quake of shivers overcame her, and she replayed their conversation over and over again. How could they think she was a demon? It was a vile accusation that had no basis in reality. Snorting, she pursed her lips. She was nothing of the sort. They had it all wrong.

Two more servants entered the hall to assist. They talked amongst themselves in hushed tones.

"Did you hear? They are preparing for war. There is a great evil coming. I heard it as I was dressing Lady Rena for the market."

Tovey craned her neck, attempting to alleviate the headache pounding at her skull. Rotten Lady Rena couldn't keep her mouth shut even with direct commands from the prince. Fool.

"Yes, but we all know purple eyes aren't real. This rumor is nothing but a scary bedtime story gone wrong."

"No, my collective sisters knew the story well. It was told that she was seen as a babe seventeen years ago, right here in Abolend, but no one has seen her since."

Tovey swallowed hard, choking on spit. A memory of Nadia counting the years plagued her mind.

"Seven more years." Nadia kissed Tovey's ten-year-old head as fall turned to winter.

"Until what?"

"You'll see."

It was like Nadia was waiting for something, the way she counted the years. Tovey had assumed it was graduation until Nadia's detestation for the collective grew. Nadia would never want to celebrate Tovey's success as a servant.

This winter would be eighteen.

Dryness encompassed her mouth as Tovey chimed into the girl's conversation. "You've never seen *anyone* with purple eyes?"

"Don't be daft." The girls rolled their eyes and moved to the doorway with trays of trash and leftovers.

"Where's Marka anyway? I'll report her to Master Daleen for missing her duties," the auburn-haired servant threatened.

"Ill. Master Daleen gave her an hour to vomit it out." Tovey smirked. "Telling her will have her sights set on you," she lied, knowing they wouldn't question her.

One lie built into two, strengthening her headache, which grew like a tumor. Tovey finished dusting the hall before leaving for her next duty. As she worked, she tried ceaselessly to remember anything Nadia may have told her, but nothing came to mind. Nadia had known Tovey had purple eyes. She had told her she saw them once when she was a baby, though there was never a time that Tovey could remember when they'd made eye contact. A smile danced across Tovey's face. She was lost in her mind while she carried laundry throughout the castle, reminiscing in the comfort of Nadia having been blindfolded too.

Tovey had always imagined she too had purple eyes, and perhaps Nadia's mother, whom Nadia used to tell stories of before Tovey turned six, was her biological mother too. But Nadia stopped talking of her mother one day, refusing to tell any tales regarding her anymore.

Tovey had believed them all to have purple eyes until the day Nadia died. The moment her face went under the water for the last time, the blindfold slipped, revealing striking olive eyes. The threat of tears prickled at Tovey's nose, and her vision blurred.

At hour twenty-three, Tovey finished her and Marka's chores, not bothering to complain. She was grateful that Marka had found a way for Tovey to pay her back for the chaos she could have caused. Doing extra duties was better than Marka reporting her to Master Daleen.

Tovey collapsed into the hay, patting it flat beneath her head. She picked a piece of straw apart. Tossing and turning, she stared at the smooth sandstone ceiling through the night. When it became too dark, she resorted to admiring her shell, getting lost in its beauty. Rumors echoed throughout the corridors and seeped from the servants' lips. Yet through all the wild theories growing like weeds, there was one shred of information everyone concurred on: purple eyes didn't exist.

7

Whispering whooshes of wind from a passing storm drove her insomnia to insanity. After hours of tossing and turning, Tovey relinquished hope that sleep would find her. Other servants slept, mouths hanging open, one with thunderous snores. One of the highborns was sure to complain of trolls storming the dungeon. With another toss of sleepless limbs, Tovey surrendered.

Perched atop silent toes, she slinked across the crackling hay to avoid waking the others. Tovey popped her head through the sleeping quarters' threshold as she tiptoed through the hall toward the laundry room. She splashed herself with warm lavender water, the same batch they used to wash dirty clothes, before wandering off into the empty corridors, traversing through three long passages to where the kitchen servants washed the mess the highborns made.

While it seemed foolish that servants would be punished for doing chores outside of their assignments, it was true; it was an act of defiance. No matter if the deed was kind or merciless, if it wasn't commanded, it wasn't allowed. The consequences didn't matter anymore, not when her world was shattering. If the kingdom wanted her dead, she'd be dead. For now, she lived. For now, she would do something kind. She'd prove to herself she wasn't a demon.

She latched on to a decorated dish with overlapping lines around the rim, scrubbing it in the dimly lit night. She yearned for the comfort she'd once had in the lemony kitchens of the collective, of home. When Nadia would tell her secrets in the cover of the night, whispers Tovey had long forgotten. Foggy memories forced their way to take over her sight. Her mind wandered back to when she and Nadia had polished the plates at the collective together.

"Nadia?" a young Tovey no more than five had squeaked.

"Yes, little lilac?" Nadia smiled, her teeth near perfect, gleaming in Tovey's direction. She had always called her lilac, after the flower. It was because of the color of her eyes, but it was their special secret.

"Tell me about your mommy."

"I'm not supposed to talk about her."

Tovey fidgeted, her toes curling and flexing in teeny boots.

"But I suppose tonight we can. Mother is a barmaid."

"Whoa."

Nadia's lips pursed. "Do you even know what that is?"

Tovey shook her head.

"So then why did you say *whoa*?" she playfully scorned.

A bitty giggle erupted as Tovey cast an infectious smile.

"Hush and listen, little lilac. My mother is a barmaid, and she lives in Abolend. That's where I used to live too." Nadia paused.

Her bruised and crooked nose pointed out the window toward the direction it lay.

Tovey stood on her toes to peer out the window, eyebrows stitching together. She saw the same old trees that stood watching the girls.

"My mother is astonishingly brave and wicked smart. After my dad died, she became the owner of his bar, a rare position for a woman in Abolend to hold. But, of course, the people love to drink the fuzzy beers my mother brews. They were afraid if they brought in a new bar owner, the townspeople and even a few highborns would never taste her concoctions again, so they let her stay. Pretty neat, huh?"

Admittedly, Tovey only understood half of the words at the time. Most of it was utter nonsense. Nonetheless, she loved hearing Nadia's comforting voice.

"It wasn't without sacrifice. King Mallum didn't want a woman holding power. He is intimidated by us, you know. So he pressured Mother to offer something valuable in return. Mother promised the most valuable thing she had, the one thing that would please a crass king like Mallum the Incompetent. Mother vowed to give her daughter to the collective, yet she always kept it a secret that I was destined to come here anyway. Foolish king. Being here with you is my fate; I was chosen to live and grow with *you*."

Tears soaked her cheeks. She'd been scrubbing the same plate for the last fifteen minutes. Nadia had been a middle person. How could she forget? The words that had once been confusing were understandable now—a barmaid. Tovey had assumed then that it was another word for a servant.

She moved to the bucket, and her hands shifted the plate

under cool soapy water before setting it aside in a leaning tower. She grabbed another grimy dish, her mind returning to the vision, aching to remember more. She hadn't remembered Nadia being so hostile toward the throne. It was heartbreaking to remember now that she'd always wanted to defect.

"Will Mommy come and visit us?" Tovey had asked Nadia when she was six.

"No, Tovey. She won't." Nadia's voice was cold. "And she isn't your mommy."

Water welled in Tovey's eyes.

Nadia's face turned the shade of a tomato. She didn't want to upset her little lilac.

"I'm serious, little lilac. She isn't. She's mine."

Tovey's head fell. She helped Nadia carry more plates to the basin.

"I'm sorry, Tovey. Sometimes it is hard for me to think about her. I made a tough decision to take care of you, and sometimes I want to . . ." Nadia's eyes reddened, lip quivering. "My mother will love you, just like I do, sister."

"Is your mommy's name Mother?"

"No." Nadia laughed. "Her name is B—"

Tovey snapped out of the memory as Gretchen walked in. She was one of the oldest servants in the castle, her hair chalk white and curled like the froth on the dishes. It was rare for a servant's body to withstand the passing strain on their bodies. Most died young.

"It's late! What are you doing here, darling?" She stepped closer to Tovey, squinting her eyes. "You aren't supposed to be in here. You're not assigned to the kitchens."

"I wanted to help. I couldn't sleep, so I figured I'd lend a hand,"

Tovey said. Her eyes fell to Gretchen's fingers, which glowed with bright pink peeling flesh. "I'm sorry."

"Sylvia, right? You are unlike any servant I've met. Risking your neck to do more chores? You are wild, and that isn't normally a compliment, but I don't care. If you want to help, help. I'm too old to bother with the nuances of rules. Our master sleeps in until seven most days anyway. Power got to her head."

A wrinkled wink from dull eyes soothed Tovey's mind as Gretchen stood next to her, drying the haphazard tower of plates, stacking them for the next day's meal. "I've seen you in here before, watching while the highborns eat. In all my years, no one has ever aided another with their chores. They aren't too keen on risking punishment for it. It's unusual, but you seem different, kinder than most. Or perhaps it is a death sentence you wish to have?" Gretchen squinted her eyes at Tovey.

"Honestly, I don't know what I wish for anymore," Tovey admitted.

"You should wish to live. You've got a lot left in your young bones."

Tovey forced a smile.

The scent of lemon filled the kitchen. The servants stood in silence, grateful for each other's company. Tovey moved at twice the speed of Gretchen, but she didn't mind.

"I have to ask, have you heard the rumors?" Tovey eyed Gretchen carefully, hoping not to offend her for talk beyond their station. But Gretchen seemed open to the idea of chatting.

"I have."

"Are you worried?"

"Heavens no." An air of safety settled around Tovey; her

shoulders dropped invisible weight. "Because I'll be dead before the final war comes. My hands can't do this much longer, and my master will have to replace me. It's a slaughtering for servants whose hearts withstand as long as mine has."

Tovey froze, jaw agape. "A slaughtering?"

"You don't think we are allowed to retire, do you? If one cannot work, one cannot live."

Squeaking from the dishes filled the air with unspoken condolences. Tovey had never known an old servant and never considered the logistics of when one became too old to work. The trainers had failed to mention that. They'd failed to mention a lot of things. The girls were always told they'd be honored, cared for, safe. Serving in a household or a business with a life full of fulfillment in knowing they helped keep Abolend happy.

A slaughtering made more sense to why a handful of girls had defected; it was the only chance at escaping a life of servitude. But their fate was sealed in death anyway with the sheer amount of bowmen stalking the woods.

Bubbles circled in the steamy air as Gretchen stalled, retreating to the cobwebbed corner, where she sat resting for a moment, breathing heavily. Tovey sped her pace, attempting to finish the dishes to give Gretchen a day off. It was the least she could do for the kind serving mate. Lemon filled her nose as her mind flowed like a river back to Nadia. She chastised herself for not remembering her mother's name. Bethany? No. Brenda? No. Birdie? No.

Cursing under her breath, she pushed at the folds of her brain hard. Like fire lit inside her heart, her knees buckled beneath her, tossing her living corpse against the wall. She gripped the stone for support.

Nadia laughed in her memories. "Her name is Breena."

Gasping for air, Tovey pressed herself to the kitchen door, trying to fill her lungs with less humid air as she stood in the steaming kitchen drowning.

Breena, the barmaid, was the middle person who'd taken the dress Tovey had stolen. Breena was the woman who'd prevented Tovey from receiving a deeper punishment from Gorv, the cruel Abolend guard. Breena was the woman who'd stared at her with questions racing across the wrinkles on her face. Tovey cursed herself for not remembering Nadia's mother's name that day. The woman wore the same chestnut hair and an almost perfect smile. She was still here in Abolend. And she knew something.

Tovey wished there were a feasible way to reach Breena and ask the millions of questions in her mind. Why was Nadia's destiny to bring Tovey to the collective? Were the rumors true? Was she a living demon? Nausea bit her tongue as she once more cursed herself.

There was no possible way to reach Breena, and even if she did, she would have to tell her the worst news she would ever let fall out of her mouth. *Nadia is dead.* She couldn't utter something so horrific to a mother, but she had to do something.

"Gretchen, I have to go. You're right. I shouldn't be here risking anything. Thank you."

Tovey snuck back to the basement, pacing the halls. It would be impossible to send word to Breena. She didn't know any servants who left the walls, and none of the highborns could be trusted. In time, she might meet someone, build trust, and be able to smuggle a message outside.

She could sneak out in the night, run to Breena and—no.

Where would she even find Breena again? How many bars were there, and how would a servant of the king not be noticed? She wore red, like a burning flag. But Breena would help her. Take care of her. She knew Nadia's secrets. Biting her nails, she pressed her ear to Master Daleen's door. Long breaths sounded from inside. She was asleep.

Tovey scanned the door Gorv had shoved her through. Tovey bolted like lightning through the corridor. Cold sweat beaded at the back of her neck. She wrapped her fingers around the handle of the door, pulling.

The door wasn't locked. It creaked open with a raucous squeal, revealing a tantalizing glimpse into the kingdom.

Footsteps pattered, echoing in the hall. Someone was coming. Tovey stepped out, refusing to glance behind her, but a hand ran through her hair, pulling her back. Marka.

"You sly little weasel. Where do you think you are going?" Marka hissed.

"Let me go. I was—"

"No. I'm tired of you. Tired of your games." She pulled Tovey through the hall before rapping on Daleen's door. "Master, wake up. We have a problem."

Daleen opened the door. Her hair had fallen out of the perfect braid she kept across her head. "What is it?"

"She tried to run. Escape through the door."

"I didn't. I heard a knock. I thought it may have been a guard," Tovey lied.

Marka shook her head. "No. I would have heard. I was organizing the closet, as you commanded me to do yesterday. I woke early to have it ready before we started our rounds."

"You must not have heard it, Marka. Someone knocked."

Daleen shook her head. "Servant. Listen to me. Don't think I haven't noticed you. You're different. I can see it in your face. You don't like rules. You don't want to serve. You have bad blood in you."

"Master, I do want to serve." For the first time, Tovey told the truth. She had yearned to serve her entire life. "My blood is of the collective. I've sworn my life to Abolend."

"Then you will understand the need for me to take Marka's word. She has always been loyal. She has never cast doubt into my mind. I must believe that there was no knock. Even if you think you heard one, you shouldn't have blindly opened the door."

"Yes, Master." Tovey trembled.

"And now you must be punished for your insubordination."

Tovey sat in darkness, dust melding with the blood weeping from her back. She received a flogging and three days without food, light, or human contact. She deserved it. She'd been reckless. Nadia was to blame. She'd lied by omission and poisoned her mind with the word *defect*.

8

Morning brought an unusual parade of sound. Voices echoed through the chambers of the castle while servants' feet shuffled with exhaustion. The steady sound of blacksmiths became amplified, a chaotic symphony of noise. The door to Tovey's prison cell creaked open, revealing Master Daleen. Tovey's eyes burned at the light pouring in from the halls. She crumpled in the corner like a used handkerchief.

"Your punishment is over. And we need you back on your best behavior. You are commanded to go straight to chores. Allowances have been made for servants to step in wherever is deemed necessary. If another master commands you, you do it, understand?"

"Yes."

"You should know, the highborns aren't in good spirits today because the king isn't happy. One of the highborns leaked a rumor that has turned Abolend on its head. A great danger is coming."

Tovey rolled her eyes. No, it wasn't. The alleged great danger was starving in a dungeon.

"Commoners are flooding the castle, begging to be heard by King Mallum."

Tovey's eyebrows pinched.

"Every morning, King Mallum opens the doors to the Reckoning Hall. Townspeople can come and plead to the king for favors, for justice, for anything. Normally he doesn't see more than a handful of citizens, but they have come by the cartful today, scared about a potential war. This is why I need you to behave. I can't risk losing any of my servants." Daleen breathed heavily, flustered.

Tovey remained still.

"Get yourself some salve, and go on. And grab food. I don't care if you fill your pockets. Just get out and be of use. Go, go!" Daleen turned on her heel, shouting commands at others, a loose cannon.

Tovey wobbled to her feet, her body aching, shivering from cold, hunger, or pain, she couldn't be sure. Trainers were never perturbed. Masters shouldn't be either.

Stumbling to the door, Tovey popped her head into the hall. Frenzied shouts from servants who had been nothing more than breathing statues bounced from woman to woman in a roar of confusion. Tovey shoved through the servants, fumbling through the hall toward food.

Gruel sloshed over the wooden table like mud, messier than if the highborns had dined there. Servants were never messy. They didn't spill anything. They would have to scrub and shine the room until it was devoid of crumbs. With the little food they were given, every bite was savored. Tovey's heart sped. It wasn't only the commoners in pandemonium. Tovey filled her mouth with as much gruel as she could shovel, but still, it wasn't enough.

Tovey pushed back into the hall, standing in a stupor as Marka stomped toward her.

"Learn your lesson?"

Tovey nodded, too tired to play games today.

"Good. A commoner in line for the Reckoning Hall spilled a basket of figs. They've been trampled over now. Go, clean it. Master Daleen has given me the ability to command." Marka smiled. "I think I might be her successor."

"Congratulations," Tovey mumbled.

"Can you clean? Have you eaten and drank? I'm sure you slept while in there . . . You know, I wasn't trying to be mean, but you needed a reminder. We all do sometimes." With a blank expression, she traced the scar on her face.

"I can clean."

Tovey stumbled through a dark passageway to the corridor outside the Reckoning Hall, carrying a bucket half filled with water and rags. She passed a crack in the foundation, light trickling in through a hole the size of a tooth. Tovey pressed her eye to the crack. It was too hard to see. She turned her head, listening.

"Get your kids inside!" a mother shouted. "Isabella, Remington, come here!"

Earsplitting screams and shouts from guards ricocheted off the stone walls. Chills covered the back of Tovey's neck, forcing her to pull away, chest heaving. Abolend was preparing for war, a war Tovey knew wasn't coming, that couldn't come, not if she stopped this madness right now.

She was a servant. She wasn't a demon. She had to put a stop to this, but she couldn't seem to find a way how. Tovey stood, returning to her duties, mind churning in a clunky grind. Her thoughts were foggy, and her mind was spent. She needed to rest, to heal. But there wasn't time for that. There was only time to wipe away the spilled figs.

Through a side door and into the chamber leading to the Reckoning Hall, Tovey entered. People were shoulder to shoulder, pushing this way and that, trying to edge closer to the monstrous doors embellished with ornamental nails studding the wood. A guard stood before them on an empty fruit box, shouting to the crowd to quiet, still, and be patient.

It was absurd that the commoners were allowed to act this way. They were out of line. Marka would have a field day.

"Aye! Servant!" a woman with frizzy charcoal hair and piercing gray eyes called.

Tovey bowed her head, padding through the crowd.

"Here are the figs. It's a shame we lost them." She pointed to the floor, where a mess of squished juices stuck like honey to people's shoes.

Without knowing where to begin, Tovey knelt to the ground, scrubbing. She listened, ears open, soaking in the conversation of the middle people.

"The line's ne'er been this long, 'as it?"

"Not that I've ever seen."

The line frequently paused. Every time the king grew tired, hungry, or flustered, he took a break, which seemed to be between every other person. Tovey bathed in the conversation from the people around her.

An hour passed as the golden sun crossed through the sky. As soon as the figs were scrubbed from the floor, someone carried in lambs to offer to the king, the creatures dropping dung everywhere.

Tovey scrubbed methodically, not wanting to leave the hall. If she had to scoop dung, then she would. She couldn't help but linger, yearning for an opportunity to speak. She wished she could tell the townspeople not to worry, that this could all be over. But they wouldn't listen to her even if she spoke.

The castle was alive in the glory of war. It was unlike anything Tovey had ever seen. Even the commoners whispered about the coming of battle. They garbled ceaselessly with conversations of fortifying their homes and requesting guards to protect their lands. With the afternoon sun setting fire to the sandstone, the banter continued.

"The demon'll feed on me pigs."

"After it sucks your eyes out. I need guards for my farm; it borders the wall."

"Shut up, you broomsticks. It's all hogwash."

"And why are you here?" the farmer said to a towering pillar of a man behind him.

"I'm here to tell King Mallum of a personal matter unrelated to your swine." He locked his jaw tight, wild red hair sprouting over his face.

"Oh, a tough one, are you? Makin' fun of us farmers?"

Tovey glanced up as the red-bearded man's fingers balled into a white-knuckled fist. His nose was crooked, and his arms were bulky, like a guard's, but by his dress, he was a commoner. He could have been a woodworker with the way his wrinkles stuck in his face as if he were squinting all the time. He shook his head at the banter, turning his attention toward Tovey. Head tilted, his gaze penetrated her. Tovey stared at the floor, scrubbing harder as she crawled forward.

"Excuse me, Servant?"

Tovey flashed a glance at the man. His forehead wrinkled into mountains.

"Wants to touch her, I bet. Can't get 'imself a reputable woman."

The man with the red beard ignored the comment. "May I ask, Servant, do—"

"Ahem." Not even ten paces away, the guard by the doors forced a pathetic cough.

The crowd ignored his attempt at directing their attention.

"Commoners, listen here!" He stiffened with his chest puffed like a bird wearing armor. The crowded line hushed, and an endless forest of eyes focused on the guard. "King Mallum is not seeing any more of you today; he is retiring to his chambers. Please come back tomorrow!"

Tovey retreated, as bewildered by the announcement as the rest of the crowd, carrying her bucket and rags away from the red-bearded man. She pushed herself into an inlet where a statue of a past king stood, allowing the commoners to leave.

The surrounding guards sang out, "Hail! Hail King Mallum, leader of the brave, father of the land!"

Stillness encapsulated the crowd. The people stood baffled, unable to process the audible information. Like a trickle turned into a waterfall, a discontented murmur encircled the hall. Individual voices rose amongst the others in a sea of noise. Apparently, the loudest one shouting was the one with the most crucial issue, the roar leaving a deafening ring in her ears. Tovey's cropped hair whipped her face as she turned to see the scowling townspeople pushing forward toward the doors. Her eyes widened. She had never seen anyone act out of line, especially an entire army of people. Her jaw quivered.

"I've been waiting all day. I've got a farm on the edge of the city at risk! I need guards!"

"I'm running low on herbs. Is it safe to forage in the forest?"

"I have come to volunteer my sons to join the collective to train them for war! The king will be pleased with me! He will reward me with safety!"

"Is the demon coming?"

The voices got lost in an entangled string of sound. Tovey watched the crowd, guilt slithering up her spine. She faced the harsh reality that they were all risking their heads, volunteering their children's lives, to rally against the danger standing inches from them, a catastrophe that didn't exist.

Tovey could stop the insanity infecting the kingdom like a ravaging plague. She could put an end to this. She could reveal her eyes to the king. If only he would see her, one last person, to put an end to this. Tovey dropped the bucket stuffed with rancid rags.

Her plan was seamless. She would stand before the guard, wait for him to command her to speak. He would be curious, wondering why she was there. She would say she had information for the king, he would see her, she would reveal her eyes, and King Mallum would command her to speak. Without a hitch, she would explain she was not a threat and the prophecy was a rumor. Arguably hearsay, it had stemmed from a midwife or a drunken middle person who caught a glimpse of her when she was a babe. The incompetent jerk must have seen her eyes and created a fantastical tale. It was silly. It was foolish. After she explained it to King Mallum, all would be well. It had to be.

The king would scrutinize the madness surrounding Tovey. He would be euphoric. The townspeople would love him for slaying the rumors of the demon. He would find amusement in realizing she was a servant and laugh the whole prophecy away, calling for the kingdom to return to its natural state. His unquestionable power and trust from the people would be reinstated. Commoners would grin ear to ear, teasing her, and it would all be forgotten in a day or two. No highborn would ever want to remember the day they'd feared a scrawny servant.

Her strategy was sound.

The guard at the front of the line shouted and pushed people back toward the entrance of the castle, moving past Tovey like she was invisible. Doors to a corresponding hallway burst open, spitting Prince Cullus into the swarming ants. He ambled through the crowd as if this were a stroll through a flowering meadow on a summer day.

"Julia, thank you for coming. Your tunics are the best in town, my personal favorite." The woman blushed. "I hope to see you tomorrow. Not to worry, I'm sure King Mallum will see you then." Her face calmed and she left the hall smiling.

Tovey was impressed.

The prince turned like he was dancing. "Ah, Hakeem, I haven't seen you for a while! How are your children?"

"Your Highness, they are good, sir. Thank you for asking. But I need to know, should we move toward the center of town? We live not three rows from the wall."

"I understand your trepidation, but consider the wall your friend. It keeps everything out, even demons. Don't forget our honorable guards walk between every battlement on the hour. Not even a mouse could squeeze through our fortifications. We are the greatest kingdom, after all."

Hakeem wiped his brow, smiling wryly. "You are right, sir. This news has got me in a tizzy."

"Not to worry, Hakeem. Tell your wife and children the royal family wishes them well."

Tovey's jaw dropped at how easily he pleased the people away with his persuasive dimples. It was amusing to watch the commoners so inundated by a young man wearing a fashionable doublet. He casually made his way toward the front with a few simple niceties, emptying the chamber of its guests.

"Disperse!" a guard shouted, shoving the last of the line away.

"Erik," Prince Cullus said, addressing the guard. "Tell me, has my father retreated to his chambers?"

"Yes, Your Highness."

"Thank you for the news. Please stand before the castle and usher anyone else away."

"Yes, sir."

Tovey sank to the floor, scrubbing, contemplating her next move. If the king was inaccessible, she could wait until tomorrow. She could petition to be stationed in the hall again. Even now, with it being empty, she had hours of work left before it would be to Master's standards.

Prince Cullus strode past Tovey without a second glance. She listened to his footsteps growing fainter as she scrubbed, her thoughts drowning out all other sounds. She surveyed the doors to the Reckoning Hall. They were menacing.

She stood before them, her fingers tracing the embellished nails, each one forged by hand.

Her neck ached, and her fingers were swollen from the water. It was the right choice to tell the king. He wouldn't kill her, not when he realized she wasn't the demon and was just a girl. She couldn't be punished for being honorable, could she? Silently, her fingers rose to the knot in the fabric behind her head. Keeping this a secret would bring more chaos to the people of Abolend in a sheer panic over nothing.

The fabric loosened on her eyes. She needed to practice what it was like to stand exposed. Tomorrow she would do it confidently, without fearing standing unveiled before the king. If she hesitated, guards might stop her. King Mallum may protest. She needed to act quickly when she stood before His Majesty.

She peeled the hemp from her face, allowing air to brush like a feather across her skin, excitement needling her cheeks. The blindfold balled in her hand. Gently, she opened her eyes, seeing the grain in the door, rich swirls of umber. Tovey touched the unwelcoming cool iron handle.

"What are you doing, Servant?"

Tovey jumped, her fingers splaying open in a flinch of surprise. The blindfold fluttered to the floor. She snapped her eyes closed, standing unwavering. She lifted her chin and filled her chest with a false sense of confidence. The hall was so silent she could hear the crackle of the torches, but she did not hear a soul.

Plunging to the floor, she met the cool marble. She pressed her palms against the polished stone, searching for the scratchy piece of fabric that protected her. Listening once more, she paused, hearing nothing. Was it her imagination that someone spoke? A fear-driven hallucination? She couldn't call out to ask if anyone was there.

Squinting in the hall, aglow with the golden sun, she searched the floor, hands flying in all directions. Through light lashes, she hunted for the blindfold. A polished leather boot stepped on the fabric scrap. She locked her eyes shut, cursing herself.

"Stand, Servant."

Tovey stood.

"Removing an impairment is forbidden. You know what the consequence is for that, don't you?" the smooth voice asked.

Tovey nodded. Quartering, a beheading, being burned at the stake.

"Good. So tell me, what are you doing standing here without your impairment?"

Tovey remained still, heart palpitating. She couldn't. She must.

"Servant!" he shouted in Tovey's face. "I command it."

Fear twisted in her chest, growing like tangled vines that choked out any words she could think of. It was now or never. *Stop the madness.* This guard, or whoever this highborn was, wouldn't let her out of this. But her plan could still work. Though it was not the king, it was someone with power. Someone who would take her to him.

"I was hoping I could speak with His Majesty, King Mallum, in the Reckoning Hall."

"Were you?" he said with surprise. "I don't think a servant has ever had anything to say . . . Well, tell me. What was it?"

She took a deep breath, and courage swelled in her chest. Tovey lifted her lids, her lashes grateful to not scrape against the hemp, eyes opening to the scene before her. A shimmery purple glow reflected off her cheeks as she met the hazel gaze of the only person left in the hall, the person who'd spoken to her: Prince Cullus.

His mouth fell agape, jaw unhinged, frozen. His pupils dilated, staring into her swirling pools of amethyst. She hesitated, unblinking. It was the first time she had made direct eye contact with someone. Ever. It was uncomfortable at first, then euphoric, creating the sensation of static buzzing through her skin, like after lightning strikes near. Heart pounding, she stood suspended in time.

Regret flooded her mind, and she began panicking. It wasn't enough that she was a servant. It didn't matter. The prince wasn't laughing it away. His eyes were penetrating, serious. Tovey lurched, snatching her blindfold from beneath the prince's boot. He stumbled in a stupor as her feet kicked the ground, propelling her toward a servants' passage. Turning her shoulders sideways, she slipped into the corridor before another second passed.

The prince dashed after her. She loosely tied the blindfold around her head, unable to steady her hands. It fell to the bridge of her nose, her eyes out in the open. Tovey couldn't close them now. She needed to see, to run, to escape the prince. Tovey barreled unhindered through the labyrinth of tunnels toward the basement. She turned left, then right, doubling back, losing the prince in the passages.

Panting heavily, Tovey winced, wishing she could disappear forever. She turned toward the basement, shoving through the door to the dirt-ridden hallway, battering straight into the chest of Marka, who clasped her into a halt.

Marka sucked air like a fish out of water, attempting to breathe. Her righteous brown eyes locked on Tovey's. As if she were being choked, she fell back onto the dirt floor, scooting away from Tovey, horrified. Tovey pulled Marka into an empty adjoining corridor away from wandering servants. Tovey's heart quaked as she refastened her impairment.

"What in the dragon's blood was that? Sylvia, your eyes . . ." She caught her breath. "Are purple."

"I know. But it isn't me—the demon everyone is talking about. I'm not the one they are looking for."

"What? Yes, it is. You must be! You are the only one. Purple eyes don't exist. Have you not heard the rumors? I heard a guard say that he was rounding up suspect people to slaughter earlier. I can't talk to you; it will get me killed." Marka's voice shook with uncertainty. "I have to turn you in. They are going to kill you," she muttered through labored coughs.

"Please, Marka, don't."

"You're a demon."

"I'm not. Marka, it's still me."

She hesitated. "Who else has seen you?"

Tovey shook her head, tears rushing to her eyes.

"Who, Sylvia? Tell me!"

"The prince."

"The prince? Of Abolend? Of course, how much worse can you make this, Sylvia?" Marka paced the cramped corridor, grasping at her chest. "What else? Tell me, what else have you done? Marched to the king to bat your eyelashes in front of him?"

"Not quite like that, but I wanted him—"

"I was joking! You didn't! Dear Abolend, we are all going to die because of you." Marka pushed her hands into her hair. "You have purple eyes. Even if you aren't a demon, you sure look like one! Having purple eyes is enough to put you to death. To put *me* to death for knowing this. And your eyes aren't even just purple,

Sylvia; they are glowing! And in case you didn't know, eyes . . . don't . . . glow." Marka gripped Tovey's arm so tightly that her muscles spasmed. "They won't believe me that I didn't know. We've served together. I've worked side by side with the demon. A blasted demon! They are going to kill me."

"Let me go. I'll disappear. Tell no one you saw me, and save yourself. You couldn't possibly know what my eyes look like. Tell them everything about me. I don't care, but let me go," Tovey begged.

"I can't lie, Sylvia."

"You must. Would you rather give up your shot at being a master one day? Would you rather give up your life? No, you wouldn't. I know you wouldn't. You must lie. One lie. It will save you."

"You will die."

"Not if you give me the chance to live."

"Before I change my mind, go!" Marka released Tovey's arm. "Go!"

Tovey lunged around Marka. She needed to escape, but she couldn't in this dress. Tovey barreled toward the laundry room. Spinning, she maneuvered like a rat being hunted. She darted into closets and corridors as other servants passed. Feverishly, Tovey tore through piles of clothing, searching for anything she could disguise herself in. She needed something basic, like what the middle people wore, but practical enough to avoid getting caught. This time she wouldn't be unprepared in the city.

She ripped off the crimson gown and cast it to the floor after ensuring she'd grabbed Sylvia's dress scrap and the shell from her pocket. Her petrified gaze fell upon a thin pair of linen pants. Pants were for men, but trousers would be more practical than traversing town in an oversize sack. Plus, all the dresses were too extravagant for a commoner to wear. She'd stick out like a sore thumb.

"Servants!" Master Daleen screeched, her voice resounding off the stone walls. "Which one of you was assigned outside the Reckoning Hall?"

Servants ran, reporting to Daleen.

"Where's Sylvia?"

"I assigned her to the hall, Master," Marka said.

"Where is the wretched girl? The prince is sending guards, asking masters to bring to him who was serving there immediately."

Heavy footsteps boomed against the dirt floor, powdering the air as Daleen's rabbit teeth chattered together. Tovey rolled beneath a table and squeezed herself behind a washing basin jammed against the wall, barely a foot wide. Like a worm, she squirmed, wedging herself like a doorstop.

Master Daleen entered the laundry room, voice screeching like a fork raked across a polished plate. "Find Sylvia. Now, girls. Find her!" A frustrated fist punched a fresh pile of laundry to the floor in a fury. "Or they will destroy me," she muttered, turning as she cantered, shouting Sylvia's name.

Tovey ran her fingers through her hair, pulling at the dried strands, worried for Master Daleen, tormented by the thought of all the servants paying the price for her eyes, not to mention the kingdom and, worst of all, King Mallum facing the horrific realization that the servants had been harboring a so-called demon.

As the hall emptied, Tovey emerged from her hiding place, arms curled into her like a mouse.

One by one, she lunged her legs into soft brown wool trousers, shimmying to adjust them properly. The pants were strange but moved with her, unlike the dress, which had weighed her down. Whipping her arm to the left, she snatched a white cotton under-tunic from the table, pulling it over her head. It hung midthigh. She slipped on her soft boots, tumbling to the half-size wooden door Gorv had shoved her through almost two weeks ago. The tunic was an undergarment for the highborns, but it resembled what Tovey had seen the middle people wear and would do well to mask her identity.

Voices echoed in the corridor, the main hall barren. She couldn't run toward the door she failed to escape from. Footsteps grew louder in that direction, forcing her to run. Tovey jumped, tossing herself toward the latrine on the opposite end of the hall. Alone in the lavatory, she locked eyes with the wooden bench. Daleen had said the toilets drained into a pond. Tovey furiously gripped the bench, lifting it from the stone to reveal a narrow vertical passage that dropped into darkness, the putrid scent of feces gagging her.

"Master Daleen," Marka called, "I have to tell you something. I know why the prince wants to see her."

Scoffing, Tovey wriggled into the tunnel, pressing her feet and back against the walls. She lowered the wooden seat steadily, alone in the passage. Slinking, she descended, her fingers gripping at bricks until her feet touched what she hoped was water before sinking into the muck. Tovey cursed, her eyes lighting the darkness for a moment. The tunnel curved. Shoving a shoulder into the water, Tovey reached her arm out, grazing an iron pole.

Tovey sank into the water, the sludge on the bottom oozing between her fingers. Pointing her foot forward, she measured the space between the iron bars blocking her exit. It was narrow, but she was tiny. Tovey held her breath, pinching her nose shut as she slid beneath the surface. She gripped the iron bars, twisting her body through the opening. Frantically, Tovey waved her hands, hunting for air. She kicked the sticky bottom of the pond, propelling herself to the top, breaching the surface.

No one was around, and for a good reason. The stench caused Tovey to vomit. Excrement baked in the setting sun, too rank for even maggots to enjoy. She paddled to the edge before walking out of the pond covered in scum. With one last gaze, she took in the castle, topped with towers competing with one another to see which one could scrape the sky.

"I'm sorry," she whispered as she slipped into an alleyway, disappearing into the twilight.

9

His face was etched into her mind. Tovey tried hard to focus on her task and not on the stench of her clothes or her growing terror. All she needed to do was escape. But this time she didn't have the luxury of Vivian making leisurely rounds; she had an entire castle, a master, a prince, and a slew of servants—which were sworn to honesty—hunting for her like ravenous wolves. Within the hour, they would discover who they presumed to be Sylvia had escaped. And she'd be hunted.

Tovey wove her fingers through her hair, shaking fringe over her blindfold to hide that she was even wearing one. The pond's mud dried like sap on her body. A man would never be impaired, but keeping her blindfold on was better than casting a glow of amethyst into the darkening night. Biting her tongue, she panicked. She needed a plan.

Jogging, she didn't stop or dare look back until she squatted in the shadows of a narrow alley three blocks away from the pond. Tucking her limbs close to her body, she became as tiny as a seed. Her lids shut as she cocked her head, taking in the sounds.

Birds fluttered through the air as the breeze carried in salt. People ambled through the streets, gabbing about their evening plans. Heated air with a sweet aroma swirled out of the shop with a stone facade ten paces to her front. A baker scrubbed his pans, preparing for a night of bread making. Tovey lifted her nose. The faint smell of meats teased her stomach from the east.

Still exhausted, drained, and in pain, she could think of nothing else. She wasn't going to defect yet again without any provisions. Barreling forward, she followed her nose until she reached the shop. A heavy man with a cleaver hacked away at a deer's corpse as he hummed a solemn tune.

A shiver trembled on the back of her neck, sending hair to stand on end, her memory taking over her eyes—the bowman. But this man was a butcher; it wasn't *him.*

Tovey scooted into the moon-cast shadows, and her body locked still. She waited, watching the man. He moved routinely— two heavy chops to remove the limb, and five slices across the meat, removing the bone. After every bone removal, he would turn and carry the remains to a measuring station, where he would meticulously poke the bloodied corpse with his finger before cutting it away into varying sections.

Dehydrated meats sat on the counter to his right. If Tovey could sneak into his shop and snag a handful of venison, she would have some time to survive before having to kill for herself. She didn't want to steal but despised the idea of having to take the life of another even more. The man turned to cut another chunk of meat into weighed piles. Tovey inched toward the doorway on all fours.

"Gerald!" a traveled woman said from the opposite side of the house.

Tovey scurried back into the shadows, cursing her hesitation.

"Aye, Cordelia." He smiled, his face turning as red as the bloodied meat. "How can I help you?"

"I came to warn you. I was selling furs near the castle a few minutes ago, and the guards . . ." She rubbed her lips together, eyes darting across the street. "Well, they seemed on alarm."

Tovey swallowed hard.

"Alarm? What do you mean exactly?"

"I mean, I don't think it is safe for us to hunt. Rumors of the"—Cordelia lowered her voice to where Tovey couldn't hear—"have surfaced. And the guards seem to know something we don't. I wanted to warn you, keep you safe, you know?"

Gerald's face transformed, becoming even redder as Tovey pushed a finger to her temple. Reluctantly tearing herself away from the scene, she changed course, heading northwest. She knew the direction where she'd entered Abolend and didn't want to wind up anywhere near the collective. Into the unknown was the only option left.

Without food or water, she needed to obtain a weapon. Her eyes watered, the ashen air from overworked forges filling her nose. The stars twinkled, paired with the squeaking of shops shutting their welcoming doors.

She wavered, crossing each street, clinging to the shadows, keeping her face turned toward the ground. A group of men not much older than Tovey walked by, playfully bantering with one another.

One sang with tenor, "Ale makes us merry, merry and—"

"Fat!"

They chuckled again as they tramped forward. Tovey tilted her head with curiosity as she twisted her body toward them. She bustled closer behind them, opening her ears to the men, who were already inebriated.

"I hope Breena's got cold brews tonight!"

"Hail Breena!"

"Breena," Tovey grunted, her eyebrows upturned. They were heading to Nadia's mother.

Perhaps she didn't know her daughter had died years ago. Tovey owed her that, and she *had* to know more about the prophecy. Nadia had known something, and the one person she could have learned propaganda from was Breena. But being against the kingdom was dangerous, and Tovey had already risked meeting Breena, which had resulted in a flogging, the beating still aching at her back.

Don't turn back. Run. Guilt nipped at her heart.

Tovey turned from her route exiting Abolend to travel deep within the kingdom's heart, where the guards stood on every corner, towering like unruly weeds in the collective's garden. She needed answers. Breena had them. As the crowd thickened, so did the stares Tovey received. Paranoia needled at the back of her neck. Did they stare because of her stench, or did they know she was out of place? Either way, it was as if the spectators were attempting to peer through her shaggy hair. They couldn't notice her impairment, something a man would never wear. Ever.

She faced the wall as she untied her blindfold and knelt to the ground, brushing aside the shell to find sandy gray dirt. She coated her fingers in the powdery soil before rubbing the sooty earth under her eyes and over her eyelids, helping to darken them and prevent the amethyst glow from shining off her cheeks. Tucking the blindfold into her pocket, she shut her eyes, stumbling forward. She relied on her other senses, which had grown categorically strong. Her ears homed in on the group of boys who kept bursting into song. She followed heel to toe, fingertips grazing the granular wall.

A young girl ran into Tovey's legs. "Oops. Sorry, mister! Phew, you smell. Do you muck horse stalls? I want to ride a horse one day."

Tovey's mouth twisted. She wasn't permitted to speak, but a commoner would reply without hesitation. She had to muster the confidence to reply.

"Something like that." She spoke in a lower voice than her standard register, hoping to allude to the false image she was portraying.

"What's wrong with your eyes?"

"I'm blind."

"Oh no! That's terrible!"

"It is terrible sounding, but it is something I am used to, and it isn't so awful."

Silence answered.

Tovey's ears strained, searching for the group of men she was following, but their voices had left earshot. "Young maiden?" Tovey tilted her head to the still air before her.

"Yes?"

"Oh, you're still here. Good. Can you help me? I'm trying to find Barmaid Breena. Have you heard of her?"

"Yes! She tells wonderful stories. Let's go!"

Tovey heard the pitter of feet skitter forward and turn left.

Tovey shuffled swiftly, sure to follow as she clung to the wall, attempting to avoid plummeting into the chest of a wandering patron of the streets. "Can you slow down?"

"Whoops, you're blind."

"Yes."

A miniature hand wrapped around Tovey's index finger, and the child pulled her arm forward. "This way, this way!"

Chest rising and falling in a roll of laughter, she was tugged along. She was capable of following the sound of the child's footsteps and did not need to be guided by young fingers, but the wild spirit of the girl made her heart swell. She wished all young women could grow up so jubilant. Tovey's stomach bubbled with uncertainty; she was ashamed of herself for questioning the sanctity of servitude.

"Here we are," the girl said.

They approached a crowded bar filled with squirming people who were dancing and laughing in the heat of spirits. Wooden chairs danced across the ground, footsteps shifted side to side, and howls of laughter emanated from the guests. Tovey's jaw fell agape as she wondered how anyone could act so carelessly. What would the trainers say if they saw Tovey amidst the bar crowd? Tovey could imagine Vivian's screeching now.

Tovey bowed her crown toward the little girl, hearing the pitter-patter of boots skip away, leaving Tovey to the tavern. Tovey wormed her way through the crowded room as she bounced from side to side until a solid counter punched her in the chest. The wood was worn and smooth against her palms. Warmth kissed her face, emanating from dwindling waxy candles placed upon the dead slab. Men yelled for ale in a tornado of growls around her, so Tovey tried the same.

"Ale," she whispered, her voice cracking with uncertainty, sounding weaker than usual. Her disguise would be ruined if she didn't perfect her demeanor. *Be powerful.* Tightening her jaw, she filled her chest with the smoke-ridden air, sucking in the palpable warmth of the bar. A low growl came out, and she even surprised herself as she shouted, "Ale!"

"Dragon's blood! I'm right here, you scrawny oaf!" a barmaid answered.

"Breena?" Tovey's voice cracked into a falsetto.

"Nope. My name's Mary. Breena's out for the night." The ocean of acid stirred in her stomach. A heavy tankard sloshed in front of Tovey, froth licking at her fingertips. "Three dragos."

Tovey went flush as she understood a drago must've been a form of payment, a payment she didn't have. Servants weren't allowed possessions, not to mention a way to pay for vain items. They weren't even taught of money. Irrelevancies were useless to the developing mind. At least that was what Vivian had always preached.

"Never mind, I was only here for Breena."

"Never mind nothin'! I already poured you the drink. Three dragos now, *sir.*"

Breena wouldn't make her pay; Breena would know she didn't want a drink in the first place. "Where is Breena exactly?"

"None of your business."

"I have an important message for her."

"If it were important, you'd know how to reach her. Three. Dragos."

Tovey walked toward the door as she was tossed haphazardly in the sea of people.

"The little one doesn't want to pay for his drink!"

Silence overcame the bar. Tovey ignored her instinct to stop walking. She attempted to push forward, ramming into sturdy shoulders and chests.

"Nothing to say, boy?"

"I didn't drink any and forgot my coin. It's not like I can see if I grabbed it or not." Tovey gestured to her dirt-covered eyes. An easiness overcame the room as chatter began again. "Let me return to my home, and I'll come right back with five dragos for the inconvenience," Tovey lied as her tongue lashed in a low voice.

"Deal!"

The bar returned to the roar of laughter as Tovey fumbled onto the shell-covered street. With a deep meditative breath, she centered herself. She would sooner find herself dead than with Breena. Tovey listened to the noise on the road, which had fallen silent aside from an owl hooting rhythmically from four rooftops away. She flashed her eyes open for a brief second, taking in the narrow street filled with shops whose lights were quenched with clasped shutters, all aside from Breena's, where the warm light cast a welcoming glow on the seashell streets.

The chiseled structures stood one story tall, some with stone and others with thatched roofs folding in and out like fancy serviettes. Searching the crooked street, Tovey saw the castle towering above the village. Breena's place sat not even a few minutes' walk to the left of her former home, so close to where she had escaped from a few hours ago. Shutting her eyes, Tovey mapped the few streets she knew into her mind. She'd visit once more tomorrow. Until then, she would need to hide.

10

The unsteady rises and falls of Tovey's chest breathed horrified whimpers into the night. She slept pressed between a foul dumpster and shelled wall not far from Breena's bar. The smell of rotting fish would keep anyone in their right mind away, and the space she'd curled up in was too minuscule for an average-size person to wander behind and catch her.

The birds whistled a cheery morning tune, bursting Tovey awake. The sun illuminated the white crumbled streets in a soft pink glow. She took in the sounds, waiting for the opportune moment of stillness in the alley before advancing into it. She waited, afraid to breathe too loud as she watched a runty rat patter across the road. It was time.

Wriggling her way out of the crevice and into the dawn, Tovey fixed her gaze on the ground, barely cracking her eyes open. She matched the pace of other commoners, sure not to draw unwanted attention. By her measure, she was three blocks away from the bar and would be there within minutes. Seagulls burst into the sky as a deafening brass bell rang out through the streets, sending stillness amongst the travelers.

Gong. Gong. Gong. Gong. Gong. Gong.

Tovey stilled, taking in the commoners' raised eyebrows and slack jaws. The collective never trained the servants on sound signals. Her forehead wrinkled sharply as she listened to the static air.

"Six," a neighboring commoner solemnly stated.

Soberly, their shoulders dropped, necks bowed, and feet shuffled. As the final brass bell sang, townspeople shifted in haphazard lines toward the castle, abandoning all plans. Tovey's heart quickened her stride. She trailed the nearby commoners, cursing them for moving in the opposite direction of Breena. And by the deflated stature of the world around her, she knew she was marching toward nothing good.

The crowd silenced, marching into the square that lay before the castle. The courtyard was massive, enough to fit half the town. The castle's peaks and gables towered above them with dragons carved in the grainy walls. Giant stone steps led to a platform where a group of people stood. Tovey reluctantly shut her eyes and was tossed side to side as she was forced to shuffle closer, pushed by the crowd. Opening her ears wide, Tovey longed to hear an explanation.

The footsteps halted, the square filling with sardines. Shoulders, both meaty and bony, broad and narrow, all whacked into her. Her nose curled as she met the oniony musk of a man covered in soot. Tovey stepped back into a woman's flowing dress, stuck in a coffin of people.

"Citizens!" King Mallum's voice resonated, sending a tremble from Tovey's shoulders to her knees. "Today we are welcomed to the Great Square of Abolend to witness an unfathomable betrayal to the greatest kingdom ever to exist, our home, our master, our love, Abolend."

Gasps filled the air as Tovey stood in the river of noise, drowning. Unable to hear, she tightened her calves, raising her head above the crowd, tilting toward the makeshift stage.

"This treasonous act is rare to see in our beloved kingdom. Before me is a traitor. Her loyalty to the crown that protects you, the crown that guides you, has withered unjustly. This serpent has infiltrated our kingdom, and now she must pay the price! You are gathered here today to witness a betrayal of the Oath of Servitude. Yet this betrayer is not just a servant who has lost their way, but one who unrightfully grasped power within the serving ranks—a servant who fermented for years with a devil growing inside her mind. A master." His voice boomed, and whispers nipped at Tovey's ears like a swarm of insects. Tovey swayed from leg to leg, consuming his every word. Biting her tongue, she stilled.

"Master Daleen, one of many master servants here, has allowed an underling servant to defect from within our halls." Another round of insects attacked the crowd, wiping away all hope of hearing the king.

"A defector?"

"A servant defected from the castle?"

"That's never happened."

"It is a sign the prophecy is true. The servants are scared."

"Scared or not, they need to remain loyal."

"Hail."

The voices dizzied her. Tovey waited, swaying in a sea of uncertainty. The whispers elevated. Something must have been happening, but her eyes were slammed shut as if that would prevent the horror. The crowd's worry churned to excitement as the townspeople tightened around her. Was he saying something? Tovey stood on her toes to hear.

"What's he going to do?"

"I hope he kills her."

"Can you see him?"

"Move, I want to watch!"

Voices settled to a soft growl as King Mallum's voice wove its way back to Tovey's open ears. "Do you deny these charges?"

"No," Master Daleen said, her voice steady. A roar of boos encircled the crowd, the guards' voices booming over the people.

"How dare you not address me properly, Servant." Tovey ripped her eyes open, unable to listen any longer. Her gaze locked on the king as the back of Mallum's meaty mitt met the cheek of Daleen, sending her to the floor. Thunder clapped, and pulsing growls erupted from the throats of commoners in a sickening war song. She closed her eyes. This was her fault.

"No, King Mallum, leader of the brave, father of the land."

"Hail! Hail!" the war-singing minions chanted.

"And do you, Master Daleen, know the name of the defector so we may all join in a town hunt?" King Mallum roared with a gleeful smile. His palms flew to the skies as the crowd echoed his endorsement.

"Yes, King Mallum, leader of the brave, father of the land."

"Hail! Hail!" Energy balled like a loaded cannon, fuse sparking away to the powder.

"Speak her name now."

"Servant."

King Mallum slapped her. She yelped, spitting blood.

"The name the servants call her. The name she will use." King Mallum's brow jutted forward, shading his face.

"Servant. We don't have names."

With a venomous sneer, King Mallum patted her on the back. "And what does this traitor to the kingdom look like?"

"Blond hair. Red dress. Impaired with a blindfold."

"Ha! An easy catch." He paused as the crowd went silent, waiting for more. Tovey's body sank in billowing fabric as hands shoved her into the onion man. "The reward for catching the defector . . ." He paused, reveling in the tension, which was tighter than a drawn bowstring. "Five thousand dragos!"

Deafening gasps pierced through her heart, spearing from citizens' throats, growing into cries of joy and jubilant screams of hope.

"There has never been a bounty so high!" a man three rows in front of her exclaimed.

The hair on the back of Tovey's neck stood at attention. The townspeople's eyes drilled into her statue silence. Whipping her arms above her head, she joined the cries, hooting with fear masked as joy alongside the rest of the crowd. Dry air ripped at her throat. She was thankful she wasn't wearing the crimson gown, which would have gotten her slaughtered on sight. Meticulously, she worked herself back through the crowd, nearing the edge of the mob so she could be one of the first to run. Tovey squinted.

"Settle, my people. Settle. I know it is a bountiful reward, but we must kick off the hunt with some excitement." King Mallum wrapped two hands around the cruciform hilt of the longsword belted to his side. A metallic shiver sang as the blade swooshed to life from the scabbard in a silvery gleam. "Master Daleen, step forward."

Tovey watched an ironclad Abolend guard march into position behind Master Daleen. King Mallum held his sword horizontally, presenting the proud gift. The executioner tightened his hands around the grip with skillful hands.

Daleen fell, her knees clashing hard into the stone steps with a bone-cracking echo that reverberated in Tovey's teeth. The king and his court stood like prideful lions, soaking in the violence. The highborns straightened their spines, the crowd mimicking their movement as they all watched with wicked grins. Lady Rena let a shrill cackle escape her blabbering mouth. The prince's face was blank.

"Are there any other betrayers?"

Tovey rubbed her nail into her thumb. She knew Master Daleen would be sworn to tell the truth. Marka alerted Master Daleen of Tovey's escape. Marka valued her position of servitude above all else, as she should. Marka would have eventually told the truth, revealing to Master Daleen that Tovey was the demon if the prince hadn't already. Though it should've felt like a betrayal, Tovey knew it wasn't. It had been an act of survival.

"No, there were no other betrayers in her abandonment of duties. I was solely responsible. I allowed Servant to abandon her usual duties, giving her the ability to defect." Tovey's jaw dropped. "I broke my oath as a master. During this day off, I alone allowed her to defect under my eye."

The king cast a wink toward the executioner. A metallic flash cut through the air, and the guard's biceps rippled with strength. Tovey faltered, knees attempting to crash into the ground like her master's, but Tovey forced them to lock still.

Time stilled to a mere stutter as iron propelled toward the slender neck of Master Daleen. The commoners cheered violently, breaking the beating war song. Tovey stumbled backward, catching herself every step. The crowd countered her movement. Commoners pushed against her, attempting to propel her toward the steps, aching to see the gore firsthand. Blood splattered the front rows of the crowd as Daleen's head tumbled away from her body like a melon fallen from a cart.

"Go fetch me the defector," King Mallum boomed.

The crowd erupted into uncontrollable waves of movement as wild limbs flew erratically, mowing people to the ground. The hunt for Sylvia had begun. Tovey barreled away from the castle, sweat dripping from her hair. Her legs moved like fire, darting to the least crowded path again and again. She turned left and then right, traversing the most barren avenues she could find. Pausing, she heaved before emptying what little contents she had left in her stomach onto the sharp ground. Filled with guilt, Tovey ran again, propelling through Abolend with squinted eyes, tears braiding into her sweat.

One thought could not escape her mind as the six bells rang in her memory. Master Daleen had broken the cardinal rule of the servants and the masters, a rule she hadn't needed to breach because she would have been beheaded either way, and Daleen must have known that.

Master Daleen had betrayed her oath. She'd betrayed Abolend. She'd given her life to protect Tovey and Marka, who, without a shadow of a doubt, had told Master Daleen everything, including Tovey's amethyst eyes. Daleen had not allowed Tovey to abandon her duties. Marka was the one who'd assign her the position. Master had not given her the ability to defect. She'd hunted her. But somehow, despite Daleen's oath to honesty and undeterred by her position within the castle, Master Daleen had lied.

11

Tovey ran through the streets, attempting to escape the maze of Abolend. Disoriented from dissonant shouting, she had woven throughout the kingdom, taking multiple wrong turns that kept looping her back to the center of town as the sun crossed the pale sky.

Minutes turned to hours as she ran. Tovey cursed under her breath. She ducked into the shadows, trying to reorient herself. Catching her breath, she wiped the sweat from her forehead and raced through barren passages, avoiding roaming middle people as she aimed toward the outer walls.

Her stomach growled as she lurched toward an alleyway that led behind two rows of houses. Eyes squinted, she searched the shutters for one that may have been left ajar. Lifting her nose, she took in a deep breath, hoping to smell the scent of a meal, but there was nothing. Most people hadn't returned yet and were out on the hunt—the hunt for her.

As she passed endless windows, one rattled in the breeze to her right. Her feet stilled. She surveyed the loose shutter. She leaped behind the window in a flash, weaving wriggling fingers beneath the panel. She pulled it open, and the worn wood creaked. With a slight smile, she tightened her calves, lifting her sights higher.

The humble home had a warm fire flickering through the window. Tovey squatted beneath the opening, waiting for someone to scold her peering eyes, yet no noise came. She tilted her head, lifting her ear to the windowsill. Nothing.

Once more, she stood on her toes, peering into the home. Though the coals in the hearth crackled, the house was vacant. Her eyes widened. She searched the tables, counters, and chairs. A stunning silver dagger sat near the window, and a loaf of bread was lying on the table ten paces from where she stood.

Tovey debated crawling into the house, but it was too risky. Someone may turn into the alley. Someone could pop their head out of the window of a nearby home and see her. Swiveling her head, she took in the empty street as a decision snapped like a thread. Without thinking any further, she darted her arm in, lacing her fingers around the dagger's hilt, stealing it.

She squeezed her eyes shut, and regret poisoned her blood, dizzying her. Her fingers dove into her pocket, pulling out one of her two possessions: the broken conch shell that resembled a rose. She peered over the windowsill once more, ensuring the home was as still as before. Arm diving in, she placed the shell where the dagger had once lain.

"Thank you." The whisper fell from cracked lips, and she tucked the sheathed blade into her boot. She was morally compelled to leave something in return. Though it wasn't dragos, it was something—a sign of gratitude. She'd remember the house and would pay it back if fate would ever let her.

A fresh taste of air rushed through her lungs as she pushed onward through the town, pausing in nooks to catch her breath. The number of guards on the streets increased and her escape felt like a distant dream. Shadows grew long as the growing darkness shrouded her from prying eyes.

The moon was bright against the black sky. Tovey's tired palms pressed against the rough sandstone border wall; she was thankful she'd finally reached it. She hunted for a handhold so she could scale the thirty-foot barrier, but it appeared to be seamless. Tovey tied the blindfold around her eyes once more, shielding the purple glow of her eyes. No one would step close enough to see she had an impairment. The blindfold blocked the lilac glow and allowed her the slightest bit of vision in the navy night.

Cursing, she ran both hands along the wall as she pressed forward, hunting in the roughness for a crack, a doorway, anything she could use to wriggle through the barrier. Walking through the front gates would lead to her immediate execution. Six bells for a girl in men's clothes. A servant who'd defected. The purple-eyed ghost from the prophecy.

Ruby liquid met her fingertips as they grated into pink rawness from the uneven stone. Pausing, she heard Nadia's voice ring through her aching skull. *Defect before failure.* But failure appeared to be the only option left. Tovey was exhausted, and her prospects were disappearing quicker than she could count.

Tovey curled into a miserable lump of embarrassment at the base of the wall. She pressed her lips to her knees as her eyes caught something behind her—a hole in the wall. Scrambling like a spider, Tovey spun on all fours and punched a fist-size opening through to the other side. Pulling her arm out, she traced the wall around the hole, her finger finding an invisible crack spiderwebbing up to the right.

Shoving her shoulder into the breaking stone, she shifted the rock loose. Spinning to gain leverage, she kicked the wall hard, her knee begging for forgiveness as pain shot up her leg. Not giving in, she smashed her feet against the city's stone cage.

Boom. The crack lengthened.

Boom. The crack shifted an inch off.

Boom. Boom. Boom. Boom. The sandstone wall crumbled, revealing a small opening.

Heart pounding, she lay down, stomach pressed to the ground, ensuring her frame would fit; the opening was barely wide enough for her shoulders. Her split nails dug furiously at the soil, breaking away at the shell, scarring the ground until she collided with dirt. She shoveled enough space for her chest to snake through before stealing a glance behind her. The alley was vacant.

A devilish grin sprung across her face as she tore away at the dirt, giving clearance for one more inch. The dry soil coated her fingers like gloves, soaking the blood that pricked at her fingertips as she lay flat on the road.

She pressed her chest against the ground, releasing every ounce of air from her lungs. She compressed herself, crawling through the tunnel, holding her breath. Her feet kicked in a fury at the soil behind her to propel her through the makeshift tunnel. Furiously, she stretched her arms out to the other side, shifting her torso from one side to the other. Her palms slapped the outer wall as she planted them with a strength she was surprised she had. A solid adrenaline-filled thrust birthed her body halfway out of the tunnel.

The forest that met her was hauntingly dark through the hemp blindfold.

With no more time to waste, she thrust her pelvis into the soil, repositioning her body to plunge through one last time. She dug her fingers into the soft mossy soil on the other side of the wall. Her grip was firm on the ground; her muscles strained to no avail. Cold fear shivered through her veins.

Like lightning, forceful fingers gripped her ankle as dizzying fear scorched through her nerves. Kicking, she wiggled, reluctant to be caught, but a second hand wrapped around her other ankle, ripping her backward through the opening. The broken rock tore at her tunic, running lines of blood across her ribs, the ground fighting against her.

Thrashing violently, Tovey attempted to escape the hands ensnaring her. She was yanked back into Abolend and tossed on the ground like trash. A dark cloaked figure released her ankles, observing the defector.

Lavishing in the freedom, she scurried to her hands, shifting backward, pressed against the wall. Without deliberation, her hand darted toward the hidden dagger tucked in her boot, and she readied herself for a fight.

Neglecting to blink, she took in the stranger before her, unable to see any details on the shrouded man. She wrapped her fingers around the hilt of the dagger, ready to pull, but before she could move, the man snatched a fistful of her tunic. Her hand panicked, releasing the blade to grip his arm as he pulled her to her feet.

The cloaked stranger pressed his forearm across her chest, pinning her to the wall. She was trapped.

"Don't yell," his smooth voice snapped.

He pressed his palm over Tovey's mouth.

Tovey twisted, squirming beneath the domineering figure. She wriggled her way out of his forceful grip. His smooth jawline was illuminated before her. A black cloak shrouded the eyes of the mysterious figure. A gentle breeze billowed the hood slightly. A shimmer of crimson and gold glinted in the starlight.

Tovey's eyes widened. Her gaze locked on the familiar dimple resting in the center of his chin. Goose bumps covered her arms as she shivered in recognition. Prince Cullus.

The prince raised his strong fingers to the back of Tovey's head. Tenderly, he untied her blindfold. He squinted with fear or uncertainty; Tovey couldn't be sure.

Defeated, Tovey abandoned all hope of reaching her dagger, aware her charade had expired. The scratchy fabric fluttered away from her eyes as she snapped them shut, unwilling to expose herself.

"Open them. I command you," his smooth voice said.

Tovey opened her eyes, and they emitted the faintest lilac light, which reflected off her cheeks in the night. A smile danced across his face as he reveled in the shimmering light. His mouth moved without words. He swallowed air and attempted to speak again.

"Where are you going, defector?"

Tovey remained silent, unsure of what to answer.

Prince Cullus tightened his lips. "I command you to answer and remind you all questions are to be answered truthfully. You should know that everything I say to you is a direct command," he growled.

Tovey shifted. The sensation of bugs crawling beneath her skin pulled at her mind.

He inched toward her, eyes darting across her face. "The truth."

"To find a way to prevent the final war. I accidentally overheard the king speaking about the prophecy."

The slightest smile flashed over his face, wrinkles forming in the corners of his eyes. "Prevent it? Explain. You can speak freely during this conversation."

Tovey had never been able to speak freely to anyone of power. Contemplating her words, she chose them carefully, bringing the confidence held in her chest when conversing with the girl she had met the night before.

"I've heard the girl with purple eyes is the catalyst to the final war. But I have no interest in causing a meaningless battle. There is nothing I want to fight for. I'm not a threat, I promise. I simply want to live fed and sheltered, and I might be able to have that if the prophecy is proven untrue. I was going to turn myself in." Tovey bit her lip. "I was persuaded to defect."

The prince huffed, shifting his body. His arm eased from her chest.

"I thought there might be a way to stop it."

Prince Cullus raised his eyebrows as he frowned, taking in her words. Hours seemed to pass in the night, though the moon never moved. Nodding, he spoke, releasing his arm from her makeshift jail. "There is a way if you really want that."

Tovey nodded erratically.

"Good. We can convince Silvis to back down. My father is too hotheaded to avoid going to war, but if *they* retreat, we can call back our forces, and the final war will be prevented. No lives lost."

"We? Who is Silvis?"

"Yes, we. You and me. The prince and the demon." Fury intensified the glow of her eyes, and Prince Cullus's jaw dropped in awe. Gathering himself, he continued. "Silvis is our enemy kingdom and lies in the direction you intended to escape to." His accusing lips tightened.

Tovey shook her head, not even having known another kingdom existed.

"Did you *not* intend on running to them?"

"No. I intended on not dying for something I haven't caused. And here, I won't survive," she snapped, forgetting her position in the tornado of fury raging beneath her skin.

"Your birth caused this, and your existence is fuel enough for Silvis to attack Abolend. We are going, and you will convince them."

"How?"

"The same way you were going to do here. We will request a meeting with their leader."

"Do I have a choice?"

"No." He smiled again, a dimple forming on his right cheek. Annoying. "Go through now. You have a bounty on your head, not only because of those"—he gestured to her eyes—"but because a servant of the king defected and admitted to it."

Tovey's heart pounded. She prayed he wouldn't command her to give away details of her escape. She didn't want to criminalize Marka.

"I am the prince, and anyone we encounter has to obey. With me, you are safe." He paused, watching a man drunkenly stumble in a nearby alleyway. Lowering his voice, he whispered, "We need supplies. Give me an hour, and I'll meet you. Go a mile straight into the woods. Wait for me there."

Tovey faltered. "Why are you helping me?"

"Why did a demon pretend to be a servant?"

Tovey's shoulders stiffened at the word *demon*. "I'm not a demon, and I *am* a servant."

"And I am your best hope. Go now! Godspeed!"

12

Prince Cullus released his catch. Tovey slipped into the hole, kicking her way through. Her feet beat the ground hard, dirt squishing beneath her soft boots, her eyes glowing the brightest purple. Tovey hustled into the forest, walking heel to toe, ensuring she was traveling in as straight a line as she could manage.

Ivy ripped at her ankles, tangling her boots in their woven spirals. After a few minutes, Tovey surveyed the forest. The sound of her heartbeat was overwhelming in the silence. Even the crickets ceased to sing their twilight song. Tovey ascended into the branches of a hickory tree, planting herself with a bird's-eye view of the surrounding woods, taking in open areas where the prince might reappear.

Indigo clouds swirled in the sky, bright-lit stars shining between them. Maples, oaks, and pines swayed in harmony with the wind, dancing in the moonlit night. She waited soundlessly, berating herself for her choice to foolishly sit like prey in a tree, waiting to be hunted by the highest of highborns. Even as prey, Tovey was the weakest kind. She didn't have wings to lift her away from an oncoming arrow. She didn't have eyes that could see through the darkness. She had to obey. Or did she?

This time she was officially a defector, a true renegade of Abolend. If she ran, Prince Cullus would kill her, but if she obeyed, he might spare her after they went to Silvis. Running her fingers through her thin hair, she pulled it hard, easing the swelling in her skull, debating with herself. Minutes passed like hours as she weighed her options: wait or run, be hunted by Abolend or work with the prince. She was trapped with one feasible option. Disgruntledly, she accepted the conclusion she'd come to. She would wait for Prince Cullus and survive.

He had a plan and would have food and supplies she desperately needed. If she left now, her only hope was to run or become a wild woman, a fabled tale of defectors who managed to survive off the land. But her skills were acceptable at best. If she made it to Silvis on her own, she'd then have to work her way into another mysterious kingdom that could want to kill her more than King Mallum did.

Deep breaths calmed her echoing mind. She tightened her muscles, pressing higher into the tree, nearing branches that would soon grow too thin to support her weight. The wind blew her cropped hair gently as the branches thinned. A refreshing breeze caressed her cheeks, easing her stress. Her fingers traced the smooth pommel of the dagger tucked in her boot.

Tovey peered through the canopy, unsure of what would greet her. A battalion of Abolend guards? A rogue bowman? The ghost of Master Daleen? Daleen would've scolded Tovey for falling into the grasp of the kingdom within less than a day of her sacrifice. Chest tied with ropes, Tovey leaned back in the tree, tracing the fissured bark with her gaze, focusing on nothing more than what was before her.

The moon shifted in the sky. More than an hour must have passed by now. Tovey searched the forest, picking at the hickory's bark. A soft clopping echoed off the towering trees. She pulled herself close to the branches, keeping her eyes peeled, searching for the approaching animal. With a swift motion, she tied her impairment on in the event she would have to play coy once more. Her fingers pressed hard against the bark to hold her place as her chest tightened, and she became one with the tree.

The plodding continued, revealing a massive dark horse weaving its way through the trees, skillfully taking its time to seek the course of least resistance. The creature avoided trampling the waxy leaves and curling ferns that littered the forest floor. The rider was in a dark cloak, but beneath it, the familiar crimson-and-gold tabard of Abolend did not sparkle back, as it did before.

Tovey's fingers wobbled, her body shifting to see the rider. Pushing higher into the tree, she lodged her foot on a thin branch that snapped beneath her weight. A reverberating echo sent slumbering birds soaring out of the canopy. Slipping, she fell backward, grating her calf like cheese against the broken limb before regaining a foothold.

The rider's horse stopped at the sound, sending the cloaked figure to crane his head upward. He shifted his broad shoulders to investigate the sound. The rider pulled the horse's reins this way and that to center the creature below the noise. The figure's head snapped, searching feverishly as the cloaked figure's gaze shot up. Tovey wrapped her limbs around the trunk, trying not to whimper from the throbbing gash and her wailing fingertips.

"I see you." Prince Cullus's familiar smooth voice chuckled through the leaves.

Tovey didn't move, unsure if he was telling the truth. Perhaps he didn't see her, and she could still run. Her muscles shook, aching from the strain as a soft whimper escaped her lips.

"Come down! I command you!" he boomed.

A ball of air sat tight in her throat. She released the trunk, skittering out of the tree, defeated.

"Why did you bother hiding?"

Tovey stood still.

"You can answer freely." He pulled the cloak off his head, revealing the soft brown cloud of hair she envied.

A lump sat in her throat as she tried to swallow without success. Tovey debated the meaning of the word *free* as she shifted her weight from leg to leg. Speaking freely did not mean speaking carelessly, but it perhaps meant speaking honestly. Obviously, the prince didn't mean to talk as she wished, because Tovey wouldn't know how to voice those thoughts and words. Bouncing her head to her internal monologue, she said, "I didn't know if you were coming to kill me." Tovey clasped her tired hands together as she bowed her head.

An airy laugh escaped the prince's lips as he smiled, dismounting his steed. "Do you not know that you are the most important person in the kingdom right now? I wouldn't kill you. Did you not hear me say you are the one person who might be capable of getting Silvis to back down?"

Tovey stared at him with a blank expression.

"Well, believe it. We've got to move. Not everyone feels the same as I do, especially since the entire town is looking for your head." He searched the trees cautiously, ensuring no unexpected lurkers stood within the darkness. With a slight bow, the prince held out an outstretched palm.

Eyebrows stitching, Tovey stood still, questioning his gesture, her head tilting to the side. A flash of white teeth materialized on his face. His knee sank into the ferns as the other remained bent. He extended one hand and grabbed her slender fingers while his other hand tapped his knee.

"Use it as a stool."

Tovey's jaw dropped before she clamped it shut with a grinding halt. He wanted her to use his body as a step to mount the horse. He was insane.

"This is Frilliam." He motioned toward the horse.

Her cheeks burned as she placed her soft dirt-ridden boot atop his knee, which was wrapped in tight tanned pants. His leg was unwavering beneath her weight as she clumsily sat on the horse. A whisper of awe unleashed itself, Tovey's jaw agape as she settled upon the creature. Its strong muscles shifted beneath her. The horse's hair was coarse, and his body was warm. Bristly fur nibbled her skin as she ran her fingers across his back, causing the flicking of an unkempt tail. The prince mounted the horse with grace, resting in front of her. His soft hands wrapped around hers as he placed them on his tapered waist.

"Hold on." He kicked Frilliam and shook the reins, launching them forward into a canter that carried them through the forest.

The creature took steady breaths as its hooves pattered against the earth. Tovey's cheeks ached from smiling so much. She had never imagined riding a horse would be so ethereal.

Honestly, she had never imagined riding a horse at all. Rarely did one venture to the collective. Donkeys were the ones to carry supplies from the carved path. But she'd dream of this forever, bouncing above the forest floor as if she were flying. The wind from Frilliam's momentum kept her hair twisting in feral spirals as they rode.

The landscape blurred into an oily blend of emerald as jarring sways in the uncharted trail forced her to latch on to the prince much tighter than she intended. When she released her grip, he would reach an arm back, pushing her to hold tighter over unsteady ground. It was unusual for a servant to touch someone, especially someone of power. It was forbidden for servants to have physical contact with trainers and masters, and even then, it was rare to touch one another. But when he brushed his fingers against her skin, it tingled to life.

Shutting her eyes, she mustered inspiration to be brave, remembering how Nadia had held her hand through stormy nights. Imagining her sister before her, she grounded herself.

The horse's hooves battered against the untouched ground, chorusing soothingly, and the pair rode deep into the ever-thickening forest as dreams painted inky plumes on the insides of her eyelids.

13

Tovey's eyes snapped open beneath the blindfold. For a moment, she forgot she escaped the kingdom and was away from the castle, far away from anything she had ever known. She was no longer on the horse but lying in a meadow. Bearded grass caressed her body, and a finely woven cloak blanketed her legs. Pulling the fabric to her nose, she filled her lungs with an aromatic scent of lavender linen, a reminder of the laundry room at the castle. It was a comforting smell despite the chaos she'd left in.

Tovey prayed Marka was safe. She wished, no matter what, that Marka would accept Master Daleen's noble move. Whatever her reasoning, she'd died for a purpose. The beating of Tovey's heart came to a steady drumming. Blades of grass wove through her fingers, and she paused at a flowering weed to take in the vibrant golden color.

She wondered why weeds were called weeds and not flowers as

she twirled the silken petals in her fingers. Was it because they grew in undesirable places and were not perfectly kept in their boxes for the highborns to dote upon? A rose out of a finely blown vase would be discarded as an unruly weed, unnoticed for its layered beauty.

"Good morning!" Wrinkles crinkled in the corners of the prince's eyes. He walked from the forest, a quill pen sticking out from his pocket. Mind rattling free from her thoughts, she watched him. He rambled into the clearing with a pile of wood cradled in his arms. With an echoing clatter, he dropped the stack near a smoldering fire that lay two paces away from her feet. It, along with his donated cloak, had kept her warm overnight.

The sleeves of Cullus's white tunic had been rolled to reveal tanned forearms. Grinning, Tovey was shocked a highborn knew how to gather wood and had the ability to start a fire. By the looks of it, he had started it the night before and tended to it throughout the night. Flattered, Tovey scurried to her knees, searching for ways to help, thankful for the unusual kindness, not only from a prince but from another being. Not even other servants assisted one another in times of need. True friends were those willing to bend the rules, willing to sacrifice their necks for someone else.

"So, we haven't officially gotten to meet. My name is Cullus, and yours is Sylvia, correct?"

Tovey's eyebrows rose.

"Rumors. We know you keep your names, and we know most of them too. A servant from Master Daleen's ranks was missing. It didn't take me long to find out who you are."

A guilt-filled lump twisted her gut like a knife had been stabbed and twisted through her torso. Her cheeky grin faded as fast as it had appeared. Visions of Sylvia's battered body lying bloodied on the ground plagued her mind, causing sickening nausea to rise in her throat.

Though Tovey couldn't have prevented Sylvia's death, she still felt responsible. She could have let Sylvia be. Tovey could have continued into the woods. But she'd accepted the burden the moment she made the wretched decision to claim Sylvia's life as her own, defaming the bowman's victim even more than his arrow had.

"I've told them you stumbled into a bear trap and, well, your body isn't in any shape for public display."

Forehead wrinkling, Tovey mulled over his words.

"So, the hunt for defector Sylvia has been called off." He winked.

A burp of bile bubbled in Tovey's mouth.

"I went back to the castle to gather a few belongings before meeting you—you know, food, shelter, the necessary provisions." He motioned to the bulging saddlebags tied to the side of Frilliam. "My apologies that it took more than an hour. I underestimated my ability to gather everything. Regardless of my tardiness, your loose ends are tied. You don't exist," he proudly noted, chin lifted in accomplishment.

"I know," Tovey muttered, her gaze falling to the weeds. "I haven't for a while now."

Cullus's forehead wrinkled into deep valleys. His eyebrows waved like the sea across his forehead. He knelt to the ground, sitting in the meadow next to her. "And what makes you say that?"

"I'm not Sylvia."

"Yes, I suppose now you can be whoever you want."

"No. I'm not Sylvia. I never was. Sylvia, she . . ." Tovey berated herself for speaking truthfully and cursed herself for not being able to admit what she had done.

Cullus's eyes widened, and his shoulders became rigid, squaring into a statue of intimidation. "She what?" he challenged. His fist balled around the meadow grass. "If you are not the defector Master Daleen was referring to, our plans will be—"

"She's dead. Sylvia's dead." Tovey stifled a tear as she attempted to level her voice. "I am the defector Master Daleen spoke of. But Sylvia, the real Sylvia . . . escaped the collective and ran three weeks before I . . ."

"Before you what?"

"Defected from my collective."

Cullus rubbed his fingers against his round jawline.

"A bowman hunted Sylvia as I watched." Tovey's voice cracked. "I did nothing besides help mutilate her body and make her person look like my own." Tears rushed from her eyes and were absorbed by the blindfold, but her reddened nose was exposed. "I was scared to die like *that*. I couldn't do it. I couldn't run. I couldn't become a defector and starve alone in the woods. I killed myself and took her place so I could serve," Tovey admitted, ashamed of her act of survival. "The collective lied to us about Sylvia. They said she graduated. I didn't know she'd defected until I saw her that night. I assumed the castle hadn't heard Sylvia had defected either, and I was right."

Cullus's mouth dropped while his brow furrowed in a delicate dance of confusion. "Your name. Tell me." He squinted.

"Tovey." Warmth filled her the second her name left her lips. It had been so long since she'd spoken her name; it was like greeting an old friend.

He shook his head, running soft fingers through his hair. "You have broken countless laws: defecting, interfering with a defector, serving in a station not assigned to you, skipping duties to mingle with commoners in the Reckoning Hall, defecting yet again!" He listed her crimes finger by finger. Surveying the invisible list, he muttered, "No wonder they say you are a demon."

Tovey's eyes welled. She had heard enough, and working with an abrasive prince wasn't worth it. She could find Silvis on her own. Determined, she stood. Spinning on her heel, she gained momentum. The bearded grass parted, her legs a blur as she sprinted into the forest, boots slapping hard against the ground. She shook her head as she ran faster. Stars of shimmering purple light blocked her vision. Her feet intertwined with the waxy vines, which yanked her to the earth. The dirt met her face with a familiar clash.

Cullus was right behind her. He stepped with high knees to avoid the tangle of growth. He grabbed the back of her stolen tunic, pulling her from the dirt. She spun, tumbling to the ground like a rabid dog, ripping her fingers through the air to grab her hidden dagger as they wrestled in a tangled brawl. Cullus grabbed her foot, yanking her toes upward before she was able to reach her weapon. He turned, readjusting his grip on Tovey's ankle in his hand, and dragged her back toward the meadow.

"Just kill me already!" Tovey roared, attempting to kick free from his grip, her fingernails lodging into the soil. She flopped against the soft ground like a fish out of water. "I know that's what you must be bringing me out here to do! I heard your father. I heard you! *Stop her. Hunt her. Kill her.*"

"That was before I came to the realization that you could stop this! Are you not listening?" He released her ankle and grabbed her hand, pulling her to her feet. Once more, he ripped the blindfold from her face. Staring straight into her eyes, he cast the scratchy fabric to the ground. "You, Tovey, are the catalyst to bring the final war, yes." He pointed his finger at her nose, inches from it. "So says some prophecy. But what if you are the catalyst to *prevent* the final war? What if the prophecy is a bunch of codswallop? They say you are a monster, but I see no scales or horns. What if we go to Silvis and they back down? There will never *be* a war. Abolend will have no one to fight. We will not lose men, and our kingdom—your home—will be secure. And we will not fight you. One cannot wage a war on the many. Plus, you are docile, are you not?"

"You know I don't want to fight."

"Then our plan is seamless."

"And what then? What about the laws I've broken? Even now, speaking freely isn't allowed. Highborns won't accept this. They won't accept me, not after what I've done."

"And I am the highest highborn—aside from my father, of course. I will spare you for your service to Abolend despite defecting. And your mouth." Wrinkles formed by his eyes as he flashed a quick smile. "Your persuasion could save countless lives—the lives of your friends, of the people in my kingdom. I stand here with a purple-eyed being straight from an old tale. Everyone is going to listen to what you have to say. Even if they don't like it, I know they will hear it. How could you not want to try?" His eyebrows turned upward as if he were pleading.

She searched his face, unsure of what other options she had. At the least, he seemed to believe in his plan, a plan that would leave her alive. Reluctantly, Tovey agreed. Her lips pursed. "Never call me a demon again," she demanded as she turned toward the fire and began tending to the coals.

Cullus scoffed while pulling sticks and fabric from a pack tied to Frilliam's side, then began raising a tent. Tovey shook her head at the idea that a tent was a necessary accommodation for him to bring. So far, nothing seemed out of the ordinary, but now his noble blood was showing.

"I sat on guard last night. I didn't have time to set up a proper camp," he justified to judging eyes.

Tovey watched him move across the camp in gentle swaying movements, as if the dirt-ridden ground were a polished floor in the kingdom. She crossed the clearing to assist him, mimicking his tent building to raise it on the other side. As they worked, his eyes bored into her like a drill. She was uneasy without the blindfold, never having been without it. She felt like a finger had been lost or a new appendage had been added and she was unsure how to use it.

"What?" Tovey blurted, uncertain why he searched her face for answers she didn't know.

"Your eyes. They glow when you are upset. It is fascinating."

"They do not," she retorted, the faintest spark of purple flickering on her ivory cheeks. Cullus smiled the annoying crooked grin that made his irritating twin dimples appear. "May I put my blindfold back on?" She yearned to hide from his prying eyes.

"No."

Tovey's shoulders turned inward.

"What is it? Please speak. I don't want to command you. It grows tiresome."

"Why lie and say that I, Sylvia, am dead?"

"Battle strategy." His eyebrows knitted. "I need to prove myself as the prince. The time is nearing when I may take the throne, and this mission to Silvis can be what secures my spot. Abolend has historically given the throne to the eldest son when they prove themselves capable. It ensures our strength as a kingdom. The new king leads while the elder guides from a distance. My father took his place when he was twenty-five." Tovey wrinkled her nose. "If I can prevent a war, I will be a hero. Winning without any deaths is a feat not even my father can accomplish."

A sliver of understanding and hope crossed her mouth. "So, King Mallum knows your plan?"

"No, which is why I said Sylvia is dead. It'll keep the commoners out of the Tenbris Forest; we'll have no unwanted visitors that way. And, if I do not tell my father of my plans, he cannot send guards, hence the guards will not take credit for what we can accomplish together."

The intricacies of Cullus's plan made her mind tick in sluggish movements. Her previous plans had been on a whim: run and survive. If she thought too hard, she'd second-guess herself. A master plan with so many assurances was boggling, but still, working with him was worth it if she got to live another day. He had power and sway, and if she could prove herself helpful, there may be a reward at the end—a comfortable placement as a servant. Perhaps she'd even be allowed to be a middle person. If Cullus didn't want death on his hands, then he could be sincere with the fact that he did not want to kill her. He could be trusted for now.

"So, Prince Cullus, are we staying here for long?" she asked, diverting the conversation.

"Cullus. Just Cullus is fine. And we are only staying until we fortify a plan." He unrolled a leather scroll from his satchel, revealing a map of Valledera. His manicured finger pointed to a place illustrated with a castle in the center of the town, showing twists and turns in the streets. Brain swelling, Tovey now understood how she kept winding up lost. The roads were more woven than a knotted ball of yarn. "This is Abolend, and this landmass is Valledera." His finger circled the continent. "Which collective were you at?"

"How many are there?"

"Fifteen for servants. Ten for warriors, because they are bigger." Tovey rubbed her dry lips together, unsure of where hers was. She studied the map while Cullus continued to mull over his thoughts aloud. It was a strange experience for Tovey, who was used to silence. "I cannot wrap my mind around why you attempted to defect only to come back to serve. It is unusual."

"I made a promise to my sister not to fail," Tovey admitted, and Nadia's screams echoed in her mind. "And you know what becomes of servants after the third test is failed?" Cullus's eyes shifted as Tovey lowered her voice. "Death. And I don't want to die." The forest fell eerily silent before she continued. "Or better yet, servants are taken away to serve in a place no one mentions. What are they then?"

"If you're asking if they are freed, then no. No one is ever free. We all must serve Abolend in one capacity or another. And I commend you for continuing to serve."

His face became solemn. He stood, disappearing into the woods, his fingers tapping his pocket. Curiously, Tovey watched him before turning her eyes to study the map. She pressed a sore finger against the smooth leather, which bent beneath the pressure. She traced the fine lines of the kingdom, searching the rivers and turns she remembered finding the night she'd defected, finding the only collective that could be hers.

A knot formed in her stomach as she touched the little square house illustrated on the map. It was so close to the kingdom. Tovey had always imagined they were days away from the city. She shook her head at the incessant mulling of status whisking in her brain. She wondered how people could grow up lavishly in a kingdom while others were beaten in filth just a few miles away. It was the way of the world. She pushed the treasonous question from her mind.

Inspecting the map once more, she saw a similar-size circle as Abolend marked with a tree. Instead of having its roads mapped out, there were bushes. Silvis. Tovey swallowed hard. The opposing kingdom also towered on the coast, but it was across the uncharted Tenbris Forest they were currently sitting in.

The sun had swept beneath the trees by the time Cullus returned. She pondered where his lone walks took him, but questioning him wasn't permitted. Spending time alone was never allowed at the collectives. It must have been the same for highborns. A moment with your own thoughts was valuable.

He paraded into camp while he tucked spare parchment into his pocket. The woodland insects started singing their bedtime songs as the sky flashed inky displays of pink and purple in the setting sun. Tovey tended the fire after moving it from Cullus's original location to the base of a tree. Nadia had once told her that the leaves of a tree can diffuse smoke and help conceal a fire. Nadia had always been smart like that, cunning in the way of survival.

Cullus eyed her cautiously, watching her every move as he took a seat by the tree hearth. Her hair rose on the back of her neck; she was not used to highborns being so critical of her work. She hadn't yet been allowed to work directly with them, and she was thankful for it. Her stress boiled, moving through her veins as she attempted to appear the perfect servant.

The two sat in near darkness, the faint embers glowing in a rhythmic pulse before them, the beating heart of the forest. A comforting smell of ash glazed the air. Tovey let her eyelids fall, breathing in perfect time with the glimmering coals.

"Tovey," Cullus whispered.

The hair on her arms stood at attention as she heard her name dance upon his lips. She loved that she was finally called by her name.

"Tell me, what was it like growing up? I've never spoken to a servant before you," he admitted before shrugging the thought away.

"Structured." Her eyes glossed as she recalled her time at the collective. She'd always known what was expected of her. "Humble." They were never taught to adore lavish clothing and baubles, like those the highborns had. They only needed the necessities—bread for most meals, hay to sleep on, tools with a bit of life.

Dull tools and near-hairless brushes could still do simple house chores like laying new stone floors or scrubbing the old ones. Maintaining the thatched roofs was easy to do with vines and a solid bite to rip them. Shining the windows could be done by standing on the shoulders of another since they didn't have a ladder and making tools was prohibited. Shoes weren't necessary for trekking through the mud to fetch well water.

Shiny useless trinkets and clothing that lacked usefulness were irrelevant to servants. She studied the familiar earthen ground dotted with bulbs of moss, her gaze moving to take in Cullus's thick fingers with kept nails, the exact opposite of her bony, bruised, cracking fingers and chipped nails. She traced his face, which was scar-free and radiant. Her finger touched her skin, where permanent impressions lay—nonerasable marks from where the blindfold had chewed into her cheeks, forming thin white lines.

Hateful tears raced toward her scars as she envisioned all the girls who had been scarred, beaten, and mutilated, unlucky because their birth was not of noble blood. Tovey speculated the servants were more deserving of lavish meals than blasted Lady Rena, who would benefit from a day of hard labor. Tovey swallowed forcefully, focusing on being honest. She had never faced the reality of her position. There was never a moment when she ever questioned it. It was the way it was.

A deep breath escaped through her nose. "It was dreadful. And I never knew that until I met you."

His eyebrows pinched as his broad shoulders turned toward her, but Tovey remained silent, letting the fire warm her skin.

Mutual understanding encompassed the pair as they sat in stillness. Even the birds and crickets had tucked in for the night, leaving the crisp air still. The fire was the only one to speak, rambling on for hours until their eyelids became too heavy to watch.

Tovey lay asleep on the ground. Her eyes fluttered open to see a dark cloak had been placed over her. Cullus paced, repeatedly circling the quarter-acre clearing. He turned to the horse's saddlebags, fishing a bell and string from the pack. Tovey shut her eyes, listening to him tiptoe closer. He wriggled his fingers around her calf, lifting it before tying a bell around her ankle.

Tovey's eyes opened, causing Cullus to still.

His face reddened. "It's so I would hear you in case you decided to run," he admitted awkwardly.

"I'm not going to run."

Cullus frowned. "You've run before. How can I trust you?"

"The same way you expect me to trust you."

Cullus's eyebrows pinched, and he took the bell and string back to the saddlebags.

Tovey tossed a fresh log onto the coals as the crickets returned to sing a calming lullaby. Her ears soaked in the sounds of the forest, and she closed her eyes once more, listening to the rustling of leaves beneath the miniature feet of rodents. Cullus retreated to his tent. Tovey listened to his blankets fluttering in the chilly air. The faintest whisper traveled in the whistling wind straight to Tovey's eardrums as the prince's smooth voice sang, "Good night."

Tovey pressed her fingers into her boot, fingering the dagger's hilt. She pulled the blade from its sheath before turning to her stomach and hiding the sharpened weapon close to her chest.

14

The sun's rays brushed the soft grass of the meadow. Birds tweeted and rustled amongst the fallen leaves, searching for breakfast. In the distance, a sizable branch snapped. The woody echo caused Frilliam to shift uncomfortably next to the tree Cullus had secured him to. Tovey woke, glaring toward the unnatural noise, the dagger still gripped to her bosom. She shook off the dark cloak and folded it neatly before placing it beside the tent where Cullus slept.

Perched on her toes, she crept toward the sound, which had sent flocks of birds fluttering. The forest was silent again. Perking her ears, she listened, but the gentle sound of rushing water in the opposing direction pulled her away from investigating the echoing snaps. It could've been a bear or a deer. Cullus had assured her no one was after them, and bowmen wouldn't be so careless as to make such a harsh sound.

Tovey's mouth was achingly dry; it felt as if she had been

licking cotton. Turning back toward Frilliam, she searched his dark eyes, knowing he too would prefer a drink over investigating the intrusive sound. Whipping her arm out, she untied him from the tree, leading him toward the water. She had seen a bear once from the window of the collective, and she wouldn't want to meet one face-to-face.

The black horse was mild mannered, and he took Tovey's lead. She followed the hum of water in the valley. The air became cooler. Trampled trails led them to the river as the thicket thinned, proof of large game. She swooned with gratitude as icy glass rushed southward to the sea.

"Drink up!" Tovey patted Frilliam's muscular side as she released his reins. She pulled a deerskin canteen from his pack and filled it with water before she knelt, relieving her thirst. Wetness sopped at her pants as she kicked aside her soft boots, inching into the stream. Smiling at the chattering glass, Tovey plunged into the water. She washed, brushing the dirt, scum, and blood from her body.

Another crack echoed through the valley as Frilliam's head rose.

"Tovey!" Cullus shouted with a terrifying howl.

Heart racing, Tovey flitted from the water, gripping her boots in one hand and readying her dagger in the other. She leapt, mounting Frilliam in one balanced movement, and dug her feet into his sides the exact way she had watched Cullus do the night before. Frilliam's hooves dug with fury into the moist soil, propelling him faster. He galloped through the forest with no guide or direction. Panicked, Tovey let go of the reins, weaving her fingers into his mane. The dagger's tip shook dangerously close to Frilliam's neck. She pushed it into her boot before tucking her head close to his.

"Frilliam! Slow down, Frilliam!" Tovey squealed as his pace

increased. "Cullus!" she yelled into the still trees, fighting the rising panic. The thought of Cullus in danger ached at her heart. It must not have been a bear. Guards must have come after the missing prince, or the huntsmen hadn't received word that who they presumed to be Sylvia was dead. They had been caught, and it was her fault for ignoring the signs.

Find Cullus, she thought, willing the horse to calm down. Frilliam changed direction back to the camp as if he could understand Tovey's boiling terror.

Minutes passed as the green blur of trees whooshed her hair into a knotty nest, her eyes wild with terror. A hand reached out from the woods, grasping the fluttering reins. Frilliam's head was yanked to the side.

"Whoa, whoa!" Cullus yelled, dragging his heels into the soil, guiding the wild horse to a halt. "What in the name of Abolend are you doing?" He scowled toward Tovey, fuming.

"Rescuing you!"

"It doesn't look like it," he scoffed.

"Where are the guards?"

"What guards?"

"You yelled, didn't you?"

"Yes, for *you.* You ran off with the horse."

"*No,* I took Frilliam to get a drink and brought you back some." Tovey's face felt warm, and she was thankful she tucked the dagger back into her boot, sure to hide her weapon. Tovey pulled the canteen from Frilliam's pack, shaking it.

Cullus released the tension in his furrowed brow. He offered a soft hand to aid Tovey in dismounting the towering horse. She slipped on her boots.

"You weren't running away?"

Tovey shook her head at the prince, and her eyebrows formed an unapologetic ridge across her forehead. She held out the canteen, thrusting it into Cullus's chest. "I'm not going anywhere. But I did hear a crack in the forest this morning. I don't think we're alone."

Cullus motioned to two short broomstick-size branches beside him, his face reddening with the rising dawn. "That was me."

Tovey twisted her head as she glared toward him. "You weren't asleep in the tent when I left?"

"No, and you were still asleep by the fire when I left. And when I came back, you and Frilliam were gone." Silence fell over them as they both smiled nervously. "So, you decided to run toward a prince in danger instead of taking off? Why wouldn't you leave?"

Tovey wrinkled her nose.

"Speak freely. I want to understand your mind. It baffles me."

"Trust."

Cullus's hazel eyes sparkled in a way Tovey had never seen before.

"And you yelled. I assumed you needed help. I didn't act with bravery for Sylvia, and I won't be a bystander again. I didn't want to see you hurt."

"I'm the prince. I can't get hurt," he said, and Tovey looked askance at the prince. "Any guard or bowman who stumbles upon us will obey me. But you *can* get hurt, which is why I don't want you wandering off without me knowing where you are. If you got injured, how would I find you?"

Tovey hadn't comprehended that someone—not just someone, Cullus—cared. She contemplated how badly she wanted him to be safe as her heart jolted. This was something more than the type of loyalty servants showed to the highborns, similar to the kind of loyalty she shared with Nadia. A friend.

"I won't leave again without telling you," Cullus promised, his fist wrapped around Frilliam's reins as he led the beast back toward the camp. "And please tell me if you leave camp." Tovey's heart fluttered as her lips parted in awe. Unable to hide a grin, she stared at him with wide eyes. "What?"

"You said please." Tovey blushed, honored for the first time in her life she'd been *asked* to do something, not told. Do this. Do that. It was always expected.

Cullus nodded to himself, and a perplexed expression crossed his face before fading away. He turned and picked up the broken sticks, tossing one toward Tovey.

She grasped the wooden shaft, her eyes widening. It was an odd shape for firewood, but she appreciated Cullus's efforts all the same. Still, he hadn't needed to throw it at her.

Cullus tied Frilliam to a hitching tree by the clearing. His grip loosened on an identical branch as he twirled it, allowing his hand to slide to the bottom. He swung it in a loop, letting it land stiff, pointing it at Tovey's face.

A crooked smile lifted wrinkles to the corners of his eyes. "Do you know how to fight?" He confidently swung the stick, and the tip swayed in fanciful patterns. His feet stepped with certainty as he performed a warrior's dance.

A mischievous grin flickered across Tovey's face. She held the branch firmly with both hands, her knuckles whitening before she loosened her stranglehold, comfortable with the weight. She stepped forward with her left foot, lurching into a spin and whacking the stick out of Cullus's hands. Defeated, the wood stuttered from his delicate hands to the earthen floor.

His mouth hung agape, and her laughter filled the air around him. His hazel eyes sparkled in the midday sun. Wishing she could unbox Cullus's mind, she bit her tongue, watching the highborn grip his makeshift sword, her stance readying for another embarrassing fumble for the knightly prince.

"I know servants are not taught to fight." A dimple bored itself into his cheek. "More trouble you got yourself involved with?"

Tovey frowned. "Is it trouble to know how to defend yourself?" Her eyes dug into Cullus, daring him to answer. "After being beaten for things you don't deserve to be beaten for, you make sure you know how to protect yourself if it goes too far. We are obedient, yes, but not foolish." She repeated Nadia's words, which were truer now than they'd ever been before.

Cullus fell silent.

"Should we continue?" Uncomfortable that she'd let her truth run wild again, she pushed forward, advancing at him. Tovey lurched, whacking him on the shoulder with a swift blow.

"Ouch!" He rubbed his arm while his other hand swung, pushing Tovey's stick into the dirt.

At lightning speed, he lunged forward with the wooden sword, switching direction like a dragonfly darting through the air. The wood fell still right next to her neck, a death blow.

"Don't think I haven't had training. I was being kind before." Cullus winked.

Tovey rolled her eyes as dimples raced across his cheeks once again. Admittedly, she liked seeing them, but she wasn't sure why their presence always made her face echo the sentiment. Heart fluttering, the warrior in training steadied herself. She placed her hand on her chest, unsure of the cause of the strange palpitation. It was now twice her heart had acted funny.

"Ready?" he asked.

Cullus led Tovey, and the two practiced tactical moves until the sun crossed the crest of the sky. He grabbed her arms, moving them through calculated acts, placing her feet in varying stances. Occasionally, he would tuck in her elbow and show her pivoting moves to ensure she could deliver debilitating blows despite her petite stature.

Exhausted, the pair retreated to the hearth as the sun dipped to the horizon, and they ate dried meats Cullus had brought from the kingdom. They chewed in silence, taking in each other's presence. Tovey assumed he wondered precisely as much about her as she did about him. Admittedly, she didn't know much about the prince's duties, politics, or highborns.

Cullus rummaged through their stockpile. He had brought a longsword for himself but also an accompanying rapier. Tovey watched him eye the smaller weapon, the blade etched with leaves, perfectly balanced and adorned with faceted tourmaline stones. He grabbed the hilt and spun it in his hand, walking over to where Tovey stood.

"You should have a weapon."

Tovey waved her stick playfully.

He shook his head solemnly. "This was gifted to me when I was young. It was the first weapon I learned how to wield." His eyes became misty, as if they were no longer fixed on the sword but a memory from long ago. "But I'd like you to have it." Turning toward her, he presented the blade as he knelt to the ground.

"I . . . I can't," she protested. Tovey pushed her fingers into her boot, pulling the dagger she had stolen from her boot's inner lining. The blade glinted in the amber glow of the forest, and the setting sun turned the leaves to honey. Crickets chirped, filling the still air with strange conversations.

Cullus sat, scooting toward Tovey, his questioning gaze inspecting the dagger. "Where did you get this?"

"A man."

Cullus squinted. "Which man?"

"A man who lives in a house."

His expression fell flat. "It is fine craftsmanship, the kind made in Abolend by a skilled smith."

Tovey's lips sealed shut.

"Hornsby made this for you? I know his prices are not cheap." He watched Tovey intently, surveying her every move.

"I stole it." Her gut wrenched.

"Any other crimes you want to admit to?" he growled at the dirt.

Tovey sat silent, her hands clasping together as her posture straightened.

Cullus laughed, his fingers racing through his hair. "I am honestly starting not to care anymore."

They met each other's gaze. Tovey stared at his eyes, which had islands of gold floating within them. Her lips unintentionally parted as his soulful gaze traced her face. Confusion clouded her senses. She couldn't comprehend what he was searching for. She pulled the sleeve of her tunic over her face. After wiping it quickly, she checked the fabric for blood or dirt, but there was nothing.

He turned his head, pulling his gaze away, forcing a cough. "It will take about three weeks to travel to Silvis, and we need to make sure we arrive before the solstice."

Tovey swallowed air. She had forgotten the reason they were out in the middle of nowhere. For a moment, it was like the rest of the world had faded away. The absurd prophecy, their class standing, any pressure—it was all gone, dissolved by the floral fog of the forest.

"Right." She paused. "Why before the winter solstice?"

"The final war is said to take place on your eighteenth birthday."

"I don't know when that is." Tovey remembered that Nadia said snow began to fall when they arrived at the collective. "But I suppose it could be around the solstice."

"It is *on* the solstice, according to the prophecy."

Tovey curled her limbs into herself. She had a birthday, a specific day when her life started, the day her cursed amethyst eyes were brought into the world, and she had no idea. Cullus placed a steadying hand on her shoulder as she wavered.

"Will you tell me everything you know about the prophecy? I'm starting to feel like you know more about me than I do." She brushed her boot against pebbles on the ground. It was as if she was one of them, a little insignificant piece of matter that was unable to see the forest full of life around them, yet everyone else saw the rock and pitied it for not having eyes.

Head bowing, Cullus motioned for Tovey to sit by the fire. They folded their legs beneath themselves as they huddled close in the rising night.

"It was a cold dark night when the earth shook," he said. "The embers from the winter's log danced into the night like a million fireflies had been released." His fingers danced in the air, illustrating the moment.

"Do you remember it?"

"It's one of my first memories." His teeth flashed. "I was three."

Crinkling her nose, Tovey imagined the prince as a toddler. She couldn't help but smile at the thought of him toddling around the halls.

"Great seers across Valledera all had identical visions that night: something powerful had risen. King Mallum was fuming, my mother always said, because he didn't want a power greater than that of Abolend to exist. Abolend's strength keeps our kingdom functioning peacefully, and without it, chaos would erupt.

"One by one, the seers were called to court and interrogated individually, and one by one, they confirmed what the others had said. A babe had indeed been born of the earth, identifiable by her brilliant lilac eyes." He paused, his face illuminated briefly by a faint purple glow.

"The king asked the seers to divulge how she could be more powerful than a kingdom so great, but they didn't know. Their sight was not all-powerful, but one thing they all agreed on was that she was a demon."

A shiver ran up Tovey's spine. She was not something of legend foretold to be pure evil from the depths of the hellish underworld. Surely it wasn't true. It couldn't be.

Cullus's mouth twitched with terror. "Of course, any threat to the throne had to be a demon." He paused with upturned eyebrows, searching her face. "That night, King Mallum started a hunt for the purple-eyed babe. Every highborn and commoner was questioned.

Every home was searched. Every mother was brought into the Reckoning Hall with their newborns. Yet she was never found. King Mallum even extended his search of all babes born within the year, but even then, Abolend's searches always came up empty."

Tovey took in a sharp breath before her jaw slacked. Astonishment poured into her brain like a leaky faucet that had broken loose. "The collectives were never searched."

Cullus shook his head. "It would be beneath the highborns to think servants held power over us. After all, why would a demon be abandoned into a life of servitude?"

"Because your father was too daft to search there." Tovey stiffened as Cullus's eyes berated her before stilling to a calm sea.

She had never considered herself abandoned, though she knew she was an orphan. After all, the collective was where she'd found family, not lost it. Who were her parents? What if they were still alive, in Abolend, like Breena? They could be searching for her, and she had never even considered the notion of finding them. Servants were forbidden to talk about their life before the collective. Still, not being able to talk about where she was born wasn't an excuse to never think about her life before. Guilt sat heavy in her chest.

"I think there is much Abolend has overlooked." Cullus brushed a stray strand of hair out of Tovey's eyes and tucked it behind her ear. Tovey shivered at his touch, the fine hair on her neck standing on end. Her heart swelled, too expansive to be confined in her chest.

"Over the years, the prophecy became a rumor. Fact turned into fiction. Some still believed the babe existed, yet others hypothesized the seers had planned this fabled event to shake the stability of our kingdom, an attempt at a rebellion. King Mallum thought the seers were traitors to the throne, and they were slaughtered." Cullus's mouth twitched. "The people we once revered became people my father feared."

Tovey's eyes raged, her body flushing. Her lip quivered, and tears rushed to her eyes. The body count she had caused rose. Again. A handful of seers. Nadia. Master Daleen. They had all died because of her. Sylvia died because Tovey was too much of a coward to do anything but watch.

"But despite the story becoming a legend, as we approached the seventeenth solstice, defector rates rapidly increased. Our influence within the collectives has been diminishing, and once more, the people began recounting stories of the fabled child. Yet still, no one had seen the babe." He paused, his eyes shifting to rest upon hers. "That is until the day a servant bravely stood before the Reckoning Hall and unveiled herself in surrender, a nonsensical noble move." A crooked smile danced across his face before fading.

"Why would defector rates increase because of an absurd rumor about me?"

"Because *you* are said to cause the final war. Servants who don't accept their place and soldiers who refuse to serve their kingdom see this, see *you*, as a sliver of hope, hope to rebel against the kingdom, to rebel against the law of life and position."

Who would be willing to fight for change? It seemed silly that servants who defected and survived would be considered dangerous. But if soldiers were defecting too, that *would* be a threat. They could build an army. Was that what Nadia had wanted? For them to defect and join a rebel army? She wouldn't. Nadia had hated the collective, yes, but not enough to ever cause harm to anyone, or would she? Tovey's theory was shattered as Cullus continued.

"The eighteenth solstice was when her true nature would be unstoppable, and Valledera would enter into the final war." He paused. "The only people we can have a war with is the other kingdom on Valledera unless our plan is right. Abolend is preparing for war. It would be useless for us to attack Silvis unprovoked. King Mallum has been secretive about his plans, but I know there must be a threat from them. They must fear the prophecy. They know you aren't within their reach, which makes you dangerous. They will come here and attack us to find you unless you can convince Silvis to back down, to not attack Abolend. You can persuade them and tell them you are not a threat." He eyed her carefully. "Though you are a thief." An airy laugh escaped his lips.

"A thief who is armed." Tovey unsheathed her dagger and pointed it playfully at him. He pushed the blade to the dirt with a solid finger. "So, does Silvis know of the stories?"

"Yes, Mother always said they have seers too."

Tovey's eyebrows rose. "I've never heard people talk of your mother."

"She died when I was young. The flu."

Tovey bowed her head. "May the light guide her."

Cullus's eyes became glossy as he peered into Tovey's soul. "Thank you. No one has ever said that. Ever. Really, thank you."

Tovey lay back on the forest floor, the soft ferns weaving in her hair as she listened to the pitter-patter of forest creatures emerging in the night. It was comforting to know they were not alone. Cullus collapsed next to her, eyes open wide, searching the sky.

"When do we leave?"

"At dawn."

15

ool fog rolled across the dew-covered ferns, the mist cascading
through the camp. Tovey and Cullus stirred by the fire. His
steady breath brushed across the back of her neck as he lay curled
behind her. From a dead sleep, Tovey's eyes widened, bewildered.
Her head swiveled from the empty tent to where Cullus shifted on
the ground, waking next to her.

"Why didn't you sleep in your tent?" Brow furrowed, Tovey
stood, once again removing the dark woven cloak from her body
and thrusting it back toward Cullus.

"I fell asleep." Cullus shrugged. "Besides, I feel bad with you
being out here."

"You *feel* bad?"

"Yes."

"Because I sleep next to a warm fire while you shiver in a tent?"
She smiled, instinctively throwing rocks on top of the coals, stifling

any airflow that would've let the heat continue. Pouring water on top would've sent a clear smoke signal into the sky, drawing nothing but unwanted attention to them.

Cullus collapsed the tent and surveyed the sizable bundle curiously. "Maybe this was too much to bring. We are running out of food. If we find some, we will need the space." He kicked his boot against a stone, tilting his head side to side.

"I will find somewhere to stash it," Tovey said. "If we end up needing it, we can always come back."

Cullus watched with wide eyes as she scooped the burly heap into her arms, a bundle that appeared too heavy to carry on her own. She stumped into the forest, hunting for a hiding spot.

A fallen tree whose core had rotted away with passing time rested in the sedge before her. Its opening was narrower than a washing basin. She pressed her palm firmly on the bark, and it didn't move, solid and study on the outside still. *Good.* Her fingers raced along the rugged scars of bark protecting the dried peeling pulp inside the log, hunting for any sign of mildew or leakage, but it was dry. Nodding to herself, she pushed the rolled tent into the hole. Tovey scampered around the nearby area, collecting massive stones and piling them before the opening, blocking it from unwanted intruders.

She spun, taking in the forest, noting the two towering trees bent toward each other on her left and a slight rock outcropping to her right. Bright yellow flowers traced the fissures in the rocks and bridged over the log. She burned the place into her memory as she plucked a flower, breathing in its sweet scent.

Trekking back to Cullus, she stepped on stones and dry land to avoid breaking any leaves. Even an expert hunter wouldn't be able to follow her trail. Her mind clouded, reminiscing on the sheer fear that had emanated through her veins the night she made her way through the thicket, escaping the collective. But now, living invisibly amongst the trees was becoming another part of her existence, like breathing.

Entering the clearing, she saw the prince squatted, scribbling on a sheet of parchment. He jumped at the sight of her. He tucked the paper away, standing suddenly, fumbling with Frilliam's bridle.

"What are you doing?"

"Just getting Frilliam ready."

Tovey swayed, uneasy with the tension. "You've been journaling?" Tovey gestured to his inky palms.

"Oh. Yes, a bit. Tracking our movement, that's all." He wiped his hand on his pants. "Ready to go?"

With a reassuring smile, she walked beside him as he led Frilliam to the river Tovey had found the day before. They filled their canteens and ate a frail piece of dried meat. Tovey's mouth watered as Cullus wrinkled his nose. Raising her eyebrows at his reluctance, she asked, "Why the face?"

"This is hard to eat every day."

"But it's delicious."

The flavorful smoked meat was a savory treat she gladly tore into, sucking out the seasoned flavor with pleasure. Cullus eyed the beef once more. "It's got nothing on the pastries the chef makes."

Tovey bobbed her head in agreement, sucking cool water from her cupped hand.

Cullus burst out with laughter.

"What?" Tovey's eyebrows pinched.

"How would *you* know what the chef's pastries taste like?"

Gulping, Tovey was thankful her mouth was too full to respond.

"You admitted to indulging in the pastries made for the highborns."

"And why is that a crime?"

Cullus laughed.

Tovey's face fell flat. "No, seriously. Why is *that* a crime? Since we've been together, we are talking freely, and the world hasn't crumbled. I've eaten your food, and I haven't died. You've lifted a finger to collect firewood, and you are still standing. So, why is it that servants are left burnt bread and are forced to scavenge for pests to live?"

Cullus remained silent.

"It's all right if you don't know. I just don't know either . . ." Her voice trailed off, spirals of thought drowning her mind, and she fell deep into introspection. It was absurd that something like elegant food was saved for the highborns while the waste was tossed into trash bins and later fed to pigs.

Why was eating leftovers a problem? And what about the commoners? They had meats, freshly baked bread, and cheeses. But nothing too fancy. Why? No one should starve while others were careless and threw away excess. They all lived in one kingdom, and it seemed like it would be more fortified than ever if they had empathy toward one another.

Cullus wiped his face off, kneeling on the riverside, lending a knee for Tovey to climb on. Instead, she put a foot into the stirrup and swung her leg over the side of Frilliam, giving him a scratch between his ears. Cullus mounted the horse, tucking himself behind Tovey, reaching around her to grab the reins.

"What are you doing?" Her voice shook, warmth filling her cheeks.

"Teaching you how to ride before you and Frilliam wind up in trouble again."

Frilliam neighed in protest.

"Yes, that is right, Frilliam. We were being silly yesterday. Of course I know how to ride," she lied playfully, grabbing Cullus's hands and placing them on her waist, as he'd done to her. "Hold on."

His light laugh tickled her ear. Locking sturdy, he gripped her waist. She tucked the loose ends of the reins under her thigh, allowing slack. She wove her fingers into Frilliam's shiny black mane, which reflected the pastel blue sky, silently begging Frilliam to walk. As if the horse could understand her thoughts, Frilliam moved through the forest, trotting happily at a steady pace.

"I don't understand you," Cullus muttered.

"Nor I you."

16

Five suns rose, and four moons fell. The two spent countless hours traveling through the Tenbris Forest, only stopping to give Frilliam a rest. They were roughly halfway to Silvis and still needed to push forward. The December air chilled the farther north they traveled to Silvis. The solstice was thirteen days away, and Tovey incessantly worried they wouldn't have enough time to talk to the leader and convince a foreign land to back down from a war they'd been preparing to fight for the last seventeen years.

Questions pounded in her mind, forcing her heart into a foot-race. She felt panic at the infinite outcomes they could face. Anger. Fear. Death. Tovey knew nothing of Silvis, and Cullus wasn't forthcoming. He, too, didn't know what they were walking into. The collective had never even mentioned another kingdom. If they did, the defector rates would be even worse. It was a place to run to.

Still, the solstice was fast approaching. Tovey sucked in the thick mist, her lungs relishing the sweet mountain air as a squirrel popped along the path in front of Frilliam, whose trot turned into a saunter, tiring once again for the day.

"Time for a break, mate." Cullus slid off the saddle, tapping Frilliam on the neck.

Filling with warmth, Tovey smiled at Cullus's endearment toward the horse. His words had changed toward Frilliam. It was apparent that he used to think of Frilliam as nothing more than a means of transportation.

Tovey unbuckled the saddlebag, diving an arm inside and pulling out the last of their food rations. Water splashed inside a canteen while Cullus drank. She turned toward the sloshing sound.

"Food low?" Cullus asked.

Tovey nodded.

"The water is almost gone too."

"I thought we'd cross another stream by now," Tovey admitted.

"Me too. I guess there is a growing reason no one travels between Silvis and Abolend."

"Is hard travel the only reason?"

"No," Cullus admitted.

Tovey pushed more than half of the dried meat into Cullus's hand. It wasn't fair for them to split the food in half. Cullus was bulkier than her. Plus, she was used to one minuscule meal a day, whereas Cullus lacked his routine pampering and sizeable meals. She made sure to cover her portion with cupped palms so he wouldn't notice, but she knew it was the right thing to do. He was still a highborn, a prince. He deserved more.

"What is Silvis like?" Tovey managed to ask. It was beginning to no longer seem strange for a question to leave her tongue, like she was becoming more fluent in speaking a foreign language she had learned mere days ago.

"Bad. They are barbarians. Savages."

Tovey shook her head, not understanding the words.

"Silvis isn't inhabited by humans."

"What?" Tovey's jaw dropped, her mind on the brink of exploding into a thousand bits. "*What* are they?" Mind bursting into a catastrophic explosion, she tried to fathom that humanoid creatures existed days away from where she stood.

"Dryads."

"Dryads?" Tovey's eyebrows pinched.

"Tall, evil, nasty devils."

"You are telling me *now* that the blasted kingdom I'm supposed to convince to back down is filled with devilish dryads? And there are creatures that live amongst us that are not human? How did I not know this?" Tovey's vision blurred, her scalp prickling.

"Servants know what they need to."

"And do commoners know?"

"No. They, too, know nothing more than what they need to."

Tovey's mouth went dry as she lashed out at Cullus in her mind, unable to find words.

"Would you have come if I'd told you?"

"No, I would have run!"

"Exactly."

Anger fumed from Tovey's ears like steam rising from a kettle. She gave the last bit of water to Frilliam before turning her back to Cullus and trailing off into the forest, letting sound guide her.

If a squirrel was near, it had to be finding a water source somewhere. Tovey trekked through thickening brush until a game trail appeared in the forest. It was matted and appeared as if deer frequently traveled there.

"Come back!" Cullus ran after her, dragging Frilliam with him.

Like a fire had been lit beneath her feet, she jogged the game trail, ignoring him.

"Tovey, please."

She paused.

"I didn't know you then. I didn't know I could trust you like I do now."

His words pulled at her heart.

"I understand." She paused. "No more secrets?"

He smiled. "Agreed."

Liquid trickled against the marble-size pebbles in the gully. As if they had one mind, they focused on each other, beaming. Cullus led the way, finding an easy decline for Frilliam to tread. Minutes of silence passed as they followed switchbacks leading to the river.

"Tell me about them. The dryads."

Cullus groaned. "They are impish creatures that live within the trees. Their society does not function on rules, at least none that are logical. Their king is called a chief, and he earns his power by fighting for it, not by birth."

"So, they earn their position?"

"Yes."

Tovey's chin wrinkled at the concept. Servants had to earn their placement. "And that is bad?"

"Obviously, a society without strong leadership can fall apart. Though someone may be physically stronger than me or have more skill in another area, no one knows the structure of Abolend better than I do. From the moment I was born, it's been my duty to serve as king when my father dies or when he sees me fit. It is something I have trained for my entire life, and though people may want the throne or feel more equipped, they are not. It isn't an easy burden to bear."

Tovey shivered, imagining Cullus calling for the beheading of Master Daleen like his father had. How could one person take responsibility for killing another? "You think your birthright is a burden?"

"I already told you, no one in Abolend is free."

His words sent a chill down her spine. Her birth had granted her glowing lilac eyes, which apparently meant she was dangerous. Like the dryads. A devil. A demon. They were all given harsh names based on their appearance.

But it seemed fair that the burden of ruling in the same fashion as King Mallum while upholding an equivalent level of respect demanded a lot from Cullus. He, too, had to obey the invisible force of society and the laws of the land. His appearance was that of a future king, and so must he be.

Tovey admired Cullus, taking in his golden skin wrapped in fine fabrics. Her eyes fell to the dimple in the center of his chin.

"Do you not find it absurd that the prince feels as trapped as a servant?" she asked.

His lips tightened. "Do you not find it absurd that you never considered we all are pawns in Abolend's chess game?"

"Cogs in the machine," Tovey muttered.

"Exactly. But there are also rooks and knights, kings and queens. There are fewer of them, and those pieces appear taller, more elaborate. Perhaps those pieces think they are special because they can make moves the pawns cannot. Still, they cannot leave the board unless they die. They are still restricted to the same squares as the pawns."

"So flip the board, end the game."

Cullus's brow furrowed, and he became taciturn.

Branches snapped beneath their feet, filling the silence as they walked. Neither Tovey nor Cullus were worried about covering their tracks. They were consumed in the Tenbris Forest, days away from Abolend. Unable to handle the leaves ceaselessly crunching in unbearable silence, Tovey let her worries flow. She longed to be open with a true friend who understood her on so many levels despite their opposing lives.

"I don't know if I can do this. I might fail."

"But you might succeed."

She let her head fall, hair curtaining her face from the outside world. He grabbed her shoulder, stopping her. He twisted her around to face him. His gentle finger fell beneath her chin, and he lifted it, letting the midday heat warm her face.

Their eyes locked. In a world of their own, they stared into each other's souls. Cullus's hand fell to her hair, brushing smooth fingers through it. He looked away, locking his gaze on a flower blooming in the air; he plucked it from the tree's branch and held it before her.

"You are a flower." A childish grin seeped across his dimpled cheeks. "Radiant, yes, but also resilient. You flourish where others cannot even dream of growing." He tucked the purple flower into her hair.

Her heart was a sparrow rapidly beating within the cage of her ribs. Her eyes darted across Cullus's face, searching every pore for answers to questions she didn't even know. His lips parted. She yearned to lean closer, to touch them with hers. Frilliam prodded the ground, pulling Cullus forward, dirt sputtering into the still air.

Tovey turned away, patting Frilliam. "Let's move quicker. Before nightfall," Tovey said as she blushed, spinning on her heel, hoping Cullus couldn't see the embarrassing heat rising in her cheeks.

She pulled the flower from her hair, admiring the deep purple veins for a moment, her fingers soaking in the silken petals. Her nose swooned in the flavorful scent of the orchid. Tucking it back into her hair, she held branches aside for Frilliam to wedge his way through.

Slipping on the rocky slopes, they clung to exposed stone, avoiding slippery moss like it was the plague. However, maneuvering around the soppy squish was more complicated than they had imagined. Tovey and Cullus kicked at the wet growth, shoving it aside to give Frilliam his best chance at not skidding to a painful halt.

Reaching the water, Frilliam lunged his face forward, submerging his muzzle into liquid, attempting to drain the stream. Tovey and Cullus cupped water in their hands, quenching their thirst.

"We will have to hunt," Tovey said. "If we travel along the bank, we should find something. Game has to drink too, and this is the only source we've found in miles." Tovey was surprised at how confident her voice sounded. Hunting was something she wished never to do. Her life wasn't worth a life. It was unfair but necessary. "Have you hunted?"

Cullus rubbed his chin. "No. It was something Mother despised. She wished me to let the citizens do the deed. Father has yet to invite me to one of his hunting parties, and I've had no interest in hosting my own."

She mulled over his words. With a steady rise of her head, Tovey sucked her teeth, knowing she could do it. They needed to survive to save thousands of people, and the farther they went, the more the plants shifted away from the ones she knew and recognized. The unknowns caused her head to ache with tension.

Her fingers laced around her dagger as twilight hit. Pulling the iron blade from its sheath, she wove in and out of the trees by the shore. Tovey sprung from rock to rock as her toes broke her steps into whispers.

She cocked her head side to side, perking her ears. Her bony fingers wiggled on the blade's hilt. Admiration crossed Cullus's face as he watched, soothing Frilliam into a statuesque stance. Finger-size branches crashed to her left. Behind the thicket, a deer pranced away.

She cursed, turning to Cullus.

"Tomorrow," he said.

Blankets of navy dyed the sky. Retreating from the path to Cullus, she collapsed, defeated.

"Tomorrow we will hunt together."

Tovey looked askance at him.

"We will," he reassured.

Cullus breathed fire to life near the river. The prince and the renegade huddled with their backs against a rock face. The heat reflected between the fire and the stone, creating a warm resting spot. Tovey scooted closer to Cullus as they leaned against the rock, staring into the night sky, stars twinkling like hanging candles.

"I wish the sky always looked like this. I missed seeing the sky when working in the castle," Tovey admitted.

"The stars are always there, even if you can't see them."

Tovey smiled, staring at the sky.

"Can I tell you something?" Cullus asked.

"Yes. You can tell me anything." Tovey saw the uneasiness teeming in Cullus's eyes. "But I can't guarantee I won't gossip to Frilliam about it."

An airy chuckle eased his mind before he paused. "I'm worried too."

Tovey's eyes widened.

"King Mallum doesn't favor me. Since my mother died and he bore another heir with Mara, the queen consort, he hasn't been the same."

"I haven't heard much of Queen Mara or your brother."

"Elias," Cullus muttered. "I raised him, but Mara is pushing him to take the throne from me. They are waiting for me to make the wrong move. That's why our plan has to work. We can prevent the prophesied war without any lives lost."

"We can. We will do it." Tovey's chest surged with power like the embers beating in the fire.

"I've spilled my secrets. You should share yours," Cullus whispered into her ear, his breath tickling her skin.

"I don't have many. You know everything."

"Not everything, I'm sure."

"There isn't much more than living for Nadia, my sister, and Vivian, my trainer. All I wanted to do was please them both, and now one is dead, and one must hate me. Do you think I'm irrational for still worrying about upsetting Vivian? She was cruel, but she was also the only mother I've ever known."

Cullus rubbed his jaw. "It isn't irrational to miss her." He paused, inspecting his nail beds. "I . . . I understand on some level, with my father." He lowered his voice. "Though I know the trainers are far worse."

She fell silent as tears welled in her eyes.

"What is it?" Cullus said gently.

"Why do you think I was left at the collective? Someone knew who I was, didn't they? Nadia knew who I was. She was a child when she arrived at the collective, so her mother must have known of me. If I'm supposed to be so important, why would no one come for me?" Tovey sobbed. "I'm alone. No family. No friends. No sister."

"You aren't alone, and you do have friends." He gestured to Frilliam. "That doorknob loves you."

Frilliam snorted.

"Sorry, steed." Cullus smiled bashfully at Frilliam. "He reacts to you in a way he would never do with me. And I am here, and I consider you a friend."

Tovey gazed through her lashes at the prince, smiling. A missing piece of her heart fell into place. "And I you. It seems silly, doesn't it?"

"What?"

"Me being friends with the prince of Abolend."

"Me being friends with . . ." He winked, not saying the forbidden word. "You."

A dimpled smile raced across his face, and for once it wasn't annoying, but endearing. Turning toward Tovey, his face grew serious. "I don't know who brought you there, how they found you, hid you, or why. I know you must want answers, but I have none."

Silence wrapped the pair in the chilling blanket.

"Tonight's cold," Cullus muttered. He wriggled an arm behind

Tovey's back as he threw his woven cloak over them. Tovey leaned her head into Cullus's shoulder. He laid his cheek atop her crown.

Tovey studied Abolend's dragon insignia imprinted into his leather jerkin, a detail she had never noticed before.

"Can I ask, why is Abolend's insignia a dragon?"

"It's an old legend."

Tovey groaned.

"Not to worry, not one that affects you." He chuckled. "It is said that our noble blood comes from a dragon."

"Dragons? Real dragons? How does that even work?"

"I haven't the faintest idea. Dragons have never existed in any history I've read. It's likely a metaphor. Anyway, the symbol of strength became our family crest and stuck throughout the centuries."

An infectious grin covered her face. "Does that make you a monster?" she teased.

"Frilliam thinks so." Cullus laughed.

Tovey couldn't stop her childish grin from showing. His arm was warm behind her, cradling her. Cullus's breathing deepened as he cuddled into her warmth. Tovey's eyes grew heavy as the fire crackled. A gust of wind sent the purple flower tucked into her hair fluttering into the flames.

17

A guttural growl snapped Tovey's eyes open. She looked at Cullus. His stomach rumbled again, causing him to shift in his sleep. Tovey untangled his arm from around her. Remorsefully, she started gathering their belongings, sweeping the dirt floor with a branch, erasing their existence as she prepared for their departure. She listened to the wind humming through the leaves, hoping to hear an animal on its way to the river. But the sun had not yet risen, and the birds were still an hour away from beginning their morning song. She ground her teeth together as she thought of today's task: to kill. Her gaze fell upon Cullus. Heaviness sat in her chest with the sacrifice he had made to aid her in her mission.

Tovey readied Frilliam before suffocating the last of the coals, pouring river water over the embers and sending smoke spiraling into the air. She watched the plume rise like tendrils, knowing they were so deep in the Tenbris that no one would see it.

Tovey knelt on the hardened ground, running her fingers through Cullus's cloud of hair as he had done to her countless times. Startled, he woke, eyes wide before settling into a wrinkle-eyed grin.

"Good morning. Let's get on the move," Tovey whispered.

Nodding, he rubbed crusted sleep out of his eyes, then sipped from the stream before mounting Frilliam. "Get on."

"No, I'll walk ahead of you. Everything will run if animals hear Frilliam too close." Tovey patted her dagger, reminding Cullus they needed to eat.

She walked fifty paces ahead, stepping delicately. She kept her head on a constant swivel, analyzing the sounds of the forest. Birds bounced in the branches above her carelessly. If she'd had a bow, they would've been fed, but she wasn't sure if she could ever fire one. Shaking her stringy hair, she attempted to scramble the imagery of Sylvia into oblivion. Her eyes traced the forest floor, searching for bedded-down sedge like the game trail she'd traced to the river.

Frozen on her toes, Tovey heard a branch snap. Raising her finger to her lips, she eyed Cullus, who pulled back on Frilliam's reins, bringing him to a pause. Knees bent, she inched toward the snap, holding her chest still, listening to nothing but the pulsing of her heart.

Crunch.

Blood pumping, she bowed her head toward Cullus, signaling him to come closer. The unseen creature moved deeper into the brush, leading her away from safety. With a flick of her wrist, she pulled her dagger from its sheath.

Snap.

Her eyes widened, tracing every leaf, searching for movement.

A thorny bush shivered to her right. Tilting her head toward the hedge, she crept. Cullus followed after he'd slid from Frilliam's saddle, leading the beast by his bridle. Tovey glanced toward them. An amethyst glow reflected off her cheeks, and her heart pounded with the adrenaline of the hunt.

Cullus raised outstretched palms to his head, asking if it was a buck. Tovey shook her head; it wasn't that massive. He pulled his fingers tight, making bunny ears, his thick eyebrows raised. Tovey stifled a laugh, shaking her head again. Her ears strained as she crept. The invisible beast crunched the leaves beneath its feet evenly, so distinctly steady that the creature had to be placing one foot on the ground at a time. The pitter-patter of weasel-size mammals or the clopping of hooves didn't fit the thump of sizable pads. It was strange; what animal would be walking on two feet?

The blood drained from her face, her body as white as a corpse as she turned back to Cullus. Tovey pointed two fingers downward as she moved them, illustrating someone walking. Her body lowered, pointing to the path on her right. Cullus tied Frilliam to a tree before sprinting toward Tovey.

"We have to climb," she whispered before ascending into the tree like a squirrel. Cullus followed behind her, unable to move as nimbly as she did. Sloppily, he neared where Tovey was perched a few branches higher than he could reach. Peering through the canopy, they spotted a game trail and followed it to the source of the skittering: a young boy.

A blossom of fear and excitement bloomed in her stomach, twisting as it grew. Eyes widened, she cast a glowing glare at Cullus, attempting to read his mind. His face sat stern, eyes pasted to the boy, lips tightened into a thin line.

"Are we close enough to Silvis for it to be a . . . you know, dryad?"

Cullus shook his head; his eyes remained locked on the boy, who disappeared into the shadowy woods. "We still have a ways to go, and no one from Abolend should be out this far."

"He appeared to be human, right?"

"Yes." Cullus remained distant. His brow cast a menacing shadow over his face. Tovey bit her tongue, holding back the endless questions racing through her mind like wild horses. His stomach emitted a rumbling growl.

"We need supplies, and we are miserable at hunting—so bad I don't think we can do it. We should track him. Maybe we can find a trading post."

"No, Tovey. Listen. There shouldn't be *anyone* out here. Citizens of Abolend are forbidden to enter the Tenbris Forest this far. There is a reason the woods are left alone. It is the barrier between us and *them*."

"But if there is a child, a human child, he has a family close by, and families have to eat. We are running out of options, and you are starving. I've heard your stomach all morning."

Cullus gazed back at Tovey, sorrow in his eyes as he took in her face. Tovey knew she must have appeared more famished than she had when they'd started this journey.

He descended the tree. Tovey landed gently, pressing forward, tracking the boy's trail. Glancing over her shoulder, she watched Cullus conceal his longsword beneath Frilliam's saddle blanket.

"What's the point?" she asked.

"The point is not everyone loves Abolend as much as we do."

Tovey felt like an icy wind blew straight through her. Pushing waxy leaves out of the way, she homed in on the sound, taking in the boy's steps when his trail went awry.

Frilliam reared his head, attempting to shake Cullus's grip on his reins. The ground became littered with sharp, rickety stones. Grass disappearing, their path turned into ivy scattered through the unsteady crannies.

"We are moving too slow. I can't hear him, and his trail is gone over this." She shifted an unsteady rock beneath her foot. "The terrain is scaring Frilliam."

Cullus frowned at the beast, whose eyes showed white with fear. Cullus spun on his heel, pulling Frilliam back to steady ground. "Stay here, you big rat." Frilliam huffed in retort. A crooked smile flicked across Cullus's face, flooding her heart.

He pushed through the branches back toward her, balancing on rocky terrain that shifted beneath his weight. The trees filtered out sunlight as the pair walked into a narrow ravine, pushing them farther along a shadowy narrowing path. The forest fell silent as the birds and insects vanished from earshot.

"This isn't a good idea." Cullus grabbed Tovey's hand. "We are surrounded by mountains with a lone child running around. This could be a trap, an ambush. Think about it. We abandoned our weapons and our horse and put ourselves in the most vulnerable position. We sound like a tale from my training—two strangers walking in the woods following a stranger. Tovey, let's turn back. Trust me, it never ends well." His finger pointed to ridges above them on both sides. "See up there? It's the perfect place to position archers."

Tovey's eyebrows swayed as she contemplated his words. "Yes, but shouldn't we go a little farther? Danger doesn't change the fact that in a day or so we will be too hungry to continue." She hesitated, pleading with her eyes. "Continue, or starve to death?"

Cullus cursed, pushing himself in front of Tovey. "Stay close." He cupped her hand inside of his, squeezing it gently.

Together they trekked, unspeaking, searching the ridgeline for any sign of impending doom that may rain from the heavens any second.

Minutes passed. The rocky path flattened, and the trees thinned, opening to a mighty valley. Hiding in the cover of the tree line, they waited, watching a rolling fog reveal no more than twenty wooden cabins placed in rows positioned in the center of the meadow clearing.

A babbling stream rolled through the bearded grass, meandering its way through the valley. Ashen smoke matching the ever-graying sky rose like a phantom from the cobbled chimney of the largest cabin resting in the center. Tovey smiled as the smell of roasting meats greeted her nose.

The boy they'd tracked hopped out of a cornfield on their left. The burly man paused chopping at the stalks, revealing a brutal burn on his forearm. The boy popped into the arms of the man. He looked toward rows of corn. From the crops appeared a limping woman who knelt, hugging the boy out of the man's grasp. A tiny hand popped from the boy's chest, and he presented his parents with a handful of berries.

The boy pointed a teeny round finger to the edge of the woods, and his parents stiffened their spines with fearful eyes. The boy was swept beneath a shawl in the woman's arms. The strangers' quick feet shuffled, the trio retreating into the smoking cabin.

"They know we are here. Tovey, we need to leave *now*." Cullus tugged on her shoulder, trying to pull her back into the shadows, but Tovey remained rooted to the ground, unable to tear away. "If they have remained hidden this long, they won't be kind to strangers," he warned.

A crowd of people exited the building, eyes peeled and necks snapping, furrowed brows searching the bordering trees.

"We need food. How many times do I have to say this? I cannot make it appear, and I am not a cook. I don't know the beginnings of which plants are edible. We both are miserable at hunting. What are we going to do? Eat Frilliam?"

Cullus smirked, lightening the situation, but his eyes darkened with an unsteady fear.

She turned her gaze back toward the people, surveying them and their weaponless hands. Tears rushed to her eyes as she took in the women, who showcased a variety of mutilated and scarred skin. She knew them, somehow, without knowing them at all.

Tovey stuttered, "Th-they are all impaired. The women are like me . . . The men all have burns right here." She pointed to the top of her wrist, above the back side of her hand. "Defectors." A sigh of admiration escaped her lips, and she was surprised by how much respect she held for the ragtag group of renegades.

Leaves broke underneath Cullus's shifting weight. Tovey watched him cower backward as his limbs collapsed beneath him.

"We shouldn't go near them. Those people are dangerous. The men burned off their brands. Look closely." Cullus pointed to a man's arm that was close enough to see. "A clear sign of defiance."

"And strength. Putting themselves through that pain *again* purely to be free."

Free. The word had melted off her lips like jelly. She craved saying the four-letter word more and more, as if her teeth brushing against her bottom lip could breathe it to life.

"Strength is serving. Cowardice is defecting." Cullus's voice was stiff in her ear, sending an itch running up her neck.

"You're wrong."

"You should know I'm right. You were brave. You continued to serve."

"And you should know that doing what we are doing now is brave. This isn't serving. I am a defector."

"You are serving. Though not a servant, you still serve Abolend. This, Tovey, is your service to the crown." The growl from his lips stung Tovey like a bee.

She lurched to her feet and exited the forest, revealing herself to the crowd of defectors. Open palms raised to her sides, the clouds in the sky parted, allowing the sun to melt away the shadows.

A forceful whisper echoed from the edge of the forest as Cullus's silhouette disappeared toward the path. "I'm going to grab Frilliam," he said on the rising wind. Turning, he boomed, "Your blindfold. Put it on!"

Tovey turned toward him, lavender light reflected off her cheeks. "If they are going to kill me, so be it. The prophecy will be over, and the world will be saved. There can't be a final war without a demon, can there? I will not impair myself in front of those who escaped their binds."

Face ignited with a heated glare, Cullus turned, his boots pounding the hard ground as he sprinted toward Frilliam. Wind rushed in his direction. Tovey wished it would help propel him faster. She was afraid to be without him, but she would never admit it.

Tovey's feet squished through soppy soil, and the drying grass licked her ankles with a wet snarl. Once again, she raised her hands toward the defectors. Fifty or so people searched her body with their stares, leaving traces of confusion across their faces. They peered around one another, arching to see her.

"I'm not a threat." She steadied her voice, pleased at how confident she sounded.

Pride swelled in her chest like rising dough. She was no longer the fearful servant she used to know.

She neared the people, who had varying expressions of confusion and alarm. Whispers swarmed through the crowd, creating a hum of uncertainty. But finally, their faces flattened into a state of acceptance at her inhuman eyes. Tovey wasn't sure what she'd expected from a defector camp, but this wasn't it.

A woman hobbled toward her from the silent crowd. She was dressed in various furs woven together to form a warm cloak. Her alabaster hair was woven around her head like a basket. Wrinkles circled her brown eyes as a welcoming smile was painted across her face.

The woman raised a calloused finger to Tovey's face, tracing the thin white scar across her cheeks where the blindfold had once bored into her skin. The woman's ghostly pale eyes became glass, her feet stumbling in awe.

She stretched her arms toward Tovey with fingers spread. "We've been waiting for you, dear amethyst child. Welcome."

Tovey's heart skipped a beat, and a dizzying swirl of confusion punched at her skull. Welcome? The word sent her heart pounding. Tornadoes of questions swelled into a hurricane, but one stood at the forefront: Why would the defectors welcome her when they knew something of the prophecy?

She regretted not taking Cullus's advice and putting on the blindfold. It would have been much easier to hide. The woman's strong and steady voice broke her thoughts. "People, it is safe. She is one of us!" A cackle escaped her lips. "Brilliantly one of us," she muttered beneath her breath, shaking her head in awe. "Welcome to Terrowin."

18

The people of Terrowin surrounded Tovey in silent fascination. Ushering her forward, the leader guided Tovey to the central wooden cabin made from downed trees. The notched edges of the structure were expertly fastened into a square. The other homes were smaller but built in the same way. Worn dirt trails crossed the ground instead of roads. Tovey swallowed hard as she neared the structure. She glanced back to the forest, searching for Cullus.

"Where is your friend?" the woman asked.

"Who?" Tovey hoped she sounded convincingly clueless.

"The one you came here with." The furred woman grinned knowingly, tilting her head toward the young boy, whose eyes shined like marbles. Tovey's heart sped. Cullus was right. They had already known they were both here. "He is welcome."

Tovey turned to the forest, letting the eyes of the villagers fall to her back. A shadow shifted in her sights, hiding from the light.

"Cul—" She forced a cough. "Collin!"

Frilliam emerged from the cover, strong and brooding, stepping with high knees through the tangled grass. Atop the saddle rode Cullus, who had muddied his shirt and scattered his hair into a tangled mess.

Tovey tried not to laugh at his strange attempt to blend in with the defectors, though she hoped they wouldn't see through his pitiful disguise. If the defectors held any values similar to Nadia's, they would hate highborns, especially Cullus. Still, his posture was too perfect, and he held an air of importance around him without trying, even when he wasn't wearing fanciful fabrics.

A few men stiffened as Cullus approached, a subconscious respect dwelling within their spines. Cullus drew his black hood over his face, casting a dark shadow over its entirety aside from his dimpled chin.

Glancing at the former soldiers, Tovey studied their faces for any form of recognition. The men traded skeptical stares as muscles tightened in their bulky arms. She cursed herself for not considering that the soldiers knew who they were serving. Servants never got to see anyone outside of the collective. The soldiers, however, were likely visited by those they were unwillingly pledging their lives to.

"Welcome." The woman paused, surveying Cullus's cloaked body. "Who might you be?"

A rock settled in Tovey's stomach. She eyed Cullus's darkened face, the weather turning sour with heavy clouds building in the skies. The charcoal sky contrasted with her eyes, brightening them in the dim light.

"He is a dear friend," Tovey interjected in the eerie silence.

Cullus bowed his head, sliding off Frilliam in his naturally graceful demeanor. Tovey forced a smile, grabbed his hand, and stepped in front of him. It was odd that she was the one protecting him now. His body was cool and rigid. Tovey squeezed his hand, hoping to communicate all was well, but she wasn't sure Cullus got the message.

"Join me," the woman demanded, turning toward the main house. "This is Terrowin, founded fifteen years ago." She turned to Tovey and winked before continuing. "I and another defector wound up here after many years as wild women. We defected from our collective as children. We ran together, surviving off the land until we happened upon this place. It provides food and water and is surrounded by towering mountains." She pivoted at the threshold, pointing toward the cliffs. "It's deep enough to protect us from unwanted visitors. Together, we replenished our bodies and made our way back to Abolend, sending word to our families. They eventually joined us, bringing back provisions and skills. That is when the first structure was built." She tapped on the heavy wooden door of the main house with her foot, kicking it open. "And from then on, defectors made sure to spread the existence of our haven carefully."

"I never knew there was somewhere to run to," Tovey admitted, wishing she could have run here all those nights ago.

"We have to be careful about who knows. We scout the woods, searching for lost defectors. But if one of us is caught, we are slaughtered by Abolend's men, and we are one less. There are fifty-three of us here, and we cannot afford to lose one. We have sworn an oath of secrecy to one another. If caught, we will claim we've been wandering mindlessly in the woods since our defection date. It protects Terrowin, and if we get captured, we're dead anyway."

Cullus tilted his head, and Tovey knew he must've been wondering about the same thing she was.

Tovey said, "So, if someone from Terrowin has been caught before, wouldn't word get out that defectors have been able to survive? Everyone I have ever heard of defecting has died the night they left, either caught or killed in some other horrific accident. It's rare for someone to last more than a few days."

"Word never makes it to the people because Mallum wants us to stay a secret just as much as we do. I'm sure he knows we are somewhere out here, but he wouldn't admit to his people or even his court that the possibility exists." She spat on the ground. "Cowardly oaf."

Tovey's eyes widened. Cullus clenched Tovey's hand in an iron grip, and she wriggled her arm, trying to shake him off. He didn't let go. She rubbed his hand with her thumb, easing the tension.

"Abolend lies to its people. I'm living proof that defectors survive," the woman said.

She opened the heavy door, letting the pungent scent of roasting onions and peppers rush through the doorway. Drying herbs hung from the rafters in husky clumps. Candles burned in long waxen tubes. A sigh escaped Tovey's lips as she stepped forward into the room, and the warmness filled her soul with a humid comfort.

"Please, sit. And tell me, how did you find us?"

The three sat around a wooden table with bench seats worn into a soft cradle, smooth against Tovey's fingers. The wooden floor creaked beneath them, it, too, seeming to question their presence, along with a few of the townspeople, who'd joined them and stood around the edges of the room, listening.

After contemplating her words carefully, Tovey began. "I am the one the prophecy speaks of."

The woman dropped her head for a moment, a friendly smile appearing on her face once more. Her unsettling grin caused an unwelcome tremble of Tovey's shoulders.

Tovey continued. "I defected from my collective, then met another defector." She smiled toward Cullus. "But Collin was much more prepared than I was, having stolen a horse from Abolend." Tovey forced a hearty laugh she hoped sounded convincing. "And we are on our way to Silvis."

"Silvis? Hmm," the woman said as a mousy-faced lady carried forward two cups of steaming dandelion tea from behind a bar. The herbs released their flowery scent into the steaming air. Tovey released Cullus's hand to hold the warm cup to her mouth, sipping at the familiar taste.

"This reminds me of home." Tovey's eyes tightened as she remembered days spent with Nadia plucking dandelions from the ground and hiding the herbs in their pockets to make tea late at night after the trainers had retired to their chambers.

The woman bowed her head toward Tovey, urging her to continue. "We were hunting, and I thought the little boy we found was a deer. Once we realized he wasn't, we followed him, hoping to find a trading post. Our rations are running thin."

The three sat in silence as Tovey sipped with gratitude, nudging Cullus with her elbow to drink the tea. He wrapped a hand around the cup and drank mechanically. Stomping hard, Tovey pressed her boot into his.

The sound of a whistling kettle was the sole noise for what seemed to be hours until the mousy-faced woman who had brought the dandelion tea sat next to Tovey. She gathered her tattered bohemian dress, allowing a leg to slip over the bench. The woman had a familiar face, yet Tovey couldn't place it.

"I must ask . . ." The mousy-faced woman's voice cracked as her nose turned red. "We are waiting on someone, a defector from the collective in the east hills. Her name is Sylvia. Have you heard of her? She's several weeks late."

Tovey released her cup, sending it clattering against the wooden surface, droplets of tea splotching her tunic in a blood-splattered pattern. Stomach twisting in a dizzy dance, tea resurfaced on her tongue. Cullus wrapped an arm around Tovey, pulling her into him, moving away from his statuesque state.

Tovey cleared her throat. "Syl—" She choked, coughing once more on the acid that fought to fill her mouth. "Sylvia is dead."

Shattered gasps echoed in a heartbroken symphony as she continued. "An Abolend bowman caught her outside the woods of our collective. She was in the same home I was in. But her death saved my life, and I am forever indebted to Sylvia and her family." Tovey bobbed her head to the mousy-faced woman, knowing why she appeared familiar. Sylvia had had the same face, narrow and pointed.

"She defected right before I did. I heard her in the woods the night I ran. I tried to follow her, meet with her, but a bowman was on her trail. He came out of nowhere and struck her with an arrow. I was too late. He took her body, so I tracked him, wanting to ensure she had a proper burial. I took the fabric from her dress and was able to ensure she had a noble death."

Tovey's voice cracked. She truly wished Sylvia's death had been a noble one and not one ending in being mauled by wolves. A single tear escaped.

"It should have been me." The pathetic whimpering of Tovey's voice struck a flat chord. Head wobbling, her chest swelled with an unnerving knowing that those five simple words were the most honest ones she had ever spoken. If it had been her, there would never have been any of these problems. No prophecy, no war, nothing. Life would have continued, and everyone would be safe.

Tovey's fingers wrapped around the drab fabric she'd kept in her pocket since the haunting night of her escape. "This was hers." Tovey pushed the material into the weeping lady's hands, the woman's face red and sunken.

Sylvia's mother pressed the blood-splattered fabric to her nose. She burst into tears, heaving broken breaths.

"It smells faintly of my daughter. My . . . daughter."

The furred leader escorted Sylvia's mother out of the house. Other villagers turned their backs to the situation, resuming their usual doings, giving privacy to the grieving mother. Unintelligible conversations happened outside the wooden door as the room emptied, leaving Cullus and Tovey alone.

Cullus leaned close to Tovey's ear, his hood tickling her cheek. His smooth, calm voice sank into her ear. "It shouldn't have been you."

19

The fire crackled as minutes passed. Tovey and Cullus exchanged a questioning expression, neither one wanting to speak in the eerie silence of the cabin. Cullus shifted, leaning close to Tovey's face, sure to keep his voice quieter than the kettle's whistle. "Tovey, listen to me. These people . . . I know you like them, and I know Sylvia has family here, but they aren't afraid of you. Isn't that a little alarming?"

"Maybe a little. But I thought it was sort of comforting."

"It isn't." He snorted. "They disrespected King Mallum, and they are defectors. They broke the law, Tovey, and now they are treating the one person who is going to cause a war kindly. Why do you think that is? They *want* a war. They want people to die."

"It is a little strange, yes, but I'm not sure if that means—"

"I'm sure. I didn't grow up as you did. My training was strategy, being three steps ahead of your enemy. They want to use you, make you into something you're not."

A crawling sensation covered Tovey's body, sending uncontrollable tremors through her veins. She didn't want to be controlled. Not again.

"What do we do?" Her eyes glowed fearfully.

"Get out of here as quickly as possible."

The heavy wooden door in the entrance of the building creaked, reopening. In a panic, Tovey stood, her eyes bursting with light, filling the room. The door slammed shut with a thunderous roar, flexing from the strain.

"You all right in there? Let me in," the older woman said from outside the door. The iron handle jangled, not budging despite her incessant tugging.

Mouth open, Tovey gawked at Cullus. He turned toward her, eyes wide. Her mind fell blank. She sat, brow furrowed at the unexplainable force.

"Ah, there I go! Blasted old door." The leader entered, sitting before the two again. "You two need time to talk? Did you slam the door?" Her gaze penetrated Cullus.

He shook his head.

"The wind," Tovey lied, her heart beating through her chest.

The woman pursed her lips. "Tell me, amethyst child, what do they call you? My name is Amile."

"Tovey," she muttered.

"And Collin, of course." Amile turned toward Cullus, ducking her head to see below his cloak, but he let his head fall toward the table, preventing her gaze. "Now, is there anything else we can do for you?" Amile smiled. Her voice was brasher than it had been before.

She scoured Cullus's forearm for a brand with her eyes. He

shifted aggressively, pulling the woven cloak farther down his arm, his fingers gripping the hem as he stiffened his shoulders. Highborns were not branded.

"We are in great need of provisions." Tovey drew Amile's attention. "I can work for trade."

"No need, dear amethyst child." She stood, moving to the doorway. Leaning out, she shouted, "Bring food for our guests. Gill, one of your woven blankets would be a wonderful gift we can give our amethyst child; the winter air is thickening. Travelers of the woods will need it." Amile directed the defectors, sending them swarming in various directions, gathering supplies. She spun toward the table. "Are you leaving tonight?"

Tovey surveyed Cullus, unsure of how she should answer. A sheltered bed would be beyond welcome, though the pressing danger may be worse than another night in the woods. Tracing his face, she found no clarity. "If you will allow us, we'd like to stay for the night and get a fresh start tomorrow morning."

"To Silvis?"

"Yes."

"But why, child?"

"To convince them not to attack Abolend. I hope to prevent the final war."

"I see . . . Collin, why don't you join Gill?" She motioned to a man who stood inches outside the propped door. "He will help you find a place for tonight and leave you with goods to load on your horse."

Cullus remained still.

"Join him. I want to talk to the amethyst child alone," Amile said, her shoulders squaring.

Though she was old, Tovey didn't want to upset the town's founder. Cullus stood, reluctantly stalking toward Gill, a man no more than twenty-five, whose arms were the size of a well-developed tree. Gill stood in the open doorway of the tavern, casting a smile at his excoriated brand, twisting it in the setting sun.

"May Abolend burn, eh?" Gill jeered. "You got one of these, don't cha? Collective men all wear one, and commoners are encouraged, though I suppose you weren't a commoner since the demon said you defected."

Cullus grunted.

Tovey's eyes sparkled, her face reflecting the light at the despicable word. Her lips tightened, now seeing what Cullus saw in the people. Traitors.

"His tongue was cut out. He defended a fellow defector," Tovey lied, fever spreading throughout her body.

"His tongue?" Amile questioned, unconvinced.

"Yes. Punishment has risen as a result of increasing defector rates," Tovey lied once more, overcome by dizzying sickness from the web of untruths she was spinning.

Amile crossed her arms.

"Sadly, I-I do think the need for us to travel is pressing. Amile, we are leaving tonight," Tovey stuttered.

"Load your steed then." She flicked a wrinkled hand toward Gill. Cullus and Gill moved to the street outside the door and began loading Frilliam's saddlebags with meats, bread, water, blankets, and other goods.

"Thank you," Tovey said, moving onto the cabin's porch.

"I need to ask you, amethyst child—"

"My name is Tovey."

"Tovey. What do you know of the prophecy?" Cullus's head tilted beneath his hood. Amile's eyes narrowed, following Tovey's gaze toward Cullus, searching him for answers. Amile lowered her voice to a barely audible whisper. "Are you in danger? I don't think you understand—"

Cullus stepped back into the tavern, pointing toward the sky. Towers of clouds tumbled like the washing basin. He motioned toward Frilliam, urging Tovey to leave. Now.

Tovey was rooted in a swirl of panic. Renegades surrounded Cullus outside the cabin, heads tilted toward the sky with curiosity. Trembling radiated out from Tovey's chest, her emotions shattering in a roll of thunder building between charcoal clouds. Darkness loomed toward them from the horizon. Thunderous bangs like a god hammering on an anvil shook the house.

"We weren't expecting bad weather," Amile muttered.

Tovey eyed Amile as she stepped into the street to lift her face to the skies alongside the rest of Terrowin. Following closely, Tovey smelled the sweet scent of rain rushing in on the horizon. Gill's scrutinizing eyes stared down at Tovey, sending a hard pulse rapping at her throat. He grunted, pushing the last of the goods from his arms into her own. Cradling the items, she turned toward Frilliam and unloaded her arms into his bags.

"Thank you for this. I won't forget it." The corner of Tovey's mouth twitched.

"No problem." Gill smiled at Tovey before he turned to Cullus. "Do me a favor, will you?" Gill's chin wrinkled into a pursed smile beneath his nose. He extended an outstretched hand toward Cullus, his open palm offering a shake.

Cullus declined, and Tovey knew the gig was up.

"I don't know what game your playin', but you hurt our demon, and I'll make sure you trip on that pretty longsword." He patted the hidden hilt of Cullus's sword beneath Frilliam's blanket.

Thunder clapped, echoing through the valley, rattling the dead structures. A low vibration shook beneath their feet. Frilliam prodded the ground, eyes white with fear from Gill's unwelcome touch.

"Tovey, not everyone can be trusted," the haunting voice of Amile warned.

Massive raindrops fell from the sky, soaking Tovey. Methodically, she ambled toward Cullus, a bolt of panic surging through her. Cool rain hit her cheeks, igniting something primal within her. She lifted her chin to the darkening skies, fury raging like a forge inside her. Cullus mounted Frilliam and lent a hand out to Tovey. Grabbing his sturdy grip, she steadied herself atop Frilliam. She gripped Cullus's waist tightly, wanting to pull him closer to her.

Cullus snarled toward Gill. "You're right. Not everyone can be trusted, especially not those who break their word to the crown." Cullus's eyes stung at the young man's scar. "By the way, defector, she's not anyone's demon."

He cracked Frilliam's reins in the crisp air. They galloped into the forest, northbound. Frilliam ran faster than he had in days, carrying them far away from Terrowin in what felt like minutes. Tovey hugged Cullus tightly, resting her head on his back. Terrowin was not somewhere she wanted to spend too much time.

"Damn it. Don't they know?"

"Know what?"

"No one calls you a blasted demon."

20

Uncontrollable laughter spiraled into the wind as they rode. A smile bolted across Tovey's face as lightning struck, illuminating the darkening forest in strobes. In the blinding blackness, they rode until they could no longer see, the deafening sound of rain and swirls of charcoal brought their travel to a halt.

The laughter faded into dizzying thoughts. Tovey's mind wove all thought back to Amile. Aching with confusion, she kept repeating her words over and over in her mind.

Are you in danger? I don't think you understand.

Frilliam came to a halt, shaking Tovey back into her body and away from the dark corners of her mind.

She heaved heavy breaths. Her gaze darted from tree to tree, sweat sitting on her hairline.

"Tovey, we are safe. It's all right." Cullus dismounted, pulling her off with him. He wrapped sturdy arms around her shoulders, steadying her.

Tovey shook her head. Despite Cullus saying everything was fine, nothing seemed right. Amile had insinuated she knew nothing, that Cullus was untrustworthy. Was it because of their hate toward Abolend? Or was it because they could see through Cullus's disguise? Bewilderment swelled into rage inside of her chest. The storm spiraled around them, the wind tossing leaves at them from all sides. Tovey pulled at her hair, squeezing her eyes shut.

"Tovey. It's just you and me. We are safe. Forget those blasted defectors. Breathe with me."

Cullus wove his fingers around the back of her head, pulling her ear toward his chest. He stilled her, resting his lips on the top of her head. She wrapped her arms around him, wishing she could disappear into him. The sturdy beating of his heart settled her mind like a steady drum in the chaos of the unknown.

"Listen to my heartbeat."

Sucking in a deep breath, Tovey steadied herself, silencing the unending questions attempting to bore through her skull. With every rise and fall of her chest, the storm stilled. The wind returned to a light breeze, the clouds parted in the sky, and the thunderous lightning dissipated like a phantom. Carefully, Cullus released the comforting pressure on her head. He gazed into her eyes, and a dim lilac hue reflected on his face.

"Tovey, I think . . ." He paused, shaking his head. "I know you have power."

"More prophecy stuff? Right now? We are soaked, and any chance at making a fire is shot." She kicked a soppy branch. "I don't want to talk about more theories."

"This isn't hearsay, Tovey. This is real. *That* storm, I think it was you."

Her face fell blank with annoyance, pupils locked on Cullus's dripping body. She was unable to find the words to ask if a branch had happened to whack him in the skull as they rode.

"Think about it. You got angry, and clouds formed out of nowhere. That overgrown defector called you a demon, and—"

Thunder cracked.

"See!" He threw his hands to the sky. "And when Amile tried to come back in, the door flew shut!"

Tovey fixed her gaze on the inky cosmos. Admittedly, the weather had been strange and unexpected, but still, there had already been a storm looming on the horizon. It wasn't like it had come out of nowhere, though it had arrived sooner than expected. Plus, they didn't know these lands. The weather could be strange here. Mountains and such could cause strange air currents, so that had to be the reasonable explanation. She stood like a statue, unwilling to speak despite the retort echoing in her mind.

"I've noticed your eyes. They glow when you get angry or flustered."

A flicker of lilac responded to his accusation.

A nervous smile flashed on his face. He licked his lips before speaking again. "It just happened."

"So what? My eyes have always glowed."

"Yes, and no other being on this world has eyes that do that."

She stiffened, turning away from Cullus. Under normal circumstances, she would've relished understanding more about herself, but now she was more perplexed than ever. She longed to connect to the defectors, but she'd been more out of place at

Terrowin than she had been in the castle's dungeons. She wasn't one of them.

They were more than mere defectors. They were rebels. Cullus was right; she was no one's demon, and the fact that everyone kept calling her one was infuriating.

"Why . . . Why does everyone say I'm a demon? Your father. Gill. *You.*"

"It's because they don't understand you. It is a derogatory word to describe you, and I'm sorry I ever did." Cullus rubbed the back of his neck. Moving to the edge of the clearing, he gathered wet logs, stacking them in a makeshift pile. "But they aren't sorry. They will do it again and again. They don't respect you. They don't lo—" He huffed in a frustrated snort as his lips tightened. "They don't know you like I do."

Tovey stood with tightened lips, nodding. The hideous name they'd called her raged inside her heart like a fire emanating from the ground. Her gaze caught Cullus kneeling on soft soil, his tanned pants soaking in the moisture. He tapped the center of a log to a silent tune.

"Why are you doing that?"

An annoying crooked smile crossed his face. "Think about it. Imagine how the defectors see you. Not for what you are, but for what they believe you to be."

Her nostrils flared. She spun sharply away from Cullus. She was done thinking about people seeing her as a demonic monster. It wasn't fair to assume they knew everything about her because a handful of people had had a vision nearly two decades ago. Her eyes closed as her chest rose before she released a resounding sigh of frustration.

"They think you are a monster."

"I'm not a demon." A crack of light popped behind her, making her spin. Terror struck her; she was too frightened to scream. The hair on her neck stood on end as she searched Cullus's rascally face. The prince lay on his back, shocked away from the now raging fire, laughing maniacally. Shivers raced up her spine. Tovey brought her fingers to her eyes, touching the skin beneath them as warm purple sparks died in her vision.

"You have power, Tovey. You have power!"

Her heart pounded as she watched the prince's excitement. She spoke the words in unison with Cullus, fearing his words were indeed true.

"I have power."

21

The bitter taste of smoke wove through the camp. A violent shiver sent uncontrollable shakes throughout her body. Tovey stared at the rambling fire, unable to sit and enjoy the heat. It was baffling how the strike had dried the wood in an instant as it released a puff of humid steam. Her eyes fell to Cullus, who shifted to the poised sitting position he favored. He beamed at Tovey with wide eyes that sparkled in the firelight. He stood hesitantly and edged toward her, wrapping his hands around hers.

Her hair stood on end all over her body, shivers racing across her skin like invisible spiders, his touch surging through her bones. The warmth of his skin was intoxicating. Cullus pulled her toward the fire, their rain-soaked clothes heating in the ember light. Sitting in silence, he waited for her to speak.

"I'm dangerous."

Cullus reluctantly nodded.

Guilt swelled in her chest like a tumor.

"But dangerous doesn't have to mean bad," he said.

As she contemplated his words, the bile attempting to escape her throat simmered back down. He was right. Being dangerous didn't make you a bad person. But it did make you a threat.

"Did the seers mention power? You didn't tell me there was more." Tovey sang, recounting the song she'd heard in the breakfast hall, her voice feathery.

The demon comes, heart of cold.
She'll rise as the seers have foretold.
With purple eyes, hair of gold.
She'll bring the final war.

The words of the prophecy echoed like a broken lute in her mind.

"No. But I'm not surprised. Your glowing eyes were enough to convince me there was more to you than even the seers could have dreamt of."

Tovey whimpered. "What if I'm really of the underworld?"

"Then the underworld must be a grand place." Cullus's face deepened in color.

Her eyebrows stitched together. "Is this magic?"

"I believe magic requires some sort of aid—a wand, a staff, herbs, spells. And even then, I've never heard of any magical person doing . . ." He paused, warming his hands by the fire. "This." Laughter filled his stomach. He gazed at the clear sky, searching for answers.

"I don't know much of magic. I always thought it was a fairy tale, something girls at the collective invented to dream about."

"It's real, though much more common amongst the dryads. Streghe haven't been treated kindly in Abolend for centuries."

"Streghe?"

"It's plural for those who practice magic. Streghe, or strega if we are just talking about one, used to be common in Abolend, but when Father first took power, he wanted every last strega dead."

Tovey stared into the fire, hoping the swirling ash would tell her Valledera's secrets. Biting her tongue, she tried to hide her fear.

"I can't control it. I don't even know how I did it."

"But you can." Cullus skittered to his knees, his eyebrows lifted. "Remember? I pointed to the log, and you sent a bolt of lightning right there!"

"I wasn't even thinking about that!"

"You were. You saw my finger. You felt the anger from those traitors." He lowered his voice to a feral growl. "Gill knew me. I met him when I toured the men's collectives. That's why he was trying so hard to see if I was branded. He knew I wasn't. I'm sure they didn't want to believe the prince had happened upon their camp accompanied by the most infamous person on Valledera."

"You're not going to tell King Mallum that Terrowin exists when we go back to Abolend, are you?" Tovey feared the worst for Terrowin; though she didn't particularly like them, she understood them.

Cullus cracked his neck, veins surfacing like ropes pulled tight beneath the surface. Tovey watched his face flicker in silent conversation, mirroring her own. The world was shaking for both of them.

"I don't have to tell him. He already knows."

"How?"

"I've had a feeling he has been keeping information from me. I've started logging the defector rate and the reports from the collectives. It didn't match. Sylvia was proof of that . . . The rate of people defecting didn't match the bodies Abolend had the guards hang. I went to Father about it, but he said I was wrong." Cullus swallowed hard. "I knew my count was accurate, so I kept counting for months, and the discrepancy was growing. King Mallum can be stubborn, but he is not dim-witted. He's been having more and more private meetings with Elias. I questioned my brother about the nature of them, but he's been growing distant."

Tovey frowned. "If he knows where Terrowin is, why hasn't he attacked?"

"I said he knows they exist. It's clear to me he doesn't know where. They would be dead by sunrise if he did."

Tovey lay back in the dirt, staring at the stars, counting them one by one to distract herself from their new reality. Cullus lay next to her. His hand brushed against the back of hers.

Amile insinuating that there was more to the prophecy pounded at her mind, growing from a whisper to a scream until it was all Tovey could focus on. Tovey hated herself for needing to ask, but she knew she had to.

"Is there *anything* you didn't tell me about the prophecy?"

"Are you serious?"

He retracted his hand. Heaviness sat in Tovey's chest, pleading for the truth.

"I've never lied to you."

"Amile acted like there was something I didn't know, like going to Silvis was a bad idea."

"Of course she did! Tovey, I've told you, they *want* the war to happen. They want to see Abolend fall. Everyone in Terrowin is filled with hate, not the false sense of freedom they tell themselves they have. Look at their camp. They built it in a mountainous cage where they hide like pests waiting to be exterminated."

He shook his head, chest rising and falling rapidly. "But if Abolend falls, so will the people. Do you think the defector camp is actually free? They aren't. They still answer to a higher power. And that higher power is Amile. If she told them to march on Abolend and die, they would do it. They aren't without a leader; they aren't without rules. They are Abolend rebuilt with a new name. She is the king with a new face. Give them a few more decades, and you'll see."

Tovey's bottom lip stuck in her teeth while she contemplated his words. Terrowin was no Abolend. Even with time, she couldn't see the defectors turning their self-built camp of fortitude into a power play of class standing complete with forced military and servants. They wouldn't. They couldn't. Her eyes darted across the ivy-littered ground as she debated the horrific thought.

"Who would escape to rebuild the place they defected from?" she asked.

"The person who doesn't want to be equal but on top."

Rubbing her chapped lips together, she wondered if Abolend being overthrown would be a negative. No. She couldn't entertain a treasonous thought like that. Abolend was an unmovable force with a fiercely loyal army. Plus, Cullus was the heir. He would rule Abolend one day. She surveyed Cullus with her eyes, tracing his round nose, taking in his smooth skin. Would he be the one beheading masters in gruesome public displays? Her gaze met Cullus's kind eyes, and she knew he could never be anything like King Mallum. Her wrinkles of fear softened into a slight smile.

"Why are you looking at me like that?" Cullus questioned.

Tovey blushed, shaking her head, embarrassed she had lingered on his face too long. But he stared back at her, unspeaking. Cullus's steady fingers wove through her drying hair.

"Why do you do that?" she asked.

"What?"

"Touch my hair."

"I'm sorry if I'm overstepping. It's just . . ." He paused. The prince tightened his lips. "You had a branch in it." His fingers fluttered something invisible away. "It's what friends do."

A wild smile lit her face. Cullus shifted closer, his arm behind her body. She sank into his shoulder, releasing the tension in her muscles, but the peace didn't last. Any sound out of the ordinary sent her mind reeling with unruly thoughts. She stiffened, brow strengthening as she gazed into the flickering light.

"We have to get to Silvis soon—before I become any more dangerous—otherwise I might not be able to convince them." She closed her dry eyes. "They won't ever back down. Not if they know I stand with Abolend's prince and wield a strange form of uncontrollable power. They will kill me before King Mallum does."

Cullus hung his head, not having to speak. Tovey knew he agreed. She'd known all along, even if she had yet to admit it, that this journey could end in her demise. But one truth had resonated within her mind since they'd begun this journey: one life was worth giving in place of countless deaths.

22

Tovey woke to see Cullus perched on his toes with his longsword drawn. She turned on all fours, spinning to see who the unwanted intruder was. Her palms scraped against the frost-sprinkled ground as she stood, readying her dagger.

Melodic laughter filled the air before Cullus spoke. "It was a precaution in case Gill got any big ideas through the night." He rolled his eyes. "Though I'm not sure he has much thought going on up there." Cullus turned, tucking the parchment and ink that had lain next to a tree into Frilliam's pack.

Tovey forced a smile, though she imagined there must have been an impending threat for Cullus to forgo a night of rest. "You sure nothing happened?"

"Nothing more than a few bunnies who got curious about the fire."

Something seemed different in his eyes—a hint of sadness or

exhaustion. Tovey couldn't tell. Thin ice dripped from a weeping evergreen, shattering to the ground. In unison, they lunged their polished blades toward the noise.

Nothing.

Running her fingers through her hair, she returned her blade to her boot.

"Let's move," Tovey suggested. She kicked hard soil toward the remaining coals before dipping her hand into Frilliam's satchel and pulling out an apple for the horse and two rolls for them.

Tovey tossed the larger pastry toward Cullus as she ate, peering past the shivering trees into the forest. After pulling the map from Frilliam's bag, she spread it out on the ground, studying it.

"That way is north." Cullus pointed. "I checked the stars last night."

Tovey's gaze lingered on the pale pink sky. The twinkling dots faded into the light, and wrinkles crossed her forehead for a moment. She knew the stars were beautiful but had never imagined they were a map. Before Tovey could even ask, Cullus continued.

"We should see the city by sundown." His tone was solemn as he rolled the map, tucking it into the satchel. "We've moved quickly. Frilliam has been resilient, and we have only been pausing at night. I wasn't expecting us to be here so soon." His skin drained of all color. "Are you nervous?"

Nodding, she watched Cullus swing his leg over Frilliam and extend a hand with a thin smile, his usual crooked grin washed away with the growing morning light. She grabbed his hand, allowing him to pull her onto Frilliam. Dread filled her body, and she felt seemingly heavier today, as if stones had been placed in her soft boots.

"What if we don't go?" Tovey joked, but she wondered what would happen if they didn't.

"Ride back to Abolend and face my father? You know we can't do that."

"I know. Plus, I don't know"—her voice fell to the gentle hum of a whisper—"how I could manage to live with you and not speak to you."

Cullus turned his chin over his shoulder. "It wouldn't be like that."

"You and I both know it would. I've been thinking, and even if this works, even if we prevent the war and you tell the kingdom I was never a threat, I would return to my position. Or I'd be placed in another equivalent position, I suppose.

"But that is if they never realize that I took Sylvia's place. Which they will. I'm a dead defector as Tovey or Sylvia. And lying is a treasonous offense for servants. Even if you are forgiven for claiming Sylvia died after the hunt, I won't be."

Cullus's jaw tightened.

"And I've thought about if I go back as me, as Tovey. Well, she died in the forest, mauled by wolves, remember? Again another lie and another attempt at defecting. No matter my options, I can't figure out how I can go back. I've trapped myself in my lies. I've exhausted every option. What am I to do? Remain silent and serve? I don't know if I can handle it. I wasn't the best servant before, and now tasting freedom . . . I think I'll be a wild woman."

"Wild women get hunted by bowmen."

"So then, what, to Terrowin?"

"Terrowin is even worse than Abolend. You will not go to them. I beg you. We will figure something out." He turned his back, nudging his heels into Frilliam's ribs. The horse sputtered forward. "I will make sure you are safe. You are bringing Abolend peace. We can change your hair, your name. You will be safe."

Tovey frowned. Cullus could change every detail except for the one thing that marked her as dangerous: her eyes. She hugged his waist, letting her head rest upon his sturdy back, breathing in his natural rose water scent. It seemed impossible that he still was perfumed after all the days of travel, but he still smelled faintly of it. Branches snapped around them as Frilliam plowed through the thicket until they found a game trail to follow.

Despite their steady pace, Tovey clung to Cullus as if at any moment Frilliam could toss her off his back and into the woods, leaving her for dead. She knew her grip was too tight, but she didn't care, and Cullus didn't seem to mind. He lent a hand backward, his hand rubbing her leg with reassuring strength.

"Cullus?"

"Yeah?"

"You don't think I could . . . you know, die, do you?" Tovey didn't want to believe that in the blink of an eye this could all be over. Survival was the one thing she clung to, but now it seemed like she might have to face the possibility that she might not make it out alive.

Death happened to everyone. Everyone was born to die. It was a part of life and was not something anyone should fear. But still, she was not ready if her day was to come.

"No." Cullus's voice trembled.

His doubt set in a deep panic. Rounds of cooling fall air burned at her lungs, filling her nose with the musky warmth of brittle leaves. The wind kissed her face as birds sang without a worry in the wavering branches of lifeless trees. How could a world with such unending beauty become so cruel?

Hours passed as Cullus's head swayed in dizzy dives. Tovey sat upright, strengthening her core. Her fingers gripped his shoulders, attempting to steady his vertigo.

"Frilliam, stop," Tovey commanded.

The horse slowed. His hooves prodded the ground as he snipped off a mouthful of wild grass. Tovey climbed off Frilliam. Grabbing Cullus's leg, she helped him swing it over the horse's back.

Cullus swayed once more. He blinked lazily with glossy eyes. Tovey reached to place her arms beneath his shoulders, her fingers digging into his ribs. Her muscles shook beneath his weight. She pushed her head into his chest, lowering him to the ground, straining as she mustered every ounce of strength she had left. Weaving fingers through his hair, she secured his head before moving him again.

"I'm tired. I didn't sleep," Cullus grumbled.

"Take a moment and rest."

She pulled him to his feet, supporting his weight as they stumbled forward. A crooked oak sat ahead with a nook to support his body. Tovey guided him toward it, kicking tangled sedge out of the way as they walked. She spun, lowering him to the ground, letting his limp body fall back into the tree.

Her fingers glided across his forehead. His head was without fever. Tovey's heart steadied. Grabbing their water, she pulled a frozen branch from the tree downward, letting the ice run into the bottle, filling his canteen.

"Drink."

She sat before him, eyebrows pinched, watching him lie still. She pulled his boots off, revealing expertly knitted socks. Unable to hide her laughter, she turned to Frilliam.

"Even his socks are fancy. Did you see?"

Frilliam snorted.

Tovey laid one of Gill's blankets over his legs. She didn't have time to make a fire, so the bundle she'd swaddled him in would have to do.

His darkened eyelids closed. Tovey sat before him, peering into dark green shadows, surveying the area. It wasn't ideal. The trees were too thick to see their surroundings, and they were less than two yards off the game trail, prey to anyone or anything that may happen upon them. Worry plagued her like frost to the dead trees. Hours passed as she plotted her speech to the tune of Cullus's snores.

"I am here to speak to your mast—king." Tovey cursed, pressing her teeth into her tongue, frustrated at her sheer lack of knowledge. She should have listened to Cullus more intently. Every time he spoke, she tried to memorize his words, but there was still so much new information that it was hard to keep it all straight in her mind. "I'm here to speak to your chief."

Snap.

The sound of a branch splitting sent her head whipping to the side as her eyes peeled, surveying every inch of the forest to her left. The emerald foliage was still, and Frilliam didn't flinch. *It was the sound of melting ice,* she told herself.

Crack.

She shook with panic. A branch broke as if someone had

cracked it over their knee. She stood. With narrowed vision, Tovey glanced toward Cullus, his face smooth and relaxed, chest moving with resounding snores.

"Who's there?" Her voice was unsteady.

Crack.

Adrenaline crashed through her. Her veins tightened with rushing liquid. She traced the perimeter, stepping softly. There was nothing. Her eyes widened. There *was* something. A dark shadow crouched behind a bush, making the faintest crunching noise as it watched her, a flicker of lilac reflecting in dark prodding eyes.

"Not this time," Tovey growled, crouching.

She inched her outstretched fingers toward her dagger. The leaves shivered, spitting the creature out of the shadows and into the broken light. Tovey let out a frenzied scream. Her nerves popped like corn kernels over a raging fire.

In an instant, her eyes cast a purple hue over the matted sedge path, rushing an icy wind into the beast's heart, flaying it open where it stood. Blood gushed from its chest, pulsing in steady spews, tainting the ground around it. The jackalope fell to the ground, shaking in uncontrollable pain. The creature's legs twitched, its eyes fluttered, and its blood pooled on the shivering ferns.

"No!" Tovey cried, her eyes welling with fear. "No!"

Throwing herself forward, she pressed her hands to the beast, blood oozing through the spaces between her fingers. Bones rattling, she tried to fix the wound, gripping at fur, yanking it together. But the gnarly gash was wider than her palm, and too much blood had already been spilled.

"I'm sorry, I'm sorry, I'm sorry. Oh, you poor thing," Tovey muttered.

The world spun around her while the helpless creature bleated pathetic snorts, crying in pain.

"Fix!"

Tovey waved her hands over the beast, hoping to spark magic to cure it. There was nothing.

"Repair!"

Tears fell from her eyes. Inching close, she squinted with a fierce glare. Nothing.

"Heal! Heal! Why can't you heal the jackalope?" Tovey slipped back into the misty moors of her memory. "Help her! Sylvia, I'm sorry."

Blinking herself away from melding memories that wove with the grunting jackalope, Tovey unsheathed her dagger with a mournful ring. Hands trembling, she held her breath. Her hand quaked, unwilling to move, refusing to thrust the dagger into its heart. Even a mercy killing was too much for her to bear.

"May the . . . light guide you," Tovey said. Visions of Sylvia mixed with the scene in front of her.

She released the dagger, dropping it to the forest floor. Stuttering away from the miserable beast, Tovey turned, chest heavy with guilt.

A snore rumbled from Cullus, his body limp on the tree. She cast a gaze toward Frilliam, whose tail flicked carelessly, unaware of the horrific act she had committed. She trembled in fear of herself, casting a resentful glare at her blood-soaked hands. She had stolen a life. Her power had taken a life.

Cullus was wrong. She couldn't control her power. She was evil. She was dangerous. And she was deadly.

Wiping her bloodied hands on her pants, she dug through the

satchel, finding Cullus's pen and paper. Tears streamed from her eyes. Kneeling beside a boulder, she pressed the parchment against the stony surface, the pen uncomfortable and foreign in her hand.

Goodbye.

Servants weren't allowed to read or write, but Nadia had forced her to learn in the wee hours of the morn while the others slept. Nadia used to write basic words in the dirt on the stone floors of the collective, urging Tovey to trace the letters with her finger. She was thankful for those lessons now.

Tovey tucked the paper into Cullus's hand, kissing his forehead the same as Nadia had once done to her. Her face lingered. She brushed her nose against his hair, the scent of rose emanating from his head. Her heart ached.

She walked toward Frilliam and pressed her cheek to his long face, running her fingers through his tangled hair.

"Take care of him."

She eyed her dagger lying in the dirt. No. She wouldn't touch it. She wasn't brave enough to use it for mercy, nonetheless for malice. Biting her tongue, she turned, leaving it in the pool of crimson dirt next to the jackalope, which was still hanging on to a thread of life.

When he woke, Cullus would return to Abolend. He must. He should know that Tovey continued with the mission. He trusted her, and he'd know she would do the right thing, just as she trusted him to carry word to Abolend.

A tear fell. Tovey prayed he wouldn't follow her.

Cullus would have to trust that she would succeed in removing

Silvis as a threat. His job was the harder of the two, convincing King Mallum that there was no threat from their enemies across the Tenbris. There was no war to fight.

Focused on the road, she slipped into the shade, her boots silent on the ground as she left, breaking her promise to her friend. An untamed wind pushed at her back as icy tears froze on her cheeks. Stumbling forward on the unsteady ground, she walked, legs burning from exhaustion.

Long shadows of trees snaked across the mountainside in the golden light. Time was running out to make it to Silvis before nightfall. Tovey staggered to the crest of the hill before her, hoping to see something more than the evergreens blocking her way.

She neared the top, the hill crumbling into a stony cliff before dropping into a gully.

"Great." She grunted, kicking a pebble from the edge.

Squinting, she searched the horizon. She sucked in a sharp gasp. A silhouette of a twisting, towering tree rose above the forest in a cathedral of power. It was taller than any tree Tovey had seen before by three times, its trunk the same size as Abolend's castle. It stood in the center of a massive grove of oak trees spanning miles. Their leaves were too green, as if they didn't realize it was nearing the winter. Her brow furrowed as she took an unsteady breath at the sharp line of trees that turned from rich greens to barren branches. Tovey clasped her hand to her face, knees buckling beneath her, crumbling at the sight of Silvis.

Tovey would not enter the strange land in the dark. She was so close, but arriving in the shadow of night could endanger her, and backtracking would cost more time. Nodding, she decided to stay the night and start fresh in the morning.

She crawled into a soaring pine, using the branches as a ladder. Finding flexible limbs, she braided the newborn branches around her legs, securing herself in the upper boughs. She rested her hollow cheek against the craggy trunk, gazing toward the kingdom, tasting the slightest hint of salt.

She traced the town's border, hunting for anything that could indicate an opening. A faint area on the outskirts of Silvis was cleared of trees. That was it. That was her entrance.

"Please let the chief be more understanding than King Mallum."

Locking her fingers around her wrist, she hugged the tree. For what felt like an eternity, she stared at the kingdom until she could no longer keep her eyes open.

23

A low vibrational horn sounded. The warning tone repeated over and over again, growing stronger with every blow. Tovey's dry eyes shattered open, surveying the ground, seeing nothing. Twisting her neck, she loosened her muscles, tilting her ear toward the rich timbre of the sirens.

The horn sounded with steady repetition. Tovey pushed aside the prickly pine needles, peering toward the dryad kingdom. Silvis appeared frozen in the morning light, yet the sound was positively coming from its borders.

She pursed her lips as she descended the mighty tree to the clearing on the hilltop where she'd paused the night before. Eyes narrowed, she strained to see past the misty rays of morn blocking her sight.

As she tightened her jaw, her head swelled with frustration. Unwilling to wait for answers, she jogged back until she found a path that led straight to the clearing she'd spotted the night before.

If the horns were sounding for her, she would show herself, give in to the mystery, and allow Silvis to be the first to know she wasn't a threat. If they trumpeted for Cullus's arrival, she would show herself and aid him in their journey once again, though she hoped he was on his way to Abolend right now. If it was for something less serious, she would still show herself and stop the madness from unfolding once and for all. Pulsing with adrenaline, Tovey stomped forward with a scowl.

Dust puffed beneath her boots as she hastily wove through the forest. The unnaturally warm breeze guided her when the path fell to disarray, fading into knotted sedge. Minutes passed before she snapped to a halt, the forest becoming still. Rooted like one of the trees around her, she froze.

Tovey swiveled her head. Birds stopped singing. Rodents weren't moving. The slight whistle of the wind whispered in the silence. The hair on the back of her neck rose from an undeniable sensation that someone was watching her.

A hand snapped out of the shadows, grasping her tunic. Her heart lurched, feet flying into the air. Her body tumbled toward the ground. She clamped her mouth shut, not wanting to scream as fear fluttered in her stomach. Tovey was dragged into darkness, unable to see the hand that bound her. Fear flooded her body.

"Are you out of your mind?" a smooth voice hissed.

Fuming, she steadied herself. She raced to brush the dirt from her pants. "Are *you?*" She spun to look into Cullus's eyes, which raged like embers.

"Am I what?"

"Out of your blasted mind?"

"Apparently, I am, because for the life of me, I cannot figure out what happened or why you abandoned me." He panted heavily. "What in the name of Abolend happened? I woke up alone, stranded, with a scrap of paper that said 'goodbye.' It's ridiculous, Tovey! You left me with a camp covered in blood, and a bear—a blasted bear!—was investigating the scene, eyeing me like I was next! Were you attacked? Did someone force you to leave? Or did you stomp away on a rogue mission you told me nothing about, breaking your promise?" Cullus's voice shook. "We had a promise."

Panic flared in her eyes, and she was unable to find the words to explain.

"Was it your blood?" He surveyed her body, gripping her arms. "Tovey, talk to me!"

Guilt gnawed at her insides as she shook her head in disbelief at her actions. She hadn't considered predators would come to the corpse; that had been her plan for Sylvia, yet she'd assumed Cullus would be safe? The thought of Cullus not realizing she'd killed the jackalope and the mere fact that she'd left willingly ripped at her chest. Cullus was right. She was out of her mind.

"What? Say something!"

Tovey's eyes burned as salty pools swelled at her lids.

"Tovey!" His gaze penetrated her as he eased her back against a tree. "What happened? Are you all right?"

"Yes, I'm fine," she snapped. Tovey searched his eyes, begging for answers. "No, I'm not all right . . . I lost control and killed the jackalope." She heaved through tears. "No, I slaughtered the jackalope. I left willingly. I was scared; I *am* scared. I heard a noise, and I thought it might have been a dryad or something else. I don't know . . . Then something like an invisible sword ripped through the air, and the poor thing blasted apart. Because of me." Snot bubbled at her nose as she wiped it on her tunic.

"I can't let myself hurt Frilliam, and I can't hurt *you*. You are the only person I care about, Cullus. I'd never forgive myself." He went to wipe a tear from her cheek, but she shoved his hand away. "Don't. Don't touch me. I feel like I'm on the verge of doing it right now, so back off." She turned away from him and squeezed her eyes shut, digging her fingernails into the tree behind her. A low rumble like thunder sounded in the ground.

"In the name of Abolend," Cullus whispered. He waited for the growl to stop before speaking again. "Tovey, I'm not afraid of you."

"You should be."

"No. I shouldn't." He spun Tovey around from the tree. "Listen to me. There wasn't a jackalope at the camp. One crossed my path as I was leaving, but it was alive and well."

"There wasn't a body? But how?"

"No. Just blood. That's why, when I saw the bear, I thought something had happened to you. Tovey, you didn't kill anything."

"Are you sure? The jackalope was dying. I saw it."

"I'm sure there wasn't any dead creature there. That bear didn't find anything either. He seemed as confused as I was."

"I didn't kill anything?"

"No, Tovey. It survived." He paused. "I wouldn't lie to you."

A sigh of relief washed over her. Cullus gripped her into a hug as her tears soaked his shirt.

"Where's Frilliam?" Tovey muttered.

"He is in a safe area by a lake. I broke off branches and fenced him in to keep him from wandering too far. If things go poorly, I don't want him to get hurt."

Tovey stumbled backward. "If things go poorly? You mean if I hurt him?" She focused her rage into the ground. Pebbles scrambled together with the vibration, the ground shuddering more violently.

"I didn't know what had happened to you. You could have been captured by the dryads. I'm stealthier on foot. I didn't leave him to protect him from you. I left him to protect him from our enemy."

Nodding with pursed lips, Tovey let her adrenaline settle.

"But, Tovey, your power is way more than I could have imagined. If you actually did that to the jackalope . . ." He hesitated. "I think you may have caused an earthquake."

"I know. It's bad. Really bad. I'm bad." Tovey's heart thrummed rapidly, her chest rising and falling into hyperventilation.

Cullus didn't bother to retort. They both knew the reality of the situation, and lying about it was useless. She calmed herself, opening her eyes to take in his round face. His face was calm, but his eyes did not lie. It was clear he agreed that she was bad. Her arms folded, and she hugged herself. She sucked in a false sense of conviction as the horns sounded once more.

"Do you know what the alarm is for?" Her voice cracked into a falsetto.

Face blank, Cullus stared at her.

"Me?"

He nodded.

"But why?"

A vein popped out in his neck. "Because of me."

Tilting her head, she shifted her legs, digging the tip of her boot into the dirt.

"I sent word to Abolend, and word must have traveled to Silvis.

We have always suspected spies in the court, and those horns are proof. They know we are here—that *you* are here."

Mind spinning, Tovey wanted to ask a thousand different questions at once. Spies? Sent word? How? Her jaw unhinged, yearning to ask everything at once, yet words failed her. Cullus grabbed both of her hands, his eyebrows turning upward with sorrow.

"I wrote a letter to my father." His voice quivered. "I've *been* writing letters to my father."

Tovey's heartbeat stuttered, her knees clanking with unsteadiness.

"You didn't think the prince could disappear unnoticed? I could make you, a servant, disappear, but me leaving court, especially without an escort . . . It cannot happen for me."

"You've been lying to me?"

"No. And I haven't told my father everything. I kept Terrowin from him."

"Great, so you protect a few people, but me . . . You were never protecting me." Tovey stepped backward, pulling her hands away from his, tears welling in her eyes.

"I am protecting you!" he shouted, stepping forward. "But you left. You left me in a camp that was soaked in blood! You could have run, you could have gotten yourself killed, you could have decided to walk straight into Silvis as they have horns blaring in some sort of alarm.

"And guess what, Tovey? You did! You ran, you hid, and you were walking straight into a death trap without any sort of weapon or protection." Cullus pulled her polished dagger from his belt, shoving it toward her. "*Me*. I don't just wield a sword. I wield a highborn position in an enemy kingdom. They cannot hurt me if

I go in for a negotiation. But they can hurt you, someone who has no shield from their wrath.

"I told King Mallum you have power, a suspicion most of us had when we heard the prophecy. If they called you a demon, you must have something that makes you strong. Those of us in court weren't sure if it was power in terms of magic, strength, influence, or what have you. And I told him I have been trailing you, not traveling *with* you. I have been holding Abolend troops back from swarming us by letting them know you aren't dangerous."

"Until now. Right?"

His round nose turned red.

"You've been telling half-truths, but if it weren't a big deal, you would have told me from the start. You would have told me this was all an elaborate plan to get to know me, to survey your enemy in the privacy of the woods. You knew what you were doing. You knew you were threatening my life. Is that what you've been doing with the parchment? I can't believe I thought you were journaling, mapping our course." She pressed her tongue to the back of her teeth. "How'd you send the letters?"

"By bird."

"Bird? In the name of Abolend, Cullus. We were starving, and you were able to wrangle a bird to send a letter? We could have eaten that!" The earth growled beneath her feet. "I cannot believe that I believed a highborn. I should never have trusted that you were tracking our path or mapping our journey for an easy ride home."

"I-I was," he stuttered, eyes glossy.

"But not only mapping."

His face turned to stone. "What am I supposed to do? It was how I could get you alone."

"Why alone? Why not an escort of a dozen guards?" Tovey's heart pounded in her throat. "We would have had better provisions. Our arrival at Silvis would be more convincing with an army backing our word. Don't you think?"

"And how do you think you would have been treated? With kindness? No." Fire raged in his eyes, face reddening. "You would have been treated as a servant, worse than that—a criminal. I wanted to get to know *you.*"

"No, you wanted to know the demon," she growled, clenching her jaw.

"I wanted to understand your power." He raised his hands, stepping closer.

She ran her fingers through her hair, pacing. "So all of this . . . running away together on some magnificent adventure has been because you wanted to be the one to discover the purple-eyed demon's powers? To get her to aid you on a mission and take all the credit? To secure your blasted throne?" She bared her teeth at him as he swallowed air. "That's it, isn't it?"

"Not anymore, Tovey. Things have changed," he pleaded, rubbing his lips together.

"Nothing's changed, Cullus." Tovey sniffed, wiping her tears.

"What do you expect me to do? I am trying to navigate this to the best of my abilities. I am the blasted prince of Abolend! Do you have any idea the kind of pressure I am under?" His voice cracked.

"Pressure," she scoffed. A wicked smile flashed over her face. Tovey shook her head. "I'm a servant who has some horse dung destiny I never even knew of until you and your friends laughed about it over crumpets. You, Prince Cullus, know nothing of pressure. I have not one but *two* kingdoms and their people's lives weighing on me! You don't have any fathomable idea of the pressure I'm under. And now"—her eyes burst into light, brighter than ever before, casting a purple hue over the surrounding foliage—"I'm uncontrollable." Her face contorted into the embodiment of anger. "I'm a demon."

Tovey's hair lifted as air swirled around her like a tornado was beginning to churn. Her eyes turned to torches of lilac, consuming her in a flash. Body wasted, she collapsed, falling to the earth like a highborn's doll tossed aside.

24

Pale morning light met the flickering embers in Tovey's eyes. The sky remained unchanged, yet her surroundings had transformed. The thorny bushes that bordered the sedge-covered path had turned into a meadow—a perfect place to camp with the trail nowhere in sight.

A steady fire rolled in the center, crackling to a silent melody. Cullus crouched over the flames, warming his fingertips. His head turned, eyes locking on Tovey's questioning gaze. Shuffling, he rushed to her side and knelt beside her. He brushed his fingers through her hair before pulling her forward, helping her sit.

"Wh-what happened?" Tovey stammered.

"You passed out." His eyes flooded with worry.

"From the power?" She blinked, dizzy.

"I think so." He paused, contemplating the scene. "It seems like it pulls energy from you. Let me grab you something to eat."

He ran over to where a heap of blankets and supplies were sitting. After rummaging through it, he brought back a bit of cheese and pushed it into Tovey's icy hands.

She bit the bitter block, and her mouth watered. Tovey's stomach twisted, growling for more. "How long have I been out?" She surveyed the sky, wobbling. The sun was an hour or so from the position it had sat in when Cullus had confronted her.

"Two days." He gripped her shoulder, steadying her. "How are you feeling?"

The world swayed beneath her, and blood rushed through her ears. Searching the site, she knew Cullus told the truth. He had moved her, visited Frilliam, and brought back resources. Ash around the fire had been brushed aside, evidence of several logs burned through to their core.

"I feel like I haven't slept in days. I'm drained." Her head bobbed side to side, unsteady. "I passed out?"

"You looked like you were leeched."

"Thanks." Tovey smiled wryly.

"But your hair sort of spiraled in a wind you somehow created around you. It was almost like you were floating."

"What?" Tovey's heart sank to her stomach. "Was I actually floating?"

"I don't think so."

Her ears grew hot. She hated this power that grew like a tumor, overtaking her body more and more every day. "Is there anything else you need to share? Anything else you've lied about?"

Cullus shook his head. "I told you, I've never lied to you."

"Oh, right. You omitted the truth from me. You're right; *that* isn't lying. It is so much better." Tovey took a deep breath. "So, do you know how my powers work? I want to stop feeling like I'm spinning."

"No. I know as much as you do. Can I grab you something else to eat?" His voice was steady and calm. He stood, not waiting for an answer. Cullus sped to the bags and pulled out meats, water, and bread. Returning, he pushed them into her lap.

Tovey broke open a roll before biting into it. Though it was starting to stale, it was still delicious and melted on her tongue. With a full mouth, she said, "How can I trust you?"

"How can I trust you, Tovey? Don't forget, you broke your promise. I'm not the only one causing problems." He shook his head, eyes penetrating her. "You left without telling me."

Her stomach clenched.

"Your eyes . . . You need to calm down."

"You need to shut up." She pressed her lips together, shooting a deadly stare at him. "We are running out of time, and if you want to be my human shield, so be it. We need to leave now."

Cullus held Tovey's shoulders down, keeping her sitting on the leaf-littered ground. His push was gentle but still unwelcome. "You need a second to recover."

"No, I don't." Tovey was surprised at how strong her voice sounded. "Don't tell me what to do, Cullus." It was odd that her vernacular had evolved into its own entity, like speaking freely was something she had always done. Like it was her prerogative.

Spiders crawled over her spine, her mind reliving the memory of standing in the dining hall watching Cullus and the other highborns eat from behind her blindfold. Shaking her head, she couldn't believe how she'd wished to be nothing more than a statue. The thought churned her stomach with a sour liquid. How could she want to live a life of silence in the shadow of someone else's game? She wasn't ready to return to servitude, yet her days were numbered.

"I'm going to Silvis. Where's Frilliam?" Tovey pushed dried meat into her mouth, searching the tree line.

"Still at the lakeside paddock I made him. He is safe, grazing while you recover."

Tovey ran her fingers through her hair. "Good. How far is that from here?"

"An hour or so on foot."

"I will walk to Silvis then. Get him after."

"You could die." Cullus's eyes were wide, like they were screaming.

"I could die right now thanks to my powers, or I could die thanks to you letting King Mallum know right where I am. I could die walking into Silvis, who may just happen to want to kill me even more than your father." She searched his eyes despairingly. "I could die at any moment. A tree could fall, lightning could strike, anything could happen. I didn't want to admit it, and I didn't even think it, but this entire time I've been marching to my death, either by Silvis's hands or your father's." Her voice cracked, rising to a falsetto. "Now I know that you knew too."

"I can't let you go," he whispered, kneeling before her.

"It isn't your choice anymore."

Tovey's feet met the soil, her torso swaying. Her throat tightened as she attempted to ignore Cullus's wide pleading eyes. Spinning, she made her way toward the path to Silvis. They were less than two miles from it, and with a steady pace, she would be there within an hour.

"Tovey, let's think for a second." Cullus's voice trailed behind her. "Maybe there is another way."

"Another way?" She turned, jabbing her finger into his privileged chest. "Cullus! You were the one, *you*, who told me I needed to come here to get Silvis to back down so Abolend won't attack. Now that you told King Mallum I have power, he's got even *more* reason not to back down. I'm not his servant, and he knows I wouldn't fight for him. Who would after the way the kingdom has treated me? But he doesn't know I won't fight for Silvis."

Cullus's face glowed red, a fire brewing beneath his pores.

"But I won't fight for them. I'm not fighting for anyone. Because I don't want a fight at all. This is our best chance. This is Abolend's best chance. Hell, this is Silvis's best chance! Everyone will calm their blasted selves down once I convince them I'm not a threat and that these powers are nothing more than sparkly irises—a deformity. And the prince who has been stalking the so-called demon was wrong all along. Everyone will forget the blasted prophecy, and we will figure out the rest then." She tramped forward, pebbles trembling beneath her feet.

"You cannot walk in there," he warned, blocking her way.

"Yes, I can. Move." She faked moving left and then dodged right under his outstretched arm.

He twisted, springing before her, blocking her path once again. "You cannot."

"And why is that, Cullus? Please tell me why, because I don't see any reason to wait." Tovey took quick breaths, not wanting a reason to stop. She shook her head, marching forward.

"Because, Tovey, I don't want to see you get hurt." He reached for her hand, stopping her once more. "They might not agree to back down. They might see your eyes and kill you before you have a chance to speak. The dryads are violent. Deceitful. What will we do then?" His chest rose and fell with a crescendo of anger. "This whole time, we have assumed. My grand plan is based on assumptions, on educated guesses, like I am playing a chess game without seeing the pieces of my opponents. Don't you understand? There is a valid reason our kingdoms are so far apart. Their morals are not the same as ours; they are downright terrifying.

"We have no idea what state their minds are in, especially now that they must know you have power. Thanks to my ignorant obedience to the crown." Flustered, his eyes watered, sparkling like diamonds in the blue morning light. "I had no other choice." He grunted beneath his breath. "I'm sorry."

Somewhere deep within the darkened corners of her heart, she understood. Cullus was a servant to the crown, the same way she'd been or still was a servant to the highborns. Even now, if Cullus commanded something, she'd do it. It was instinct. It was her born fate, and her innate need to please was not a reprimand-able fault.

Tovey dug the tip of her shoe into the ground. "I'm sorry for leaving you. I wanted to protect you. I don't know what I'd do if I hurt you. Cullus, I promise I will do my best to survive." Her stomach lurched. She didn't know if she could keep that promise.

"You have to do better than that." Cullus's eyebrows pinched.

Tovey shook her head, unwilling to promise anything more than she already had.

"You have to do better than that, Tovey," he pleaded, running his fingers wildly through his hair before rubbing the back of his neck. "I need you to walk out of that forsaken kingdom with me."

He stepped closer, his brown hair fluttering in the breeze. He stepped so close they breathed the same air. She tasted the sweetness of an apple on his breath. He paused before Tovey, his eyes silently speaking visceral words of comfort, compassion, and understanding. She connected to him in a way that she'd never connected to anyone else, like he was a part of her somehow.

His gaze shifted from her eyes to her lips, which were pursed with frustration. Cullus's warm fingers traced from her wrist to her cheek. She breathed in deeply, her muscles releasing tension. She shut her eyes, focusing on nothing more than the featherlight touch of his skin against hers as he outlined her jaw. He released a breath, tickling her cheeks.

She opened her eyes, shaking her head at his dimpled smile. She hated how she could be furious at him one moment and the next feel as if nothing else existed besides the two of them. His hand fell back to his side as confusion swept over his face.

"What?" she whispered. Tovey was unsure why he always touched her so gently, as if she was something to be cherished.

It gave her an unsettling awareness that he cared for her life more than a friend should. Maybe he did. Tovey hadn't spent much time contemplating her affection toward Cullus, though her heart knew what she thought of the ridiculous cloud-headed highborn without even needing to question the matter. A smile swept across her face. She was unable to deny the fact that she admired him, that she understood his faults and flaws. He was imperfect, like her.

Cullus's boots met hers. He stood inches away from her. The lightest freckles, barely noticeable on his skin, revealed themselves on his nose. His thick eyebrows turned upward, eyes racing across her face before locking tight on hers.

Warmth bloomed like a spring daisy in her chest. Butterflies stirred in her stomach, sparking energy inside of her. She grabbed his tapered waist as if they were atop Frilliam. But she wasn't steadying herself from any movement other than the trembling of her steadily pounding heart.

Cullus wove his fingers behind the base of her neck, pulling her in closer. Goose bumps raced across her skin. Inches of static air between them vanished by the second. Her lips parted as his lips brushed against hers, softer than a petal. She leaned into the kiss as sparks of lightning burst in her mind. Their arms tightened, pulling each other closer, somehow never grasping the other close enough. His lashes brushed against her cheek as she breathed him in.

Trees rustled in the fall breeze, humming with delight as time vanished. Parting, they swayed. A crooked smile shimmered across his face, and familiar wrinkles bunched by his eyes. Heat rushed like a river through her cheeks.

"I-I think," Cullus started. "No, I know. Tovey, I . . . I love you."

The words fell out of his mouth like a blissful mistake, a whisper of wind whooshing through sweet grass, purring the silence away. Sucking in the savory scent of familiar breath, Tovey was more alive than she had ever been before. She brushed her nose against his.

Her heart pounded, resounding throughout her body. She was sure Cullus could hear it, but somehow the drumming sped faster, and she didn't care. This was love.

She loved her sister, but this was different. This love was pure, like a rainstorm in summer. She traced Cullus's face, soaking in every detail, wanting to memorize every inch. He was complicated and flawed yet was somehow more perfect than Tovey could have dreamt. She stood on her toes, drawing her mouth to his ear, teasing her lips across his skin.

"And I you."

25

The moment shattered like glass. Cullus turned away, ripping a piece of fabric from his sleeve. Cullus pushed the thin material into Tovey's hands, but she didn't grasp it. It was clear what it was: a blindfold. Shaking her head, she refused. Pain pricked at her heart, which had fallen from the top of a mountain into a ravine of darkness.

"That kiss meant nothing?" Tovey muttered.

"It did."

She shook her head. "No. The world still spins, and I'm still your blindfolded servant." A shiver raced down her spine.

"You were never my servant. We went into this as equals. This"—he waved the blindfold—"is a precaution. We don't know what the dryads know or what their course of action will be, but hiding you as a servant protected you before, and it can protect you again."

Tovey stretched her neck. "I don't want to."

"You must. Trust me." His eyes pleaded, apologetic and serious.

Wishing she could live in the kiss forever, she shook her head, knowing their fantasy wouldn't last. But now everything seemed so much harder, so much more pressing. The pressure was exploding from her skull, sure to erupt. Silvis had to back down.

Her eyes had enjoyed taking in the little nuances that were hard to see from behind the scratchy fabric, like how dust sparkled in the sun as if it were glitter, or the slight glint in Cullus's hazel eyes when she caught him tracing her lips. And those freckles, a secret from the world, kept from everyone aside from her.

"Cullus?"

He blinked at her, waiting silently.

"Nothing."

"What is it?" he asked.

"It isn't anything," she lied.

"Tell me."

She shook her head. Their eyes wallowed in sorrow and regret. She knew that some deep part of him wanted to run like she did, run away from their lives, duties, and obligations. They could live in the Tenbris together, abandoning all duties to the crown. She wanted to ask him to give it all up—the war, the throne, his life in Abolend—but she couldn't.

Silence stiffened in the air. Cullus watched Tovey pour water from their canteen over the frayed hemp before molding it to her face with a tight knot. The fabric scraped at the white scars on her cheeks. With perked ears, Tovey took in the somber gulp from Cullus before he muttered unintelligibly in hushed tones.

She didn't bother asking. She knew Cullus also hated the

blindfold, but it would've gone against everything he'd been taught to admit it, like how he'd confessed he loved a servant. It was a disgrace—the most beautiful and heart-filling dishonor in Abolend's history.

"I hate to have to do this to you, but you'll be less of a threat." Cullus held out a red dress, the linen the putrid color of death. Her mouth hung ajar, but air couldn't enter or escape Tovey's swelling throat.

"How? How do you even have this? I've been in our bags . . ."

"There is a secret pocket. If you lift the seam on the left bag, it opens to the lining. I pressed it flat in there so that it felt like nothing more than padding. I'm not trying to hide anything from you. This was a precaution when I left that night.

"We could have left it somewhere for bait, made you look dead if the rumors hadn't stuck. After seeing you dressed like a commoner, I figured it would be good to have on hand, though getting to the laundry room in the dungeons was no easy feat. All the servants were swarming on high alert, looking for you that night."

"Don't look." After snatching it from his hands, Tovey wiggled off her pants, casting them aside. She'd miss them. The way they moved with her legs was something a dress would never allow. She could be stealthy, mobile, and most of all, free. Imagining Cullus tramping around the servants' quarters was amusing and brought a little bit of light into a darkening world. "I can't picture you down there." Tovey smirked, knowing Marka would have been overcome with every emotion burning in her heart at once.

"And I cannot picture you there either."

Her teeth ground together, jaw flexing. How could Cullus not picture a servant in the servants' quarters? And if he couldn't, then there was something wrong with anyone being in those conditions. Nothing made her special now, aside from his love, which was unseen. If this was true, was it possible that servants didn't need to be servants? No. She couldn't think like that, like a traitor to the crown.

Tovey silenced her thoughts. Despite the blindfold, she could see Cullus trying not to watch her dress as a smile flickered over her face. It was strange to know that his lingering gaze and the butterflies that lived in her stomach were symptoms of love. Stepping into the dress, she pulled the top over her bosom, covering her chest as she shimmied out of the loose tunic. The shirt, too, gave her a comfortable sensation of being one with the wind instead of bound in heavy unbreathable fabrics, a treat she would sorely miss.

Being dressed like a servant made her whole body cringe at the awfulness of it. Never before had the dress degraded her, but now she knew she was nothing but a toy waiting to be shoved along by a nobleman's manicured finger, a little doll dressed in smothering fabric the color of blood to hide all that would spill. Ingenious. A haunting laugh escaped her gritted teeth as she remembered her former self standing in the dungeon gasping with elation at the new uniform. How conditioned she had been to admire the garb of servants.

"I don't like seeing you like that either," Cullus stated, seeming to read the infuriated expression on her face.

Tovey didn't reply. She bowed her head as her hands folded in front of her. The way her subconscious took over her body was horrifying, as if the moments of free speaking had never happened and the moments they'd shared had been obliterated from history in a flash. She shook her hands, trying to break free of their muscle memory. Tovey ached to scream, but instead, a whimper sounded.

"It will be fine. We will make this quick. Remember, with me, Silvis cannot touch us. If they did, they would immediately start a war that wouldn't end until Abolend avenged my death. Even with the war coming, they won't kill royalty. Not yet. Even our deepest enemies understand the importance of my life while I'm unarmed in their court. Rules of negotiation."

Bobbing her head, Tovey listened and agreed. Highborns were immune. The cannon fodder, like her, were the ones worth killing. A messenger was always easier to kill than the king—or the king-to-be, in their case.

Side by side, they walked, the woodland chatter filling the silence along with the churning of the ground beneath their boots. Cullus wrapped a steadying arm around Tovey's waist, but she shook it off.

"Don't touch me like that," she said harshly, her tone even scaring her as it flicked off her tongue.

"I'm sorry, I wanted to—"

"Don't. Not like this." She didn't want to remember he loved her. Not while she was playing nothing more than a servant. Not while she was someone who would be forced into loving him back despite her personal wishes, even if they were reciprocated in reality. The guise of highborn and servant turned her stomach sour with bile.

Once more, the crickets filled the place of conversation as the miles shrunk into feet. They stood before the wooden arch of Silvis. Ancient trees wove toward each other, forming an arch like an ancient knot of power, welcoming outsiders to their earthbound kingdom. The trees' bark was smooth and twisted in tidy spirals topped with green leaves, unchanged by autumn.

"How is that possible?" Tovey muttered.

"Magic."

Tovey's eyes widened beneath the shroud. No guards were present, unlike Abolend's arches, which overflowed with buckets full of men posted at all three entrances. Tovey shifted her shoulders toward Cullus, twisting her head, attempting to see through the new fabric, though the tight weave was much more challenging to see through than the loosely woven hemp she had grown accustomed to.

Still, she could see thorn bushes running along the kingdom's perimeter, dividing the Tenbris, which was deep within fall, from the emerald greens of the trees within the border.

"We should go in. The dryads likely know we are here. Those evil devils are one with the forest. The trees could have already betrayed us."

Tovey's thoughts churned. She ached to ask questions, but her outfit had convinced her mind she was wearing a muzzle—one she shouldn't dare tamper with. Memories of floggings flashed in her mind. It was something she'd buried within the folds of her brain, neglecting to dwell on painful memories since being on the run.

Vivian had taken great pleasure in hurting anyone who ever asked a question or muttered out of turn. That child often happened to be Tovey.

She dug her teeth into her tongue.

As she stepped through the threshold of Silvis, a vibrating buzz of invisible humming resounded throughout her body. It was nearly palpable, as if somewhere a war drum was banging, yet the area was silent. Gold sap dripped from the woven branches, highlighting gnarled ridges on the trees, illuminating them in the midday sun. The air was oddly warm, rustling through green leaves as if an invisible hearth were somehow heating the entire kingdom. A fragrant herbaceous scent filled the air around them.

Her feet stilled. Tovey tilted her head, trying to hear the silent vibrational charge whirring through her body to no avail.

"I feel it too," Cullus said, eyes darting around. "This is going to sound strange, but I sensed this same sort of thrumming in the dining hall. When you were serving and hiding behind that tapestry, I could feel a buzzing, almost like I knew you were there."

Tovey recalled the heat of his gaze toward her that day. She remembered thinking even then that his senses were unusually keen. Instead of pressing for more answers to the questions building in her mind like an unstable tower, she hung her head low and took steady steps inches behind Cullus.

It wasn't custom for servants to walk in the same line as their master, for that would give the illusion they were equals, and they obviously were not. The subordination ate at her, pain seeping through her soul, deadening her spirit with every step.

The kingdom was stunning and unnaturally bright, with stone-cobbled streets and moss growing between every placed rock. Trees stood where buildings should've been. Their trunks were massive enough to dwell within. Knots of severed branches formed various-size windows within the tree homes, lights flickering within them. Doors half the size of humans were nested into the bark. Tilting her chin upward, she traced the landscape, peering out from beneath the blindfold, hoping to learn more.

Large-eyed creatures with colorful skin, from greenish shades of moss to brown tones of bark and the pastel glow of flowers, walked from the shadowed bark structures. They folded in half to move out of the doors and into the light. Tovey followed close to Cullus's heels, her chest tightening. The dryads towered above them, most standing a head or more above Cullus.

They were beautiful, similar to humans but with enlarged eyes filled with questions. Their hair was long, falling in shades of black, brown, yellow, and pink. They were curious. She would have been scared, but their faces held a softness she couldn't explain. They didn't appear to be devils at all but appeared as if trees came to life before them. She suppressed a relieved smile. Cullus was wrong.

The inquisitive strangers watched the two intruders press forward on the meandering streets. Filling her nose with the sweetest bouquet of an unfamiliar note, Tovey savored every moment. It seemed impossible that Silvis was so unequivocally similar to Abolend on the outside. The irony was amusing. Walls of stones to bushes of thorn. Structures of shell and towers of bark. Yet if this were Abolend, guards' spit would have already showered them instead of gentle faces of curious beings.

Tovey tucked her chin to her chest, focusing on the individual stones rubbed smooth from wear. In every cobblestone, a different symbol was etched, each twisted in a strange knotted pattern. Tovey's eyebrows stitched together. She tried to visualize the moss and ivy on the ground sprouting golden flowers, leading her to a safe place where she and Cullus could escape to, away from their burdens instead of into the mouth of the beast.

26

A crowd of dryads circled them. Uneasiness encapsulated Tovey from the weight of their gaze. Their enemy did not seem aggressive, and the kingdom was serene, as if no one would ever dare speak above a whisper. At least sixty dryads had come to see who had entered their kingdom. Tovey thought they must have perceived her the same way she saw them, both curious about the other, wanting to know more. If humans were not to come here, this was the first time they'd seen someone like her too.

The dryads shuffled, their bodies tightening any gaps in the circle around them, blocking Tovey and Cullus from moving any farther. The dryads stilled as if they were trees planted in the ground, unmoving. Tovey strained to see the creatures through the fabric, but it was difficult to make out more than towering shadows. Together they stilled. Cullus held his hands beside him in the air, palms spread.

"I am Prince Cullus of Abolend. I have come here to speak to the chief. It is an urgent matter. I do not come with any intent to harm." His words dripped off his lips diplomatically. Another person than the one she had grown to know stood before her, spinning in a circle. He flashed a coldly polite smile. Tovey swallowed hard, knowing Cullus was undoubtedly nervous, though she hoped the dryads couldn't see it.

The dryads exchanged glances, unheard conversations bouncing soul to soul as one of them stepped forward, nodding a bald head.

"I will take you. My name is Firth, and I am the hand of the chief." The dryad straightened his spine for a moment before collapsing into his hunched demeanor. "And who is she?" His crass voice spoke with a slight accent. She wouldn't have noticed it if her ears hadn't been soaking in every word. His curled finger hooked toward her.

Tovey kept her head facing the ground and her hands folded, waiting for Cullus to reply. Her hair covered her in a blanket of fortitude, allowing her to take methodical breaths while focusing on nothing more than the moss on the stones beneath her shoes.

"She's my servant."

The words cut like a stinging bee at her heart even though she knew this was all a ruse. No matter what she told herself, the words that fell from his lips were excruciatingly valid. It hurt.

"And why would a prince bring a servant with him to meet with a chief?" Firth waddled in a circle around them, tracing the circumference of the curious dryads. "To cook? To set up your camp along your journey? To hunt or to be hunted?" the dryad snapped, his tongue flicking on his lips with disgust.

Tovey clenched her teeth, stopping her jaw from dropping as her heart punched at her chest. She wondered how the dryads knew that servants were hunted after defecting when Cullus knew nothing about them.

Cullus stood still, allowing the verbal barrage to occur.

Firth smiled. "Ah, yes. We know much about your kind. Tell me, Prince, is this servant here for your personal pleasure? We've heard highborns like to . . . indulge in things they don't have consent to touch."

Tovey shivered with disgust.

"I'd watch yourself, or the chief may lose a hand," Cullus jeered, his stance aggressive as he leaned toward the dryad. Tovey inched toward Cullus, grateful she still had the dagger tucked in her boot. Cullus had walked in without his sword, and his display of submissiveness would be a sign of trust. Hopefully.

"A hand!" Firth cackled, and the other dryads stood wordlessly watching the spine-tingling scene as if it weren't happening before their empty gaze. "And you may lose *yours*."

Firth's long fingers gripped Tovey's throat before she detected the dryad had moved from his hunched stature. Her jaw dropped as her chin lifted, and she sucked at the air, trying to breathe without success.

Visions of the Abolend guard, Gorv, choking her before she went to the dungeons of the castle echoed in her mind; she was a helpless servant once more. But Breena wasn't here to save her this time.

Within the second, her fury turned to flame, igniting her blindfold. The scent of burnt paper filled her nose. The blindfold burned to ash in a wave of amethyst glory. The crowd of dryads gasped as Cullus moved toward Firth, gripping the creature's wrist. Cullus spun unerringly. His arm locked tight around Firth's body. Cullus sent the dryad's arm backward in a twist as he ripped the foul being away from Tovey's neck, sending him falling to his knees.

Cullus pinned Firth in a kneeling position. Tovey stood before the crowd, her eyes glowing for the dryadic kingdom to see. Their purple radiance shimmered around her face. Tovey lunged toward Firth, and her tiny fingers lodged in a bony grasp at the base of his neck. Cullus threw Firth's arm to his side. A wicked gaze glinted in his hazel eyes as Cullus let Tovey have him. His chin lifted as a slight smile crossed his face, proud of his protégé.

"I am the one they call the amethyst child."

Several dryads beamed in awe as others remained blank. Tovey searched their eyes, an energy of acceptance wrapping her despite her grip on the flesh of one of their own.

"And you are going to take us to your leader." Her words hung in the air.

The dryads shifted, eyes darting from one to the other. Tovey's mouth went dry, and she was unable to keep her grip on Firth. She let go, stepping back, waiting for something to happen.

A sneer crossed Cullus's face. "I'd listen to her if I were you."

Tovey glanced toward Cullus with a swift bow of her crown, grateful for his interjection. Static buzzed between them; they both knew she was never going to hide again. It was a sentiment she was grateful to see reciprocated in his swooning eyes.

"Pleased to meet you," Firth said sincerely, expression serious. He gave an enigmatic smile as he stood, bowing deeply, folding his body in half as the rest of the dryads knelt.

Spinning, Tovey stared at the dryads, mouth agape. Her breath grew thin and ragged, knees trembling beneath her. She wanted to kneel with them, but Cullus shook his head. The dryads smiled at her like they knew her somehow. Tovey's lip quivered. They must have heard the wrong prophecy. They must've been confused.

Tovey glanced over her shoulder, taking in the face of each dryad. Other than the colorful undertones and lengthened limbs, the dryads were nearly identical in shape and form to humans. Were the dryads as devious as Cullus had claimed? They had to be. Firth had attacked her, unprovoked.

But now, they remained bowed to her. She was consumed with the sensation that ants were crawling over her skin, uncomfortable from their unblinking gaze. No one should bow to her. That was something reserved for people who demanded respect. She was not someone to be respected. She was someone to be feared. She dug her nails into her palms, the moment lingering for an eternity.

She wrinkled her brow, looking to Cullus for guidance. His face radiated optimism as he, too, lowered his crown to Tovey, taking a knee and mirroring the dryads' sentiment before he stood once again. She stepped closer to Cullus and moved her lips next to his ear.

"Never bow to me." Her nose grazed his cheek intimately before kissing the rounded tip of his ear gently. Her spine straightened as she caught the fiery glare of Firth. The dryads rose as a devilish smile overcame his face, curling his green-hued skin into an unnerving grin.

Cold sweat formed at her hairline, and her hands became clammy. She was unable to read the dryads. Cullus's jaw tightened, and his chest puffed. Tovey knew something had gone horribly wrong.

27

Firth flicked his tongue across his lips like a lizard. He peered down his hooked nose toward Tovey. Raising the corners of his mouth, Firth revealed rotted teeth as if he wanted to eat Tovey alive. Cullus's spine became rigid as he edged in front of Tovey.

"Follow me," Firth croaked. He promenaded down the stone path, weaving through a corridor of tree homes.

Tovey admired the natural state of Silvis as if it were a camp of people living within a petrified forest. Removing Firth from the scenario, it could be somewhere she would enjoy exploring. She reached for Cullus's hand as they moved forward, but he shook her away, casting a dangerous glare, his eyes widening threateningly.

Tovey had never seen him be so aggressive toward her.

"What's wrong?" she mouthed, not letting a noise out.

Cullus shook his head, warning her with his eyes.

Frowning, Tovey walked, taking equal steps with Cullus. She

wasn't playing servant anymore—the gig was up. His aggression was unnecessary, but there was likely another plan forming. She shook off his strangeness and continued.

The afternoon sky darkened as they followed the cobblestone road beneath a towering canopy of leaves. The road meandered to the gigantic tree in the kingdom's heart. It soared stories above the others. Deep emerald leaves the size of rabbits cast an unsettling green glow on the cool stones beneath her feet.

Though she should've been afraid, she wasn't. She couldn't help but smile as they approached the hollow tree, examining the branches to see the life it still had. She traced the fissured bark from the leaves to weaving roots. Awestruck, she ascended the monumental steps rooted in the twisted foundation.

Worn from ancient feet, the stairs dipped. Tovey savored each step as she approached the ornately carved doors with a dryadic guard standing on each side—a man and a woman with toned muscular bodies. They stood with their shoulders pulled back, eyes locked ahead of them. They wore natural flowing fabrics, free of armor or weaponry. A smile flickered over Tovey's face as she noted the woman warrior, something Abolend lacked.

Tovey searched Cullus's face for the same sentiments, but his expression was a statue of perfection without a hint of emotion. She flicked her chin over her shoulder, gazing behind her. Dozens of dryads had followed behind them in a parade of curious tranquility. The guards bowed toward Tovey, noses plunging to the ground.

"Enter." Firth gestured toward the doors as they opened, revealing a grand chamber. Carvings wove their way across every inch of the bark. Candlelit lanterns and plants tangled in and out of the wooden walls. "This is our great kapok," Firth announced.

Tovey tapped her fingers against her leg, staring at a carved throne in the center of the room, sitting empty. It reminded her of standing before the doors of the Reckoning Hall. The world had grown so much since then.

Tovey turned to watch Cullus enter behind her, his face devoid of emotion and his spine straight. He maintained an unshakable rigid posture, refusing to show any form of weakness. Cullus's life had been spent training for moments like these. She wished she understood him more when he acted this way.

Wooden hinges creaked. The sound snapped her gaze to a simple wooden door sunken into the wall behind the throne on the right of the room. The door flung open, revealing a dryad whose skin matched the warm walls. The dryad was imposing, passing Cullus's height by half a foot. He was shirtless, and loose linen pants flowed around his legs. Tall woven sandals wrapped his calves.

He sauntered forward, long midnight hair flowing behind him in knitted braids. His brow jumped in surprise, and he gawked for a moment at Tovey as if she were not real. A welcoming smile steadied his face. His eyes were green like the forest and teeming with life. He sat on the throne, throwing a cape made of moss to the side.

Tovey's jaw unhinged. She was unable to believe that this dryad was the chief. He was so informal. She'd expected someone like King Mallum, face hardened and hungry for death. But this dryad was the opposite. She tilted her head, observing the man as he settled into a hunched position. He casually rested his arms on his knees with his hands folded before him, ignoring the illusion of power that Cullus held. The chief looked young. He couldn't have been much older than she was.

"Welcome to my kingdom." He nodded toward Tovey. "Cullus. Not so welcome." A chuckle from his jab rose from his full lips. His voice chimed like an instrument playing in the barren tree. He eyed Tovey. "Tell me, love, what brings you here?" His gaze snapped back to Cullus. "And tell me, Cullus, what idiocy has caused you to dress the prophetic one in the garb of your servants?"

A muscle in Cullus's jaw twitched.

"I'm a servant," Tovey said flatly.

"You are not really a servant though. Playing dress-up?"

"She is a servant of Abolend," Cullus stated.

Anger and disapproval washed across the chief's face. "Is this true?" His midnight brows pinched as he leaned toward Tovey.

"Yes, I am a servant of Abolend. I serve King Mallum and his court."

"And it has never crossed your mind that he should be the one serving you?" the chief growled. His face was serious, but his words made Tovey's face twist in confusion.

The chief released the tension in his face, clapping his hands. "You've enslaved the demon. How adorable. Is it working out for you, Cullus?" He flicked the prince's name off his tongue, his lip pulling upward with disgust.

Tovey wanted to fight the degrading comments, but she swallowed the insult as a purple hue flickered before her. She bit her tongue. Her respect for the chief was dwindling faster than grass on fire.

"Cullus, Cullus, Cullus," the chief chimed. He sprung to his feet, letting his muscles ripple threateningly. Circling Cullus, he eyed him aggressively. "Now, I've heard of you, but you, poor boy, are so much less than I was expecting." He paused, peering down his nose at Cullus. "And to let you in on a little secret, my expectations weren't high."

A stifled bark came from Firth, who stood to the left of the throne, watching the scene unfold with glory.

"But you, now, I have heard of you too." He flashed a charming smile at Tovey. "And you are much more than I was expecting." He winked. Spinning on his heel, he returned to his throne. "I am Chief Arden." He bowed his head before flicking a braid from his face.

"Thank you for introducing yourself, sir, for I have never heard of you." Cullus bowed sarcastically before locking his spine once again.

"*Chief*," Arden snapped. "So, Cullus, tell me, are you the same breed of uneducated swine as your dear old father?"

Cullus stiffened.

"Hmm, a little intelligent, I see. Good boy." Wrinkles formed on his forehead as he focused on Tovey. "Why have you come to Silvis?"

Tovey eyed Cullus for confirmation to speak. He bowed his head, a friendly dimple encouraging her. Firth leaned over and whispered something into Chief Arden's ear. Listening closely, Tovey couldn't hear anything. Arden let out a howling laugh, looking between Cullus and Tovey with a devilish grin before settling once more on the throne.

"Sorry for that. A joke." Arden tapped a long finger on his lips. He settled into his hunched position, a wide grin overcoming his face as he repeated himself. "Why have you come to Silvis? And you, love, don't need your master's permission to speak to me."

Cullus's hands balled into fists.

"My name is Tovey." She shot Cullus a dangerous look.

"Tovey." He smiled softly.

"And I don't need his permission to speak," she said with force.

"Understood."

The tension in Tovey's shoulders released.

"So, Master is being kind today?" Arden sneered.

Her expression shattered into a scorned glare.

"Continue, dearie."

She bit her tongue hard, water filling her mouth. Arden's irritatingly pompous voice echoed in her head. She wanted to rip at him. He'd crossed the line over and over, and she and Cullus were doing their best to remain respectful to a chief who didn't deserve it. She didn't need permission from anyone to speak. Cullus had never been her master. Since she'd met him, she'd been free from the binds of a servant.

Tovey stifled her rage as her eyes shone brighter. She was here on a mission, and she needed to play by the rules. "I'm here to ask you, Chief Arden, a favor on behalf of Abolend's people."

"Isn't that *his* job?" Arden snarled at Cullus.

"No. It is mine." Tovey stepped forward. "I'm assuming you know the prophecy."

"I do."

"So you know, then, of the final war." She paused, her heart hammering in her chest. "They say I will bring it, that your kingdom will come to attack mine because you fear me, the same as people in Abolend fear me. They hunt me based on old words, but . . ." She hesitated as perplexity crossed Chief Arden's face. "I don't want a war to come. I'm not a threat to you or to Abolend. People in my kingdom do not need to be attacked."

Arden's head tilted.

"Unfortunately for you," Cullus said, "King Mallum is readying for war as we speak to prepare for your unwanted advances, and the power of Abolend is unbeatable."

"Debatable," Arden scoffed.

Cullus's voice was solemn. "It isn't. I've come here of goodwill." Cullus's eyes pleaded with the chief. "I don't want my people or yours to die."

"We ask that you have Silvis back down." Tovey's voice wavered. Though the dryads had greeted her with respect, Cullus was confident that they had plans to advance on Abolend. After all, why else would Abolend be preparing for a fight?

Cullus straightened his spine. "If you, Chief Arden, would consider a surrender before our fight has begun, it would mean no war. I'm sure you can see Tovey is no threat to your kingdom or mine."

Chief Arden shifted in the wooden throne, nodding rapidly, his face contorted. "If we back down, Abolend won't attack? Then there will be no war. Interesting." An unreadable smile crossed his face.

"Yes. I'm not a threat." Tovey raised her hands. "I am a servant of Abolend."

Arden's eyes narrowed.

"I'm a maid. Nothing more."

Arden pushed his shoulders back. His mouth twitched, unable to settle. Lunging sideways in his chair, his hand blocked his mouth, and he whispered indistinctly toward Firth. Hushed tones encircled the room, and anxiety twisted in her gut. Days seemed to pass as time crawled, the conversation between the dryads finally ending.

"I didn't think you'd come here asking something so great of us. It doesn't sound like a good deal to me. You've given me news that Abolend is preparing to attack, that you are preparing to come to my home, yet ask that I pull back all defenses against a kingdom that is already prepared to fight. On a promise by the king's little boy?" A whistle of air rushed between his full lips. "No."

Tovey's heart pounded as her breakfast sat in the balance of her stomach and mouth, fighting to escape. Chest heaving, her breathing labored, her eyes flickered with fear. A responsibility surged deep in her heart. She needed to win this debate not only for her own sake but for Cullus, for the people of Abolend, and even for the dryads of Silvis. There was no reason for blood to be shed. Her lips parted instinctively as she spoke in an authoritative tone. "You will not refuse my request."

28

Silence filled the room. Tovey puffed her chest out, accepting the words she had spoken. For once, anxiety and fear didn't plague her; instead, a calm stillness settled in. She waited for Arden to speak, refusing to plead for him to reconsider. Tovey did not ask. She commanded.

"You impress me," Arden said.

A smile crept over her face. "This war has nothing to do with anything between Silvis and Abolend. You weren't fighting before this, and you shouldn't fight because of it."

Arden's face went blank. "Love, we've fought each other for centuries."

Not knowing the history of war, Tovey cursed Cullus for the lack of information. "But you aren't fighting in this instant. Correct?"

"Correct," Arden stated.

"And war is rising because of the prophecy?"

"Yes, dearie."

"So this war has everything to do with me. All because I was born with eyes like these." Tovey's fingers graced her face before falling to her side. "You called me a demon, but I am not one. Why would anyone fight a war over a fable that couldn't be further from the truth? I'm not a monster. I haven't come from a hellish world to wreak havoc. I'm a girl who wants to live in peace alongside my people.

"I don't want your people or ours to die over something useless. Why should the kingdoms fight? Over what? None of it makes any sense. If I am the catalyst to fight, please allow me to be the cause to back down and away from the fear of an old prophecy."

Chief Arden smiled, his perfect teeth shimmering. He stood and walked to her side. "Unlike Abolend, we still have humanity." Arden lowered his voice so Cullus couldn't hear. "I don't understand this game we are playing. How did you convince him you were a servant?"

Tovey's mind ached, not understanding. "Chief Arden, I've told you, I am."

He shook his head, wrinkles crossing his forehead. "I will consider your plea."

"Thank you."

Arden turned his back, returning to his throne.

"If you agree, I promise on my life that Abolend will back down," she said powerfully.

Cullus scowled at her as Arden sat, shaking his head. "That's a bold promise."

"But a promise I am willing to make. My life." Tovey meant it. It was the only thing of value she could offer the dryads.

Arden lifted a hand, snapping. "Firth, prepare a room and a change of clothes for Tovey."

Firth scurried forward, gesturing Tovey toward the wooden door behind the throne. He shuffled across the floor, eyes wide.

"Not without Cullus," Tovey said.

Cullus cast a sardonic smile at Chief Arden, who raised his thick eyebrows.

The chief's full lips pursed before he bobbed his head eagerly. "All right, all right. Bring her dog too."

Cullus's smile turned into a glare. He dragged his feet, letting his boots scuff the ancient floor of the kapok, looking askance at the chief.

Firth led them through a narrow passage lined with unmarked doors. The hallway ended at a spiraling staircase ascending to the top of the tree. They didn't stop climbing until they'd nearly reached the top. Firth creaked open a heavy door to a lavish room complete with a bed, dressing drawers, and an oversize washing tub filled with steaming water.

Tovey blinked rapidly, taking in the beauty of the wooden room with leaves popping from the walls. She had never seen a room so extravagant. Tovey's feet carried her as if she were floating to the edge of the bed. She touched the blankets, relishing in the soft, fluffy fabric beneath her skin. Pressing her weight into her palm, she sank into the bed, beaming toward Cullus.

Firth spoke before she could. "Never slept in a bed before?"

"No," Tovey mumbled.

Firth shuddered like her response had somehow slapped him

across the face. Fishy breath brimmed the room when his jaw dropped. "I was joking. I apologize. Where'd you have the girl sleeping?" Firth snapped.

Cullus puffed his chest, stepping eye to eye with Firth.

Regret canvased Firth's face. "Apologies, Prince Cullus," he muttered.

"Leave us." Cullus's face turned the color of a cherry. "I don't need to answer to you."

Firth stepped backward out of the door. "It will be locked." He snickered, slamming the wooden door. "I'll be back with clothing! Ticktock, back soon!" His voice echoed in the hollow tree.

"He makes me uncomfortable," Tovey admitted.

"Yes, honestly, me too. If that is Silvis's hand, Arden does not have a handle on his kingdom. I would never trust Firth in my court." He paused, forehead wrinkling. "Are you all right?"

Tovey nodded.

"You were uncannily brave out there. I cannot believe you told Arden he wasn't allowed to say no. I nearly fell over." His smooth laugh soothed her nerves.

"I didn't know what else to do."

"You did wonderfully. I knew you could do it, but I think you made progress with him."

"Do you think he will reconsider?" Tovey asked honestly, not sure if she could trust Arden.

"Yes, otherwise we wouldn't be here. Arden will deliberate for hours to days."

"Days?" Her jaw dropped.

"He isn't sharp. He could barely keep up with our conversation, acting like he had no idea what we were even asking of him. It will take him days to understand what is happening."

Tovey glared at Cullus.

"What is it?"

"Don't you think this is strange? Why did they bow? Why did *you* bow?" Tovey's stomach twisted at the thought of standing before the crowd.

"You scared them. Your blindfold burned off your face, and you defended yourself with Firth. If they hadn't bowed, you could have incinerated the entire town." Cullus smirked.

Tovey scowled. "You know that isn't true."

"But they don't know that." A spark ignited in his eyes. "I bowed because I saw someone in front of me who deserves my respect." Tovey's heart fluttered. "Don't forget these are the people who want to attack Abolend because you exist."

Tovey huffed. "I haven't forgotten, but they don't seem to be preparing for anything."

"A ruse. If they came to Abolend, we wouldn't show our hand either. My father wouldn't be preparing to invade a kingdom unprovoked."

Tovey nodded with uncertainty.

"Why don't you rest? Get comfortable."

Cullus stood still at the door for hours. He'd never resembled a guard as much as he did now. He closed his eyes, and Tovey undressed, shedding the skin of a servant. Carefully, she lowered herself into the milky water of the tub resting in the corner of the room.

"You can open your eyes." Warmth filled her soul. Her fingers washed the layered dirt from their travels away with heated mineral water. Cullus kept his eyes directed out the plate-size window in the room, where a knot had formed in the tree.

"This is incredible," Tovey said, delighting in the water.

"What?"

"The bath. We always splash clean. It is rare to sit in a basin, nonetheless a warm one. This"—she cupped the water—"is like I am floating like a feather in the sky."

Cullus's face twisted with anger. Tovey knew he envied Silvis for offering more hospitality in one minute than Abolend had given her in her entire life.

His eyes darted to her before locking on the round window once more. "If you lean back, it is easier to wash your hair than splashing it like that."

"I . . . I don't think I can." Tovey shook her dry head, eyes welling with tears.

Cullus locked eyes with her. "What's wrong?" He frowned.

Tears ran down Tovey's face. Cullus left his post. He sat on the floor next to the tub, dipping his hand in the water to hold hers.

"I promised my sister, Nadia, that I would defect."

"I remember."

"The collective drowned her in front of me." Tovey relayed the story of her sister's murder to Cullus as her tears rushed like a waterfall.

"You won't drown in this tub." Cullus rubbed his thumb on her hand.

"I'm terrified of it."

"You won't, see?" He raised his hand laced with hers from the tub. "I won't let anything happen to you."

Heart pounding, she steadied her thoughts, thinking of nothing more than his touch, his voice, how she trusted Cullus with every fiber of her being.

"Sink into it, just a little." Cullus kept his eyes locked on hers as she lowered into the basin.

Tovey sank, sure to keep her neck above the water.

"Do you want me to wash your hair?" Cullus asked. Turning red, Tovey bit her cheek. Cullus shifted behind the tub. "I'm going to let go of your hand, but I'm right here."

"Don't." Her voice cracked.

"I won't. Not until you are ready."

The two sat in silence. Tovey leaned back over the basin, and he rested his lips on her forehead. He sank his other hand into the tub, cupping bubbly water to pour over her scalp. He rubbed her head, sending warmth surging through her body.

Finishing, he released his hand from her hair. Tovey sat hunched in the water. In the reflection of the mirror above the dressing table, Tovey watched Cullus survey her skin, stretched thinly across her back. She knew what he saw, deep lashes of purple and white. His fingers traced the fissures in her skin.

"Don't touch them," she snapped. She hated the scars. They were embarrassing, a sign of her inability to please.

"Sorry. How did it happen?"

Tovey snorted. "Which one?"

Cullus's mouth shut. His eyes welled.

Tovey watched him process the notion that every scar had been a different event. She knew he didn't understand the severity of the brutality she'd faced before they met. "So . . ." Her shoulders sank beneath the water. "What do you think?"

Cullus raised his eyebrows. Unspeaking, he sat beside the tub, his sleeve drenched with water as he held her hand. His eyes met hers with questions.

"Of Chief Arden," she clarified, her face reddening. "This is your first time meeting him, right?"

"Yes." Cullus fell deep into thought. "He is dangerous, and I hate that waiting here is our only option."

"Me too." Biting her lip, Tovey tilted her head. "He seemed to know a lot about Abolend. And you."

"I knew Silvis had a chief, but we've been unsuccessful getting spies here. Humans in disguise don't work, and it is impossible to reach anyone in their kingdom. It is like they have a hive mind, all loyal to the chief without even a shred of uncertainty. I know they function differently than us, but I had no idea he was so . . ." He paused, unable to find the right word.

"Young?" Tovey suggested.

"Immature. Dryads age slower than we do. They live twice as long. Arden looks young, but he has had the throne my entire life. My mother mentioned the chief took the throne two years before I was born. She tried to tell me stories of the dryads, but Father didn't want me to hear of them."

A knock on the door caused them to jump. Water sloshed onto the floor. The door unlocked. With a creaking clang, Firth popped his head into the room, surveying Tovey.

"Get out!" Cullus widened his shoulders, rushing to the door. He palmed Firth's face, pushing him backward. Firth squawked, dropping a pile of clothing onto a stand beside the door. He peered down his nose, his haunting giggle filling the stagnant air. Firth's eyes darted from Tovey to Cullus before he disappeared with another clunk of the lock.

"What's with him?" Tovey's head shifted sideways, and she wrapped her arms around her body.

"He saw you kiss my ear after I knelt for you. And in the hall, you addressed me as Cullus, neglecting my title."

Tovey rubbed the back of her neck.

"So they know, Tovey." Cullus's eyes were sorrowful.

"Know what?"

"That the prince of Abolend has a weakness."

Her body pulsed acid through her veins, rocking her as if she were a leaf in a river. That was why Cullus had pulled his hand away in the street. That was what Firth had whispered to Chief Arden. She berated herself in her mind. She had been trying so hard to follow these new rules of negotiation, of freely speaking and being honest, that she hadn't even considered how dangerous it was to show weakness.

"I'm sorry. I didn't realize . . ."

"Don't be. I'm sure word is already on the way to Abolend as we speak. What's done is done, and I'm not sorry for it." A dimple formed on his cheek, but his eyes were filled with sadness. "The heir to the throne betrayed the crown by falling in love with a servant. I'm sure we will hear Lady Rena screaming from here."

"Lady Rena? Why her?" Tovey croaked.

"She's the highest highborn woman, the person I'm expected to wed and bear heirs with."

"*Her?*" Tovey's stomach twisted. "Do you like her?"

Cullus shook his head. "Love doesn't matter in a marriage. Not for princes. Even if it does for me." He gulped air. "Come. Get dressed."

Cullus handed Tovey a towel and then turned his back to her. She wrapped herself in it, watching him remove his shirt and lean over the tub, scrubbing his arms. Water dripped from her skin to the wooden floor.

"You can get in if you want to," Tovey suggested.

"No, I don't want to let my guard down for too long." Cullus had a glint of danger in his eyes. "There is a lake by Frilliam. I will bathe there after we leave."

She brightened, leaving puddled footsteps trailing from the tub to the dresser. She sorted through the pile of clothes Firth had delivered.

"They are all dresses." She groaned, taken aback by how much disgust sat in her throat.

"What were you expecting?"

"Pants." She grimaced. "I like the ones I took from the laundry."

"Men wear pants," Cullus said plainly. "I'm not surprised they didn't bring you any."

"And why is that? Doesn't it seem silly that I'm supposed to walk around the woods in a heavy dress?"

"Women aren't supposed to walk around the woods." He laughed, but Tovey remained stern.

"But we do. *I do.* I wear pants and walk around the woods."

"Then we will retrieve them. You can change when we leave. Until then, we are still playing their game. Don't forget that. You have to stay calm and act like you aren't a threat."

Tovey huffed. She sifted through the clothing, veering away from every gray- or red-toned item. Her heart lurched as she saw a golden dress sparkling like the sap on the trees. It fell to the floor and had embroidered leaves, like the Tenbris. The bodice had one strap that crossed the front of the gown, leaving the other shoulder bare.

Slipping the sparkling dress over her head, Tovey was elated with the gown. The fabric was light and smooth, like it was made of air. It was snug from her torso to her waist, where it loosened into a gentle flow, allowing her legs to move freely. A polished hair stick topped with a carved sparrow sat on the dresser.

"I've always wanted to try one of these," Tovey said, grabbing the stick. "We were allowed to tie our hair in knots if it needed to be out of the way, but we weren't allowed to use any objects. Vanity is a right reserved for highborns." Tovey twisted the stick into her hair, wrapping what little was left of her hair, keeping it off her neck.

Cullus shook his head, teeth gleaming. A flyaway hair popped out at her hairline. His smooth fingers twirled the soft hair into a curl. He lowered his mouth toward her skin, kissing her bare shoulder. Shivers raced from his kiss, vibrating through her body. He inched his way up her neck, kissing with a feathery touch until he found her lips.

Filled with warmth, she swooned at him through her lashes. His head tilted as his lips parted. She mirrored him, butterflies fluttering in her chest. She pressed her lips against his. Unlike before, they kissed hungrily, like they may never kiss each other again. Her body was pulsing. He pulled her in closer, his heart pounding against her chest.

The world and the problems they faced melted as their mouths moved as one. Tovey brushed her nose against his as they pulled apart. She pressed her ear against his chest. His heart beat faster. She clasped her eyes shut, and her lower lip trembled.

"I'm scared." Her voice cracked.

Cullus tightened his arms around her, squeezing her gently. He rested his cheek atop her head. His fingers grazed back and forth across her back, soothing her.

"How can so much power live in such a tiny body?" he joked, attempting to lighten the mood.

"The same way so much smell can linger in Firth's eight teeth."

Howling with laughter, the two plopped onto the bed.

"I think I could sleep for the rest of my life," Cullus admitted.

Tovey curled into his arms, letting her eyes close. "Me too."

29

A frenzied knock on the door woke them. Tovey and Cullus sat up, scrambling away from each other on the bed. Without invitation, Firth popped his annoying hooked nose into the room once again.

"Chief Arden has made a decision." Firth bowed. "Come, come." He put forth a wavering hand, ushering the two out of the room.

"Of course, as soon as we fall asleep, he decides to make his decision." Cullus yawned, rubbing his face.

Tovey glared at Cullus, silencing his banter. She slipped her worn boots on, neglecting to choose any of the impractical sandals sitting below the dressing table. The dress was enough of a compromise to please the dryads. Her fingers grazed the hilt of her dagger tucked in her boot, ensuring it was ready in case of emergency. Tovey stepped out of the threshold, smiling coldly toward Firth, who eyed her with a satisfied grin.

"Chief Arden will be pleased to see you." Firth winked.

"And I hope I'm pleased to hear his decision," Tovey said, returning his sentiment.

Cullus stifled a laugh as they waded through the twisting herbaceous halls. Tovey's heart sped. The throne room was more intimidating than standing in line with the commoners waiting to see King Mallum. Chief Arden was unpredictable. Every time Tovey had thought she had him figured out, he'd changed course. King Mallum was calculable. Tovey traced the rings on the steps, hoping to distract her mind as they descended the spiraling staircase in a dizzying labyrinth of spins.

Tovey's heart raced as the three entered the throne room, where Chief Arden sat hunched. He sat upright when his sights fell upon Tovey. His eyes seemed to smile even when his mouth did not. Tovey and Cullus resumed their positions before the chief.

"Have a fun few hours?" Arden asked.

Tovey and Cullus neglected to reply, both wanting to please the chief in the unlikely scenario that he could still be swayed in their favor one last time.

"Puppy, go sit." Arden flicked his wrist, shooing Cullus. "This is a conversation for those who actually hold power."

Arden sneered at Tovey. Firth ran behind the throne. After fetching a wooden chair, he placed the seat in the corner of the room, and Cullus sat. Like a punished child, Cullus followed commands while he shot a terrifying snarl toward Chief Arden.

"Good boy, Cully." The chief clapped.

Tovey's mouth dropped as veins popped from Cullus's neck, tightening beneath his skin.

"Now, Tovey," Arden said, "I've considered your request."

She bowed her head, forcing her face into a relaxed smile, the same fake grin Cullus had worn upon entering the forsaken kingdom.

"And it is a no."

Her chest deflated. Tovey wasn't surprised. She had suspected Arden's denial. Her mind spun with questions, eyes buttoning shut.

"Tovey." Chief Arden's voice rang in her head.

Tovey peered at his warm face behind a solemn mask. A too-perfect smile still sat on his face. "Yes, Chief Arden?"

Cullus cracked his neck, his lips tightening.

"Chief Arden? No need to be formal. We all hold power, do we not? Well, all of us besides your pet over there." He winked at Cullus before turning back to Tovey. "You do hold power, don't you?"

Tovey remained silent.

"Firth," Arden snapped.

The hand lumbered to the side of the room where Cullus sat. Firth pulled a bow from a concealed rack before stringing an arrow.

Tovey's gut twisted, her body trembling at the sight of an archer. The strength she had mustered was disappearing, melting back into the terrified defector who had watched Sylvia die. Shivering, she surveyed Arden.

"I'm going to ask you one more time. Do you have power, Tovey?"

"No."

Firth straightened his arm. In a flash, he had pulled the string, creaking the bow's limbs, aiming it at Cullus. The wooden arrow shot with a flick of Arden's finger, splitting the air. The arrow bolted toward Cullus's head. Tovey's infernal scream raked the walls in the room, her eyes casting a purple hue as they flickered in a flame of vibrancy. Her blood boiled with anger and fear.

The arrow grazed Cullus's hair, sticking inches into the wall behind him.

"That was just to scare you," Arden hissed. "Nice shot, Firth."

It was barely a miss, and Tovey had done nothing. She hadn't stopped it. She didn't know how. If Firth were not an exceptional shot or if Cullus had shifted, he would have been dead, and it would've been her fault.

Cullus's hands rushed over his head too late. He was in shock, his face draining of color as he popped out of his seat.

"Sit down, Cullus!" Arden barked.

Cullus stood still, unspeaking, surveying the room.

"Oh, come on, puppy. Sit." Arden laughed. "Let me ask you one more time, Tovey, for good measure. Do you have power?" He paused, inspecting his nail beds. "I do. I'm the chief. That's my power." He smiled, standing to circle the room once more. "Now that I've shared mine with you, please show me yours, dearie." He lifted his finger to Firth, who nocked another arrow on the string. Arden lowered his voice to a whisper. "He's not going to miss this time, love."

Spiders crawled under Tovey's pale skin. She darted her eyes from Cullus to Arden, both of which were unreadable statues well versed in hiding all signs of stress. Of course, she knew she had power, but there wasn't a way to control it, and there wasn't a way to use it on command. The earth could shake, the clouds could roll in, or she could blast straight through everyone in this room, leaving the wooden hall dripping in blood. The dryads had seen her incinerate her blindfold. They already knew.

Eyeing Firth's shaking bicep, straining from the resistance of the bow, she blanked. Any form of deception leaked out of her mind. She needed to save Cullus.

"Wait!" she shouted. "Yes, I think I might have some form of power."

"Tovey, don't," Cullus pleaded.

Arden's long finger hushed Cullus. "Thank you for being honest. I already heard that you do. And I heard it is quite illuminating." He winked with a sickening knowing. "My ears are everywhere, Prince." He smiled toward Cullus. "Firth!" He flicked his wrist, and the arrow released.

Tovey's mind flashed to Sylvia as the arrow soared toward Cullus. He sat frozen with fear for a second too long before throwing himself to the side. The arrow was too fast, and he would be hit no matter how he maneuvered. Time didn't exist as her voice ripped through the frozen air. Her hellish scream was disconnected and distant. Cullus's eyes widened, and he stared his death in the face, the bolt inching toward his nose.

Amethyst lightning lit the room. The arrow caught on fire in a blaze of lilac, just as her blindfold had done, burning to ash and dusting Cullus's face with soot. Her legs buckled, brain throbbing in her skull before she fell to her knees, her palms pressed against the floor. She curled her nails, biting at the ancient wood.

"Brilliant!" Arden shouted. "All right, I agree. We will back down from Abolend."

"What?" Tovey muttered, pulling strength from the floor of the kapok, attempting to steady herself.

"I said I agree. We won't attack. Cullus, go tell your father he is safe." He lowered his voice. "For now, of course."

Eyes wide, the cinder-dusted prince rushed to Tovey's side, helping her stand on her feet. "You've lost your mind!" Cullus growled at Arden. "You could have hurt her! You don't understand the toll that takes."

"He was going to kill you," Tovey whispered.

"Calm down, Cullus. I wouldn't hurt Tovey. We are friends, after all. Aren't we?" He cast a slight smile at Tovey. "That's why she's going to stay here with me until I hear from my ears that you've held up your end of the bargain."

"No." Cullus gripped Tovey tightly. "She comes with me."

"Not if you want me to agree to your terms, sweet dog. Now you have to agree to mine. Tovey stays with me."

Tovey steadied herself with Cullus's broad shoulders. She scowled, scorning Arden. Her face twisted into a snarl of hate. Tovey despised the chief, but she couldn't forget her mission: to save lives. She was here to protect Abolend, no matter the cost.

"I accept," Tovey announced.

Arden smiled with joy.

"You can't," Cullus muttered before raising his voice. "She cannot accept. First and foremost, we are here together, sent from Abolend. Our presence constitutes the laws of war are abided by, and keeping a member of the parley committee hostage nullifies that law. I do suppose you know the laws. Don't you, king?"

Arden scoffed.

"Oh, sorry, I forgot. You are no king." Cullus curled his lip. "Merely the current team leader. Bravo."

Chief Arden cast a questioning glare at Firth, who lowered his head in agreement with Cullus. Arden's fingers tapped his leg. "But Tovey is her own person representing herself, is she not?"

"She's not. She's my servant, and you have no right to interfere, again the laws of war, or need I remind you?"

"I know the laws!" Arden growled.

"You don't. You put my life—a prince's life—in danger. You've already negated any trust on our side. You claim you don't trust our word, but had Tovey not performed a miracle, Abolend would've been here in days to avenge me, and your kingdom would've been in ashes."

Arden's jaw jutted forward. "Take your servant if you must, but, Tovey, if you ever wish to be free, you know where I am." Chief Arden bowed his head toward her. "One day, you will face the painful truth, and these comforting lies you tell yourself will crumble around you. Infatuation isn't love, dearie. Remember that."

Comforting lies and painful truths . . . Tovey shook her head at the chief, too exhausted to engage with him anymore.

Arden stood before the throne, his chest filling with air. "My word still stands, Tovey. I will back down from Abolend for you, not for him. But I need to receive word immediately."

Cullus's dimples applauded with a satisfied grin.

"Oh, and Cullus, if I ever hear Tovey is removed from her status as a servant or treated any differently, as we all know you treat her, be sure that your father will find out. You won't have to worry about attacks from Silvis. Abolend will tear itself apart over your blasphemy."

"Mind your business," Cullus snapped.

"Tovey is my business." Arden stepped toward Cullus.

Cullus spun on his heel and stomped out of the chamber. Tovey followed. He shoved the heavy doors open, revealing swirling cobbled paths filled with dryads' dulcet conversations while children played in the streets. Tovey watched a little girl who giggled and spun in dizzying spirals while her father strummed a stringed log. Plucky music rang in the statically charged air like a festival of energy.

Tovey was wrong; Silvis was Abolend's antithesis. A stitch pulled at Tovey's heart. Would it have been the right choice to stay in the foreign kingdom while Cullus confronted King Mallum on his own? Arden wasn't someone she wanted to be around, but he made a lot of valid arguments, including some points Tovey didn't want to simmer in her mind much longer.

The faceted gems adorning Tovey's dress caught in the sunset, shimmering like she was made of gold. The dryads watched with kind faces. Children waved at her, and a few of the adults bowed their heads. It was unsettling and invigorating to be treated like a person, an actual respectable human being. And yet it was still more than that. They treated her the way people in Abolend acted toward highborns, toward Cullus, toward the king.

She was no longer a useless invisible object that could be cast aside and replaced without a second thought. In Silvis, she wasn't a servant. She was alive, seen, heard, and respected. Chills covered her skin.

None of the dryads were disfigured, impaired, or bound by inhumane rules keeping them oppressed and subdued. They all seemed jovial, their lives seemed meaningful, and most of all, they were free. The warm breeze carried the scent of cedar, and it filled her nostrils. She cast a sincere smile back toward the dryads, bidding them a goodbye that felt all too soon. The dryads bowed to her simultaneously, and her heart swelled with warmth for those she didn't even know.

Tovey whispered, "Until we meet again."

30

A strange sense of emptiness enveloped Tovey. The sensation of static energy dissipated the moment Tovey and Cullus passed through the woven tree archway, the warm grasses of Silvis leaving her nose for the familiar musky scent of fall. Coolness pricked at her skin, triggering a race of goose bumps around her body. Craning her neck for one last view, Tovey took in the kingdom, grateful they were more understanding than Abolend despite Arden's brashness.

For once, an air of peace fell over the two. They shuffled through the bushy terrain, heading straight toward Frilliam.

"Can you believe it?" Cullus wiped the ash from his face, staining his tunic.

"No." Tovey smiled with glee. For now, they had succeeded, but still, the taste of sour milk tickled the back of Tovey's tongue. There was no justifiable reason to worry. Chief Arden had agreed to stop any advances, and now King Mallum had no reason to fight. Silvis was not going to attack. Tovey had proven herself trustworthy despite her untamed power. All was well.

Tovey glanced toward Cullus, worry in her eyes. "Your father will stop the war, right?"

Cullus grabbed both of her hands, stopping their walk. "Yes, there is no threat to Abolend. He wouldn't fight unprovoked. We've won, Tovey. You've won." Cullus beamed.

Tovey forced a smile, her chest tight. "Do you think everything will calm down now?"

Cullus touched the back of her neck, drawing her attention to his eyes. "Absolutely. We aren't going to wage an unnecessary war."

"Is any war necessary?"

Cullus frowned at the question.

"I'm sorry. I know I should be happy. I-I'm not sure what's next. For me, you know?" Tovey focused on the ground.

"We will figure it out, don't worry. We need to celebrate!" Cullus lifted Tovey off the ground, spinning her in a circle.

The sun sparkled off the gems on her dress, casting little rainbows that bounced off the trees around them. The hazel sparkles in his eyes caught the light as his melodic laugh melted the tension. It was official: the final war was over before it had begun. Tovey's lips curled into a relieved grin as she took in Cullus's face. Stepping closer, she leaned her head into his shoulder.

"I can't wait to tell Frilliam!" she said.

"I'm sure he misses you. I know I would."

Beaming, Tovey couldn't find words, her heart swollen with bliss.

"Let's go get your pants back."

"That can be our next adventure. Pants for the masses." Tovey laughed, free from guilt.

She watched his dimpled grin disappear like smoke. Stone-faced, Cullus no longer reflected the laughable sentiment, instead stilling into a statue of a hardened king. His brow shaped forward, shadowing his eyes. His gaze shot into the forest like a spearhead. His knees bent as he moved in front of her, silent as the wind.

"What—"

"Don't speak," he commanded.

Tovey eyed the forest around her, fingers pulling the flowing fabric of the golden gown into a ball, ready to run. A voice growled from the darkness of the bushes as an ironclad guard dressed in a crimson-and-gold tabard stepped before them on the path. He raked his beady black eyes across Tovey, nose wrinkling at the sight of her.

"Disgusting." He spat at Tovey's feet before kneeling to the ground before Cullus. "Prince Cullus, we were sent here by King Mallum. All hail!"

Tovey questioned his plurality, but the answer came faster than a throwing dagger. The guard welcomed two more Abolend soldiers, who moved into a triangle around her. The evening sun reddened the skies, lighting their blood-colored garb aglow. The guards lumbered out of the shadows. A sickening clanging sea of men stood before them. Boisterous voices began chanting.

"Hail! Hail King Mallum, leader of the brave, father of the land."

"The king wished us to be hasty about bringing back the cargo." The guard kept his eyes away from Tovey's gaze, reluctant to lock eyes with her.

"Cargo?" Prince Cullus questioned, his gaze settling on Tovey.

"What do you think he meant, brother?" A boy dressed in a bloodred tunic laughed, jumping from behind a tree. He was blond, stood with arrogance, and had the same crooked smile as Cullus.

"Elias? What are you doing here?" Cullus's brow furrowed.

"Father sent me to get the job done. He knows I'm more capable than you," Elias teased, prodding a finger between Cullus's ribs.

"I don't think you are." He shoved Elias away, attempting to be playful, but Tovey could read the fear in his eyes. "I still don't understand. What are *you*, specifically, doing here? Father wouldn't send you out to aid me. Two princes away from the kingdom? I'm sure the battalion of men was more than enough. Do not think you are wise enough to fool me, Elias. What are you doing here?"

"Oh, come on, Cull. I'm helping you! You are getting a team to help you procure the cargo while I may be leading another team. Secret mission stuff." Elias surveyed Tovey with icy blue eyes. He lowered his voice. "Does it bother you that *it* almost looks human? And why is it dressed like that?" Elias choked. "I could vomit." Cullus locked eyes with Tovey, who was unveiled in the forest. "When Father said a demon was on Valledera, I expected something a little scary, not some ugly hag."

Tovey bit her lip, limbs folding into each other, wishing she didn't exist.

"Well, soldiers, I hate to be the bearer of bad news, but I will be escorting her myself. Please return ahead of us to let King Mallum know of our arrival. Please ensure my path is clear. I have an important message to bring to him—one that cannot be written, for I fear ears of the dryads have infiltrated our ranks."

"Spies?" one of the men asked. "But how?"

"That is something for me and the king to discuss. Clear our path." Cullus gestured for the men to move.

Elias twisted his face in disgust as the group shifted, the men unsteady in their shoes.

"Your Royal Highness, King Mallum told us not to leave your side, even if you protested. Our mission is to escort you." A potato-nosed man raised a hand and gestured to the forest, which came alive with metallic rattling. Another handful of guards appeared from the darkness.

Men surrounded Tovey, growing like weeds around her. Dust muddied the air as horses led squealing carts of supplies, haphazardly making their way over young saplings, scarring the land. Tovey was isolated in the sea of men. She, too, would be nothing more than a scarred sapling, never getting the chance to grow from beneath Abolend's boot.

She wanted to cry, but she knew emotional outbursts led to more punishment. Tovey rubbed her shoulder where the trainers had whipped her for mourning Nadia's death. She had cried too much, according to Vivian. She wouldn't act irrationally now. Her hands folded in front of her.

Cullus shuffled on the dirt trail, an audience of eyes analyzing his every move, waiting for direction. Standing silently, Tovey didn't dare speak, knowing Cullus would handle this. He would fix the insanity that had befallen them.

Elias clicked his tongue at his brother shamefully. "This is why Father says I'm going to be king. Your strategy is miserable at best. Must have gotten that from your mother."

Rage burned in Cullus's eyes. "Guards, distance!" he shouted.

The guards stepped a few feet away. He lowered his voice. "You know the throne is mine, little brother. Tell me, what is this secret mission?"

"It wouldn't be a secret if I told you." Elias grinned.

"You have to tell me. I outrank you." Cullus pushed a finger into his brother's chest, leaning to be eye to eye with the boy.

"No, Cull." Elias shook his head. "Father said I can't tell you."

Cullus rubbed his lips together as the wind blew through his hair. He raised his dimpled chin, taking in a deep breath. Cullus thrust a fist of white knuckles into the air as his smooth voice rang out. "Hail! Hail Abolend! Hail King Mallum!"

"Leader of the brave, father of the land!" the guards echoed, and Elias joined in, tilting his head with squinted eyes.

An insolent smile formed on Cullus's face, sending rancid bile racing to Tovey's whitened lips. Her heart palpitated, chills consuming her body as she cried dry tears. Cullus had never resembled his father until now.

Face as hard as granite, he shouted, "Soldiers, secure the cargo."

31

Tovey gripped the crimson gown that had been shoved into her hands. She stood frozen, numb with shock. She had no thoughts or feelings. There was only emptiness. One of the iron guards placed his stout hand behind the small of her neck, pinching her with meaty calluses.

"Change out of those rags, Servant." The guard's flying spit splattered the elegant dress she wore. "Change, now!" Tovey's vision blurred, searching for Cullus. She didn't bother to wipe the guard's spit from her arms. None of this felt real. Metallic helmets bobbed in the sea of men as Cullus stood behind the front row, watching.

She wanted to scream for him, but she didn't. Instead, she just existed, like her soul had left her body, leaving an empty vessel standing in her place. The guard pulled the sparrow from her hair, tossing it to the dirt.

"No weapons."

Tovey looked suspiciously at Cullus. He grabbed the stick, nodding toward the soldier before he turned, disappearing into the crowd.

A guard shoved Tovey into the soil, his heel pressed against her spine. "Get dressed, now."

He kicked her in the ribs, the blow bringing her mind back into her body. Coughing, she scrambled, eyes locked on the ground. She scurried to her knees, wriggling out of the dress. She held the fabric to her chest while the scars across her back exposed themselves.

"Disgrace!" someone shouted.

"No one is afraid of you, demon!" Another laughed. "Look at her. Not even her trainers liked her."

Tovey's fingers trembled as she stepped into the garb of a servant. Tovey had always wanted the trainers to like her, to love her. They were, in a twisted way, her family.

"Abomination! You should go back to hell, where you came from!" a man's voice croaked.

They were right. She was an abomination. With or without her eyes, Tovey would never stop being the demon everyone saw her as. These guards didn't know what horrors she could cause or that a terrifying power loomed somewhere inside her, waiting to strike.

Someone threw a blindfold made of the familiar scratchy hemp. Tovey stood, eyes closed as she tied the fabric around her eyes. Tears wet the fabric as she wept silently. Her twisting stomach screamed for Cullus to do something, yet he did nothing. She refused to watch him, locking her eyes on the grassy path instead. She never wanted to see him amongst his people.

"Cull!" Elias shouted. The boy pranced after his half brother. "I'm leaving if you can handle this."

Men shifted. Cullus must have been moving through the crowd, inching closer. Tovey's heart sputtered, wishing this were over, that he would save her.

"Leaving where?" Cullus asked, less than an arm's reach away from her.

"Nice try, brother." Elias punched Cullus in the arm before scampering off into the foliage.

Cullus shook his head as he wove through the cavalry of men to the front of the soldiers, surveying the ranks, leaving her side once again. She wanted to call to him, but her lips didn't move. Tovey prayed he would figure something out soon.

Becoming Abolend's servant once more was worse than swimming through the muck under the latrine. An executioner was likely awaiting word of her arrival. She'd never signed up to be treated this way. None of the girls did. Even the girls who were so-called volunteers were forced to do so. Enough was enough; Cullus needed to take charge, be a leader. Now was his time to show Abolend his heart.

The guard snapped his hand at the base of her skull once more. Again, the guard shoved her. She plummeted toward the hardened dirt. Her face met the rocks, and they bit at her cheeks. She spat blood. His boot pummeled between her shoulders as he pinned her to the ground. He wrangled her arms, twisting them behind her back. Chains choked her wrists. She was pulled to her feet wearing a belt of metal, tethered to a horse whose rider didn't even bother to pass her a glance.

"Move!" someone shouted. The line of soldiers propelled forward in an explosive uproar of metal that clashed with the stillness of the forest. "We don't stop until Abolend!" The chains yanked at her waist, pulling her forward, and she stumbled behind the horse.

The night passed as Tovey was tugged along by the horse, which endlessly yanked her hips forward as her feet scuffed over the battered ground. Three guards trailed behind her with drawn swords, prodding their sharpened tips against her back. They never stopped moving.

The iron men treated her as if she were about to grow wings and burn them alive like the golden dragon on their chests. That wasn't her. That was their beloved dragon, Cullus.

Her ears ached from sifting through the noise of squeaking wheels and rattling armor, searching for the familiar smooth voice she longed to hear. It never came.

The sun floated above the hilly horizon in a shifting sea of white, the morning as gloomy as her deadening soul. Her heels chafed, desperate for a break.

"The prince is impressive," a young guard said from behind her.

"Couldn't agree more, Calvin," a prominent voice said.

The third grunted in agreement.

"I would never have thought of using the demon to infiltrate our enemy's kingdom. Who would have thought such a powerful weapon would be hiding in a girl's collective? Incredible."

Trembling overcame her body. She hated them. She hated the word *demon*.

"Would you have thought of that, Rus?"

"No, Calvin. Shut your yap. We get it. Prince Cullus is admirable," the blustering voice boomed.

Tovey raised her eyebrows. She agreed with Rus. Calvin needed to stop talking. It made everything worse.

"He is more than admirable. We now have information on the intricacies of Silvis. Prince Cullus, all hail, followed the devil into the heart of our enemy kingdom. He somehow convinced her to do his dirty work, and now he is bringing back the prize, a monstrous girl who has already begun helping us destroy an unsuspecting kingdom. It's brilliant. When the time is right, I know King Mallum will have us crush those humanoid brutes into a pulp while they are none the wiser."

Tovey tripped as the tip of a sword prodded into her back, piercing her skin. Spiking pain shot through her nerves, but it was admittedly more diminutive than the agony of her shattering heart. Cullus had betrayed her. No, this was deeper than betrayal. He had used her as a pawn. This entire time she was nothing more to him than a chess piece in a game she couldn't see.

The plan to defuse the tension hadn't been real. It had been a mission to walk straight into Silvis's throne room and survey Arden's weaknesses. Closing her eyes, she envisioned Silvis. It was peaceful, silent. There weren't blacksmiths banging armor or weapons on anvils. There weren't armed guards. She and Cullus had walked into the place without even a question from a dryad. Cullus had even admitted that Abolend knew nothing about Silvis. They hadn't even known Arden's name. But now . . . now they knew everything.

Abolend was always going to attack. It wasn't Silvis that

wanted to wage war against them because of Tovey. It was Abolend wanting to destroy kind people. Mallum might have known that they would treat Tovey with kindness. Though they'd called her a demon, they hadn't tried to imprison her. Arden hadn't even seemed afraid of her. He was more curious than anything. Mallum's plan was to kill Tovey. He hadn't been able to find her, so his second-best option was destroying the place that would harbor her.

Abolend guards hadn't come after them because they'd already known Cullus was with her. All those nights of hiding the smoke from their fires and covering their tracks . . . It was useless. The days spent jumping at every unseen noise were pointless. They'd been running from nothing. They'd been hiding from no one. The guards had been a day or so off their trail the entire time, following them in a battalion of men.

Cullus had admitted to sending letters to his father, but it wasn't like he'd said. It wasn't to keep King Mallum at bay; it was to keep him informed of their location, of Cullus's blasted progress in the grand scheme of war. He must have commenced plotting when he first noticed her in the dining hall, the day they first met. Cullus was smart. The blindfold had given her guise away then, and she'd fallen for his wicked game.

Cullus hadn't used her to prevent the final war; he'd exploited her to spark it. Everything they had been through was nothing more than a lie—comforting lies and painful truths.

Arden was right. Cullus didn't love her.

Her raging mind spun. Sweat rained down her face, loosening the fabric of the blindfold.

Nadia had warned her. Marka had warned her. Amile had

warned her. Gill had warned her. Even Chief Arden had warned her. This entire time, everyone had tried to wrench her out of Cullus's slimy grip, but they were afraid, horrified by the massive force Abolend presented. No one was a match for their power.

They were all fearful that she was already too far lost within the brainwashing that Cullus was putting her through. The world feared her.

Storms amassed in sunny skies when she felt threatened. Who wouldn't be terrified of that? She spat, disgusted with how she'd willingly kissed Cullus's deceitful lips, the taste of his breath still on her tongue. She'd foolishly admitted to loving him. She had fallen so naively into his trap, had fallen for his charm, his fake smile, and those annoying dimples. It was all part of an elaborate scheme to use her as a weapon.

He'd forced her powers out of her. He'd channeled them, encouraging her, telling her they could be harnessed. As if something as wild as a licking flame could be tamed. Apparently, she was so in control of her powers that the soldiers had had no other choice but to resort to imprisoning her with chains. She was a prisoner of war after saving Abolend from destruction. No. She'd saved them from nothing. She'd given them the power to know where to attack. She wasn't a hero. She was a tool. She wouldn't be aiding Abolend in anything. Not anymore.

"Boys, I can't stop thinking about Prince Cullus's plan, can you? How long do you think it took him to muster up a plan so deceitful? It will no doubt go down in history!" Calvin continued.

Tovey wanted to punch him square in his nose. She tripped again, a sword slashing at the back of her neck, and a white light of pain ripped into her vision. Twisting, she shot a blindfolded glare at the guards behind her. Mud blurred her sight of the three cretins as a blade slapped her cheek forward. Blood lapped across her chin, the irony taste of blood dripping across her lips.

"Mind the cargo, chap," Calvin muttered.

"Can't damage her too much," Rus added.

Heat churned in her chest, twisting her gut. She wasn't cargo. A blaze of amethyst light illuminated the inside of her blindfold. Craning her head side to side, she wriggled the soppy blindfold to the bridge of her nose and took in her surroundings for the first time. A rider sat on the horse in front of her, led by another six guards in rows of three. In front of that group was a carriage of supplies pulled by another horse and a rider. Farther ahead were another eight guards positioned in a square around a rider in a leather jerkin whose hair bounced carelessly on top of his head. Cullus.

Tovey's teeth ground together, and she huffed. Ears perked, she soaked in the sound behind her. Shutting her eyes, she counted as many feet as she could distinguish. There were at least a dozen men in front of and behind her. She was in the middle of a soldiers' parade—one girl against more than thirty trained guards, plus Cullus. There was no hope of escape.

She was tugged a few more steps forward as she battled within herself. She heard Nadia's voice in her head: *Never fail, Tovey. Defect.*

Her mind flashed to Terrowin. Cullus had said they wanted a war, but the people were already survivors of a war fought on an individual level. They didn't wish to use Tovey as a weapon. They wanted to offer her safety, like all the other defectors who had found a home there.

Her brain replayed the dryadic children playing in the streets of Silvis as the plucky music echoed in her memory. She shook her head at the freedom they had—the freedom she'd never experience. The dryads had had no weapons at the ready. No guards had swarmed the streets. They weren't ready to defend themselves. Arden had been playing them. He didn't want a war he wasn't even ready for. Arden's kingdom would perish because of her. Unless she did something. Soon.

32

The weather turned sour. Icy rain showered the company, and Tovey cursed the winter weather. With every drop, her body froze, turning blue. She was miserable. The men's worn boots trudged through the building sludge relentlessly. They were machines, and she couldn't keep up.

"Keep moving!" someone shouted.

If Tovey's hands hadn't been tied behind her back, she would've reached for her hidden dagger and fought her way out. She would've failed, but the idea gave her something to ponder other than the annoyance of mud pulling at her gown.

Tovey repeatedly crumbled to the ground. Exhaustion and hunger tore at her soul, diminishing her will to fight with every raindrop that cried from the sky. She lost count of the days.

The sun remained shrouded by charcoal smears of mist that made morning and night seem as if they were one. She stopped hoping she would see Cullus, and she wasn't sure what she would say if she did.

Calvin never stopped yapping about Cullus. The men were growing tired of him. Tovey wanted to yell at Calvin too. All he did was spout off about how wonderful Cullus was for turning her into a fool who was wholly inundated by his charm. Her mind clouded around the prince, and her brooding brain swirled more than Cullus's careless hair did.

"I can't stop thinking about how amazing Prince Cullus is. Can you?" Calvin paused. "Did you see the way she was dressed? The prince let her be paraded around like a princess in Silvis. What a smart idea. He let the servant feel secure right before he ripped it all away from her. She's nothing to us. Nothing but a weapon of destruction. She will be used until there is nothing left of the dryads, and then she will be thrown away like the highborns' leftovers. Trash."

Hateful thoughts toward Calvin filled her mind. She wanted to hurt him, to inflict pain as harmful as his words felt to her. A shiver from her evil musings nipped at her heart. She couldn't think like that, like one of them.

"Calvin, shut your blasted trap! We get it! Prince Cullus is a tactical mastermind. Now stop your yapping before I tie you up like her," the guard's booming voice snapped. The tip of his sword jabbed into her back, sending pain through her as it cut her skin.

"You wish you could tie me up like that, don't you?" Calvin chortled as Rus's snicker echoed.

"Shut it. I'm serious."

Calvin continued. "Too bad I'm not a weak, pathetic excuse for a human being. Imagine being so useless you couldn't even manage to be a servant, the lowest position in Abolend. She deserves to be treated like garbage. She asked for it. Don't you agree, Rus?"

The man grunted.

"For once, Calvin, you are making sense," the swordsman boomed.

"Good. Glad we all agree that the demon deserves to be shaped into a weapon." Calvin paused. "She chose this, and I think she'd choose it again."

Eyes on fire, Tovey let the piercing pain from the sword tip fuel the simmering coals in her chest.

"I chose none of this," she growled.

Her teeth ground together as she turned to face the guards. Her gaze fell upon the guard's sausage fingers wrapped around the hilt of the sword. The guard recoiled in recognition.

"Wait a minute. I-I know you!" the guard stammered.

"And I know you, Gorv," Tovey spat. Her teeth chomped together at the man who had beaten her in the alley the day she'd arrived in Abolend. She should have recognized his voice, but she'd tried hard to forget she'd ever encountered him.

"You're the bloody defector who is supposed to be dead! Boys, she's the defector," his blubbering lips stuttered. "What's her name? That master, she described this girl. I heard rumors of her. They called her Sylvia. She ain't dead. She's supposed to be dead!"

Tovey hated hearing Sylvia's name in his mouth. She held back a scream of frustration, sending out a low thunderous rumble that shook the swampy ground, sending pebbles scattering and plonking through puddles on the path. Hearing Calvin drone on for days about the mastermind Cullus was one thing, but the irrefutable pain paired with his headache-inducing rants was too much. Knowing that Gorv had been the one shoving a blade into her muscles broke her tolerance. She was done suffering.

"No, Gorv, I'm not dead." She smiled wickedly. "Haven't you heard? I'm undead," she lied, reveling in his fear. Embracing the forsaken name, she said, "I'm a demon." It felt good to say it in this context. The word didn't harm her now. It protected her; it gave her strength. "And my name's Tovey." She shook her head, the blindfold falling around her neck. "And don't ever let me hear you speak my name, or I will rip that sword from your hand and cut your slimy tongue out!"

A vile grin came over Tovey's face as fury burned through her pores. A purple hue grew before her eyes, sending a pulsating rumble across the forest and shaking the caravans to a halt. Guards wavered, trying to steady their swaying legs on the shifting puddle of mud.

"Wh-what was that?" Rus questioned, searching the forest for the mysterious rumbling that vibrated their feet.

"It's an earthquake," Gorv grumbled. His husky feet sent tidal waves of water splashing across Tovey's dress.

"No, Gorv," she growled. "It's me."

She steadied herself, toes curling. She shut her flaming eyes and sucked in the wet earthen air. Her chest lifted, and her head leaned back into the invisible energy that buzzed within her bones like a moth igniting in flame. The earth's energy grew like vines from the ground, sending tendrils of power into her. The energy fed her soul as if she were one with the world beneath her feet. Focusing, she toned out the cacophony of the men. Her mind centered on one thought: getting out of here.

"Tovey!" Cullus's voice shattered through the crowd, seeming to wiggle its way through a crack in her mind, breaking through her meditative silence. It had been days since she'd heard his forsaken voice, yet somehow it spearheaded its way through the spiraling wind to her heart.

She ground her teeth together, her jaw flexing. She blocked out Cullus's traitorous voice, forming a brick wall of power in her mind. A monstrous growl seeped through her teeth, turning into a banshee screech that ripped out of her throat, louder than the roar of wind slashing at the skin of the guards. They gawked at her, jaws flapping open at the ungodly sight, their weapons falling to the ground.

The guards blanched, watching the demon with fearful eyes. Her hair lifted in the gust, a tornado of hellish proportions spiraling around her. Examining her shackles, Tovey wiggled one foot at a time through her arms, maneuvering them to the front of her body. Holding her wrists in the air, she focused on pulling the chains apart. The wind broke the forged iron links. She yanked outward, her muscles flexing as the wind roared. A rush of dizziness overcame her before adrenaline washed it away. She was free.

Tovey's hair whipped in the cyclone. She ripped the blindfold from her neck. Turning on her heel unerringly, Tovey stared into the eyes of Calvin, Gorv, and Rus. Two were terrified, yet Calvin echoed her wicked grin with a horrific stare. He wasn't scared. Heart stuttering, she stilled, frozen by Calvin's pale face.

"Run," Calvin mouthed. His black eyes darted from Gorv to Rus, ensuring their vision was glued to her.

Tovey's evil grin faded. A perplexed expression covered her face.

"Tovey!" Cullus's voice rang desperately.

Calvin's forehead wrinkled at Cullus's plea. His jet-black hair clung to his forehead in a wet matted mess.

"Run!" he mouthed again, his lips curling at her.

Calvin's endless bantering flicked like a match in her mind. He knew to enrage her. He knew how to fuel her anger until her power burst at the seams. The rogue guard had been trying to boil her blood. For the last few days, he'd been pushing harder and harder, egging her on. He was trying to help her. But before Tovey could contemplate the strange comradery in the soldier or how he could understand her hidden power, her ears reveled in Cullus's voice once again.

Tovey pinched her eyes shut, hoping it would close her ears too. The tornado of whipping wind shot outward in a burst of energy, shoving a handful of men to the ground. Leaping into action, she ran, slipping through the mud like a newborn child learning to walk, disappearing into the darkness of the forest. A few seconds' head start was all she was able to manage, but fearful energy poured into her ropelike veins, pumping hardened fury throughout her body and pushing her forward.

Her gaze snapped toward the canopy, seeking any hiding spot to shield her from the oncoming warriors. She feared the men coming after her. An old knotty tree stood before her. Tovey's chipped nails drove into the bark. Squirrel-like, Tovey scampered up the tree, forcing herself to use every last ounce of strength to climb high enough, fast enough. She reached the upper branches the moment Abolend guards swarmed the forest in an outstretched line.

"Search until you find her! We cannot return to Abolend without the demon!" a guard yapped.

"This way! I saw her run this way!" Calvin pointed in the opposite direction from where Tovey had run.

"You dumb oaf! I saw her run this way with my own eyes!" Gorv bantered.

Calvin's face fell flat. "Gorv, did someone not explain to you that the demon possesses magic?" His eyes were wide, face serious. Shaking his head, he strutted around Gorv. "Poor, sweet Gorv. Such a big body to hold one itty-bitty brain." Calvin sarcastically patted the giant's shoulder. "But honestly, she must have opened a portal or something! I swear she went this way," Calvin urged. "Go on, men!" He bowed his head to the south.

"Hurry! Follow Calvin's lead. He saw the beast." Cullus rode an unfamiliar horse in front of the men, pointing a longsword in the direction of Calvin's false heading. "I, too, believe she has the power to transport locations." He wore an iron cuirass, complete with pauldrons and vambraces. He was dressed like a king. "She showed signs of the skill before I could send another letter to King Mallum. It is one of the affairs I need to speak to him about urgently. I apologize for not informing you all immediately. I was afraid if we moved too quickly around her that we'd scare her into using demon magic, but you can all thank Gorv for provoking the beast. Your insubordination will be dealt with." He leaned into Gorv's face, shouting, "Now, onward!"

Calvin furrowed his brow at the prince. Tovey tucked closer into the tree. Calvin bolted into the distance, sword drawn. "All hail King Mallum!" he chanted, leading the pack away. His agile body skittered into the distance, leading a group of men.

"Hail! Hail King Mallum, leader of the brave, father of the land," the remaining guards shouted, drowning all sounds of the forest with their voices. The chant allowed Tovey to climb higher, concealing her position. She shook her head, stilling herself with awe.

The rest of the guards trampled off, following Calvin's false lead. The men moved farther away from Tovey by the second. Cullus was the last to follow, hesitating beneath the tree. He could always tell, like another sense, that she was near. He must've known that she was barely out of reach. Tovey ached to confront him but instead bit her tongue.

"Yes, hail!" Cullus shouted to the backs of the guards cascading away in muck-covered boots. "Hail King Mallum!" he yelled. The guardsmen responded with another riotous chant of useless words. Watching the men trail away, he sat, his steed shifting with twitching muscles beneath him.

His gaze darted through the trees, hunting her. He spun his horse, searching the ground for tracks, but it was no use. His guards had trampled the land into a pulp. Tovey watched him, concealed in needles.

Vehemently, he said, "Hail. Leader of the brave." He looked upward toward the trees, searching the canopy with upturned eyebrows. Her cheeks burned hot with anger. She waited for him to finish praising his father, but he didn't finish the mantra. She swallowed hard.

He didn't mean *she* was the leader of the brave. If he did, it was a sign he was still on her side. Flustered, Tovey gripped the tree's trunk, wishing she could vanish into the bark. Cullus waited. The sound of the horse's hooves grew impatient as they sloshed in the mud. She didn't dare move a muscle or even take a breath.

She wondered if she should say something. No. Cullus was a traitor. But what if he had honestly referred to her as the leader of the brave? Her heart swooned. He was still playing a game—a twisted game, but a game all the same.

Cullus was wrong. She wasn't brave. She was nothing more than a scared servant. She led no one.

Coldness washed over her body. It could've been a trick, and she couldn't let her heart lead her into danger. But if it wasn't a trick, if Cullus's words were true . . . Tovey couldn't suppress her smile, her heart fluttering as if it could lift into the sky and fly. It was the kindest thing anyone had ever said, and it was enough to know he was still on her side.

Cullus's horse powered off, following the men. She was alone. The forest was so quiet that she could hear a rodent's teeth crunching on leaves and the flutter of dragonflies' wings. A smile crept across her face. Such sweet sounds they were.

Sealing her eyes shut, she rested in the tree, holding on to a thread of consciousness. With the bit of energy she had left, she listened for the guards, ensuring Calvin had successfully saved her life and aided her escape. The whooshing wind brought the song of the crickets, and navy blankets hung across the night sky.

Mucky clouds of gray parted for a cold moon. The forest floor glistened with puddles. Tovey wrapped her legs around the trunk, pulling her arms out from the horrid blood-colored dress. She tied the empty sleeves around a sturdy limb, securing herself to the tree.

Violent shivers overcame her in the night. Sleep teased her as she drifted in and out of slumber, watching needles brush against the sky through heavy lids. Every time rest found her, nightmares teased her with the sound of Cullus's smooth voice. Each time she awoke, she was still alone.

Stiffening, she sat upright, searching the trees for iron and red. No one was there. Her fingers grazed the smooth hilt of her dagger, and she was thankful she had something that was still hers.

She pushed Cullus as far as she could out of her mind. He wasn't allowed to cloud the decision she needed to make.

She blinked rapidly, watching a beetle crawl across the tree. She put her finger out, and its needlelike legs pricked at her skin. The beetle wasn't particularly beautiful at first glance, but upon further inspection, violet and indigo hues shined on its body in the glimmer of the moon.

An arrogant person like Mallum would squash the beetle, afraid of it because it was different, scary. But Tovey knew beetles helped decompose the leaves in winter and bring back life in the spring, working to aid the earth. The beetles protected creatures who weren't grateful for the misunderstood bugs. Tovey grew tired and let the beetle return to the tree, comforted to have company.

33

Cracking stiff bones, Tovey shook awake. Sunlight poked through the evergreen, warming her face. Perking her ears, she took in the birds singing, thanking the sky for the drops of sunshine in the cool morning breeze. It was like the earth knew she was free of oppression, the sun shining for the first time in days.

Tovey searched the tree for Cullus. Picking sleep from her eyes, she remembered the past few days. For a moment it had felt like it was all a nightmare. Dropping to the ground, Tovey turned toward the direction where Frilliam would be waiting for her. Frowning, she pitied the poor horse for having to bear the storm alone in the last few chaotic days. She marched forward, her mind bubbling with headache-inducing thoughts.

She wanted to scream and let all the stress burst out of her before it ate her alive, but screaming into the forest would alert everyone within miles of her location. Frustrated, she simmered her exasperation, pushing her rage deep inside and tying it up in a little box.

She couldn't risk revealing her location to the guards, assuming they weren't already waiting for her by Frilliam. Cullus would know she would head straight toward the steed. She wouldn't be able to traverse the mountains without him. Tovey would need his speed and resilience. If she was going to survive, she needed to think like the enemy, like Cullus. The thought sickened her.

Despite Calvin's corrupted efforts, the crimson Abolend cock-roaches could have swarmed closer than she had expected. Cullus knew Tovey better than anyone. He would know she would do one of three actions: become a wild woman, join the band of renegades at Terrowin, or betray him wholly and run straight into the arms of Silvis. But they all began with Frilliam. If she could reach him, then she'd—

Tovey paused as she listened to the grumble of her stomach. She'd eat whatever Frilliam had left in his packs.

Tovey kicked at the dirt, forcing her muscles to increase her mo-mentum, thighs burning as her deliberation ran with her. Becoming a wild woman would be impossible with the weight of what she now knew. Abolend was going to attack Silvis. King Mallum was insatiable. He would never stop trying to extinguish any threat to Abolend, real or imagined.

Going back to Terrowin would put the defector camp in dan-ger. They had already escaped a life of fighting. If she ran to them, it would only be a matter of time before Abolend troops found her.

Her heart ached for Silvis. The whole kingdom was waiting to be slaughtered because they believed her word. They trusted their chief, and for whatever reason, Arden trusted her. Going back would mean betraying Cullus. He'd resent her. But she must. She couldn't stand by and watch an innocent kingdom suffer. The least she could do was warn them.

Her sprint turned to a jog. If Cullus was still on her side, would he agree? No. He wouldn't. No matter the circumstances, Cullus would never agree to betray his kingdom. He still wanted the crown. No matter which way she spun it, she was turning her blade against Cullus. But if Calvin *had* been telling the truth, he had already betrayed her and used her as a pawn. A cold sweat covered her body, her heart aching. Warning Silvis was the right thing to do. Betrayal or not, she must take the side of the greater good, and that was Silvis.

Nodding, she decided to warn Chief Arden that the war was coming. Tears raced from her eyes. Pausing, she heaved, imagining Cullus's face when he found out she was working with the enemy. The heartbreak he would feel when he realized he was now her enemy. How his face would harden into stone as he processed what Mallum feared. She accepted her sweet, tainted fate of being a traitor to Abolend.

Wiping her tears, she sprinted. Abolend wanted to call her a monster, a defector, a demon. Well, that was what they would get. She gripped the edges of her gown, letting her bare legs run free. Tovey's lungs burned as the wind cut at her face. Fall was almost over, and the temperature continued to plummet the closer they came to the solstice. Winters were never too harsh, and they rarely saw significant snowfall, but the inclement weather still drained the heat from her body, nipping at her bare shoulders. Trees passed by in a blur, her feet bouncing from rock to rock, her steps soft and springy. Tovey didn't waver as she ran toward her friend.

Fallen trees formed a makeshift pen in the meadow clearing. A glinting lake lined with reeds sat still in the forest, a blissful land devoid of any political danger. It was too perfect. A dark horse drank by the lake. His head shot upward as grass crunched beneath Tovey, and he took her in with fearful eyes.

"It's me, Frilliam, it's me!" She scurried toward her friend, wrapping her arms around his thick neck, which arched under her grasp. "I've missed you so much. You have no idea."

Frilliam knelt his knotted knees into the sandy shore, lowering his body to allow Tovey to mount him swiftly.

"Where'd your saddle go?" She scrubbed the tuft of hair between his ears as he stood.

Frilliam stared blankly at Tovey.

"Cullus took it, that's right." She scowled.

The blanket and packs had been removed days ago when Tovey had passed out. They'd left their supplies in the clearing where she woke. Her head ached as she searched the perimeter. She had no idea which direction that lay. Bears would have ravaged the camp by now. No food would be left, and if there was, it would waste too much time to try and find it.

Whispered curse words fell from her lips. Her pants and tunic had disappeared with the stash. Fluffing the crimson skirt behind her, she sat on Frilliam's bare back. He pranced around in a circle, muscles moving under his skin. He searched the woods for their third.

"He isn't here, and he isn't coming," Tovey said solemnly, her tired fingers patting the bristled hair on Frilliam's warm neck.

The horse huffed, sending a cloud of steam spiraling into the midmorning air. Strands of hair blocked Tovey's dry eyes, which burned from the incessant tears. She laced her fingers through his mane, unable to cry any more.

"I know, sweet Frilliam. I miss him too. But he is gone. And he is never coming back." Her voice cracked.

A horsey snort retorted.

"Don't blame me. It isn't my fault. I said he isn't coming back! Why can't you accept that Cullus is gone? He left you. He never loved you! He was just another one of them, a highborn twat doing everything he needed to do to look good for the king. He is—"

Frilliam prodded the ground, his muscles tightening as his tail whacked invisible flies away.

Gulping, she shook her head. "You're right. None of that is important. Not anymore."

Tracing the makeshift pen, she noticed the storm had knocked one of the branches to the ground. She pointed toward the exit.

"Let's go, Frilliam. We are heading straight to Silvis." Guilt twisted in her throat.

Frilliam rose onto his back feet with an unleashed neigh, powering his body ahead. He leaped over the fallen tree in a graceful flash of movement. Cantering, he sped gleefully, letting his legs propel them forward at full speed, heading straight toward the heart of the dryadic kingdom. Tovey tightened her body into his. Frilliam's hooves beat against the ground like a drum, pairing to the sound of Tovey's beating heart.

Salty sweat covered her face. Eyes fluttering, Tovey prayed the dryads would accept her back—that Arden would take her back. He was unpredictable, but he was her only option. To be fair, Chief Arden had promised she was always welcome. She hoped he'd meant it.

Tovey scoffed at the thought of Arden's reaction. He'd been right all along. Infatuation with a weapon was not love. It never was. She would have to break through the chief's thick skull and make him accept, by any means necessary, that his reluctance toward Cullus was not unwarranted. She had changed sides, and she was in Silvis with a pure heart. She was no longer a tool in someone's shed. Abolend was waging an uncontested war, and from the opposing side, Tovey would stop it.

She growled, "You will regret this, Cullus."

34

The ride to Silvis progressed much quicker than Tovey had anticipated. Her bloodshot eyes watered as she searched with unmatched determination for the crimson tabards of Abolend. A sense of ease crept across her skin as the arch of Silvis appeared. The arched trees still stood, untouched and safe from Abolend. Not a soldier was in sight.

Onward she and Frilliam marched, the warm cedar air brushing against her skin with the familiar static buzz. A slight smile crept across her face. She swung her feet to the side, dismounting Frilliam, walking step by step beside him to the kapok tree Firth had taken her and Cullus to days ago.

The cobbled streets were empty. The midday sun burned at her skin. There were no crowds of dryads or children playing in the street. The sound of music had vanished.

A scuttling noise sounded behind her. Spinning, Tovey heard

naked feet clapping against the moss-carved stone as a rose-colored dryad approached and stood eye to eye with her. His green eyes widened as he rushed to the center of the street, blocking her path. The young dryad was no older than twenty, in Dryad years. His feet planted, toes wiggling into the mossy gaps, as he raised his palms in front of her, blocking her stride.

"What is it?" Tovey snapped, exhausted. Her jaw slacked, and she was surprised at how annoyed she'd sounded.

The dryad shook his head, which was devoid of any hair, and stumbled backward.

"I'm sorry, I didn't mean to be rude. I'm tired."

The boy stood, unblinking.

"What's wrong? I'm Tovey." She smiled, lightening the tone of her voice. "And this big boy is Frilliam."

The boy's brilliant green eyes darted side to side, peering at every window and door of the surrounding tree homes before looking askance at Frilliam.

"Do you want to pet him?" Tovey offered, wanting to move past the child. Anxiety swelled in her chest. She yearned to reach the chief. Every second mattered.

The dryad's eyes locked onto Tovey as if he could see into her soul, covering her with the sensation of spiders crawling up her spine.

"What's wrong?" Tovey knelt, surveying the boy. She, too, searched the homes that lined the narrow street, finding nothing. "Are you looking for someone? Are you lost?"

His wide green eyes stared, unblinking. Frustration with the young dryad needled at the back of her skull. She shook her head at the disturbed child.

"I'm going to go now." She stood, lacing her fingers in Frilliam's mane and leading him around the boy.

"Wait," he squeaked, sounding as if he were a mouse talking to her and not a boy.

She spun around, forcing an exhausted smile, irritated with the dryad. Her knees trembled, and agitation nipped at her heels. She needed to slip into Silvis and meet with Arden before the Abolend troops beat her. If she weren't in a rush, she'd sit on the rune-strewn cobble and wait patiently all day for the boy to talk, but today was not the day to stall her.

"What is it? You can tell me."

The dryad squatted, curling his rosy fingers, ushering her near. Tovey knelt on the stone, her face nearing the little boy's. The dryad's skin was thick like wood. He scrambled to her side, placing a hand on her bent knee. He propped himself higher as his lips brushed uncomfortably against her ear, hot breath tickling her ear canal.

"A new beginning is coming," he whispered.

Tovey tilted her head, her eyes fluttering. "A new beginning? What is that supposed to mean?"

The boy closed his eyes for a brief inhale. He held his breath, chest full as he thrashed around the street before falling still. His eyes shattered open with a wide unnerving stare. The corners of Tovey's mouth fell into an appalled frown as he ran off. Turning back to Frilliam, she rubbed her thumb across his muscular neck.

"Maybe this wasn't a good idea." She ran her fingers through her hair, attempting to brush out the fear that blanketed her.

She glanced over her shoulder at the entrance of the kingdom, contemplating her choice. Frilliam's glossy brown eyes stared back at her. She wished he could speak, give her words of advice or encouragement or tell her to turn around. She wished Frilliam could tell her that she was irrational like Cullus would have. Was Silvis the wrong place to go? She should have turned back and tried to find Terrowin once more. Defectors would understand her more than anyone. Her forehead met Frilliam's.

"Blink once if you think we should leave and twice if we stay."

Frilliam blinked once.

Tovey took in one last summer taste of the woody air, accepting Frilliam's well-thought-out decision. She turned away from the towering trees, facing the archway. Silvis was an ancient kingdom. They didn't need help from a defector. Like Cullus, Arden played games, twisting words and keeping conversations spinning to his advantage.

What if the child was right? A new beginning was coming, and that beginning could be her living in peace, away from any talk of war. Silvis could fight their own battles. She didn't have to pick any side at all. To Terrowin it was.

Tovey took one step, and dread twisted in her gut. Silvis would fight a battle because they would be defending themselves. The reason they would have to defend themselves was because Mallum would think she was there. They would die for her.

"We can't leave them, Frilliam. I decided to come here, and it is the right thing to do. It is my painful truth. I'm responsible for the dryads' danger."

The pitter of bare feet slapping against the cobbled stones returned, but this time it was a symphony of them, not just one little boy's. Dryads rose from their houses to watch Tovey with wrinkled brows and gaping mouths. The heated breeze brushed against her skin, billowing her crimson gown, the sleeves wrapped around her neck in a makeshift halter.

Guilt poured into her gut while sweat beaded at her hairline. Turning toward the dryads, she saw seven children scamper ahead, running toward the chief's tree.

Groaning, she whispered, "I have to do what's right, Frilliam."

Abolend wanted to use her, and they had. They still were. Her fear was because of them. Her hesitation was their making. She was the key to leaving Silvis unarmed, destined to fall to Abolend's men. Exactly as Nadia was drowned, bound. And Sylvia, skewered by an arrow, unarmed. And Master Daleen, beheaded by a sword for a crime she hadn't committed, not to mention the gruesome deaths of the seers before her.

All unarmed, all innocent, and all put to death by Abolend. The dryads couldn't fall to such a harmful fate. Tovey stepped forward, the clacking of hooves marching behind her. She wasn't going to be responsible for anyone else's death. She was going to be brave.

Tovey's eyes widened as Firth hurried onto the street from an adjoining alley. "Tovey, you are back! You should be halfway to Abolend by now. I must say—"

"Take me to Chief Arden."

The crowd of dryads planted to the ground around them, stiffening.

"Return to your activities. She is welcome here. All is well," Firth announced. "Go, go, children of the forest. Go." He stepped so close to Tovey she could smell his fishy breath seeping from his nose. He lowered his voice and kept a disingenuous leer on his sunken moss-toned cheeks. "Is the prince with you?"

"No." Tovey shot a wide-eyed stare she hoped even Firth could understand.

Terror overtook Firth's face. He spun on his bare heel, scuttling across the cobble toward the doors of the kapok tree. Firth grabbed Frilliam's mane as he bowed. "I will take your horse to the stables. He will rest well."

"Thank you." Tovey smiled meekly. "Be good, boy. I'll be gone for a minute." Stepping on the threshold, she wrapped her fingers around the wooden handle and pulled the squealing hinges open.

"You should wait," Firth squawked.

"I'm not waiting for anyone anymore." Tovey strode confidently into the wooden chamber, gliding toward the throne cradling Chief Arden, who sat with a giggling woman on his lap.

Coughing at full blast, Tovey made her presence known. A deep echo resonated in the hollow hall from her soft boots, a masterful feat. Chief Arden snapped his gaze away from the woman and glared toward the intruder.

He patted the woman's side, ushering her away. The giddy grin fell from the dryad's face as she exited through the door behind the throne. Tovey stood still, face hardened as she watched the woman leave. Arden waited for the door to shut. The hall was empty. Flickering waxy candles hissed in the silence.

He moistened his lips. "Tovey. I wasn't expecting to see you again so soon."

"Nor I you," Tovey admitted.

"Is Cullus here?"

Her voice lowered. "No."

Arden shifted in his throne. "What's happened?" he asked, concerned.

The bravery she held melted in her chest, words failing to form.

"Tovey." Arden's voice shivered with worry. He stood, his eyebrows knitting together. "Why are you dressed like that? He didn't actually make you his servant again, did he?" Arden's face twisted with disgust. "I know I threatened him, but I didn't think he'd do it. Cullus isn't the brightest, but he didn't seem this cruel."

Heart rate elevating, Tovey closed her eyes, steadying herself. Arden placed a comforting hand on her arm. Together they knelt, sinking to the floor. His hand was warm against her skin.

"He . . . Cullus . . ." Her voice cracked before she fell silent.

"We can sit here as long as you'd like." He removed his hand, sitting cross-legged before her. "I want to hear everything you have to say, and please tell me if there is anything I can do."

"I'd be appreciative if you wouldn't mind providing new clothes." Tovey smiled weakly.

He lifted his eyebrows, nodding. He waited for more as he leaned toward Tovey.

"Cullus has betrayed us. Abolend is still preparing for war and never had a single intention of stopping. They used me, asked me to talk you down, and I assure you I had no idea that they were not sincere. I had every intention of stopping this war. I—"

"You *had* every intention of stopping the war?" He cut her off, voice booming.

"I *have* every intention. That's why I'm here. To warn you that I've failed."

Arden flashed a devious grin. He stood, and Tovey followed, watching him curiously. He took elongated steps across the wooden floor as he paced the chamber.

"So, dear sweet puppy finally bit your hand, and what? Now

you want solace here? For telling me what I already expected of the brute? It's a little funny, isn't it?" he snapped.

Heavy pounding shattered against her ribs inside her chest, shaking her lips. "It isn't funny," she growled, voice barely above a whisper. "I want this all to be over. Please. I can work here. I can help however you need me. Food and shelter. That is all I need."

Arden shook his head, circling Tovey in a whirlpool of thoughts. His tongue clicked. "No."

"No?" Tovey was taken aback. "I've risked my life to—"

"No. You don't get to be normal. What even is normal? A foolish word from a foolish girl. No. You don't only need food and shelter."

"I do," Tovey pleaded before Arden stopped in front of her, leaning to eye level.

"No. You *need* new clothing too." An airy chuckle escaped. "Of course, you are welcome here, but you won't be working, not like you were in Abolend. Not a servant. And since we are talking about needs, I need you to work on something else."

Confusion spiraled in her mind as she waited to hear his request. She watched his face illuminate with a mischievous smile.

"I need you to work on honing your power."

35

Tovey gawked in disbelief. Candles hissed as the scent of clove swirled into the air. She was grateful they filled the silence as she blinked excessively, trying to fight off anxiety. She stared into Arden's earnest gaze, wondering if she had heard him correctly.

Stammering, she said, "S-sorry, did you say—"

Arden's eyes were wide, eager with excitement. "I did say you will work on honing your power."

"I'm not using my power," Tovey snarled.

Arden rested his hand upon her shoulder. "You will."

"I won't." She shrugged off his touch.

"You don't have a choice. You want food, right?" Arden smiled, sniffing the air. "Ah, smells good."

Tovey breathed deeply, mouth watering from the scent of roasting fish, something she had never tasted but that smelled so alluring. She muttered, "Yes."

"Then you are going to learn how to hone your power."

"No." Tovey was relentless.

Arden rubbed his jawline, casting a questioning glare at Tovey. "I recall you promising your life on the fact that you would get Abolend to back down."

"I did," Tovey snapped.

"Yet you've failed that promise." Arden carelessly surveyed the end of his braid, a slight smile forming as he waited for her response.

"I didn't fail." Tovey ran her fingers through her hair, easing her forming headache. "There was never any chance at it. Cullus betrayed me." Her voice cracked. She coughed, gathering herself. "I still stand by my word. I don't want there to be a war. That is why I came here to warn you. I didn't have to come, you know." She stepped close to the chief, lowering her voice. "I could have left you to figure out Abolend was coming when they marched through your archway and started killing your people."

"Still, a promise is a promise."

"Not when I could never fulfill it."

"Fulfill it by honing your power. You promised your life, did you not?"

Tovey remained silent.

"So your life is mine. All you have to do is learn how to use your power, and the promise is fulfilled. Your debt will be paid." He smiled. "It's easy."

Tovey gazed into Arden's calculating eyes. "Fine. I will learn how to control it so I can suppress it."

Arden shook his head. "Not to suppress it, Tovey."

Tovey thought about Cullus. He had tried to help her learn

how to control it, and it had seemed to work, a little bit at least. The focus he'd taught her had been enough to let her dial in on creating some sort of distraction to allow her to escape the Abolend soldiers without killing any of them—a feat she was beyond grateful for. She considered attempting to understand her power a little longer until she could find a way to free herself from its invisible chains.

Arden gripped her shoulder, drawing her entire focus into him. "Control means using it. Does it not?"

Tovey's mouth twitched.

"I have a hunch you'll want to use it."

Tovey shook her head in protest, shaking off his touch once more.

"Why don't you go rest?" Arden pointed toward the door to the staircase. "The room is yours if you want it."

Tovey huffed.

"What is it?" He tilted his head, eyebrows knitting together.

"I come here and tell you Abolend is going to attack your kingdom, and all you care about is me learning how to hone my powers. What about the war? I don't see any weapons, and none of you are wearing armor. What about your people?" Her mind ached.

His expression was blank, unreadable.

"Do you not care at all?"

Arden lurched forward with discontent. "Things are different here. And I don't need an outsider without a kingdom of their own telling me how to run mine. Watch your tongue. I have been kind to you, and you'd do well to remember that." His fingers grazed the amulet around his neck—a wooden pendant carved in a knotted pattern similar to the strange shapes on the cobble. "Besides, we don't need shiny armor to keep us safe. We will fight when they come—if they come. Tides change, Tovey."

Guilt and frustration loomed in her brain. She never had any idea what Arden was getting at as his tongue flicked around the point.

He continued. "Asking you to understand your powers *is* me caring. I don't need you to set fire to a kingdom made of wood or shake the earth and loosen our roots. You endanger us by not having your gifts under control."

"Gifts," Tovey scoffed.

"Yes. It is baffling that you pretend not to understand that. I care about the threat at hand, and that threat could still be you, but I'd like to believe we are still friends." An exhausted smile crossed his face. "Go rest and eat something, and tomorrow, when you've considered it, let me know if you will learn to use your powers. I need a new promise. You must say that you are willing to learn how to use them, not learn how to suppress them."

"Why not suppress?" she asked.

"You can still find control without burying them away. You would not keep a child from walking if they were afraid of falling. Instead, you encourage them to find their balance and confidence, and soon they not only walk but run." He smiled playfully. "Need for need, Tovey. It is an exchange, and that exchange is one you should take." He snapped a long finger, calling Firth from outside the entrance. He skittered into the hall. "Take her to her room. Give her whatever she wants." He smiled at Tovey. "Within reason."

"Yes, Chief. And your horse, Miss Tovey, is in a paddock down the road." Firth bowed toward Tovey before ushering her toward the wooden door behind the throne. Tovey looked over her shoulder, catching Chief Arden collapsing into the throne, face falling to his hands, braids sweeping the ground.

Firth and Tovey ascended the spiraling steps. Tovey's lungs took in the woody scent of the hall. Fire-flicking candles lit their way, flames as unsure as her mind. She had one choice. But Tovey couldn't help but sense there was another option. For now, it eluded her.

Firth bowed low, cracking the wooden door to the familiar room. "I had our cook leave food on the table. If you want more, ask, and I'll have someone fetch it. I will be right here." A hair-raising giggle wormed through his chapped lips.

Tovey was too awake to sleep and too tired to process any more information. She stood motionless, staring into the reflective glass mounted above the dressing table. So much had changed since she saw herself in the river's reflection the night she defected.

She ran her fingers across her head, searching for horns. Nothing, thank the skies. She was still Tovey, a girl with purple eyes. They flickered at her like they knew something she didn't. Chills raced across her arms. Hunger nipped at her as she picked up a berry, sticky and sweet, from the carved tray the cook had left.

Tovey bit into the fruit, letting its juice melt in her mouth. She tried another, which was equally as intoxicating, before pulling a flaky piece of fish from the plate. It was tender and warm. Tovey ate the most delectable meal she'd ever had, but she refused to break eye contact with the monster in the mirror for even a second.

Though she couldn't see much difference on the outside, she felt like she was looking at a whole different person whose soul had inhabited her body. She wondered if she looked like someone who had betrayed someone they loved, someone who sat behind enemy lines, reveling in the food of their domain, living in a room suited for a highborn. She was undoubtedly someone she thought she should fear.

36

Hours passed as Tovey paced in her room. She had not yet allowed herself to sink into the tub or rest on the bed. Her gaze lingered on the ivy-strewn wall, and she drew her fingers to the waxy leaves. The leaves vibrated against her skin as if filled with invisible energy. Gravely, she tried distracting her wandering mind.

Learning how to understand her power wasn't something she wanted to do. But Arden knew she'd have no choice. Her power was evil, only capable of destruction. Tovey rubbed the back of her neck. What if accepting to learn her untamed power was the last nail in the coffin of the final war? It could set the prophecy in motion. But if she learned how to use it, she could use it for good, to stop the war before it began.

Tovey ripped the red dress from her body, tossing it to the floor. She stepped into the steaming bathwater, warming her skin. A rapping on the door sent her deeper into the water.

"May I enter? I have clothes," a voice croaked.

Tovey popped out of the bath, wrapping in a towel. "Yes, Firth."

It was silly having Firth wait on her. Imagination reeling, Tovey thought this must be what it felt like to be a highborn—days spent in lavish accommodations with nonessential items pouring out of every surface served on silent hands, or not so silent in Firth's case.

Firth entered, surveying her, pausing on her bruises and scars before turning to the dressing table. He shook his head solemnly, setting a selection of dresses in the room.

Tovey rolled her eyes.

"Is this not satisfactory?" Firth eyeballed the wares.

Tovey was hesitant to ask a favor, but she couldn't help herself. "It is nice, thank you, but I was wondering . . . I lost my pants out in the woods. Any chance you have any of those?"

"Lost?" Firth giggled at the idea. "How could one lose something that they are wearing?"

"Misplaced." Tovey scowled.

Firth's mouth twitched.

"Well, if anyone happens to find them, I'd appreciate you letting me know."

Firth's yellow eyes glistened. "Sometimes, Miss Tovey, scouts leave the kingdom, but it is rare for us to leave Silvis. If they scavenge anything, I will let them know it belongs to you."

"Thank you." Her mouth twitched into a slight smile.

Firth tapped his fingers on his cheek. "We have pants our warriors wear if you want. Arden wanted clothes close to what you wear at home. To make you comfortable."

Tovey recalled the woman warrior standing outside the kapok. "No . . ." Her voice wavered. "I don't want to look like a warrior."

Firth bowed and returned to his position behind the locked door. Tovey shuffled through the dresses, finding one made of soft white linen and slipping the sleeveless fabric over her body.

She turned to the bed and plopped onto it. The soft mattress forced a cheeky grin onto her face. The feathery comfort was the best friend she'd had in days, aside from dear Frilliam. Her eyes closed.

Hours deep into the night passed. The candles cast haunting shadows onto the wall. Nightmares prodded at the backs of her eyelids, convulsions shaking her awake. Lying still, she tried to rest, but a strange noise jostled her awake. She listened.

Clink.

Tovey turned over, readjusting.

Clink.

Her eyes shot open, searching the wooden walls for the strange noise. Nothing was there. She flipped in the bed again, letting her lids fall.

Clink.

Her naked feet landed on the floor before her eyes could open. Head spinning, she searched the room for the noise. The glass rattled once more as a teeny object bounced outside the window.

Tovey neared the hole, her breath steaming the window as she pressed her nose against the surface, which was icy against her skin. She peered out into the twilight. The trees were dark, lights extinguished from every dwelling. The streets were barely illuminated in the blue of nightfall.

Clink.

A pebble hit right in front of her face, and she jumped back. Pulling a blanket from the bed, she wiped the window clear of fog. Cupping her hands on the glass, she blocked the fluttering candlelight of her room. A dark cloaked figure stood in the shadows, alone in the alley like a ghost. Her heart jolted at the shape of the person; they had broad shoulders and the posture of someone with status. She pressed herself closer to the glass, whispering, "Cullus?"

The figure stepped deeper into the night.

Heart racing, Tovey circled the window with her finger, attempting to find a latch, but there was none. She turned back to the room, searching the cage for a way out. Scampering to the door, she pressed her ear against the hardwood, focusing. The soft shuffling of Firth's feet echoed as he muttered nonsensically to himself, inches away. She tiptoed across the room to the window, searching the streets for the figure.

The streets were empty. Slapping her face, Tovey shook herself awake. She stared into the night. There was nothing. Cullus wasn't there. Rubbing her eyes, Tovey lay back into the bed, wishing she could feel him beside her as the darkness settled in. Drifting for a moment, she dreamt of his voice.

Clink.

Bounding out of bed, she stared into the streets with dry eyes, her gaze locking on the shadowy figure. The figure stood still. His finely woven cloak billowed in the night's wind.

The dark hood fell from a cloud of brown hair before he pulled it back over his round face. Cullus waved a hand frantically, ushering her toward him, pointing from her to the ground. Lurching forward, she stopped herself. Was this a trap? Tovey searched the streets, realizing Cullus was incontestably alone.

He'd said something right before leaving her in the canopy. He'd called her brave. He'd aided Calvin in steering the guards away from her. He was back in Silvis without guards. He was here to help.

Heart stuttering, warmth flooded her body. She peered through the window at Cullus once more. He'd never betrayed her. He couldn't have. She had to go. Running away with Cullus was her second option, her freedom to escape being a servant of Abolend and the choice to forgo learning her powers.

Tovey listened to Firth, who paced the hallway. Counting his steps, she memorized his strides. Tovey wrapped a towel around her hand, protecting it from the oncoming blow. Calculating Firth's movement, she waited for him to be at the farthest point from her door. Tovey coughed before letting out a resounding sigh, preparing Firth to ignore any noise to follow. She threw her fist into the round window with a swift punch, coughing once more.

The glinting glass fell to the cobbled street like glitter, clattering sharply on the ground. Wind needled her cheeks as she leaned out of the window into the moonlight. She searched the knotty tree for a feasible way down.

"Cullus?" Tovey whispered, her torso hanging out of the tree.

The cloaked figure swirled like smoke from the shadows as he ran to the bottom of the chief's tree. His cloak fell off his head to reveal his fearful hazel eyes. A smile crossed her face as she breathed a breath of relief, knowing it truly was him.

"Tovey, they want to use you. It is a trap," he said, his voice barely audible.

Tovey's smile faded as she spun around, surveying the locked door. Firth's footsteps had quickened. She had to act now.

"Get out! It is a trap!"

Brushing shattered glass from the sill, she peered out, planning her first steps before she shimmied out of the window. Locking her fingers tight on the bark of the hollow tree, she swung out of the window. Tovey found a knot the size of a leaf, barely able to balance a toe on. Limbs darting from vine to branch, she descended the kapok flawlessly.

She dropped six feet to the ground, landing on the mossy cobble, feet aching from infinitesimal glass shards. She turned toward the shattered window, surprised by her escape. Firth leaned out into the night from her room above. He let out an ear-splitting howl.

"Let's go." Cullus looped Tovey under his arm, shielding her from the night as they ran.

Tovey tried to speak through sprinted breaths, unsure of what to say or ask. Her heart and mind battled, battering coherent thoughts into oblivion. They ran north, opposite the entrance of Silvis and deeper into enemy territory. Cullus had to have a plan, one he hadn't let her in on.

"Cullus," she huffed through labored breaths, her feet icy from the stone. "Where are we going?" She peered into his hardened face, his eyes aimed at the path ahead. She wasn't sure he'd heard her. "Cullus, talk to me! What did you mean it's a trap?"

His face was as still as stone. He pressed forward. Cullus's fingers dug into Tovey's ribs, guiding her through darkened avenues.

No lights were lit inside the dryads' homes. Though it had to be roughly an hour until midnight, the village was eerily still, as if a sleeping spell blanketed the streets. Tovey tripped between uneven cobbles, sending spirals of shivers oscillating up her spine.

"What about Frilliam?" Tovey whispered through panting breaths. "We can't leave without him."

Cullus grabbed her hand, pulling her into a crevice between the scraping bark of two trees. Their chests pushed together in the light of the rising moon. His smooth fingers tucked a stray hair behind her ear as he rested his head against her forehead, ignoring the sweat slipping between their faces.

"I'm sorry for how the soldiers treated you," he muttered. "I had no other choice but to obey. It was unfair for me to do so, but if I revolted, they would have imprisoned us both. I had to——"

"I know." Soured guilt pooled on her tongue, and she questioned if she would have done the same if the roles were reversed.

"You don't know, Tovey. It hurt to see you that way, and I can't imagine how you felt. You know I never stopped being on your side, right?"

Tovey nodded solemnly, but every cell in her body, even now, was filled with unmeasurable doubt. She wanted to tell him that it had hurt her to watch him treat her like she was nothing, that he couldn't imagine the pain she'd felt from the heartbreak, the fear, and the blades that had poked at her like she was a pincushion. Tovey rubbed her waist, still bruised from being pulled from the chains. She wouldn't have made the same choice. She would have fought for him.

Cullus's eyes were wide with fear. "I was worried you thought I'd betrayed you, but I didn't. I swear. But, Tovey, I need to know, how do you know Calvin?"

"Calvin?" She was caught off guard. "I don't. I thought he might have known you."

"No. I've never even spoken with him." He swallowed air, blinking quickly. "You promise you don't know him?"

"Promise."

Cullus cursed, lowering his head, darting his eyes to the moonlit road, the dark cloak falling over his face.

"What is it?" Tovey asked, watching the corners of his mouth twitch.

"One minute after midnight marks the solstice."

Her legs quivered.

"Yeah, tomorrow is your birthday, and tomorrow is going to start the final war. It's coming. Calvin is a sign of that. He's a defiant guard who didn't defect but infiltrated our men. He wasn't out there for himself. He was out there for *you*." The muscles in his jaw tensed.

Tovey stood silent. She watched the blood pump through the pounding vein in Cullus's neck. A wet tear met her cheek, but she was unsure why she was crying. Guilt. Pride. Fear. Every emotion was somehow trying to bore through the surface. Her eyes locked on Cullus's darkening face, and a dangerous look brewed in his eyes. She knew within the depths of her soul that something was wrong—incurably wrong.

"I didn't ask anyone to fight. You know that. You know I've been trying to prevent this. Calvin isn't my fault. But you writing to your father and telling him where we were wasn't helping anything.

He sent Abolend to come to attack Silvis. Tell me, did you know the guards were going to meet us on the outskirts of Silvis?"

"No. I didn't know. I planned to get you home safe, but what am I to do in front of my army? I promise you, I had no choice. Do you expect me to tell them I've fallen in love with the creature they've feared their entire existence? The beast they came to capture? And what then? Expect thirty armed guards to accept it?"

Tovey scoffed, shifting away from him. She didn't have a home.

"My little brother and his power of deception could have tilted them against me. They are machines of Abolend, and their minds are not yet aligned with mine; they are with Mallum. I had to retain any sense of power before I lost control of them." He gripped her hands in his. "I would love to be able to parade you down the streets of Abolend and tell the world that I've fallen in love with you, tell them that you are the most extraordinary person I've ever met and that you've changed me in a way I can't even explain. But I can't, Tovey." He lowered his voice. "We'd have been killed. I had to lie and say it was all part of a made-up master plan. No one is that smart." His face turned to stone. "You know there was no other choice."

Her ears burned with anger. "You always have a choice—"

"I *still* don't have a choice," he growled.

Tovey shook her head, fuming. "I was shackled to a horse, prodded with blades."

Cullus's face twisted, turning red as tears fell. "I'm sorry. I didn't know what to do." His voice wavered. "They could have killed you. If I'd shown you sympathy . . . I-I could have lost you. I'm sorry." He sniffed. "I don't expect you to forgive me."

"I thought you . . . I didn't know if it was all a game," Tovey admitted, still unsure if she could fully trust him. She would never subject him or anyone to such cruelty. "I didn't see you for days. What were you doing? Anything?"

"Was *I* doing anything?" Cullus shook his head, stiffening. "Yes, trying to figure out how to save you, but apparently, you know a lot more about your powers than you led me to believe."

Tovey's jaw dropped, her heart shattering. "No, I didn't know I could do that! It came out of nowhere."

"Just like that rogue guard who is better at rescuing you than I am?" His jaw tightened. "I didn't know if you were playing me either, you know. After Calvin, I didn't know if you were friends or if you were a part of a rebel cause."

"I didn't even know Terrowin existed."

"And what if there are more?"

She paused. Tovey had never even considered there to be more rebel groups. Tovey focused on Cullus, his expression questioning. "No one's that smart, Cullus." She threw his words back at him.

"Fair." Cullus laughed meekly. The smile she loved flickered across his face like lightning. "Tovey, you've got me messed up. I can't think straight around you. Everything I've believed and learned is unraveling before me. I've never felt like this before. This great evil I've been ready to extinguish my entire life is this beautiful, strong woman standing in front of me. Do you know that I don't want the throne if that means losing you?"

"You have to take the throne," Tovey said seriously.

"I won't win the kingdom over, not like I know you want me to. I couldn't save you. You were tortured. I have failed you." He sniffed. "I won't be able to change Abolend's infrastructure. It isn't only the king who gets to decide right from wrong. The highborns hold power. They control the money. If I push too much, Elias will take my place." He gripped Tovey into a hug as she closed her eyes, breathing him in. "I'm sorry . . . deeply, truly sorry. For everything." He released her. His eyes were soulful. "We need to leave. I will explain everything as soon as we are out of Silvis. Where is Frilliam?"

"Firth said he's in a stable down the road by the kapok. We have to go back."

"You stay here." Cullus shifted a woven crate in the alley in front of the crevice. "Duck, and don't move until I come back." He pressed his lips against her forehead.

"Let me come with you," she pleaded.

"Not this time. I'm not risking them getting their hands on you again. The world will burn if I lose you."

Tovey swallowed hard. "Cullus?"

His brow furrowed.

Tovey smiled wistfully. "Don't take longer than an hour."

Cullus's teeth glinted in the moonlight as he melded into the darkness. She listened intensely to every howl of the wind, the rattle of leaves, and the rise and fall of the strange vibration. Minutes passed as she watched the still street, unblinking.

Materializing from the shadows, a boy with haunting pale eyes stepped into the opening, kneeling in the nook with her.

Elias smiled. "Hello, demon. We need to talk."

37

Silence trapped the two in unnerving stillness. Tovey glared at Elias, his face still plump with youth. She tasted the salt in the wind. The ocean breeze was gentle against the tension. With sealed lips, she waited for the prince to speak. Elias's mouth twitched as beads of sweat formed on his upper lip.

"I followed Cull here." His eyes shifted. "And I know you put a spell on him."

Tovey shook her head, biting her tongue.

"You did, demon," he growled.

"Elias, I— "

"Prince! How dare you neglect my title." He silenced her with a haughty glare. "Like I said, I followed Cull here. I saw you two . . . It's disgusting. I understand that you aren't the demon everyone pictured, but you are a demon all the same."

"Listen to me," Tovey interjected, leering toward the boy.

"Cullus has a plan. I'm not evil, wicked, or a demon. We are going to stop the war."

"Stop it? My brother's gone mad. Entirely." A smug smile flicked across Elias's face, eerily similar to his brother's. "Do you know the prophecy?"

"I do."

"Then how can you pretend to be noble when you are nothing more than a rat in disguise?" There was a hint of honesty behind Elias's words, as if he wanted an answer.

Tovey fumed.

"You are destined to kill us all, and you will. Starting tomorrow." Elias glanced down the alley before fixing his attention on Tovey once more.

"Tomorrow? No, I'm not," Tovey said from between gritted teeth.

"He didn't tell you." Elias laughed. "What do you know? The first verse?"

"Of the prophecy? There's more than one verse?" She shivered violently, wondering if there were more than the four lines she had been replaying in her head.

"Obviously, demon. Keep up," Elias snapped.

Her fists clenched as she swallowed dryly. It seemed impossible that there was more. No one had ever mentioned it.

Elias knelt close to her ear, his voice a mere whisper. "Mother would sing this to me every night. Listen."

The demon comes, heart of cold.
She'll rise as the seers have foretold.
With purple eyes, hair of gold,
She'll bring the final war.

On eighteen years past this day,
The babe's power will come out and play.
She'll take away life from land.
She'll bring the final war.

Diablerie, don't take me.
I am not a threat, please, I guarantee.
Spare my children, my wife, just flee.
Don't bring the final war.

The demon slew us today.
The dead line the streets, horrid display.
She took our friends' lives away.
The final war has come.

Prince Elias, save the town.
Hold your head high, you will wear the crown.
Tell the demon to retreat.
Elias saved the day.

Elias sat back and rested against the wall, his expression smug. Uncontrollable tears raced down Tovey's cheeks as the wind blustered them away. Her body drained of all fight.

"Eighteen years, demon. Like I said, tomorrow your story begins." He paused. "Or ends." A wicked sneer crossed his face.

Defeated, Tovey stilled, numb to Elias's words.

"Did Cullus tell you Father prefers me to inherit the throne? It's because of my part in this. And I'm telling you now, retreat." He smiled, face relaxed.

Tovey didn't waver.

"Exactly. I know you won't, so it is your fault we are moving to my next plan."

Tovey's jaw hung open before she shut it once more. She sucked in the cool wind, recalling her experiences with younger girls at the collective. They hadn't experienced enough to understand how life worked. Tough problems always had simple solutions to them, to the naive. Elias was still a boy.

She squared her shoulders. "I am telling you, Prince, I don't want any part in this."

"Truly? Would you do anything to save everyone, including Cull?" He wore a mischievous grin.

"Yes," she said, her mind pounding.

"Anything?" Elias smiled, his eyes empty, devoid of a soul.

Tovey rolled her eyes, growing tired of his game. "What do you want me to do?"

"Follow me." Elias pounced to his feet, surveying the alley before leaving the den. Tovey glanced at the alley, frowning. "Before he comes back, let's go. I will meet with him later, don't worry."

Without a feasible way out of this, Tovey paced behind the prince.

A light popped on inside one of the trees. Then another. And another. A golden glow filled the streets. Elias turned to Tovey, face twisted with surprise. Pumping their arms and legs harder, they ran, leaping stone to stone as if the ground were falling out beneath them.

Hooves battered the cobble behind them, and a horseman whipped from the alley, gaining on them. Tovey gripped Elias's arm, tugging him down a narrow side street. She pressed her finger to her lips as they melted into the shadows.

Frilliam pranced into the opening in front of them. Cullus's reddened face locked eyes on Tovey. Her eyes cast an amethyst hue in the darkness. Her shoulders relaxed.

"Elias? What in the name of Abolend are you doing?" Cullus shouted, ignoring the town blustering to life around them.

"She's got to die." He stood in front of Tovey.

"D-die?" Tovey stammered. "You didn't say anything about dying!"

Cullus shoved Elias aside. He cast out a hand, pulling her on top of Frilliam. "You, brother, are sick in the mind. Can't you see she is a human? She isn't the demon they said she was. For the sake of Abolend, stop acting like a child."

"I'm sick?" Elias laughed, snapping his fingers around Frilliam's reins. "Me? Me! You, Cull, put your lips on that *thing*. She's a demon in disguise." He waved his hands erratically, highlighting every word. "She's going to turn against you. Demons have their own game to play, and we don't know hers."

Tovey shuddered, causing the air around the three to stir faster.

"You see this?" Elias asked as his hair swayed in the wind. "It's like the prophecy said. Her powers are coming out to play, and I don't want to play with that. None of us do."

"What are you talking about?" Cullus barked at Elias.

"The prophecy!" Elias slapped his forehead. "Cullus, I told her the full song." Puffing his chest, he sang, "Elias saved the day." Sneering he said, "You know what that means, Cull? No more Diablerie."

"What did you say?" Cullus's face twisted, growing ashen.

Elias's face wrinkled with confusion. "You didn't know?" Elias cursed under his breath. "My mother is right. You will never wear a crown." He chuckled as if they had missed a joke.

"Wh-what is that? What is a Diablerie?" Tovey interjected.

"A demon." Cullus's jaw dropped. He stared at her with haunted eyes, like he was seeing her for the first time. Like he didn't recognize her.

Tovey clutched her arm, digging her nails into her skin.

Sweat lapped at Elias's hairline. "She's eighteen at midnight. What do you think is going to happen tomorrow?"

"We don't know," Cullus muttered.

"We do. Cull, we know. Father said her powers now are the side effects, symptoms of what is to come. Once we pass midnight"—he stole a glance at the moon—"who knows what?"

Cullus's spine stiffened. He shoved his boot into Elias's arm, kicking his grip off Frilliam's reins. Cullus's eyes narrowed at Elias. "Find your own way home." He dug his boots into Frilliam's sides. Tovey pushed her fingers into Cullus's ribs, holding tight. They turned through twisted passages, barreling to the shore. The dryads' homes turned into smears of umber as they ran.

"What's a Diablerie?" Tovey questioned.

"We will discuss this later. First, we leave." He leaned into Frilliam, galloping faster. "I don't know what Elias said to you, but his version of the prophecy is wrong. It never speaks of him or a Diablerie."

Tovey was silent, her eyes peeled wide. She gasped as the cobble turned to sand. The grains sparkled in the sea breeze. A vast tide of swirling azure poured before them, stretching farther than her eyes could venture. She smiled feebly as she saw what she had always smelled: the ocean. Somehow, despite the feverish panic that flowed through their hearts, the sea still managed to calm her.

A two-person wooden vessel sat on the shoreline, abandoned. Tovey's eyes locked with Cullus.

"Where do we even go?" Tovey asked.

"There's got to be something out there. My mother used to tell me of an island north of Silvis that's filled with gryphons." Cullus smiled briefly before frowning. "There might be a shred of truth to it. Land could be there."

"Frilliam won't fit." Tovey pointed out the obvious.

"We will have to go without him." Cullus scratched Frilliam between the ears, searching for any other feasible way of escape.

Frilliam huffed in protest.

They could run, but back into the Tenbris was useless. Their private world no longer existed.

"Let's go," Cullus commanded.

Tovey jumped from Frilliam's back, feet sliding in the sand as she ran toward the rowboat. She turned back toward Cullus, and his face reflected her horror. Crashing came from the alley as Elias and a crimson guard barreled forward on two warhorses adorned in armor.

"Stop, demon!" Elias shouted. "There is nowhere to go! Nothing else is out there!" He smiled, enjoying closing in on his prey.

"No, you obey me," Cullus said to his brother. He stepped in front of Tovey. "By the order of Abolend, I demand that you retreat."

The guard shifted his gaze from Cullus to Elias, stiffening his shoulders.

"You see, brother? I told you. I'm here on a mission. And that mission overrides *you*." He raised his hand. "Kill her."

The wind snapped as the reins shook on the warhorse powering toward Tovey. The guard drew a broadsword from his side, circling the tip in the air before locking his arm steady. He raised the blade as he charged toward her. Tovey gripped her nails into Cullus's shoulder, pushing him to the ground as she stood planted, toes bending into the sand. She breathed deeply, pulling in the salty air. She closed her eyes. A gentle buzz started in her fingertips, the same sensation wriggling beneath her feet: the earth's vibration. She drew up the power like a flower drawing water. A thrumming of energy coursed through her, and her body grew hot.

Thunder sounded on the horizon. Static from lightning hung in the air. She focused on the thunder, letting the chaotic energy become one with her, wishing it would help her. She opened her eyes, casting a purple hue on the shore. The sword was inches from her nose.

A shivering scream rushed from Tovey's lips. Particles of sand vibrated upward, carrying a bolt of lightning from the ground to his blade. It flickered past the cross guard and down to the pommel. Burns blistered on the guard's hand, forcing him to drop his cruciform. His body fell from the horse, rigid as a log, convulsing with guttural moans of pain before his muscles relaxed. His body was still on the ground.

The full moon rose in the night. Dizziness overcame her, and she was faint from the burst of energy as the world darkened around her. She didn't process what she had done as shades of blue melded into blacks. She stumbled backward into the sea, exhausted. The water nipped at her back, sucking her in.

Somewhere, as if on the other side of a long corridor, she heard Cullus yell her name, but she was blind, and her body was numb. The water pulled her deeper, and she was swept away in a riptide, without a sense of which way was up. Tovey blinked in the endless sea with limbs too weak to move.

38

Cullus thrashed at the sea. He watched the faintest lilac light descend into the shifting ocean, sinking to unbounded depths as he swam after the only sign of Tovey. He couldn't lose her. He refused. Scrambling, he lurched over each new wave, fumbling after her without success. He dipped his head under the crashing waves, the noise deafening, further spinning him into confusion. He popped his eyes open, and they burned in the salty water. Darkness met him. He was unable to see anything, including his fingers, which were inches in front of him.

"Tovey!" he screamed into the water.

He rose to the surface. Over and over again, he caught his breath before diving as far as his feet would propel him. His throat ripped, screaming for Tovey before he breached the surface for another breath.

Cullus removed his bracers and leather jerkin. He didn't care about losing anything other than her. He shouldn't have let her push him out of the way. He should have taken the sword. He should have died for her.

"Cullus! Come back here before you drown!" Elias yelled, voice cracking as he ignored the dead man. "Cull, I'm not kidding!"

Cullus broke the surface, gasping. The purple sparkle of her eyes had vanished. He shouted, pushing himself on as he tried to swim, but his muscles were frozen, refusing to cooperate. Elias was right. If he stayed in the frigid waters, he would drown. Chest heaving, he kicked back toward the shore. Every inch was a betrayal, a step farther from her.

He tossed his body onto the sand, heaving in unsteady whimpers. Despite knowing Tovey was gone, he reached in one last time, praying to the heavens he would grab her body, that her tender hand would grip him back, that she would be inches beneath the surf, smiling at him, her pointed nose red, blushing. He cried tears as salty as the sea. Cullus was met with nothing but a handful of water.

"This changes things, brother," Elias said.

Cullus stared back at his brother, his heart icy like the wind. Bile turned in his stomach. He was disgusted with the monster Elias was growing into. "You're right. This changes everything." He gripped his brother's shirt, pulling him off his horse, legs thrashing in the air. "And unless you want to be like your friend right there"—Cullus kicked the lifeless guard—"you will listen to me." He growled, tossing his brother with ease to the sand. He stood above him, unblinking. Hate plagued his heart. "Stand."

Elias scampered backward. He hesitated for a moment too long.

"Did you not hear me?" Cullus growled. "I said stand."

Elias clambered to his feet.

"She was the key, Elias. And you forced her to defend me. Her powers weren't without limits! She just sacrificed herself for *me*. Because of you."

Elias's eyes were wide with fear.

"The world will cry for her," he promised. "Everyone is going to feel the pain of losing her." Cullus shook uncontrollably.

Elias whimpered. "Cul—"

Cullus shot him a deadly glare, his heart devoid of humanity. "*Prince* Cullus. And before you know it, I'll be your king." Cullus spat next to his brother. "Show some respect."

"She had to die, Cull. You know this. She was the Diablerie," he protested.

"*She* was the savior!" Cullus screamed, gripping his brother's shirt. "She wasn't going to harm anyone! The stories were wrong. She wasn't going to destroy the world; she was going to make it better. How could you not see that?" He shook his brother violently.

"I saved the day. My mother was right," Elias grumbled under his breath.

Cullus released his brother before backhanding Elias to the ground.

Elias yelped.

Cullus kicked him in the stomach. "You saved nothing." He kicked him again. "You were a coward." He delivered another blow to Elias's stomach. "You're responsible for the death of the only person I've ever loved." Cullus grabbed his brother, who was bloodied and bruised, before tossing him toward the dead man's horse. "Question anything I do, anything at all, and I will destroy you."

Elias cried silently, looking at Cullus as if he were now a demon.

"Do you understand me?" Cullus asked.

Elias nodded.

"Get on your horse. We are going home."

39

Tovey sank into the ocean. An otherworldly silence surrounded her. Her body swirled in an endless cascade to the depths of the void. Salt burned at Tovey's open eyes, forcing them to seal. Her body, devoid of air, buried itself into the powdery silt, dusting the water around her, lungs burning for air.

She thrashed, instinctively searching for the dagger in her boot. She knew she was barefoot and weaponless, but it didn't stop her from searching for something. Refusing to breathe, she trembled in the water, her limbs flailing around her, screaming for help. She inhaled, and the first gulp of water filled her lungs. It burned like she'd swallowed fire, but she couldn't stop it. Tears cascaded from her eyes, but no one would ever know the demon had drowned in a sea of sadness.

There was no place in the world for someone like her, someone with power, someone whose life could threaten the world's existence. She kicked upward, pushing off the ocean floor in a fight for her life, somehow sinking to the bottom yet again.

Her mind wandered. The seers, Master Daleen—none of their deaths would be in vain. They'd helped put an end to Tovey's destruction. And Sylvia was the true hero who'd saved Tovey, the hero who never knew she was a hero. She'd given so much to Tovey, and Tovey would never forget the blessing she'd given her. Sylvia had given her the chance to live, the chance to love.

Tovey deserved to die. She'd taken a life. The Abolend soldier could've had a family, friends, children, someone at home who loved him and would be met with the news that his life had been snuffed out by a monster. It was cruel. She could have disarmed him, but she didn't. She could have stopped herself, but she wanted to remove the obstacle that stood in the way of her and Cullus.

With minutes to the solstice, her mind silenced, melding into the turning tide, visiting those who mattered most in her uncelebrated goodbye. Recollections of Marka filled her mind's eye. Tovey smiled, wishing her well. Yearning, she imagined she could have introduced Marka to Cullus or that he even knew her name. Two strangers connected by another who would live in the same dwelling for the rest of their lives and never know it.

Frilliam made her heart ache. She yearned to ride him one last time, to gallop carelessly through the woods on a wild adventure. The first time she rode him was magical. She'd felt airy and free, unlike now. She coughed on water, gripping at her chest. She wanted to hold Cullus. *Oh, Cullus.* Tovey blinked rapidly, writhing like a shrimp on a hook.

She could see him in front of her, his brown cloud of hair weightless even underwater. Had he come to rescue her? Perhaps there was another way out. No, it wasn't Cullus standing in the water before her. The image of the ghostly figure became clearer the more she coughed on the ocean. It was a chestnut-haired specter. Nadia. She smiled a familiar welcoming grin, warm like the sun. She reached a hand toward Tovey, pulling her forward with her compassion.

"You're drowning," Nadia said, her face stern.

"I know."

"Do you have to do everything I do?" Nadia laughed.

"Of course. You're my big sister."

Convulsions took over Tovey's muscles. She sucked in the water and spat it back out, drowning in the sea of loneliness. Her lungs filled over and over again. For a moment, it was like she could breathe again. She blinked at Nadia, wanting to be near her sister again.

"Fight, little lilac." Nadia's voice echoed in her head, but Tovey was no longer able to see her. "Golden flowers, lemon tree."

Tovey's body stilled, the thrashing thankfully over. Nothing moved aside from the tide pulling at her hair in the gentle pulse of the sea around her. Purple mist danced in the currents as her essence filled the ocean, freeing itself from worldly bonds. Tovey's eyes clouded, staring ahead absently as the water turned red. Her heartbeat stuttered to a fermata. She listened to the gentle whoosh-ing of the sea as it swayed her lifeless body into an eternal sleep.

40

Arden stood planted at the water's edge. His moss cape billowed in the sea breeze. Arden's eyes were locked on the horizon. He watched the orange sun rise from the sea in company with hundreds of dryads. Word had spread of Cullus killing the amethyst child before fleeing the city with his brother and a trove of Abolend guards. Rumors had hardened into fact, as dryadic stares had watched the scene unfold several hours ago.

Arden paced the shoreline, kicking his bare toes at the lapping water, cursing his enemy's skill. How easily Cullus had managed to bring the fabled Diablerie to death was astounding. Cullus's plan was so formulated, so seamless. It irked Arden to his core. Dryads surrounded the water, staring into the winter's first morn, the songbirds soaring above the waves whistling a mournful hymn.

"Has anyone seen him?" Arden whispered to Firth, who hobbled beside him. Firth's guilt-scorned eyes searched the shores, for he and he alone was responsible for Tovey's grand escape. Arden gripped him, drawing his attention.

"No, Chief. But I sent watchers, and I have our ears ready to alert us if he manages to find his way back to Abolend. The forest and seas are under watch." Firth's eyes fell to the ground as he muttered, "A better watch than me."

Arden ignored the comment. No one could have stopped Tovey if they'd wanted to. "I want to know the moment he finds his way home. *If* he finds his way home." Arden's eyes passed over his people. He cast a tight smile, lowering his voice. "If anyone finds him before then, they have permission to kill him on sight."

Arden waded into the water, the surf surging around his body. He pressed his open palms against the water. A strange thrumming of energy vibrated through the water, different than the usual ebb and flow. The ocean had a heartbeat.

Arden stumbled, falling backward onto the sandy shore before scrambling to his feet. "Back!" he barked at his people, who stood with their toes in the water. "Get out of the water! Now!"

"Get out of the water!" a chime of voices echoed. Families clambered over one another, moving from the shore to the cobbled roads, panic biting their cheeks. Arden ran, yanking a young girl no more than four from the water's edge, cradling her in his arms.

"Everyone, stay out!" He handed the dryad to her father before turning back to the sea, perplexed by the beating sensation.

"What is it, Chief?" Firth squawked.

Arden's hand rose, silencing Firth and the people. Arden pointed to the horizon. They watched in silence, waiting for something. Today was the shortest day of the year, or the darkest, as Arden would remember it. Indigo mixed with rose, and charcoal clouds built above the water in layers of foreboding mountains as they towered and crumbled together. The sea whirled in spirals, touching Tovey's watery grave to the sky in a wavering wild spout.

Arden's lips twitched, hope blossoming in his chest. Red light, without a source, burst from the bottom of the waterspout, elevating the unearthly glow to the center of the tornado. Dizzying spins of sea swayed side to side, waltzing to the shoreline, bringing storm clouds marching behind it—a funeral procession fitting for a fallen demon. The ruby glow in the center of the spout remained still.

An uneasy smile crossed Arden's face as he stepped backward, ushering his people to do the same. They retreated from the soft sand, finding familiar rune-carved cobble. Every single dryad had their eyes locked on the spout. The wind whipped furiously. Mothers sheltered young children in their arms while others retreated toward their homes. Others froze in time, stilled in awe, taking in the strange sight. Water from the spout rained on the shore, splattering drops of sand in every direction.

Arden stood in front of his people like a statue. As instantaneously as the spout had formed, it dissipated, spewing a crimson seed onto the battered shore. The red glow faded into oblivion, revealing nothing more than a pale wash of linen.

"What is it?" Firth muttered to the chief.

Arden shrugged, but he thought he knew. He had heard stories. Arden raised a hand, gesturing for his people to hold steady. Tiptoeing, he approached the clothing, prodding the dress with his foot. Something fleshy met his skin. With wide eyes, he knelt into the wet sludge, unfolding the fabric.

"The fabric. It's ours," Arden announced to a silent crowd, the people holding their breath.

Firth shifted closer as Arden unfolded the ocean's gift. He revealed pale skin, flaxen hair, and Tovey's sunken face, blue and bloated. Swallowing the hard lump that balled like hair in his throat, he took in the ghastly sight. Firth squawked with horror, unwilling to accept the tumultuous trepidation rumbling from his chest.

Arden glared at Firth. "Don't scare our people!" Turning to the crowd, he announced, "All is fine. Stay back."

Arden pushed the hair from her delicate face. He wriggled his arms beneath her body, folding her against his chest. She was childlike in his grasp, pathetic in a way Arden had never perceived her in life. His chest filled with sadness, but he refused to let his people see. The chief focused on relaxing his face, but he yearned to scream. He was strong, and his people would never doubt it.

Arden spun toward the dryads as he cleared his throat. His chest filled with air as he prepared to announce Tovey's death to the people. But for once, he couldn't find the words to speak. His lips danced without words. The dryads mutely watched the fumbling buffoon who was Chief Arden, fearful and shaken. Firth skittered to the chief's side, jaw dropping to reveal rotting teeth, his eyes taking in Tovey's hollow corpse.

"Move the people away, Firth. We don't gawk at the dead here. I'm taking her home," Arden said firmly, walking toward the kapok with the dead girl. Firth didn't speak as the dryads formed a procession following Arden silently.

Hanging his head, he saw Tovey up close for the first time. She seemed younger now than she had when she'd stood before him in the hall. She was once so full of life, stubborn and bold. Traits most didn't possess. And now, the bountiful life that had dwelled inside was gone, leaving nothing but the barren casing of the girl she'd once been. Cullus was despicable. Abolend had gone too far. It was his time to be a leader, to take charge as he had never done before. This was why he'd conquered Chief Kalo. He wanted the ability to lead people in the time of war, and now the time was here.

"The Diablerie has fallen." His voice boomed in the streets, echoing across the trees, bouncing his words far across the kingdom. "Tovey was tolerant to the way our enemy kingdom, Abolend, treated her. Her tolerance was not from fear but from respect, from the pure love she held for those who treated her as nothing more than dirt. She let her heart weaken her mind, yet it was her heart that allowed her to see so much more than any of us could dream of seeing.

"We can all learn from Tovey, the amethyst child. We will not forget the Diablerie. We will not forget how she bravely stood against her kind for our people, for you, for your children. She stood against everyone, including her inner judgment, to warn us of Abolend's aggression toward our kingdom. Her words were not left unspoken. And we will heed her message. We will fight. We will be relentless. We will embody the spirit of the Diablerie."

Cheering echoed in the streets.

41

Nine moons had risen since the Diablerie's body had been undressed and wrapped in a mossy tomb. Every sunrise, Arden marched to the room deep within the roots of the kapok tree where her grave sat. He carried bundles of ivory candles to the death chamber. Like a dance, he placed candlesticks across the floor and on stumpy knots in the walls, lighting them with a wave of his fingers, tracing an invisible triangle with a line in the air.

"May the light guide you," he muttered, spinning from candle to candle, waxy runs puddling on the floor. Rapping at the door snapped his braided head to the wooden entry. "What is it?" he growled.

"Others would like to see her—honor her," a croaking voice muttered.

"I've told you. No one comes into the tomb aside from me! Let me be, Firth."

Firth shut the door, shuffling on the other side. "Won't let anyone see the Diablerie. Won't let anyone look at the creature. Obsessed with a rotting body that we should have burned."

"Firth! I can hear you!" Arden snapped, annoyed.

Arden knelt, staring at the moss-wrapped body, petrified like the tree she was encased in. Sucking in the humid air infused with the scent of sweetgrass, he bowed his head, whispering prayers in another language over her.

Firth leaned against the door, and it flexed from his weight.

Arden growled. "Just come in then."

The hand entered, eyes darting around the room before falling on the chief. "You mustn't be guilty. It isn't your fault. It is mine. I let her go. I didn't watch."

"It isn't your fault. It is Cullus's. He entered our kingdom, and I didn't sense it. None of us did," Arden admitted, rubbing his brow.

"A spell? Some magic?"

"I don't know . . . He has made me question everything. How could he pretend to love her and never tell her who she was? I should have told her the day she walked into the hall, but you saw the way he had her dressed—"

"A servant," Firth grumbled. "Disgusting."

"I thought she had Cullus fooled. I had no idea she truly believed herself to be a servant until she seemed confused with my questioning. How did we not have spies search every single collective? We didn't bother to look there. We were fooled as easily as Mallum was. I don't understand why anyone would abandon the Diablerie, why they wouldn't train her, teach her . . ." Arden fumed, his blood pounding through his veins.

"We assumed her dead. She never came. No word ever came." Firth sniffed, head sinking into his hands.

Arden paced the chamber before placing a hand on the moss that wrapped her. "It was a mistake. We overlooked her existence, and we weren't prepared for war." He paused, his voice cracking. "We had nothing to back down from."

Firth nodded shamefully. "We need better ears and to recruit more humans. We need to infiltrate the castle, not just their kingdom."

"Exactly." Arden rubbed the back of this neck. "I wish we would have found her as a babe and raised her as our own."

Firth shrugged. "We can't change it now, but I do have news."

Arden's gut twisted with panic as he held his face still, waiting.

Firth licked his lips, shifting uncomfortably. "Cullus arrived at Abolend and has spread word that he killed the demon."

Arden punched the wall, and his knuckles busted open. "We must fight in her honor. Let the final war come," Arden scoffed. "She thought the final war was a bad thing, that being called a demon was an insult. The humans twisted her mind."

Firth scowled.

"She had enough power to stop everything." Arden cleared his throat and sang.

The demon comes, heart of bold,
She'll rise as the seers have foretold,
With purple eyes, hair of gold,
She'll bring the final war.

"She was lost and confused, and we did nothing. I did

nothing to help." Arden rolled his shoulders, attempting to shake the sadness out of his body. He couldn't be weak, not even in front of Firth.

Arden surveyed the candles, ensuring they all remained lit. He stroked his long midnight braids, soothing himself, in the comforting musky air. He ushered Firth out of the tomb.

"Until tomorrow." Arden shut the door behind him before pulling a grand skeleton key from his pocket and securing the door.

"You can't keep her body in there forever," Firth muttered. "We can't change what's happened. She is going to decompose." Firth shivered. "She has to burn like the last Diablerie. Her soul needs to be released so in a hundred years the great one can come again."

Arden shook his head. "The moss is slowing the process. She isn't degrading as fast as I thought she would. I felt something in the water, something different. Think of the stories of Diableries of the past." He rubbed his neck. "She's different, Firth."

"She *was* different," he corrected.

Arden shook his head. He leaned close to Firth's face. "I'll burn her when I'm ready."

Together they stood outside the door. Arden watched Firth squirm. A headache needled at the back of his neck. "What?" he snapped.

"Tovey's dead. That rot isn't her. Let's burn it and move on."

Arden shoved Firth. "Leave her be."

"Talking to a corpse. It's creepy, creepy, and most of all, creepy."

42

Arden's footsteps echoed in her tomb, leaving nothing but the gentle whistle of a hissing flame. As if an accelerant had been released, amber flames grew to pillars of blue, sending wild drips of weeping wax into puddles of white. Smoky darkness filled the tomb. Something shifted, peeling itself from a mossy cocoon, thudding to the ground with a solid weight, shaking the kapok with its power. Her eyes snapped open with fury. Two ruby eyes lit the room aglow as they rose in the darkness.

Her bare feet stuck to the waxy wood as she stepped toward the door, skin as pale as a cadaver's. She moved toward the door, willing it to open as the lock melted beneath her touch. She walked into the hallway alight with a crimson glow.

A hair-raising laugh filled the tomb, resonating throughout the hollow chambers of the kapok as her voice cracked, repeating the words of the little dryad. "A new beginning is coming." She smiled. "He was right."

She couldn't help but grin, knowing that a young seer was alive and well. Mallum had tried to kill them all, but he hadn't reached them in Silvis. Mallum's power was not as strong as he led the people of Abolend to believe. Mallum wouldn't take any more lives. He would not reign with an iron fist. Hope filled her chest as she walked toward the throne room.

"I will no longer be tolerant to intolerance."

UNSPOKEN
Chapter 1 Preview

1

A sinister cackle growled in the hollow corridor outside the vacant tomb. Tovey's fingers traced her cracked lips, searching for the origin of the laughter. The shrill and unsettling voice bellowed from her mouth once more, but the voice didn't sound like her. Her voice was that of a demon.

With her eyes screwed shut, her hair-raising laughter ceased, and untethered terror tore at her mind. Staring at her feet, she wriggled her bare toes, which were coated in beeswax and herbs. She was naked, covered with nothing but bits of emerald moss. Her arms wrapped around her, shielding her bareness from the smoky air with hints of clove and sweetgrass. Coughing, she noticed a shattered wooden door surrounded by human tracks pressed into hardened wax leading to where she stood.

Scratching her head, she searched the tomb laden with weeping candles. At the base of a polished catafalque was an empty cocoon of bulbous green moss. She grasped the moist blanket, holding it to her skin, matching it to the remnants left behind. Tovey couldn't remember why she was asleep on the table, or how she'd seemingly shattered the tomb's door, or why she stood beside a catafalque as if it were supposed to be displaying a corpse. Her corpse. Perhaps the dryads had poisoned her or believed her to be dead. Tovey wasn't sure.

Trembling, she searched her memory.

"The seer was right," she muttered, her voice hoarse and scraping.

She thought of the dryadic boy who'd predicted a new beginning was coming. Tovey wasn't sure if this was the new beginning or why her first thought focused on a boy who could see the future. She'd believed all the seers were dead. King Mallum of Abolend had slain everyone who'd possessed the gift when she was born.

Seers had prophesied her future, claiming she'd bring war, devastation, and woe. They were wrong.

Wavering, she wobbled out of the tomb and into the hall, tugging at her shoulder-length flaxen hair to relieve her skull's incessant throbbing. Her thoughts were blurry; the last memory that clicked was trying to escape this forsaken kingdom: Silvis.

Fury pulsed fire through her veins, harsh and searing. The hall flickered red, and she didn't see the source of the eerie hue. Tovey's shoulders scraped against the furrowed bark walls as she trudged unsteadily.

She must find the throne room. It was the most feasible way to escape. Dizzily, she turned through the labyrinth of tunnels. There was one thing she knew for certain: she needed to find Cullus.

Stumbling, Tovey ducked beneath waxy leaves sprouting from thick umber vines and shifted around ornately carved candelabras.

Tovey didn't remember how she'd become trapped inside of the hollow tree that stood like a castle in the center of the dryads' wooden kingdom, yet here she was, toddling like a child, her legs unsteady as she hesitated between each step, jerking from side to side, gripping any twiggy protrusion from the wall for support. She was utterly useless. Pausing, she stretched, her body sore and stiff like she hadn't moved in weeks.

A barking cough stung her dry throat, and tears wet her cheeks. Her lungs pleaded for clean air. The thick, clotted smoke, heavy with incense, prevented her from taking a full breath. She blinked hard, clearing her blurry vision. The halls were lit by the flickering glow of hissing flames and were void of windows. Her toes brushed against the moss carpets, spongy and moist, laid haphazardly in the hall. She stumped toward the end of the corridor.

Stairs, Tovey thought. I must find stairs. It took every bit of effort to move one step farther. Her muscles wailed, her lungs ached, and she collapsed. Crumpling to the floor like a used handkerchief, she trembled as the world became smeared into shades of umber. Growling, she refused to relent.

Like a spider, she crawled on all fours until she reached the end of the tunnel. There were no stairs leading down, only up. She was within the roots of the dryads' fortress, the kapok. With a deep breath, she ascended the creaking spiraling stairs sluggishly, as one would expect a living corpse to do. Was that what she was now? Undead? She laughed bitterly in disbelief at what her life had become.

Barely over a month ago she'd been nothing more than a servant living in the collective. The collective was a group home for children who were sent to its wretched halls to honor their kingdom, Abolend. Tovey's stomach churned. She gritted her teeth. The collective was nothing more than a forlorn torture chamber that stole children to do King Mallum's bidding. Within the cobblestone walls mashed together with cracking mud, the young girls were beaten into docile servants, too fearful to move, think, or breathe without the command of those above them. And everyone was above a servant.

Some months ago, her time had been spent hoping with every morsel of her soul to pass her third attempt at graduation. She dreamt of being granted a wholesome assignment that would allow her to live her life in service to Abolend, the kingdom she'd once called home. The only kingdom she'd thought existed.

It seemed as though a lifetime had passed since she'd defected and escaped into the Tenbris and learned of a prophecy that said she'd be the one to bring the final war. She'd fled from her kingdom and been stopped by the prince of Abolend, Cullus, whom she'd feared would be a foe but had turned out to be her . . . Well, she didn't know what he was to her. Not anymore. Not since she'd hidden from him, nested in the bough of a tree, unsure where his loyalties lay.

Before then, she and Cullus had stumbled upon a camp of defectors in a village called Terrowin. Finding the town of vagabonds dwelling in humble cabins had been like seeing a rainbow after a rainstorm—enchanting. She'd been optimistic for the first time in forever when they discovered there was a place where servants and guards alike could live freely. A place full of hope. But she and Cullus had refused to stay because they were traveling to Silvis.

Cullus had convinced Tovey to beg Chief Arden, the dryads' leader, to stop the final war. So, she'd pleaded with Arden for a cease-fire, and Cullus mused if no one fought, a battle would cease to exist. It was a simple thought, and they both knew it had weaknesses, but it was nonetheless a thought they both believed. And so, Tovey had succeeded in convincing Chief Arden to relinquish his role in the battle. All was right.

Then, on their return home, Abolend guards had surrounded Tovey and Cullus, taking her prisoner under the guidance of Cullus's cruel child brother, Elias, whose pale blue eyes were as icy as his heart. Cullus had allowed them to capture her, refused to speak for her, and neglected to free her. She considered the harsh reality and uncomfortable truth that Cullus had betrayed her.

She'd realized Abolend would attack Silvis anyway, even if unprovoked, and their plan was useless. Imprisoned and hopeless, a rogue Abolend guard had aided her escape. She'd fled the battalion of men and raced toward Silvis to warn them of Abolend's betrayal and to beg for hospitality. She'd given her trust to the dryads fully.

Chief Arden had agreed to protect her in exchange for learning to master her magic, which she wasn't keen to understand. Reluctantly, she'd taken the deal. Then, as soon as she thought she was safe in a room high in the branches of the kapok, Cullus had appeared like a specter in the alleyway below, warning her that Silvis was a trap. He'd urged her to escape. Desperate, terrified, and with a shred of hope, she'd trusted him once more and fled.

And then . . . Then it was blank, like unused parchment surrounded by a fog as thick and heavy as the clouds in the misty moors. She'd gone against her instinct to trust Cullus, to believe in him and have faith in his virtue. She yearned to flee to a place beyond the woes of Valledera, leaving behind the carnage that followed her.

She'd discovered she was the one person on this forsaken planet with purple eyes. She'd possessed power too, but her magic wasn't splendorous like the fables she'd heard whispered by servants in the collective. There were no wands, unicorns, sparkles, or happiness. Her power was nothing but an internal thrumming that seemed easy to touch and call upon in the darkest of nights. And now she was nude in the belly of Silvis, searching for the prince of Abolend, for her friend, for Cullus, and for a life beyond this.

TOLERANT

Cinematic Audiobook

Step beyond the page with the cinematic audiobook adaptation of The Diablerie Trilogy. Brought to life with immersive soundscapes, a haunting emotional score, directed and produced by the author herself.

Not just read.
Not just told.
This is the story as you've never heard it.

With exclusive author interviews after every episodes for a look behind the pages, let the world of Tolerant surround you in rich atmosphere and raw emotion as you journey into a kingdom where silence is survival and truth is rebellion.

Now streaming wherever you listen to podcasts.

For ad-free episodes and bonus content, join on Patreon at Patreon.com/BethanyStahl

About the Author

C.J. Sparrow is an author and artist passionate about creating mystical worlds. As a neurodivergent storyteller, she explores themes of resilience, identity and power.

She has wandered through some of the world's most haunted locations and S.C.U.B.A. dived in underwater caves alongside sharks and alligators, always chasing adventure.

Her debut novel, Tolerant, is a gripping tale of survival and the darkness that lingers beneath the surface.

When she isn't writing, C.J. enjoys traveling and spending time with her husband, three cats, and dog.

Learn more on BethanyStahl.com